CANINE CLASSICS

Graphic Classics® Volume Twenty-Five
2014

Edited by Tom Pomplun

Associate Editor
John Lehman

EUREKA PRODUCTIONS

8778 Oak Grove Road, Mount Horeb, Wisconsin 53572
www.graphicclassics.com

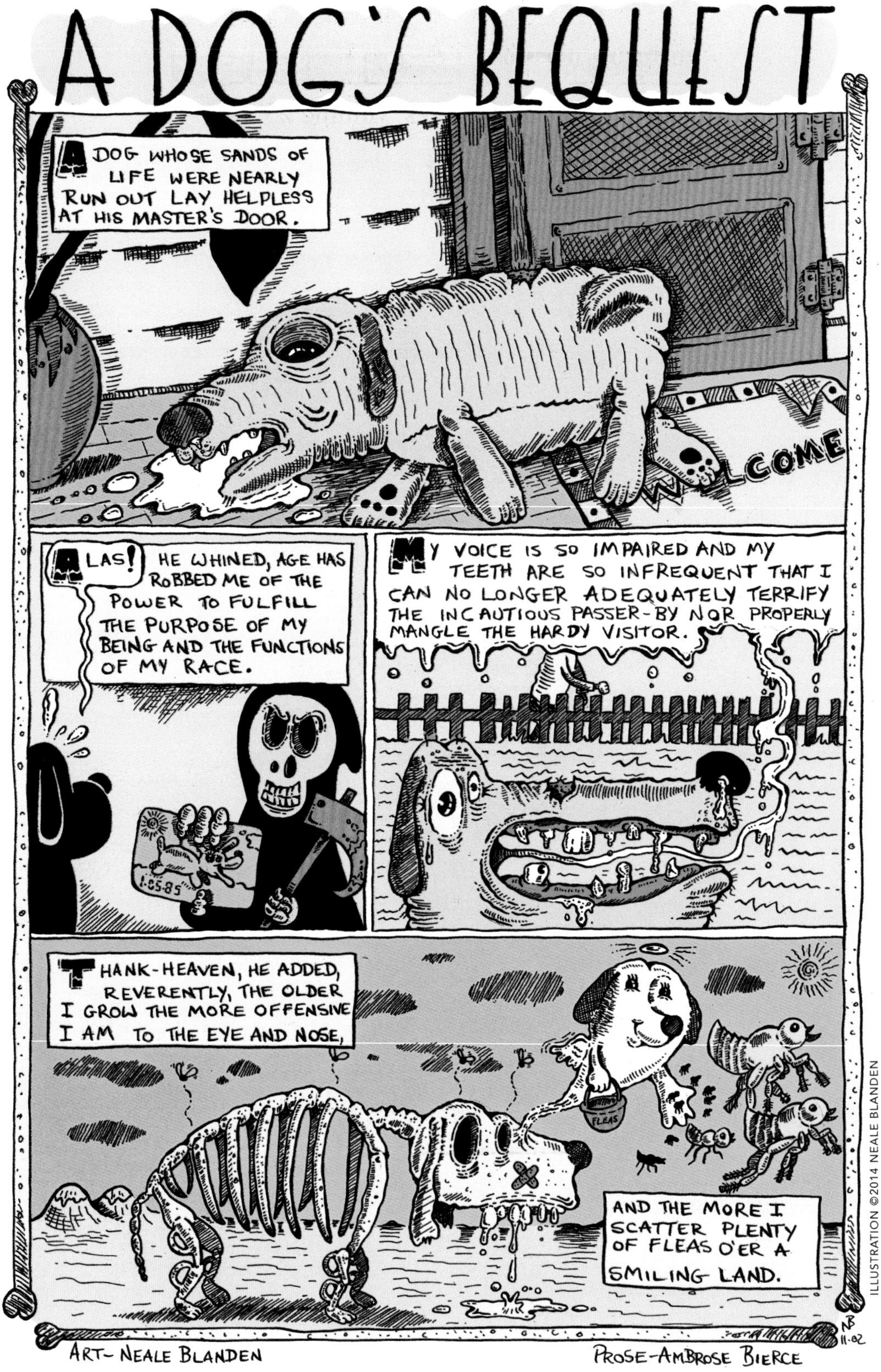
A DOG'S BEQUEST
A DOG WHOSE SANDS OF LIFE WERE NEARLY RUN OUT LAY HELPLESS AT HIS MASTER'S DOOR.
WELCOME
ALAS! HE WHINED, AGE HAS ROBBED ME OF THE POWER TO FULFILL THE PURPOSE OF MY BEING AND THE FUNCTIONS OF MY RACE.
MY VOICE IS SO IMPAIRED AND MY TEETH ARE SO INFREQUENT THAT I CAN NO LONGER ADEQUATELY TERRIFY THE INCAUTIOUS PASSER-BY NOR PROPERLY MANGLE THE HARDY VISITOR.
THANK-HEAVEN, HE ADDED, REVERENTLY, THE OLDER I GROW THE MORE OFFENSIVE I AM TO THE EYE AND NOSE,
FLEAS
AND THE MORE I SCATTER PLENTY OF FLEAS O'ER A SMILING LAND.
NB 11-02
ART- NEALE BLANDEN
PROSE-AMBROSE BIERCE

C O N T E N T S

CANINE CLASSICS

Graphic Classics® Volume 25

ILLUSTRATION ©2014 DRAGAN KOVACEVIC

Cover illustrations by Toni Pawlowsky

Page C-1 illustration by Evert Geradts

Page C-3 illustration
DoggyLand by Dragan Kovacevic

Canine/Feline Classics: Graphic Classics Volume 25, ISBN 978-0-9825630-8-3 is published by Eureka Productions. Price US $19.95, CAN $21.95. Available from Eureka Productions, 8778 Oak Grove Road, Mount Horeb, WI 53572. Tom Pomplun, designer and publisher, tom@graphicclassics.com. John Lehman, associate editor. Lisa Nielsen Agnew, editorial assistant. Permission to print H.P. Lovecraft's *The Cats* in this volume has been granted by Lovecraft Holdings, LLC. Permission to adapt *The Emissary* ©1947 by Arkham House, renewed 1975 by Ray Bradbury, has been granted by Don Congdon Associates, Inc. Permission to adapt Joe R. Lansdale's *Dog, Cat, and Baby* ©1987 Joe R. Lansdale, has been granted by the author. *What I Learn from Cats* ©2014 John Lehman and *What I Learn from Dogs* ©1998 John Lehman printed by permission of the author. *The Beast from the Abyss* ©1971 Robert E. Howard Properties Inc. ROBERT E. HOWARD and related names, logos, characters and distinctive likenesses thereof are trademarks or registered trademarks of Robert E. Howard Properties Inc. Graphic Classics is a registered trademark of Eureka Productions. For ordering information and previews of upcoming volumes please visit the Graphic Classics website at http://www.graphicclassics.com. Printed in USA.

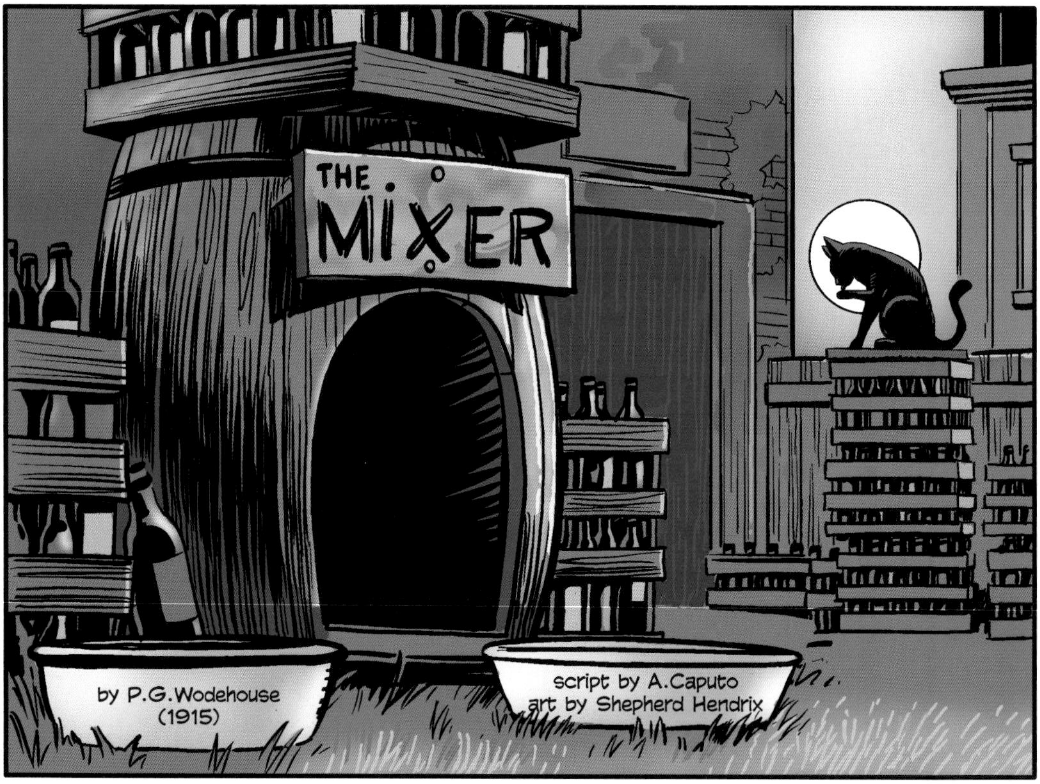
THE MIXER
by P.G.Wodehouse
(1915)
script by A.Caputo
art by Shepherd Hendrix

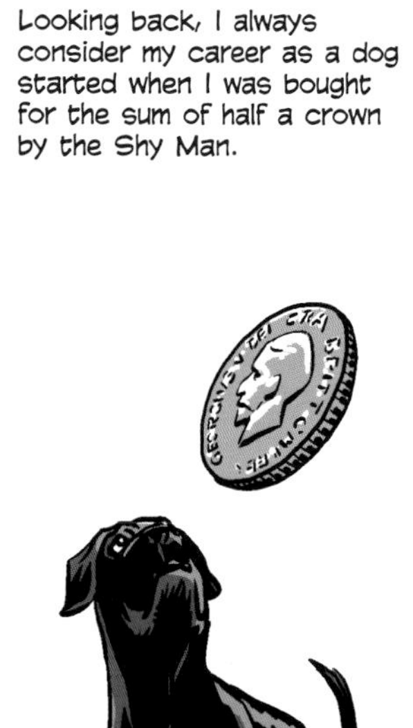
Looking back, I always consider my career as a dog started when I was bought for the sum of half a crown by the Shy Man.

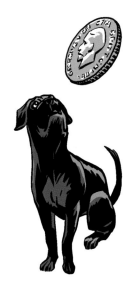

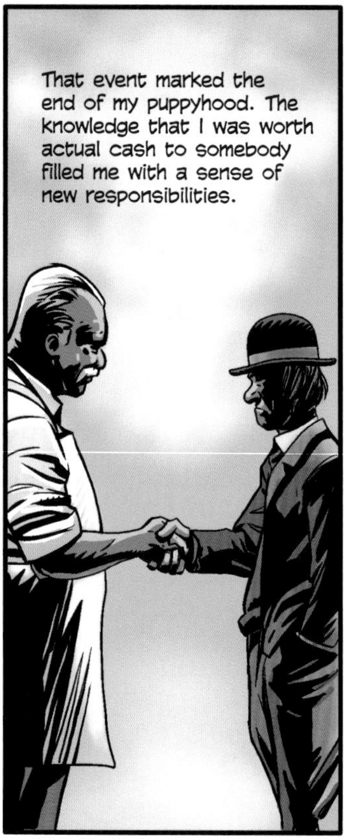
That event marked the end of my puppyhood. The knowledge that I was worth actual cash to somebody filled me with a sense of new responsibilities.

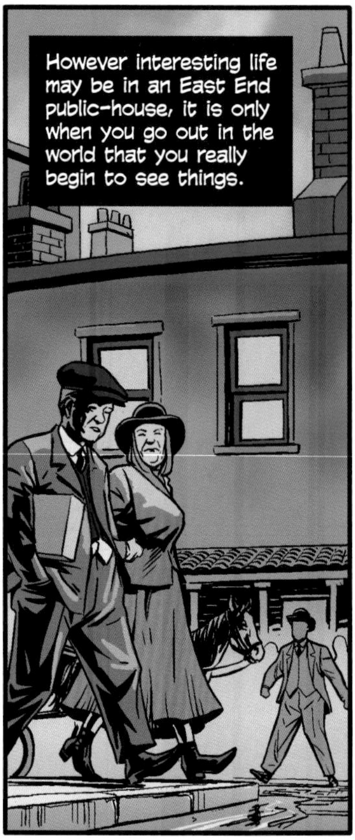
However interesting life may be in an East End public-house, it is only when you go out in the world that you really begin to see things.

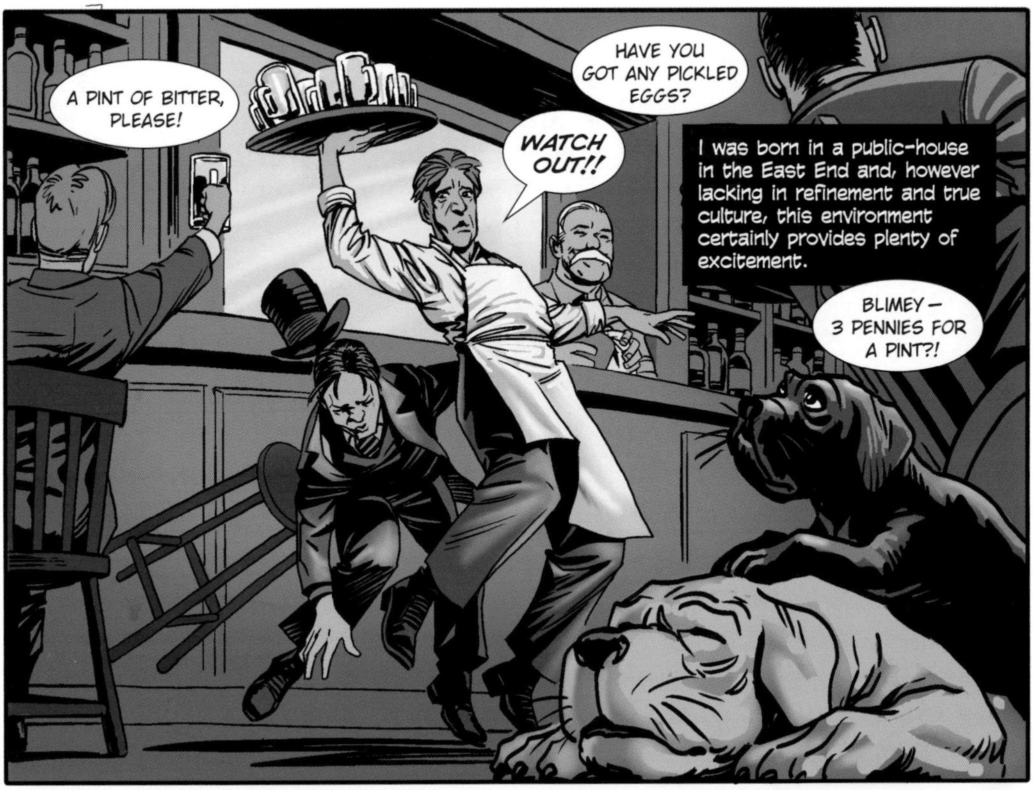
A PINT OF BITTER, PLEASE!
HAVE YOU GOT ANY PICKLED EGGS?
WATCH OUT!!
I was born in a public-house in the East End and, however lacking in refinement and true culture, this environment certainly provides plenty of excitement.
BLIMEY — 3 PENNIES FOR A PINT?!

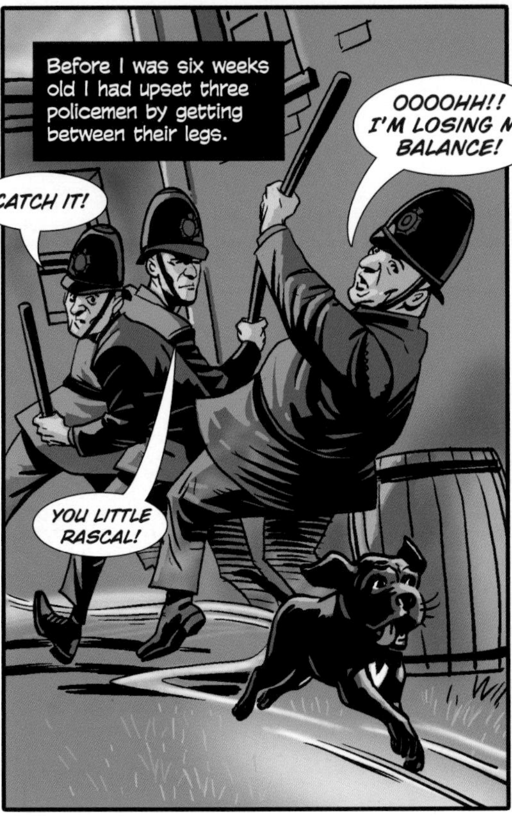
Before I was six weeks old I had upset three policemen by getting between their legs.
OOOOHH!! I'M LOSING MY BALANCE!
CATCH IT!
YOU LITTLE RASCAL!

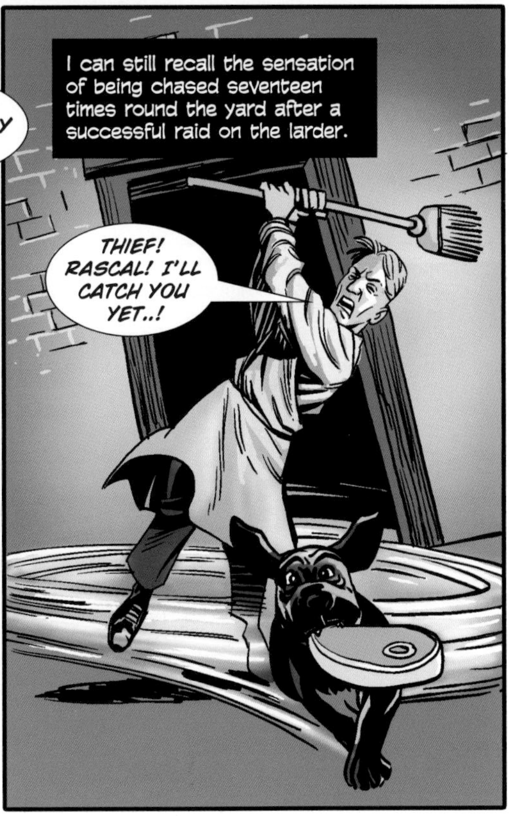
I can still recall the sensation of being chased seventeen times round the yard after a successful raid on the larder.
THIEF! RASCAL! I'LL CATCH YOU YET..!

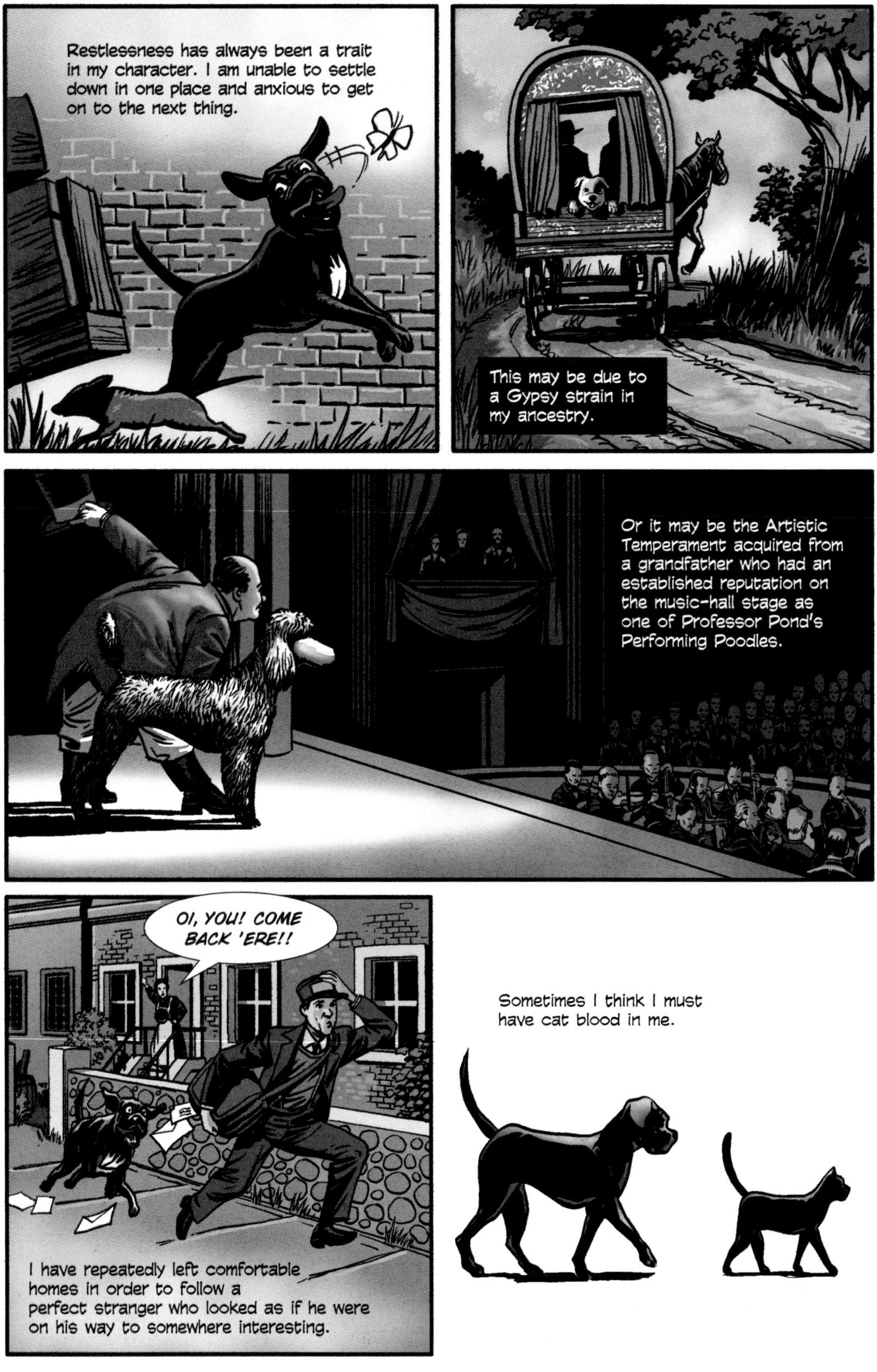
Restlessness has always been a trait in my character. I am unable to settle down in one place and anxious to get on to the next thing.
This may be due to a Gypsy strain in my ancestry.
Or it may be the Artistic Temperament acquired from a grandfather who had an established reputation on the music-hall stage as one of Professor Pond's Performing Poodles.
OI, YOU! COME BACK 'ERE!!
I have repeatedly left comfortable homes in order to follow a perfect stranger who looked as if he were on his way to somewhere interesting.
Sometimes I think I must have cat blood in me.

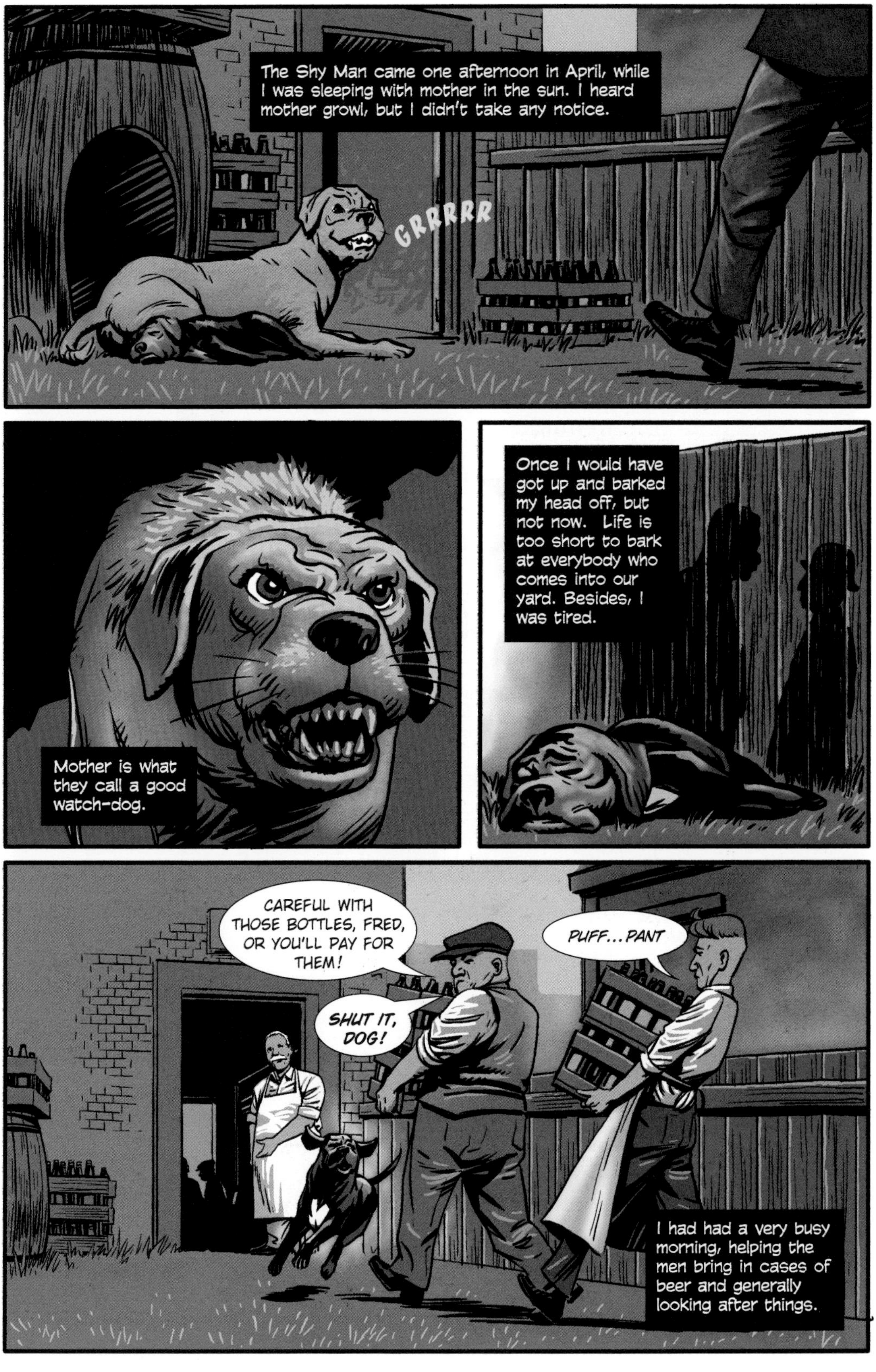
The Shy Man came one afternoon in April, while I was sleeping with mother in the sun. I heard mother growl, but I didn't take any notice.
GRRRRR
Mother is what they call a good watch-dog.
Once I would have got up and barked my head off, but not now. Life is too short to bark at everybody who comes into our yard. Besides, I was tired.
CAREFUL WITH THOSE BOTTLES, FRED, OR YOU'LL PAY FOR THEM!
SHUT IT, DOG!
PUFF...PANT
I had had a very busy morning, helping the men bring in cases of beer and generally looking after things.

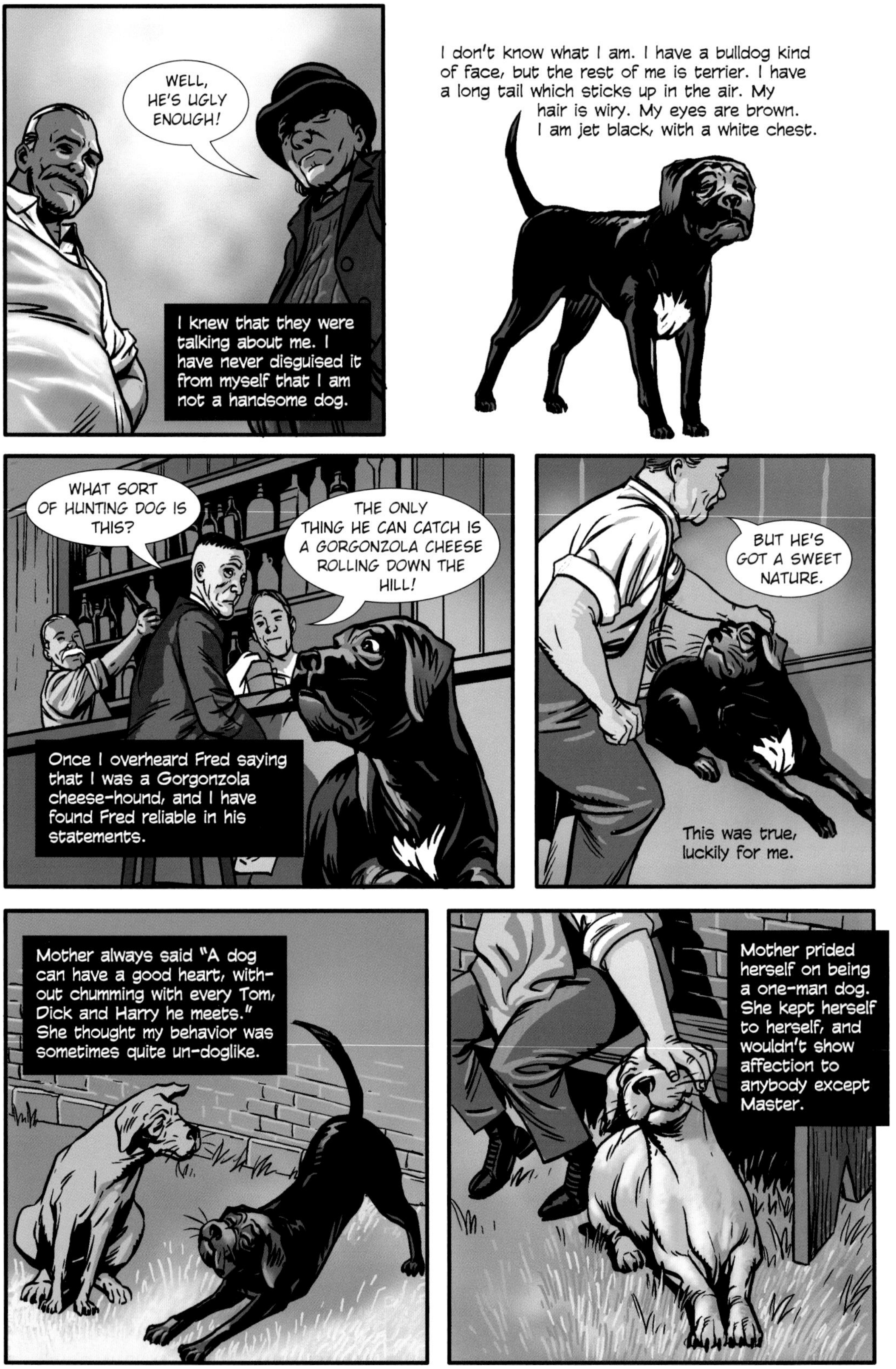
WELL, HE'S UGLY ENOUGH!
I knew that they were talking about me. I have never disguised it from myself that I am not a handsome dog.
I don't know what I am. I have a bulldog kind of face, but the rest of me is terrier. I have a long tail which sticks up in the air. My hair is wiry. My eyes are brown. I am jet black, with a white chest.
WHAT SORT OF HUNTING DOG IS THIS?
THE ONLY THING HE CAN CATCH IS A GORGONZOLA CHEESE ROLLING DOWN THE HILL!
Once I overheard Fred saying that I was a Gorgonzola cheese-hound, and I have found Fred reliable in his statements.
BUT HE'S GOT A SWEET NATURE.
This was true, luckily for me.
Mother always said "A dog can have a good heart, without chumming with every Tom, Dick and Harry he meets." She thought my behavior was sometimes quite un-doglike.
Mother prided herself on being a one-man dog. She kept herself to herself, and wouldn't show affection to anybody except Master.

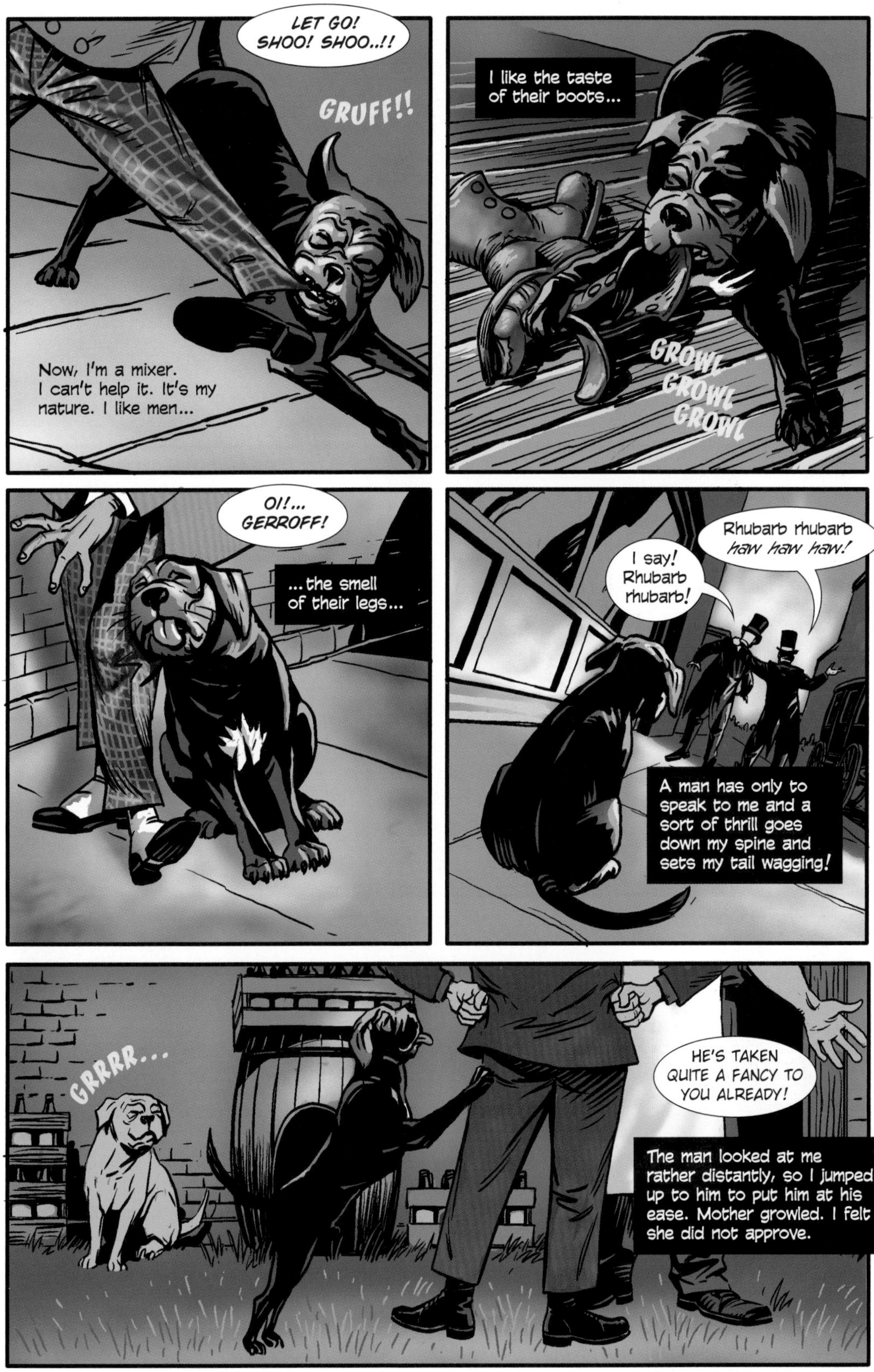
LET GO! SHOO! SHOO..!!
GRUFF!!
Now, I'm a mixer. I can't help it. It's my nature. I like men...
I like the taste of their boots...
GROWL GROWL GROWL
OI!... GERROFF!
...the smell of their legs...
I say! Rhubarb rhubarb!
Rhubarb rhubarb haw haw haw!
A man has only to speak to me and a sort of thrill goes down my spine and sets my tail wagging!
GRRRR...
HE'S TAKEN QUITE A FANCY TO YOU ALREADY!
The man looked at me rather distantly, so I jumped up to him to put him at his ease. Mother growled. I felt she did not approve.

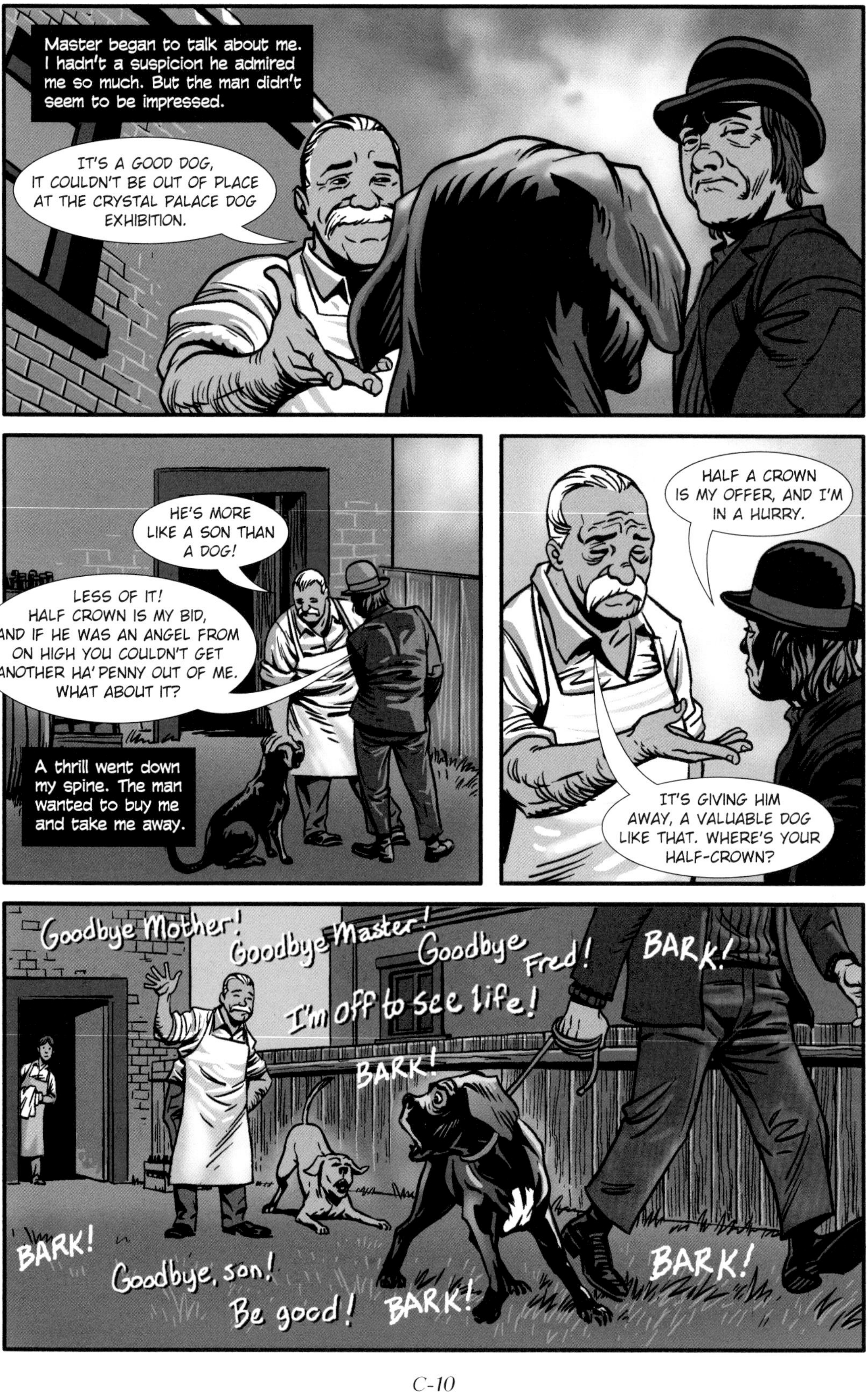
Master began to talk about me. I hadn't a suspicion he admired me so much. But the man didn't seem to be impressed.
IT'S A GOOD DOG, IT COULDN'T BE OUT OF PLACE AT THE CRYSTAL PALACE DOG EXHIBITION.
HE'S MORE LIKE A SON THAN A DOG!
LESS OF IT! HALF CROWN IS MY BID, AND IF HE WAS AN ANGEL FROM ON HIGH YOU COULDN'T GET ANOTHER HA'PENNY OUT OF ME. WHAT ABOUT IT?
A thrill went down my spine. The man wanted to buy me and take me away.
HALF A CROWN IS MY OFFER, AND I'M IN A HURRY.
IT'S GIVING HIM AWAY, A VALUABLE DOG LIKE THAT. WHERE'S YOUR HALF-CROWN?
Goodbye Mother!
Goodbye Master!
Goodbye Fred!
BARK!
I'm off to see life!
BARK!
BARK!
Goodbye, son!
BARK!
Be good!
BARK!

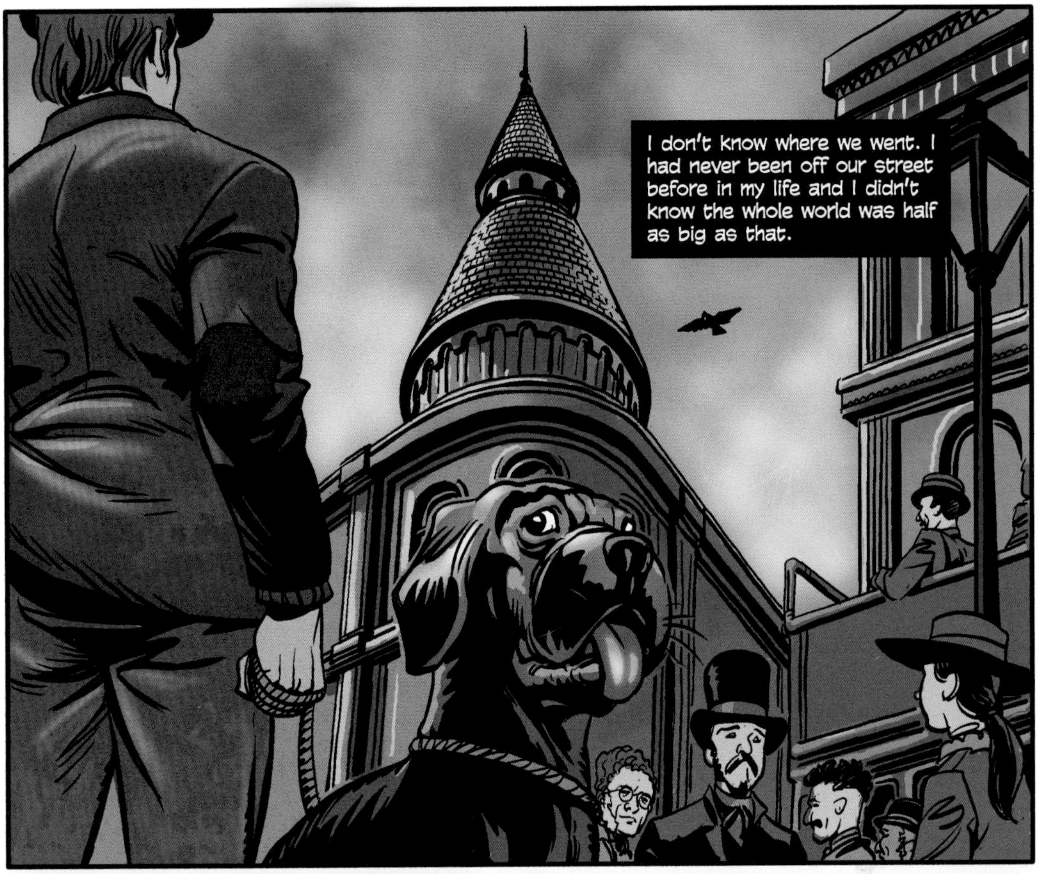
I don't know where we went. I had never been off our street before in my life and I didn't know the whole world was half as big as that.

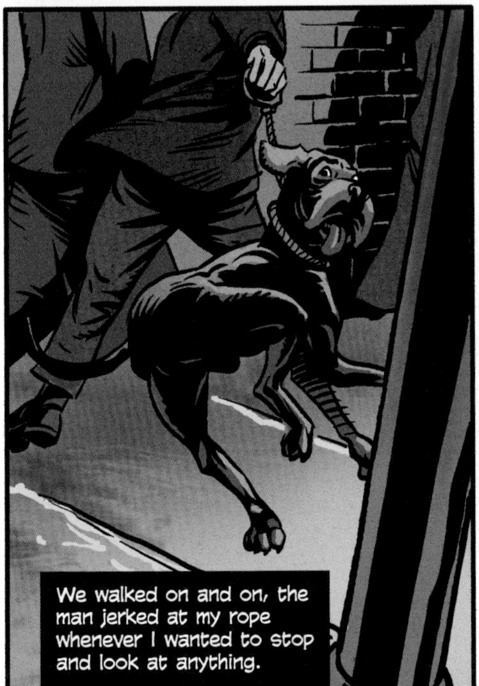
We walked on and on, the man jerked at my rope whenever I wanted to stop and look at anything.

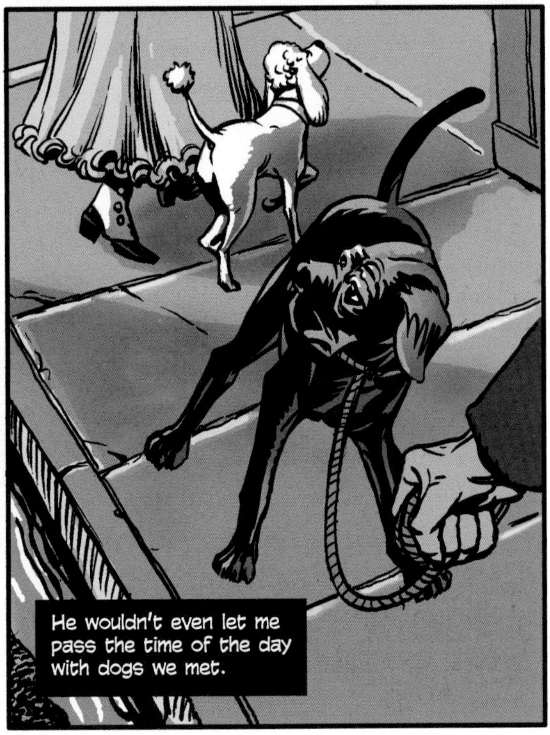
He wouldn't even let me pass the time of the day with dogs we met.

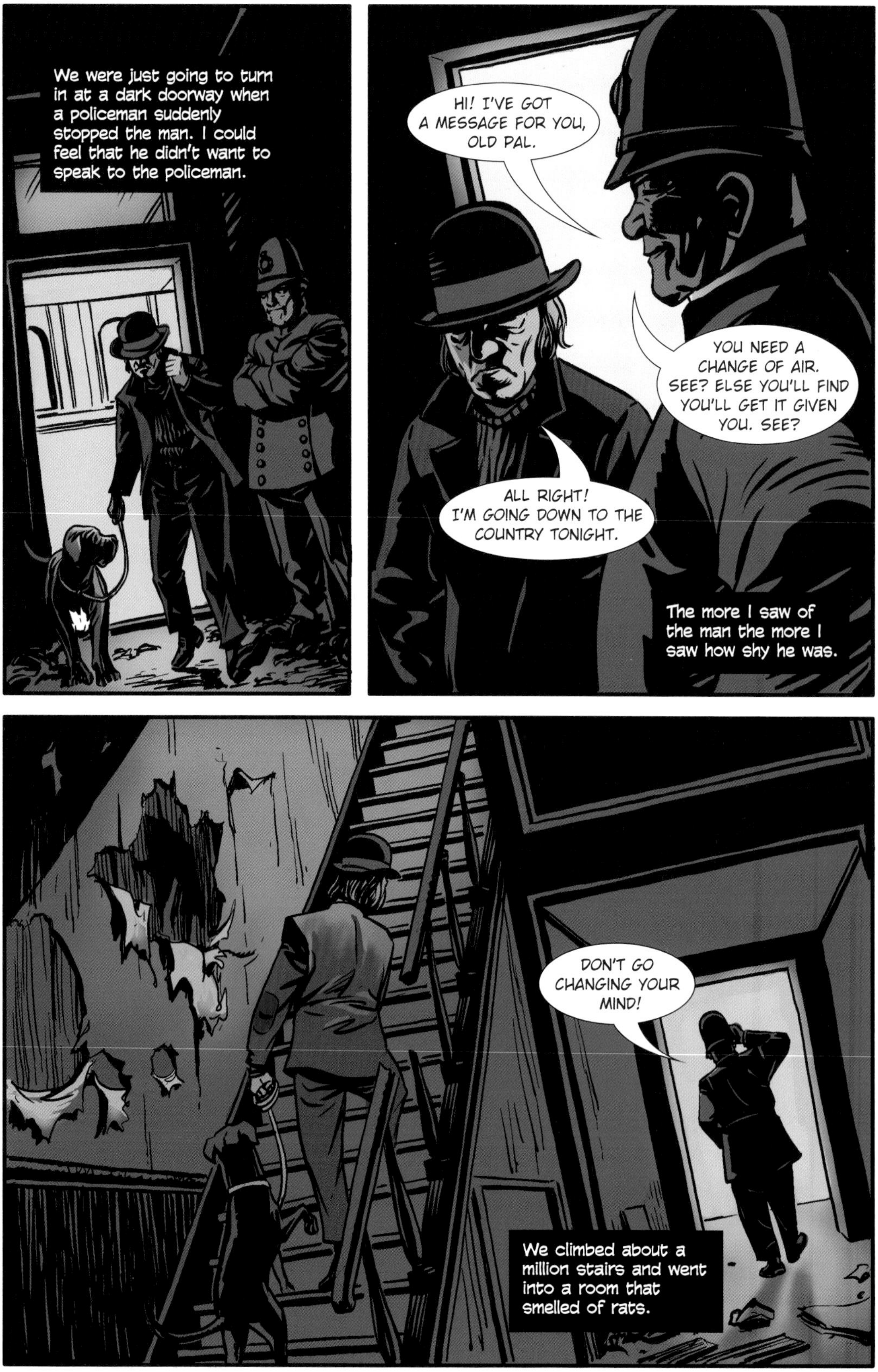
We were just going to turn in at a dark doorway when a policeman suddenly stopped the man. I could feel that he didn't want to speak to the policeman.
HI! I'VE GOT A MESSAGE FOR YOU, OLD PAL.
YOU NEED A CHANGE OF AIR. SEE? ELSE YOU'LL FIND YOU'LL GET IT GIVEN YOU. SEE?
ALL RIGHT! I'M GOING DOWN TO THE COUNTRY TONIGHT.
The more I saw of the man the more I saw how shy he was.
DON'T GO CHANGING YOUR MIND!
We climbed about a million stairs and went into a room that smelled of rats.

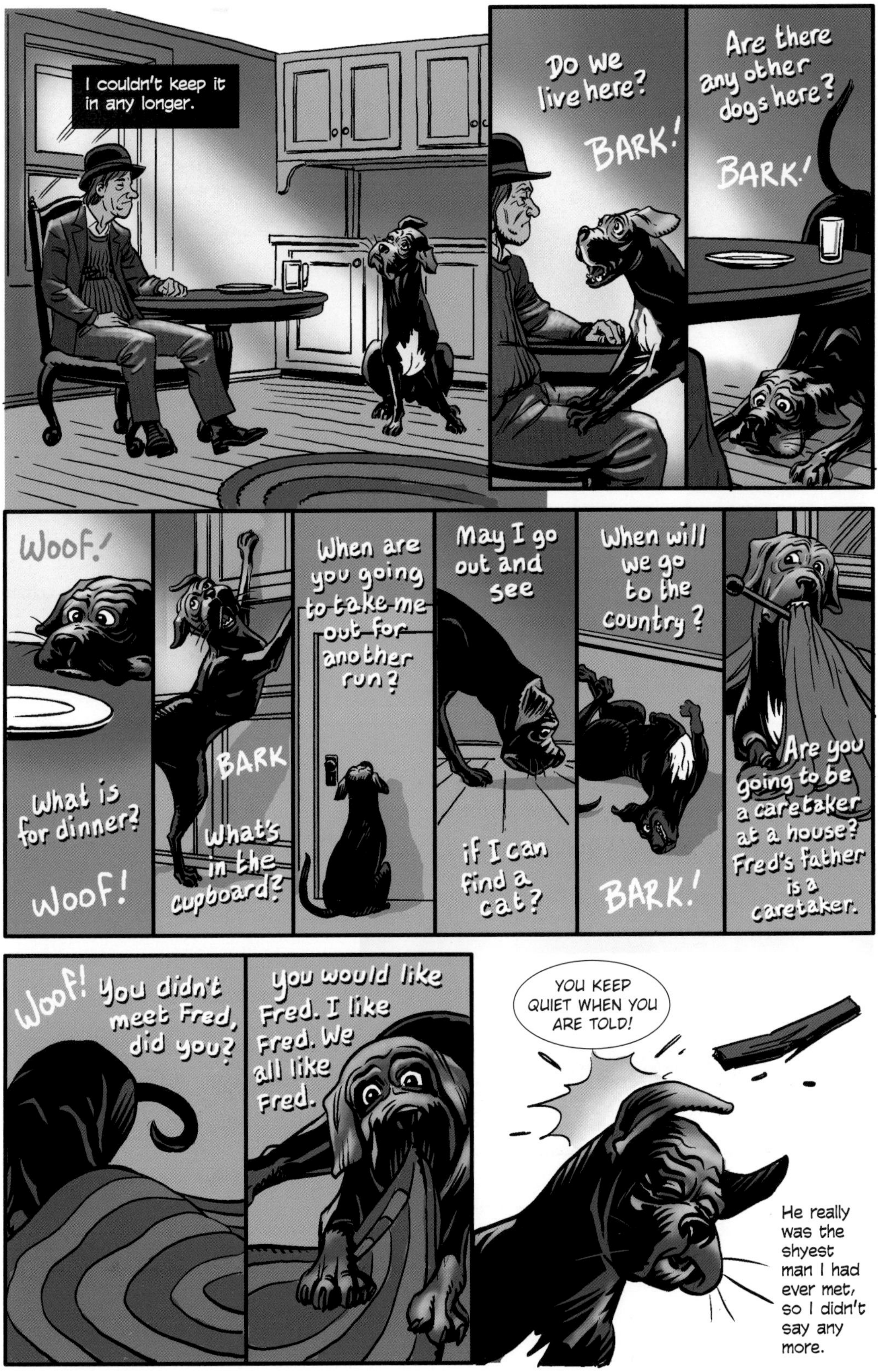
I couldn't keep it in any longer.
Do we live here?
BARK!
Are there any other dogs here?
BARK!
Woof!
What is for dinner?
Woof!
BARK
What's in the cupboard?
When are you going to take me out for another run?
May I go out and see
if I can find a cat?
When will we go to the country?
BARK!
Are you going to be a caretaker at a house? Fred's father is a caretaker.
Woof!
You didn't meet Fred, did you?
You would like Fred. I like Fred. We all like Fred.
YOU KEEP QUIET WHEN YOU ARE TOLD!
He really was the shyest man I had ever met, so I didn't say any more.

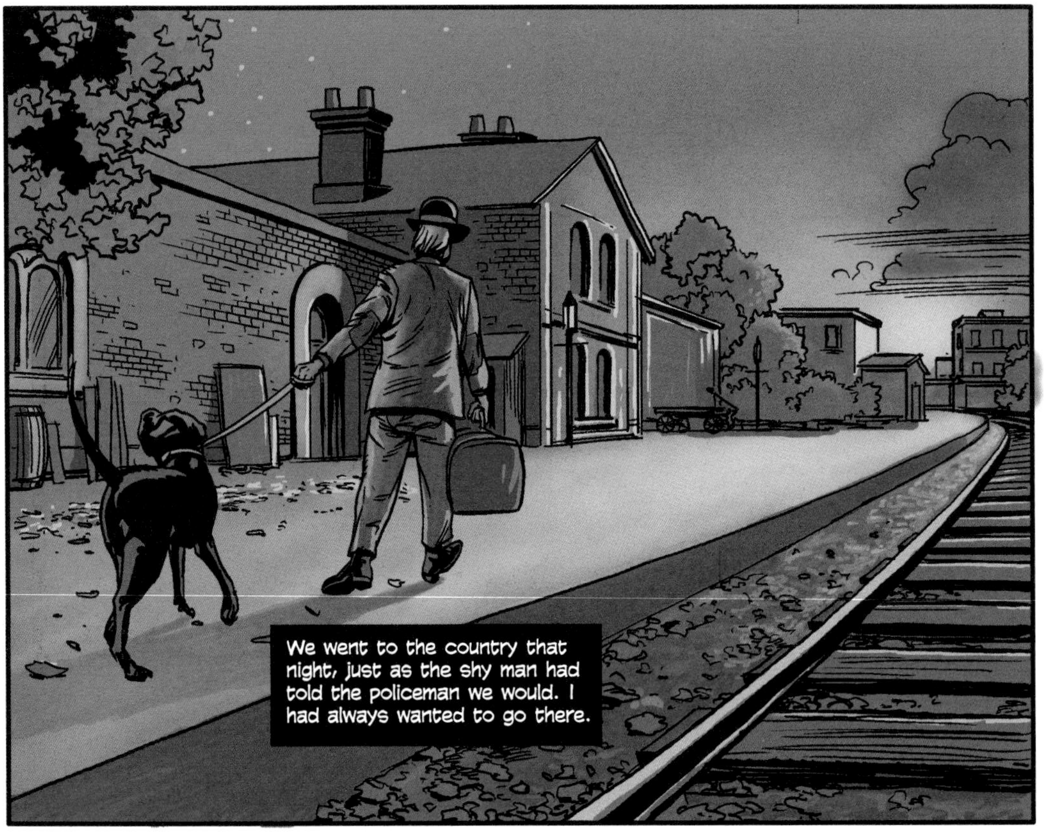
We went to the country that night, just as the shy man had told the policeman we would. I had always wanted to go there.

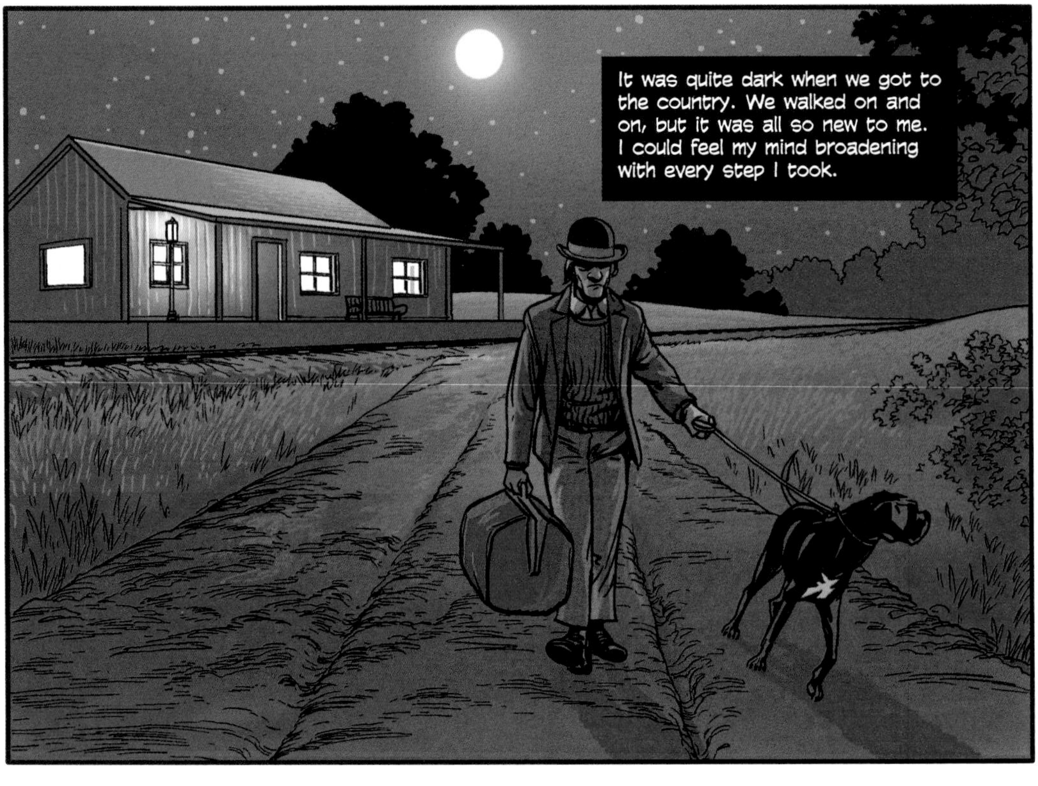
It was quite dark when we got to the country. We walked on and on, but it was all so new to me. I could feel my mind broadening with every step I took.

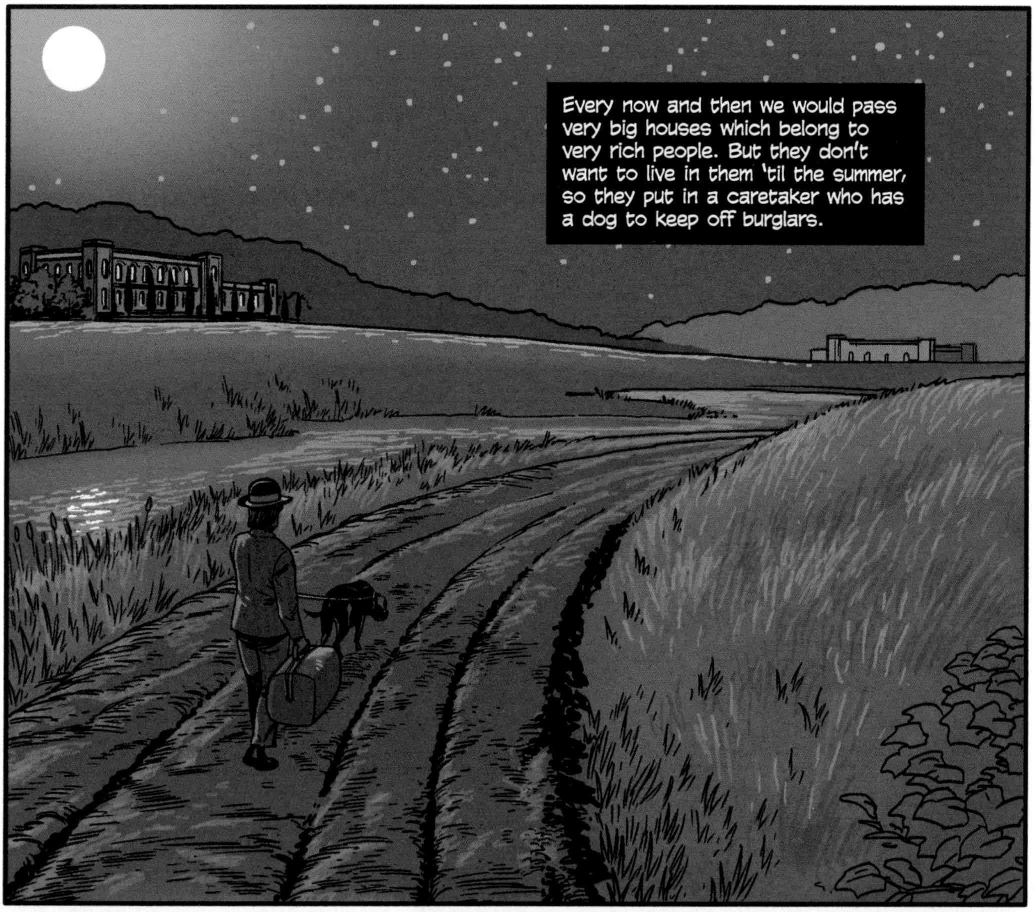
Every now and then we would pass very big houses which belong to very rich people. But they don't want to live in them 'til the summer, so they put in a caretaker who has a dog to keep off burglars.

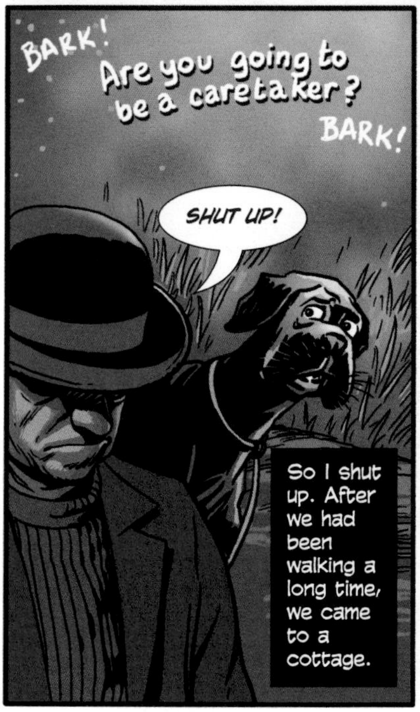
BARK!
Are you going to be a caretaker?
BARK!
SHUT UP!
So I shut up. After we had been walking a long time, we came to a cottage.

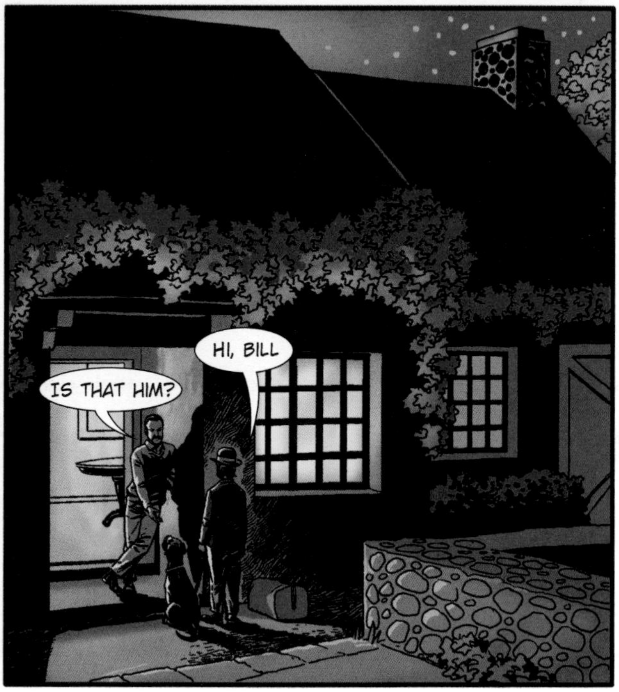
HI, BILL
IS THAT HIM?

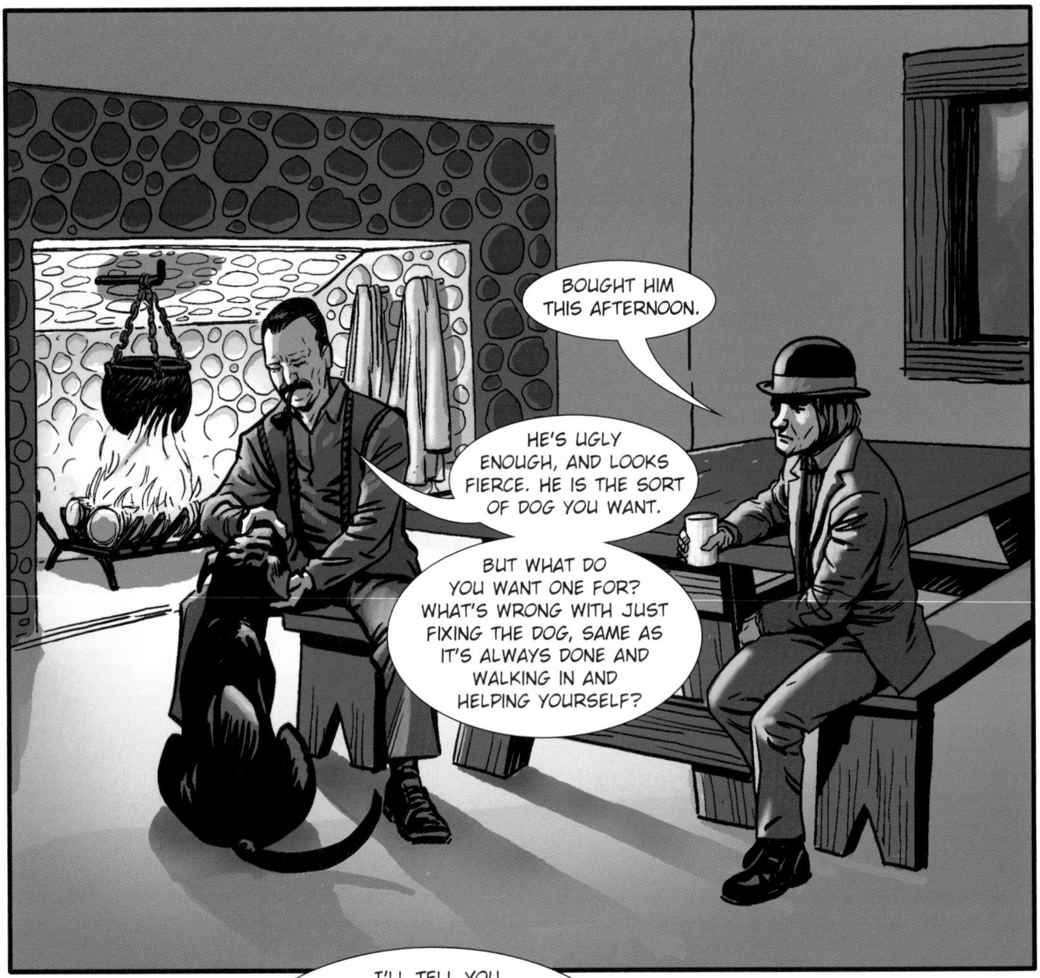
BOUGHT HIM THIS AFTERNOON.
HE'S UGLY ENOUGH, AND LOOKS FIERCE. HE IS THE SORT OF DOG YOU WANT.
BUT WHAT DO YOU WANT ONE FOR? WHAT'S WRONG WITH JUST FIXING THE DOG, SAME AS IT'S ALWAYS DONE AND WALKING IN AND HELPING YOURSELF?

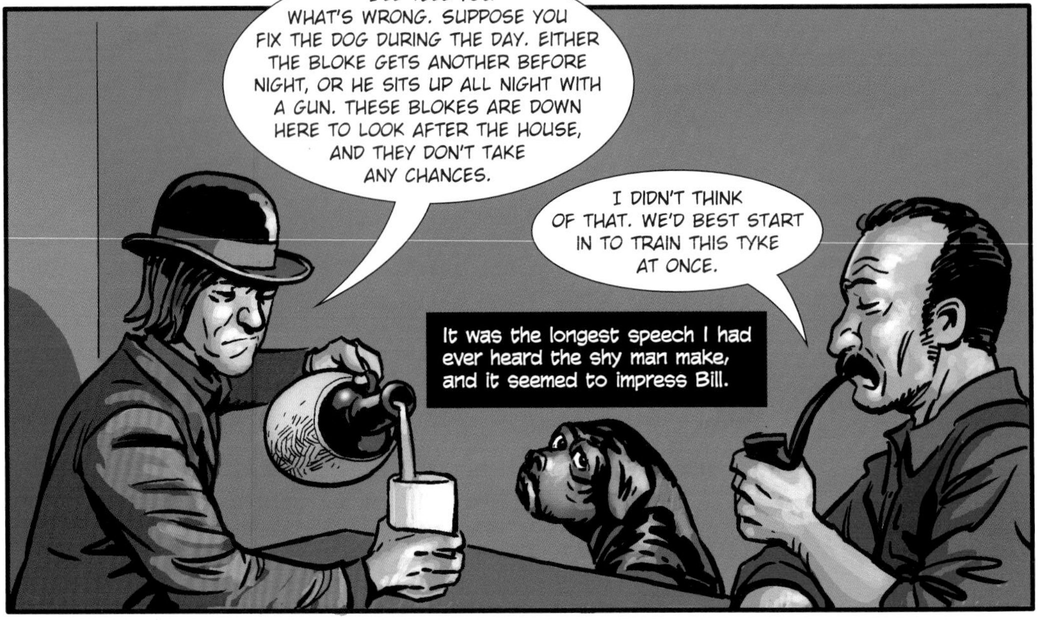
I'LL TELL YOU WHAT'S WRONG. SUPPOSE YOU FIX THE DOG DURING THE DAY. EITHER THE BLOKE GETS ANOTHER BEFORE NIGHT, OR HE SITS UP ALL NIGHT WITH A GUN. THESE BLOKES ARE DOWN HERE TO LOOK AFTER THE HOUSE, AND THEY DON'T TAKE ANY CHANCES.
I DIDN'T THINK OF THAT. WE'D BEST START IN TO TRAIN THIS TYKE AT ONCE.
It was the longest speech I had ever heard the shy man make, and it seemed to impress Bill.

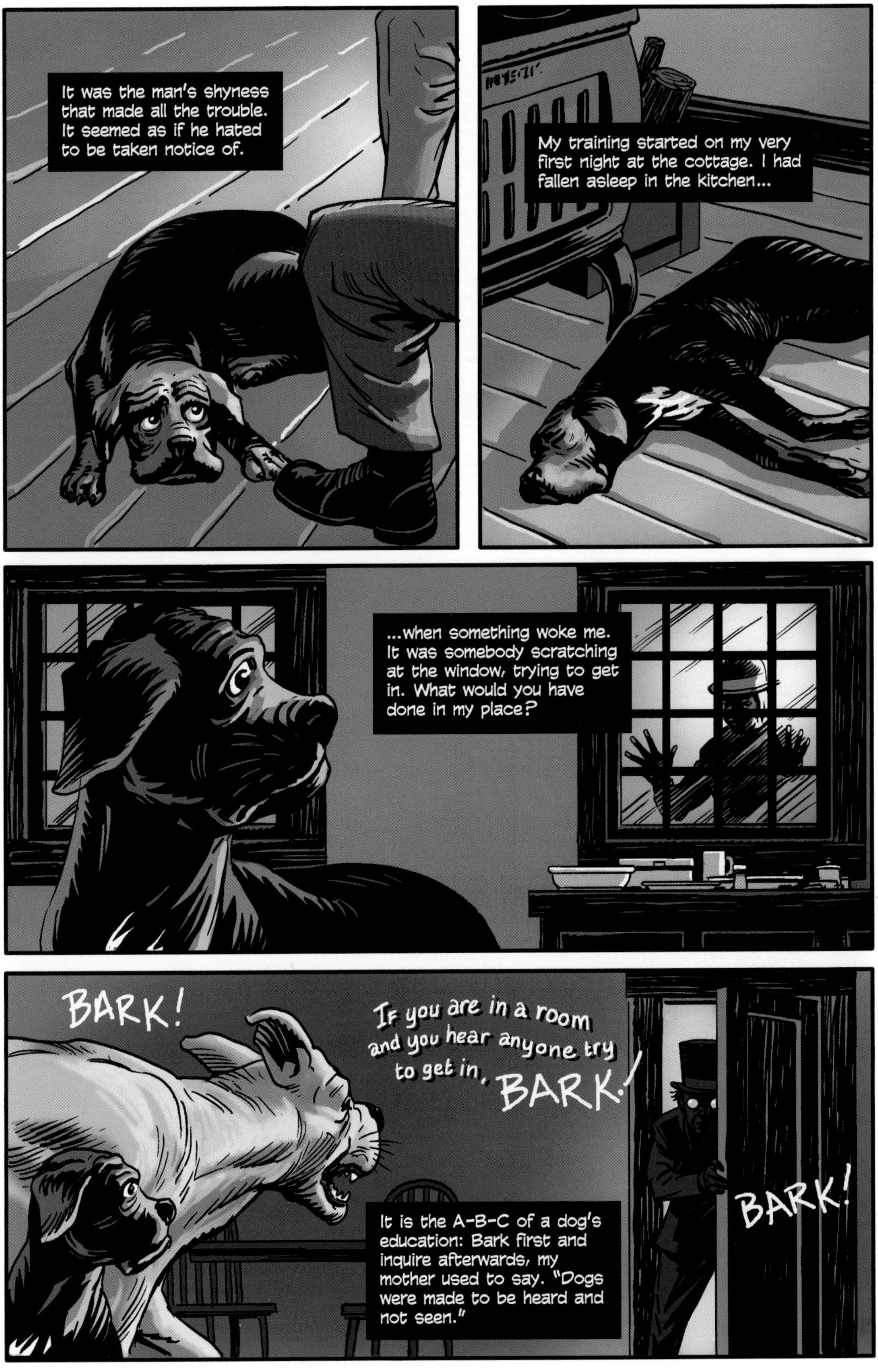
It was the man's shyness that made all the trouble. It seemed as if he hated to be taken notice of.
My training started on my very first night at the cottage. I had fallen asleep in the kitchen...
...when something woke me. It was somebody scratching at the window, trying to get in. What would you have done in my place?
BARK!
If you are in a room and you hear anyone try to get in, BARK!
It is the A-B-C of a dog's education: Bark first and inquire afterwards, my mother used to say. "Dogs were made to be heard and not seen."
BARK!

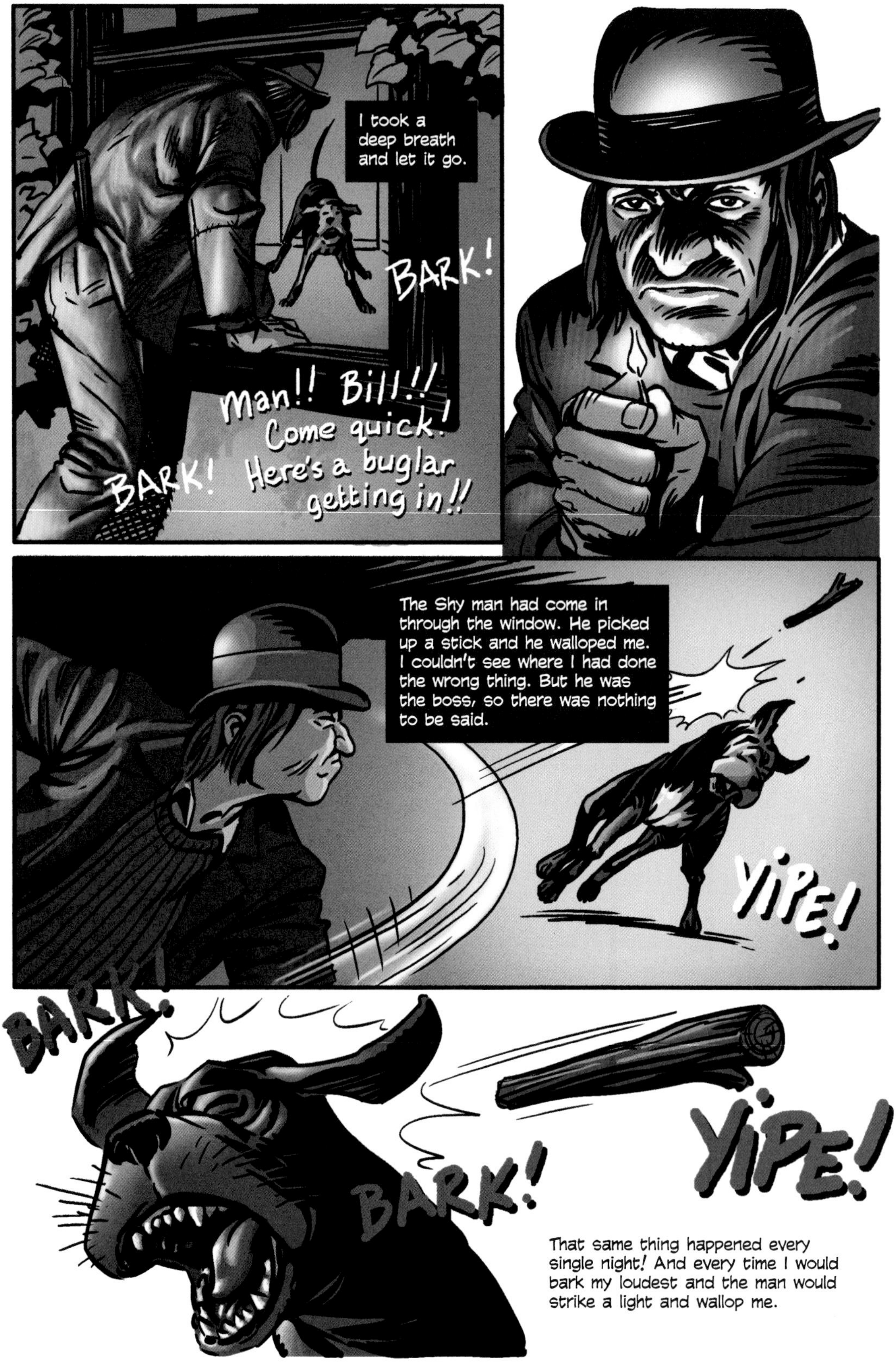
I took a deep breath and let it go.
BARK!
Man!! Bill!! Come quick! Here's a buglar getting in!!
BARK!
The Shy man had come in through the window. He picked up a stick and he walloped me. I couldn't see where I had done the wrong thing. But he was the boss, so there was nothing to be said.
YIPE!
BARK!
BARK!
YIPE!
That same thing happened every single night! And every time I would bark my loudest and the man would strike a light and wallop me.

I couldn't possibly have mistaken what mother had said to me. Bark! Bark! Bark! And yet, here I was getting walloped every night for doing it.

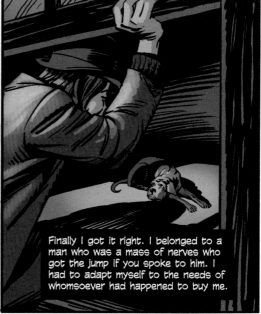

Finally I got it right. I belonged to a man who was a mass of nerves who got the jump if you spoke to him. I had to adapt myself to the needs of whomsoever had happened to buy me.

GOOD DOG! NOW YOU CAN HAVE THIS!

So the next night, when I heard the window go, I didn't even growl. Someone came in but I smelt that it was the shy man. I didn't ask him a single question. The man came over to me and gave me a pat and let me lick out the saucepan in which the dinner had been cooked.

After that, we got on fine. Whenever I heard anyone at the window I just kept curled up and took no notice. And every time I got a bone or something good. It was easy once you had got the hang of things.

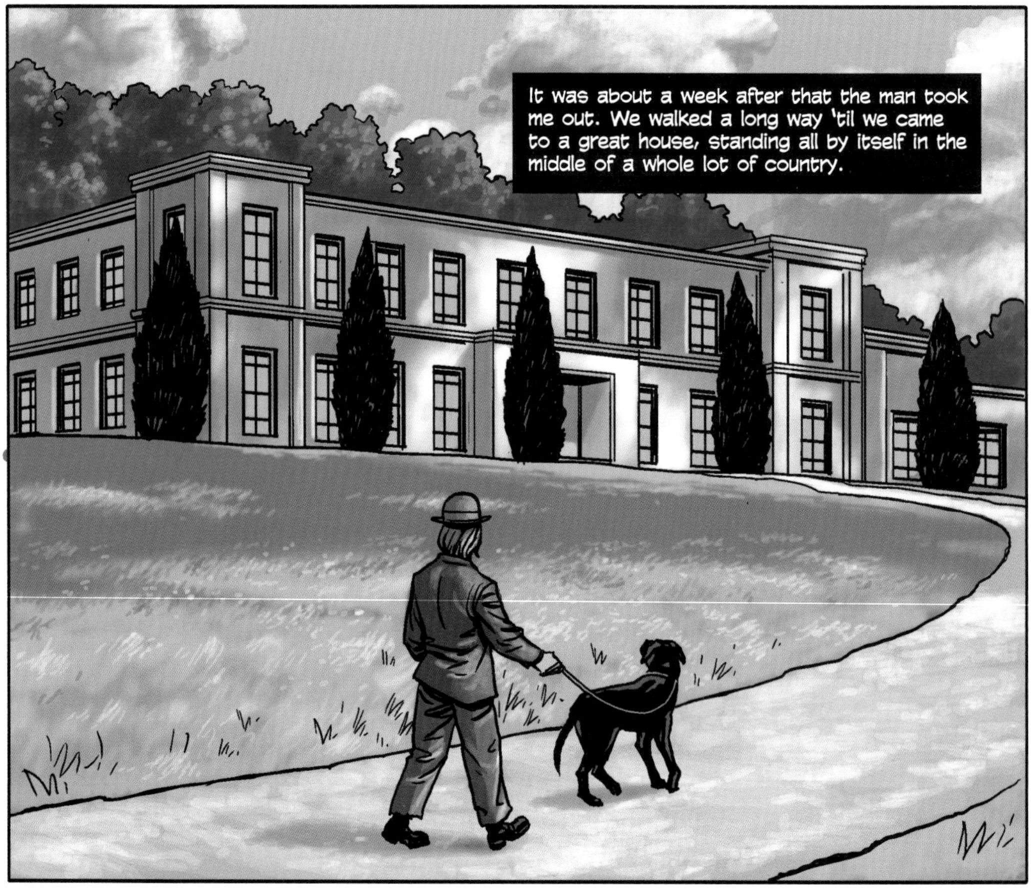
It was about a week after that the man took me out. We walked a long way 'til we came to a great house, standing all by itself in the middle of a whole lot of country.

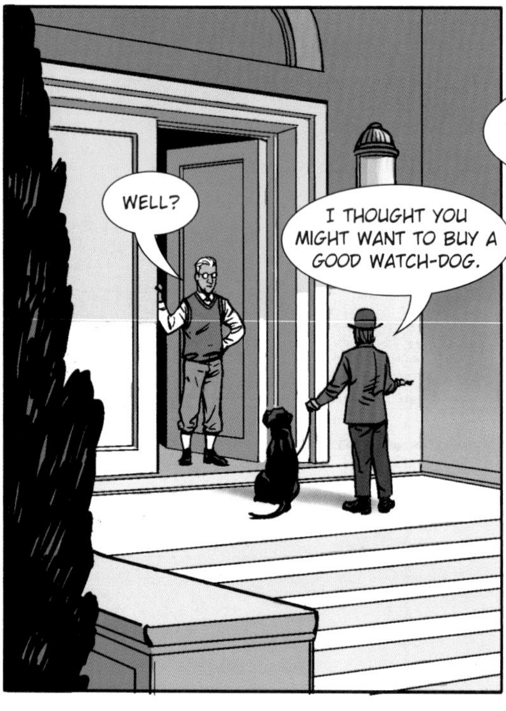
WELL?
I THOUGHT YOU MIGHT WANT TO BUY A GOOD WATCH-DOG.

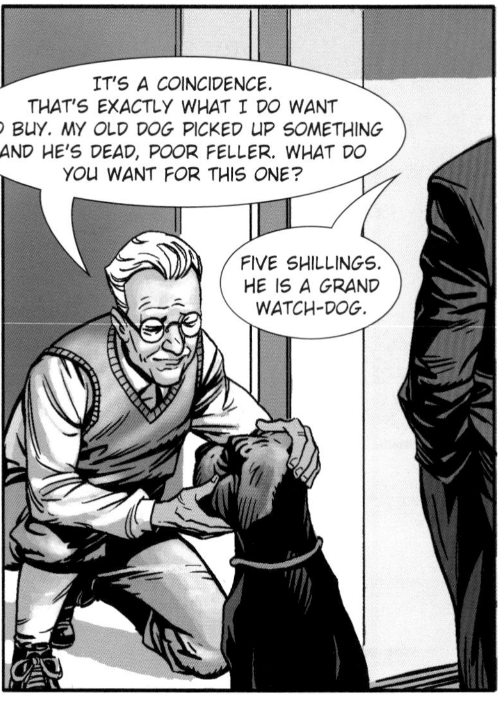
IT'S A COINCIDENCE. THAT'S EXACTLY WHAT I DO WANT TO BUY. MY OLD DOG PICKED UP SOMETHING AND HE'S DEAD, POOR FELLER. WHAT DO YOU WANT FOR THIS ONE?
FIVE SHILLINGS. HE IS A GRAND WATCH-DOG.

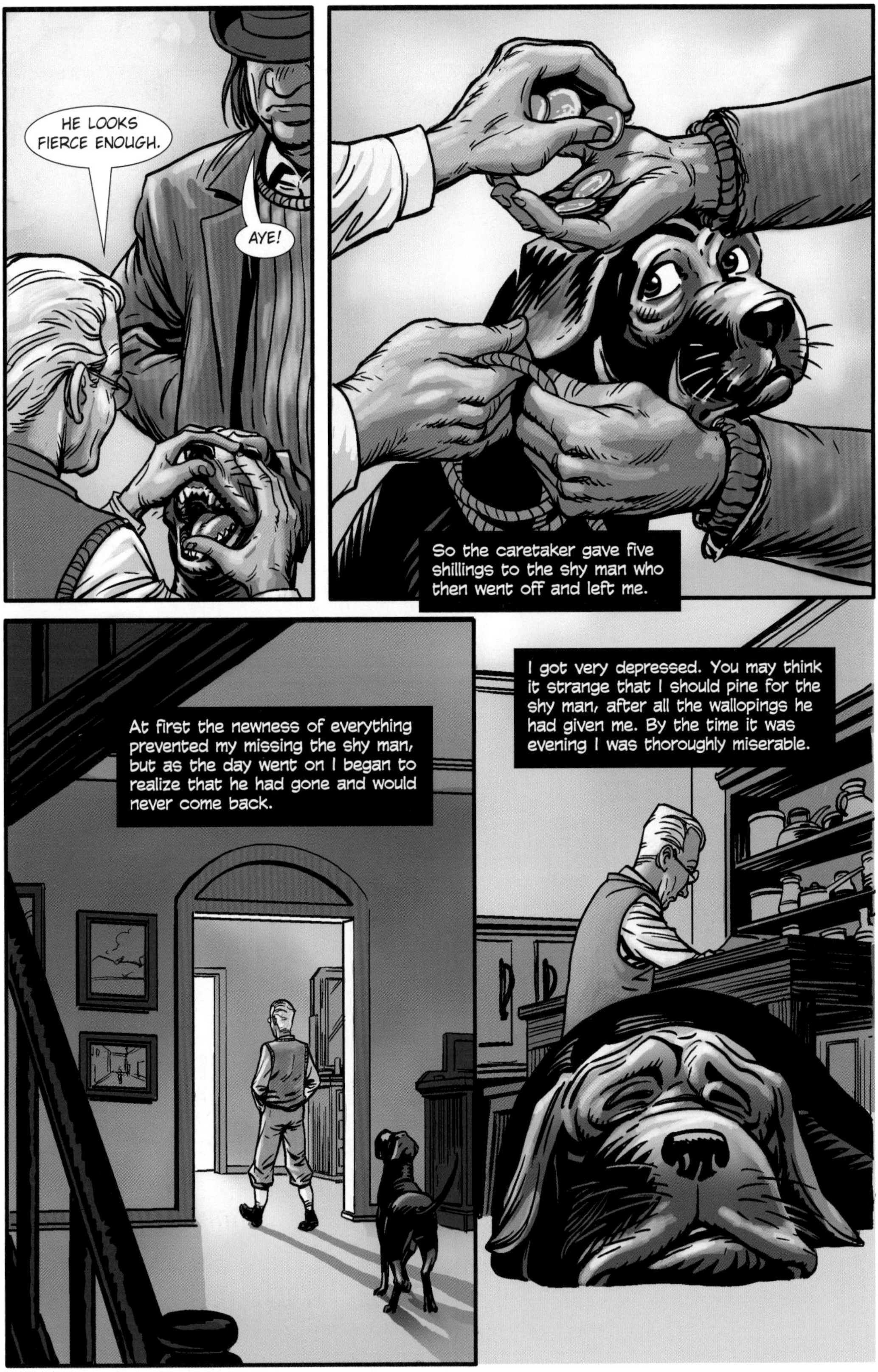
HE LOOKS FIERCE ENOUGH.
AYE!
So the caretaker gave five shillings to the shy man who then went off and left me.
At first the newness of everything prevented my missing the shy man, but as the day went on I began to realize that he had gone and would never come back.
I got very depressed. You may think it strange that I should pine for the shy man, after all the wallopings he had given me. By the time it was evening I was thoroughly miserable.

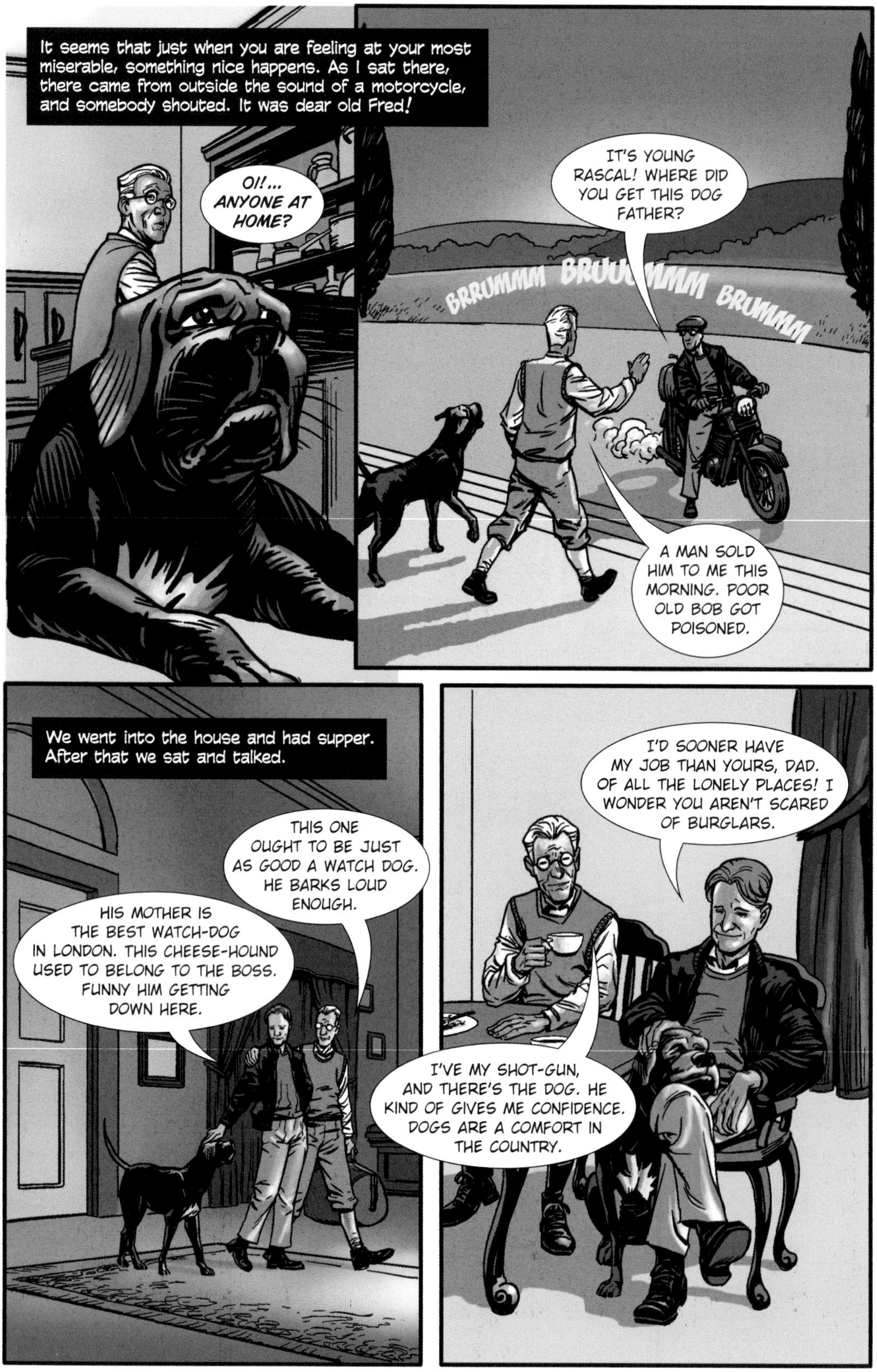
It seems that just when you are feeling at your most miserable, something nice happens. As I sat there, there came from outside the sound of a motorcycle, and somebody shouted. It was dear old Fred!
OI!... ANYONE AT HOME?
IT'S YOUNG RASCAL! WHERE DID YOU GET THIS DOG FATHER?
BRRUMMM BRUUUMMM BRUMMM
A MAN SOLD HIM TO ME THIS MORNING. POOR OLD BOB GOT POISONED.
We went into the house and had supper. After that we sat and talked.
THIS ONE OUGHT TO BE JUST AS GOOD A WATCH DOG. HE BARKS LOUD ENOUGH.
HIS MOTHER IS THE BEST WATCH-DOG IN LONDON. THIS CHEESE-HOUND USED TO BELONG TO THE BOSS. FUNNY HIM GETTING DOWN HERE.
I'D SOONER HAVE MY JOB THAN YOURS, DAD. OF ALL THE LONELY PLACES! I WONDER YOU AREN'T SCARED OF BURGLARS.
I'VE MY SHOT-GUN, AND THERE'S THE DOG. HE KIND OF GIVES ME CONFIDENCE. DOGS ARE A COMFORT IN THE COUNTRY.

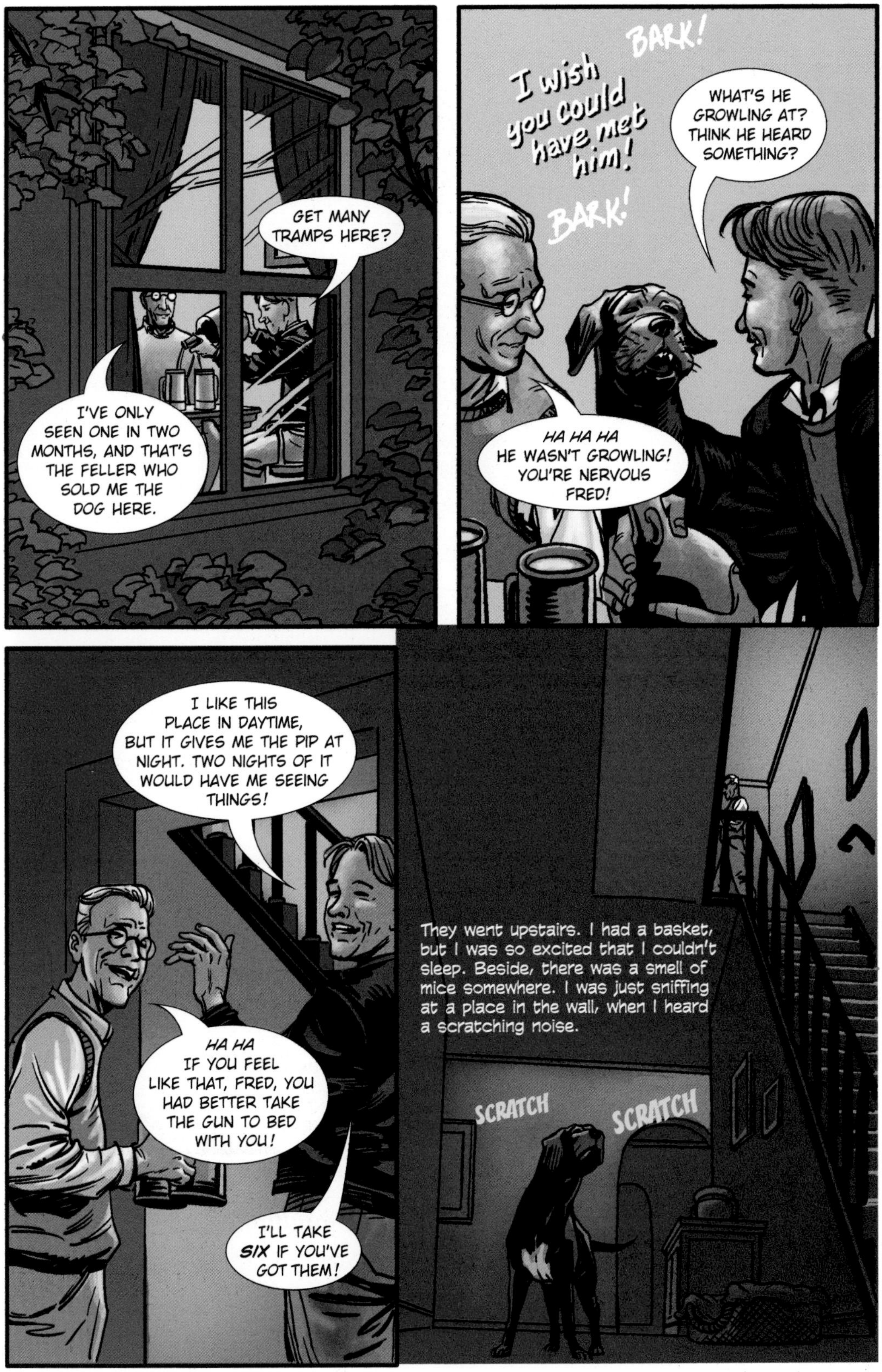
GET MANY TRAMPS HERE?
I'VE ONLY SEEN ONE IN TWO MONTHS, AND THAT'S THE FELLER WHO SOLD ME THE DOG HERE.
BARK!
I wish you could have met him!
WHAT'S HE GROWLING AT? THINK HE HEARD SOMETHING?
BARK!
HA HA HA HE WASN'T GROWLING! YOU'RE NERVOUS FRED!
I LIKE THIS PLACE IN DAYTIME, BUT IT GIVES ME THE PIP AT NIGHT. TWO NIGHTS OF IT WOULD HAVE ME SEEING THINGS!
HA HA IF YOU FEEL LIKE THAT, FRED, YOU HAD BETTER TAKE THE GUN TO BED WITH YOU!
I'LL TAKE SIX IF YOU'VE GOT THEM!
They went upstairs. I had a basket, but I was so excited that I couldn't sleep. Beside, there was a smell of mice somewhere. I was just sniffing at a place in the wall, when I heard a scratching noise.
SCRATCH
SCRATCH

I found that the sound came from the window; somebody was doing something to it from outside. I didn't bark, I stopped where I was and listened.

GOOD BOY! DOWN!

Somebody began to climb in, I gave a good sniff and I knew it was the shy man. I was disappointed that he didn't seem more pleased to see me.

I could see him moving about the room, picking up things and putting them in a bag. He was very quick and very quiet. It was plain he didn't want Fred or his father to come down and find him. I couldn't help feeling that the man carried shyness to a point where it became morbid and he didn't give himself a chance to cure himself of it.

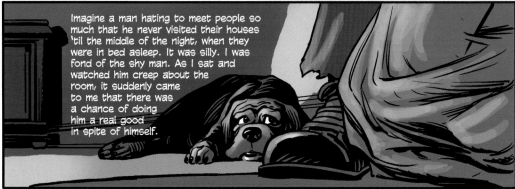

Imagine a man hating to meet people so much that he never visited their houses 'til the middle of the night, when they were in bed asleep. It was silly. I was fond of the shy man. As I sat and watched him creep about the room, it suddenly came to me that there was a chance of doing him a real good in spite of himself.

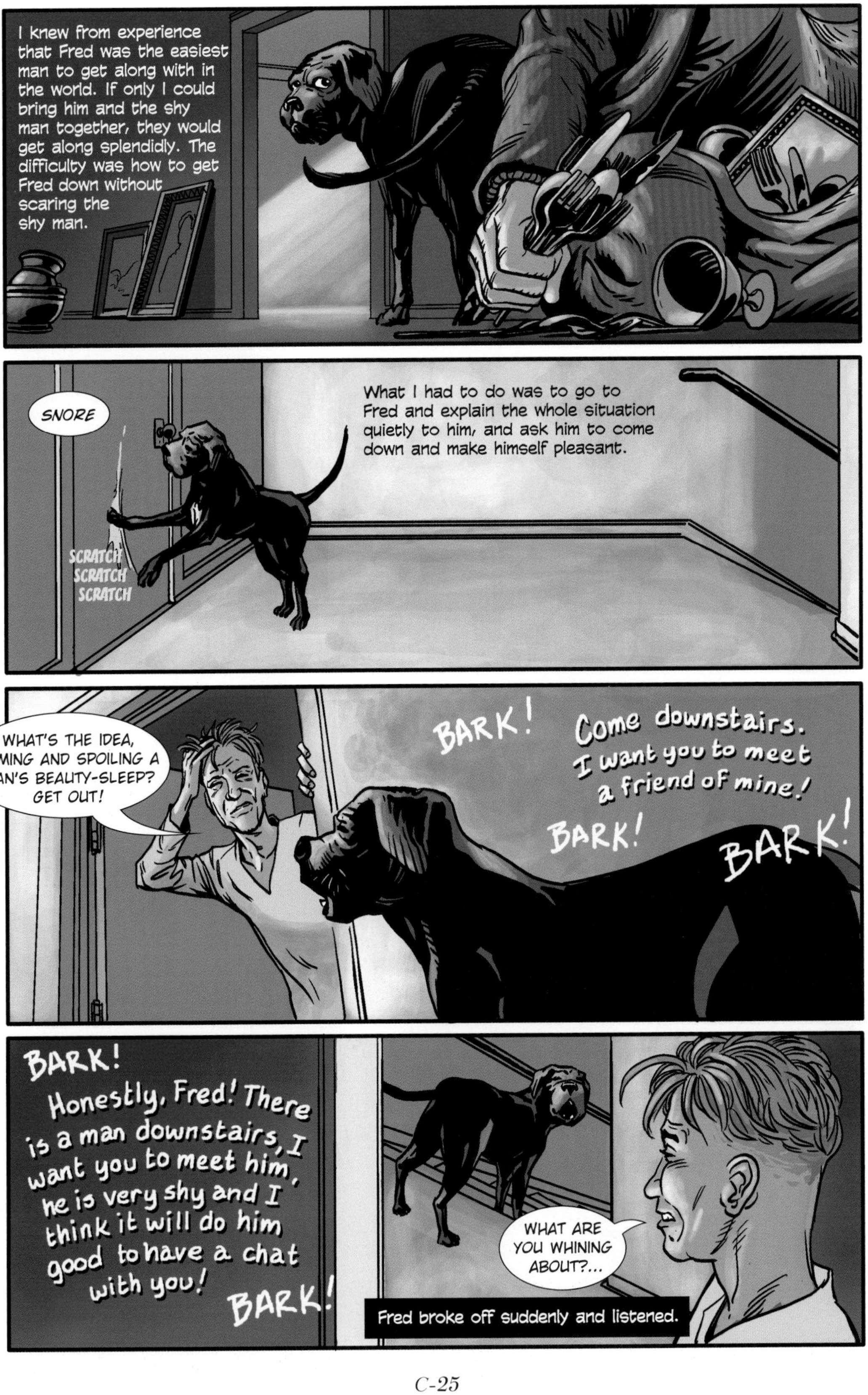
I knew from experience that Fred was the easiest man to get along with in the world. If only I could bring him and the shy man together, they would get along splendidly. The difficulty was how to get Fred down without scaring the shy man.
SNORE
What I had to do was to go to Fred and explain the whole situation quietly to him, and ask him to come down and make himself pleasant.
SCRATCH SCRATCH SCRATCH
WHAT'S THE IDEA, COMING AND SPOILING A MAN'S BEAUTY-SLEEP? GET OUT!
BARK!
Come downstairs. I want you to meet a friend of mine!
BARK!
BARK!
BARK!
Honestly, Fred! There is a man downstairs, I want you to meet him, he is very shy and I think it will do him good to have a chat with you!
BARK!
WHAT ARE YOU WHINING ABOUT?...
Fred broke off suddenly and listened.

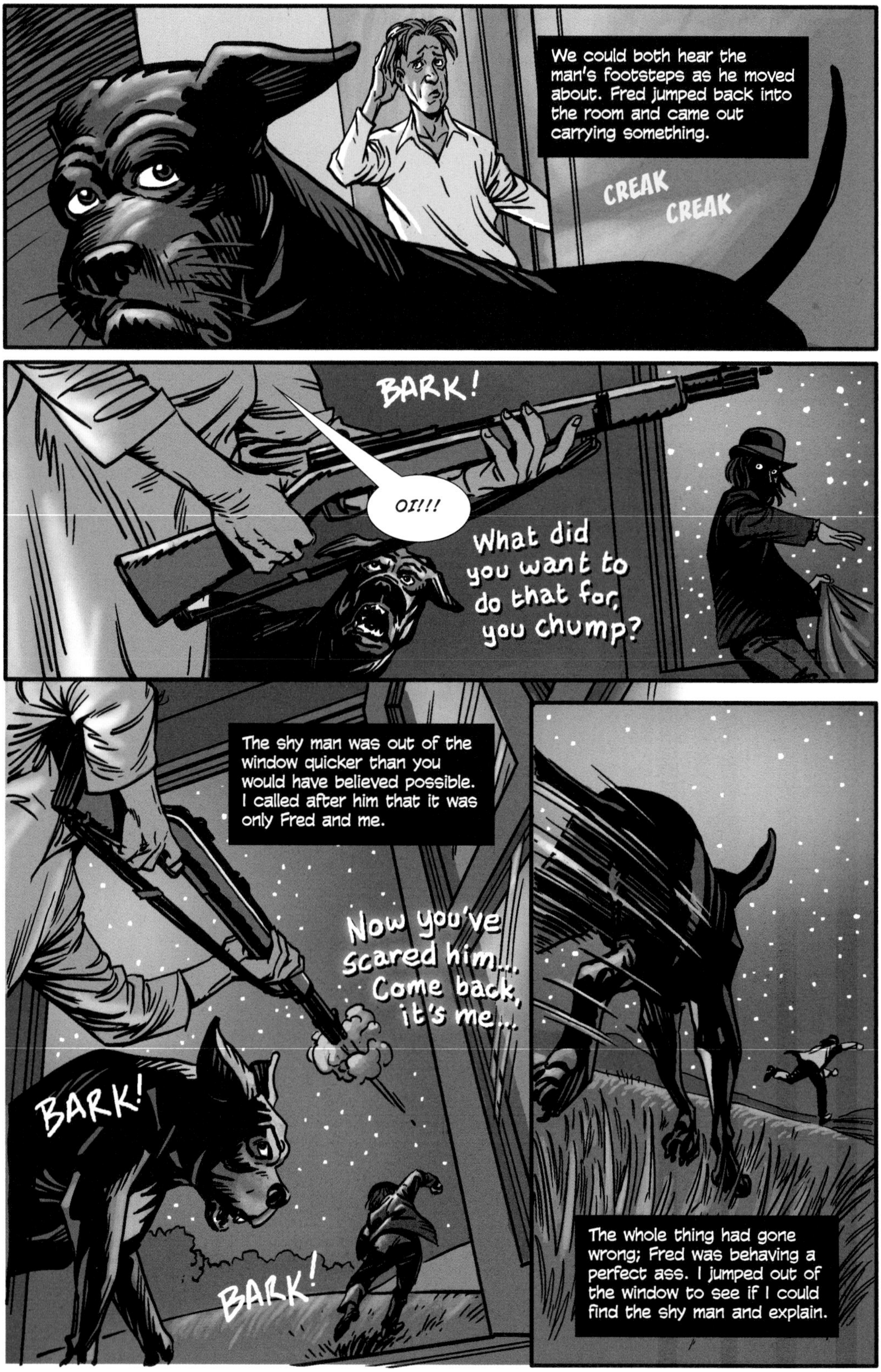
We could both hear the man's footsteps as he moved about. Fred jumped back into the room and came out carrying something.
CREAK
CREAK
BARK!
OI!!!
What did you want to do that for, you chump?
The shy man was out of the window quicker than you would have believed possible. I called after him that it was only Fred and me.
Now you've scared him... Come back, it's me...
BARK!
BARK!
The whole thing had gone wrong; Fred was behaving a perfect ass. I jumped out of the window to see if I could find the shy man and explain.

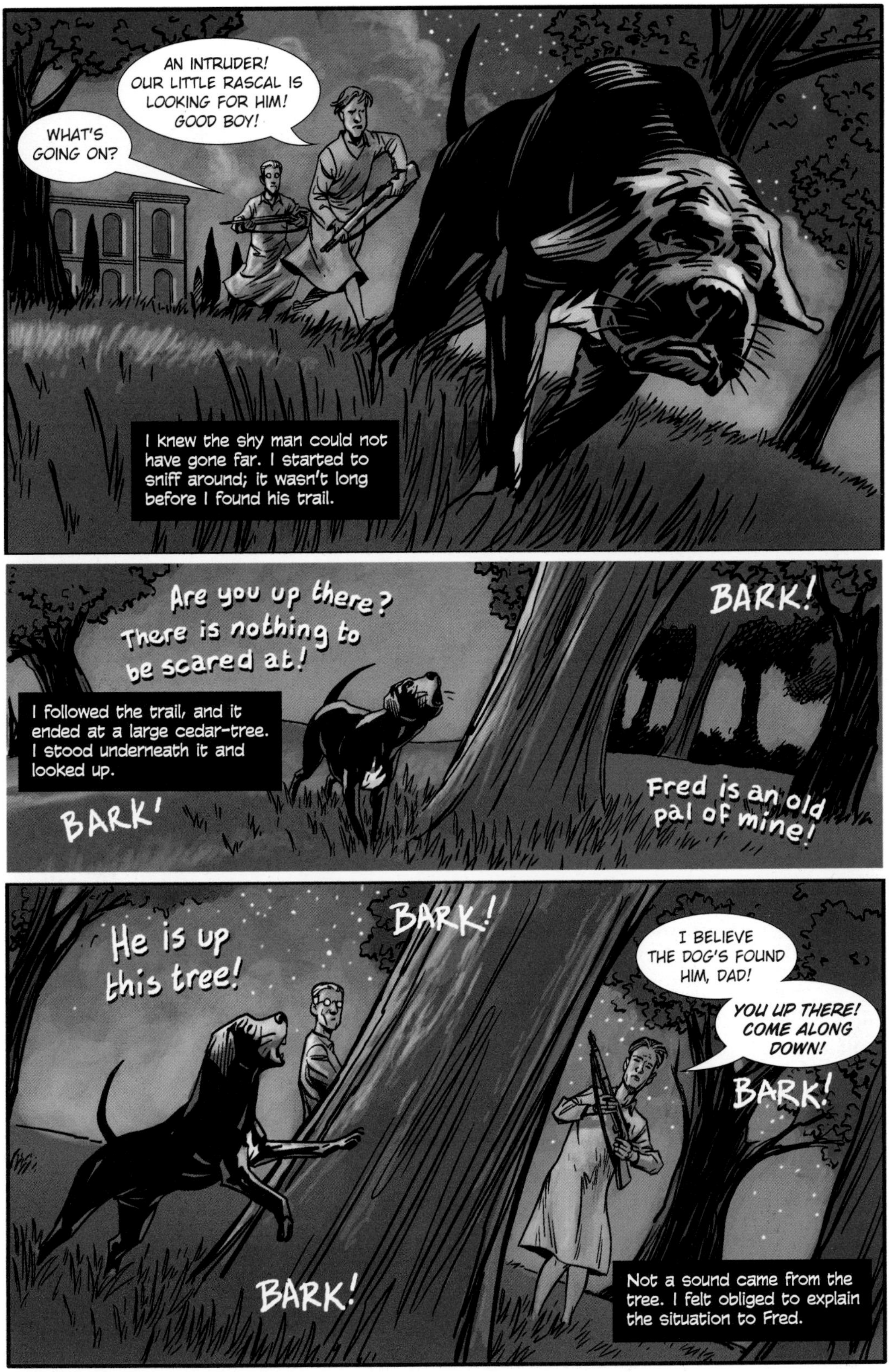
WHAT'S GOING ON?
AN INTRUDER! OUR LITTLE RASCAL IS LOOKING FOR HIM! GOOD BOY!
I knew the shy man could not have gone far. I started to sniff around; it wasn't long before I found his trail.
Are you up there? There is nothing to be scared at!
BARK!
I followed the trail, and it ended at a large cedar-tree. I stood underneath it and looked up.
BARK!
Fred is an old pal of mine!
He is up this tree!
BARK!
I BELIEVE THE DOG'S FOUND HIM, DAD!
YOU UP THERE! COME ALONG DOWN!
BARK!
BARK!
Not a sound came from the tree. I felt obliged to explain the situation to Fred.

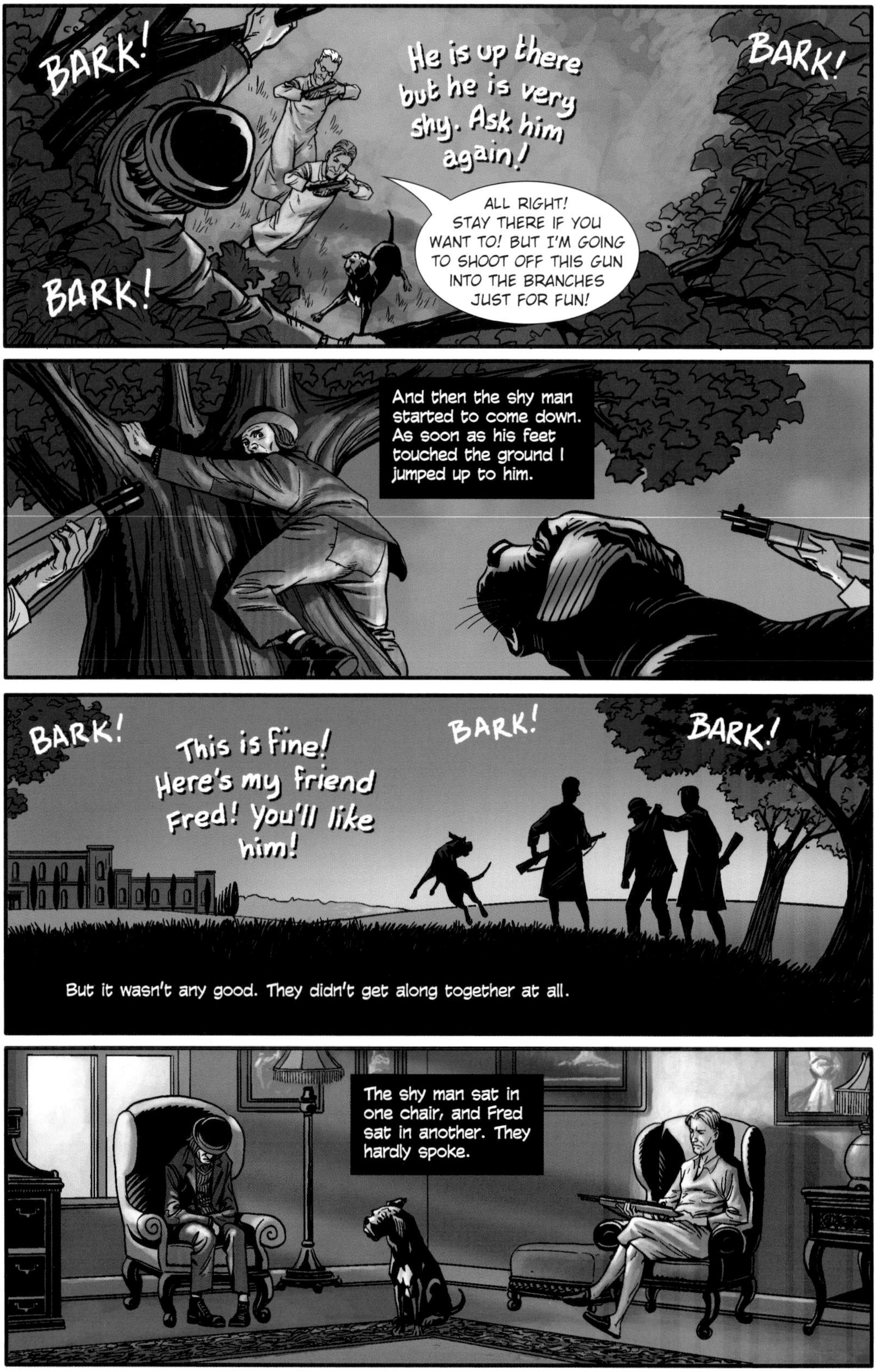
BARK!
He is up there but he is very shy. Ask him again!
BARK!
BARK!
ALL RIGHT! STAY THERE IF YOU WANT TO! BUT I'M GOING TO SHOOT OFF THIS GUN INTO THE BRANCHES JUST FOR FUN!
And then the shy man started to come down. As soon as his feet touched the ground I jumped up to him.
BARK!
This is fine! Here's my friend Fred! You'll like him!
BARK!
BARK!
But it wasn't any good. They didn't get along together at all.
The shy man sat in one chair, and Fred sat in another. They hardly spoke.

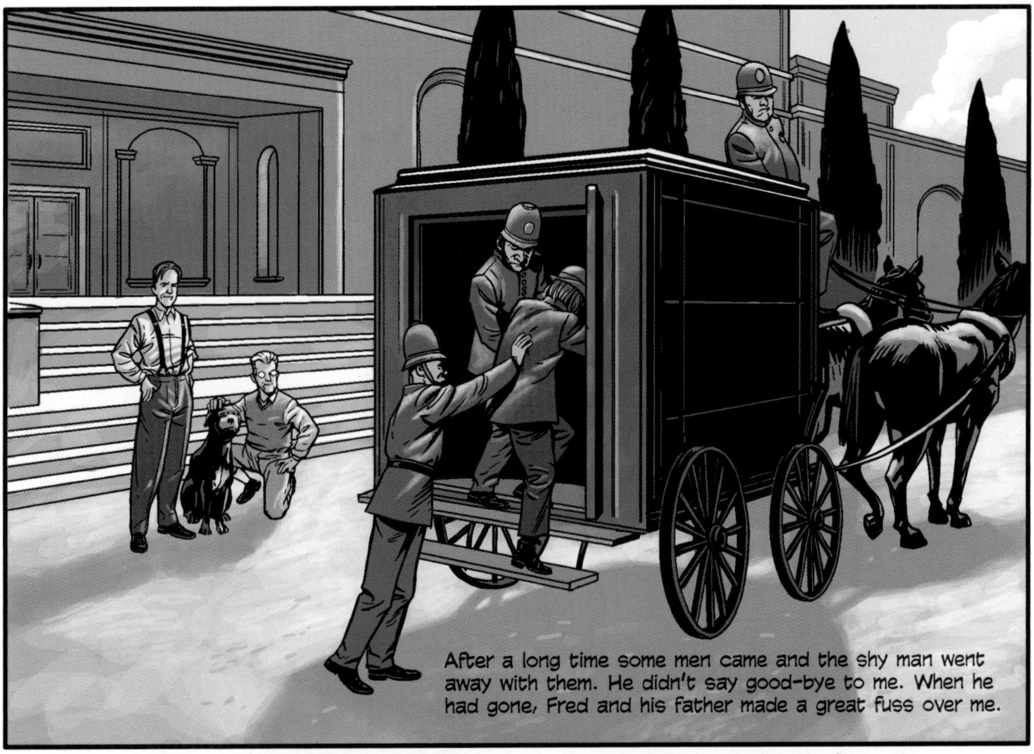
After a long time some men came and the shy man went away with them. He didn't say good-bye to me. When he had gone, Fred and his father made a great fuss over me.

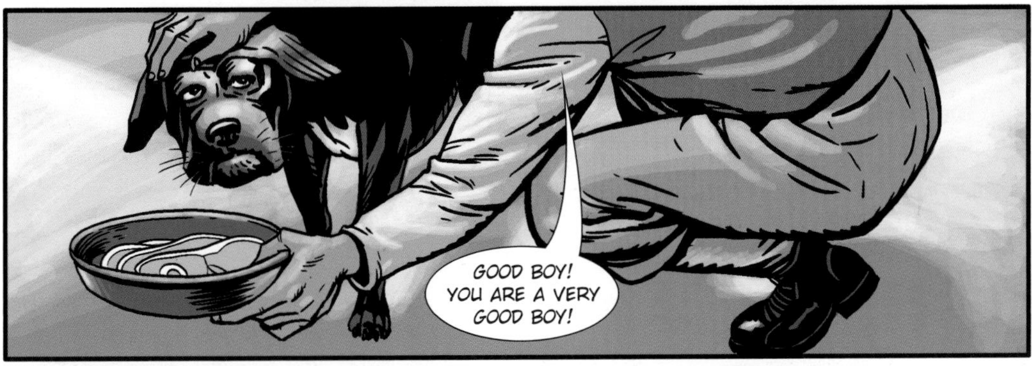
GOOD BOY! YOU ARE A VERY GOOD BOY!

Men are so odd. The shy man wasn't pleased that I had brought him and Fred together. But Fred seemed very pleased with me for having introduced him to the man. Fred's father gave me quite a lot of cold ham. So I stopped worrying over the thing.

As mother used to say: "Eat your bun and don't make yourself busy about other people's affairs." Mother's was in some ways a narrow outlook, but she had a great fund of sterling common sense.

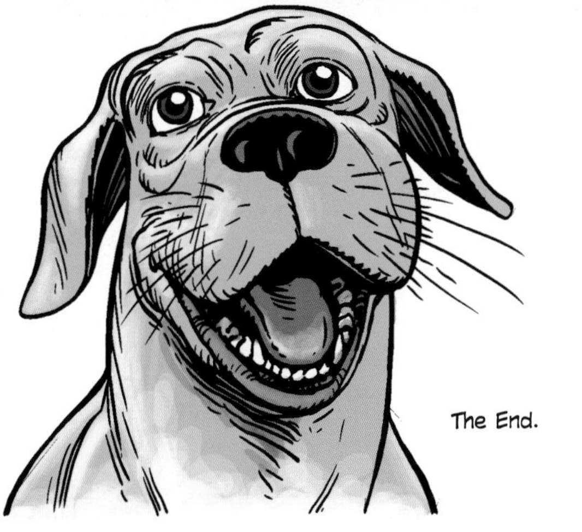

The End.

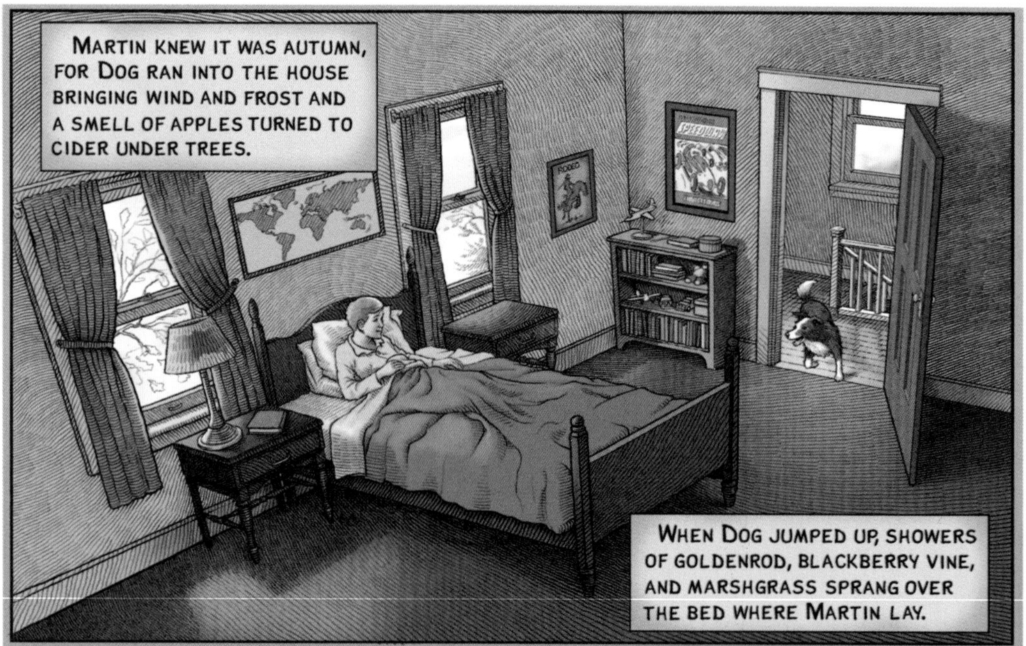
MARTIN KNEW IT WAS AUTUMN, FOR DOG RAN INTO THE HOUSE BRINGING WIND AND FROST AND A SMELL OF APPLES TURNED TO CIDER UNDER TREES.
WHEN DOG JUMPED UP, SHOWERS OF GOLDENROD, BLACKBERRY VINE, AND MARSHGRASS SPRANG OVER THE BED WHERE MARTIN LAY.

adapted by Tom Pomplun **illustrated by John Findley**

The Emissary

by Ray Bradbury (1947)

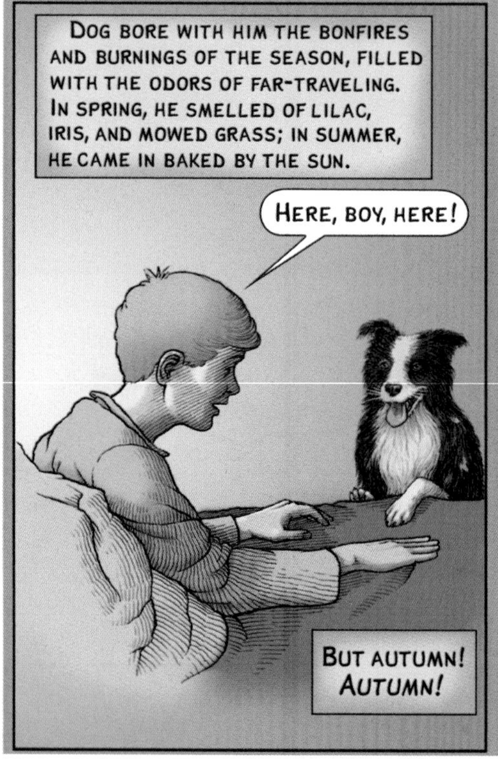
DOG BORE WITH HIM THE BONFIRES AND BURNINGS OF THE SEASON, FILLED WITH THE ODORS OF FAR-TRAVELING. IN SPRING, HE SMELLED OF LILAC, IRIS, AND MOWED GRASS; IN SUMMER, HE CAME IN BAKED BY THE SUN.
HERE, BOY, HERE!
BUT AUTUMN! AUTUMN!

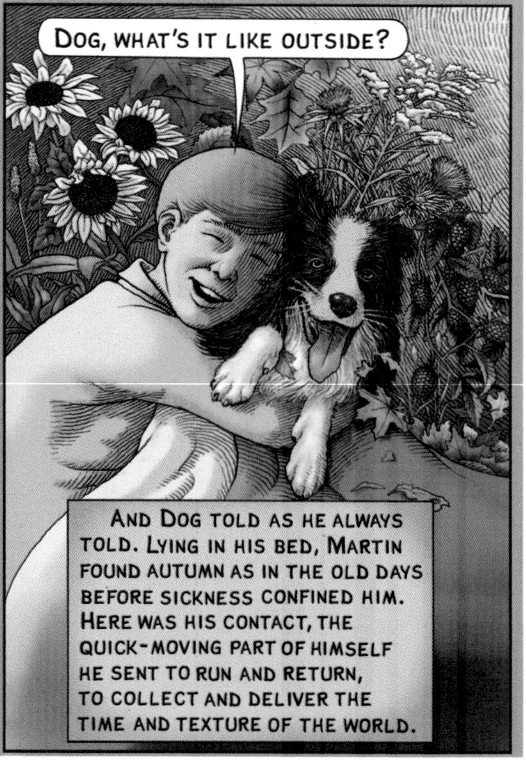
DOG, WHAT'S IT LIKE OUTSIDE?
AND DOG TOLD AS HE ALWAYS TOLD. LYING IN HIS BED, MARTIN FOUND AUTUMN AS IN THE OLD DAYS BEFORE SICKNESS CONFINED HIM. HERE WAS HIS CONTACT, THE QUICK-MOVING PART OF HIMSELF HE SENT TO RUN AND RETURN, TO COLLECT AND DELIVER THE TIME AND TEXTURE OF THE WORLD.

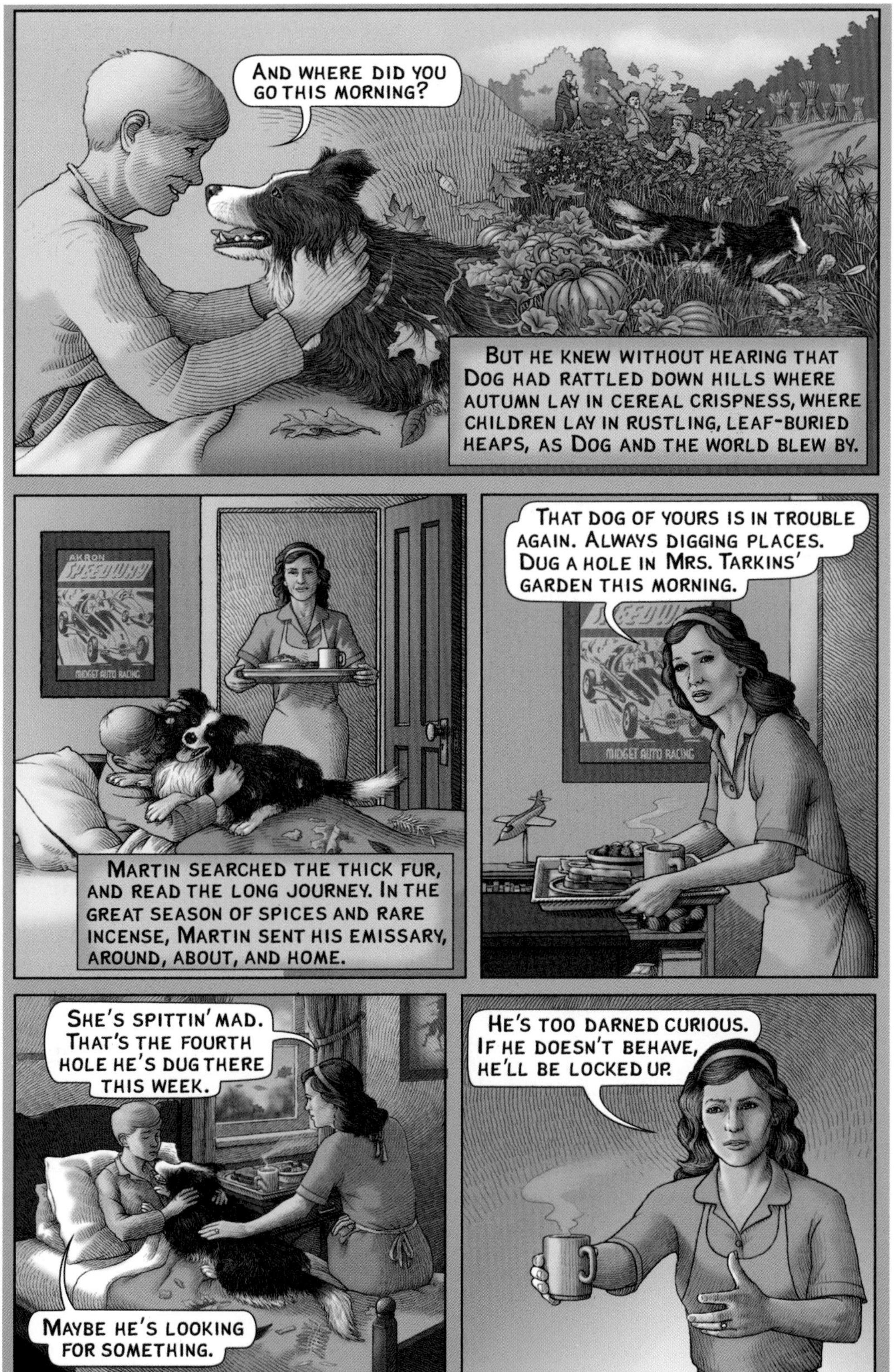
AND WHERE DID YOU GO THIS MORNING?
BUT HE KNEW WITHOUT HEARING THAT DOG HAD RATTLED DOWN HILLS WHERE AUTUMN LAY IN CEREAL CRISPNESS, WHERE CHILDREN LAY IN RUSTLING, LEAF-BURIED HEAPS, AS DOG AND THE WORLD BLEW BY.
AKRON SPEEDWAY
MIDGET AUTO RACING
MARTIN SEARCHED THE THICK FUR, AND READ THE LONG JOURNEY. IN THE GREAT SEASON OF SPICES AND RARE INCENSE, MARTIN SENT HIS EMISSARY, AROUND, ABOUT, AND HOME.
THAT DOG OF YOURS IS IN TROUBLE AGAIN. ALWAYS DIGGING PLACES. DUG A HOLE IN MRS. TARKINS' GARDEN THIS MORNING.
MIDGET AUTO RACING
SHE'S SPITTIN' MAD. THAT'S THE FOURTH HOLE HE'S DUG THERE THIS WEEK.
MAYBE HE'S LOOKING FOR SOMETHING.
HE'S TOO DARNED CURIOUS. IF HE DOESN'T BEHAVE, HE'LL BE LOCKED UP.

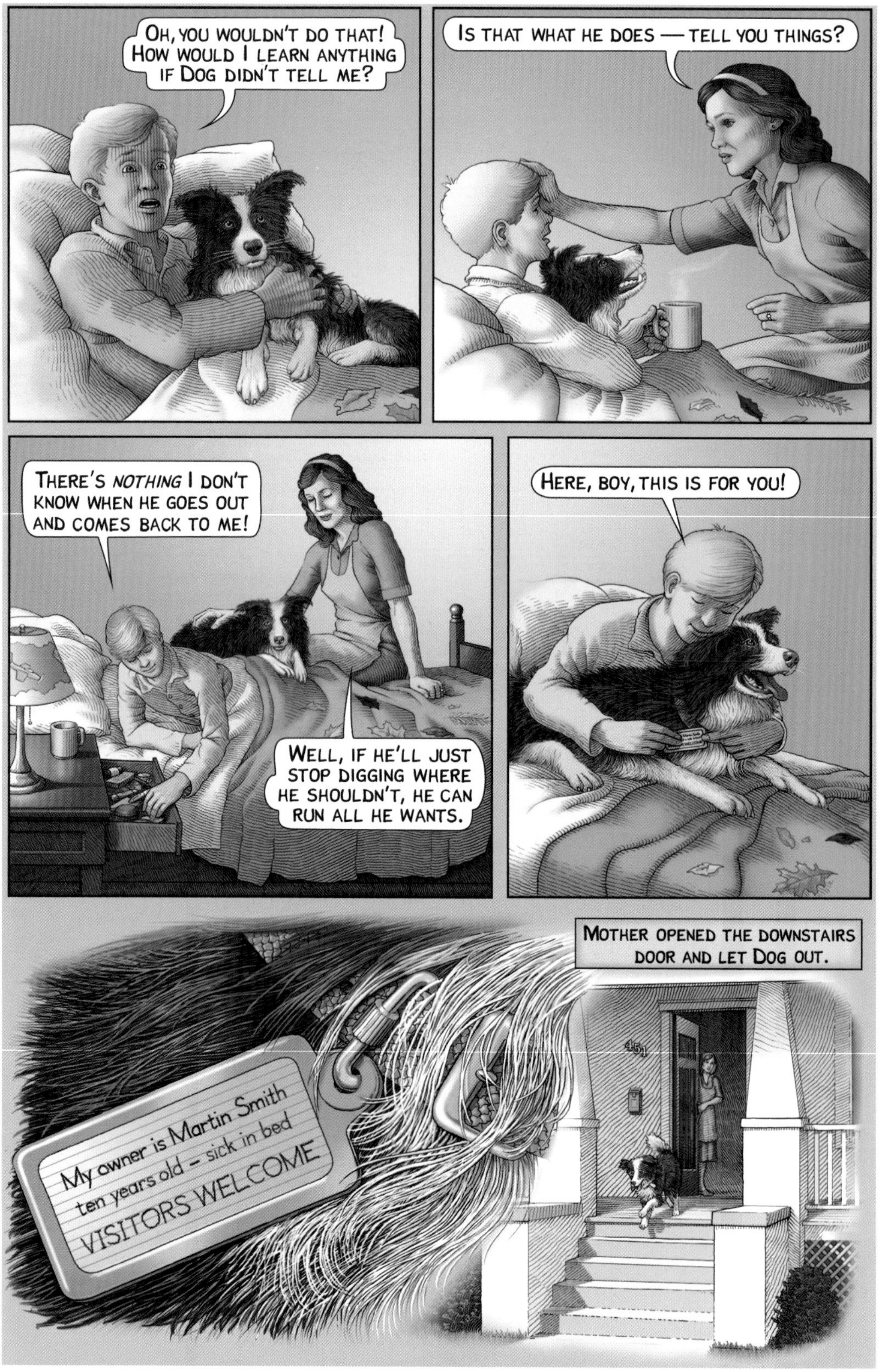
OH, YOU WOULDN'T DO THAT! HOW WOULD I LEARN ANYTHING IF DOG DIDN'T TELL ME?
IS THAT WHAT HE DOES — TELL YOU THINGS?
THERE'S *NOTHING* I DON'T KNOW WHEN HE GOES OUT AND COMES BACK TO ME!
WELL, IF HE'LL JUST STOP DIGGING WHERE HE SHOULDN'T, HE CAN RUN ALL HE WANTS.
HERE, BOY, THIS IS FOR YOU!
MOTHER OPENED THE DOWNSTAIRS DOOR AND LET DOG OUT.
My owner is Martin Smith
ten years old – sick in bed
VISITORS WELCOME
451

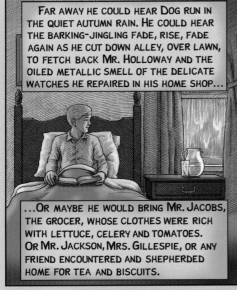

FAR AWAY HE COULD HEAR DOG RUN IN THE QUIET AUTUMN RAIN. HE COULD HEAR THE BARKING-JINGLING FADE, RISE, FADE AGAIN AS HE CUT DOWN ALLEY, OVER LAWN, TO FETCH BACK MR. HOLLOWAY AND THE OILED METALLIC SMELL OF THE DELICATE WATCHES HE REPAIRED IN HIS HOME SHOP...

...OR MAYBE HE WOULD BRING MR. JACOBS, THE GROCER, WHOSE CLOTHES WERE RICH WITH LETTUCE, CELERY AND TOMATOES. OR MR. JACKSON, MRS. GILLESPIE, OR ANY FRIEND ENCOUNTERED AND SHEPHERDED HOME FOR TEA AND BISCUITS.

MARTIN HEARD DOG BELOW, AND THE DOORBELL RANG. MOM OPENED THE DOOR, AND A YOUNG WOMAN'S VOICE LAUGHED QUIETLY. MISS HAIGHT, OF COURSE, HIS TEACHER FROM SCHOOL!

MARTIN HAD COMPANY.

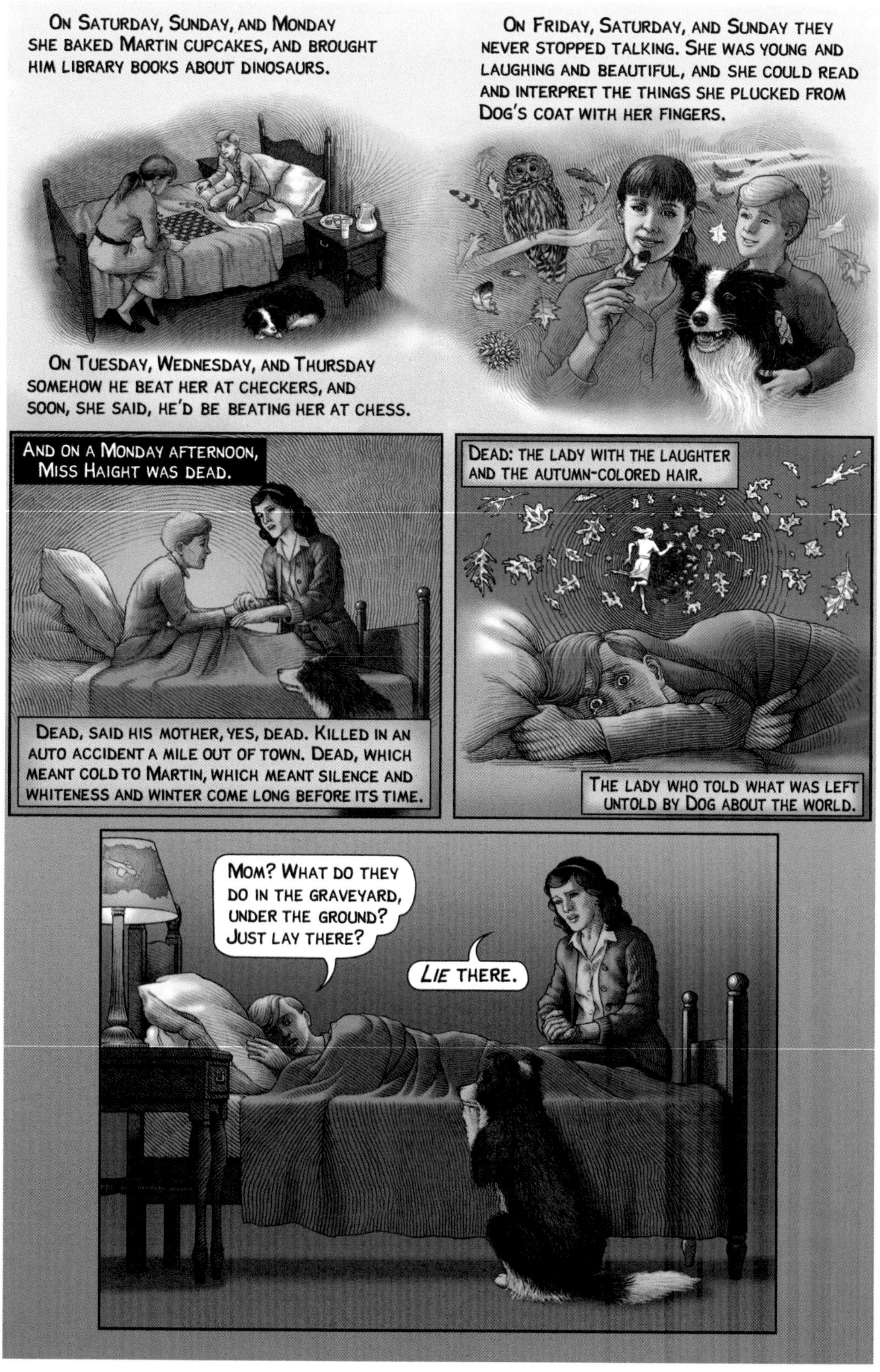
ON SATURDAY, SUNDAY, AND MONDAY SHE BAKED MARTIN CUPCAKES, AND BROUGHT HIM LIBRARY BOOKS ABOUT DINOSAURS.
ON TUESDAY, WEDNESDAY, AND THURSDAY SOMEHOW HE BEAT HER AT CHECKERS, AND SOON, SHE SAID, HE'D BE BEATING HER AT CHESS.
ON FRIDAY, SATURDAY, AND SUNDAY THEY NEVER STOPPED TALKING. SHE WAS YOUNG AND LAUGHING AND BEAUTIFUL, AND SHE COULD READ AND INTERPRET THE THINGS SHE PLUCKED FROM DOG'S COAT WITH HER FINGERS.
AND ON A MONDAY AFTERNOON, MISS HAIGHT WAS DEAD.
DEAD, SAID HIS MOTHER, YES, DEAD. KILLED IN AN AUTO ACCIDENT A MILE OUT OF TOWN. DEAD, WHICH MEANT COLD TO MARTIN, WHICH MEANT SILENCE AND WHITENESS AND WINTER COME LONG BEFORE ITS TIME.
DEAD: THE LADY WITH THE LAUGHTER AND THE AUTUMN-COLORED HAIR.
THE LADY WHO TOLD WHAT WAS LEFT UNTOLD BY DOG ABOUT THE WORLD.
MOM? WHAT DO THEY DO IN THE GRAVEYARD, UNDER THE GROUND? JUST LAY THERE?
LIE THERE.

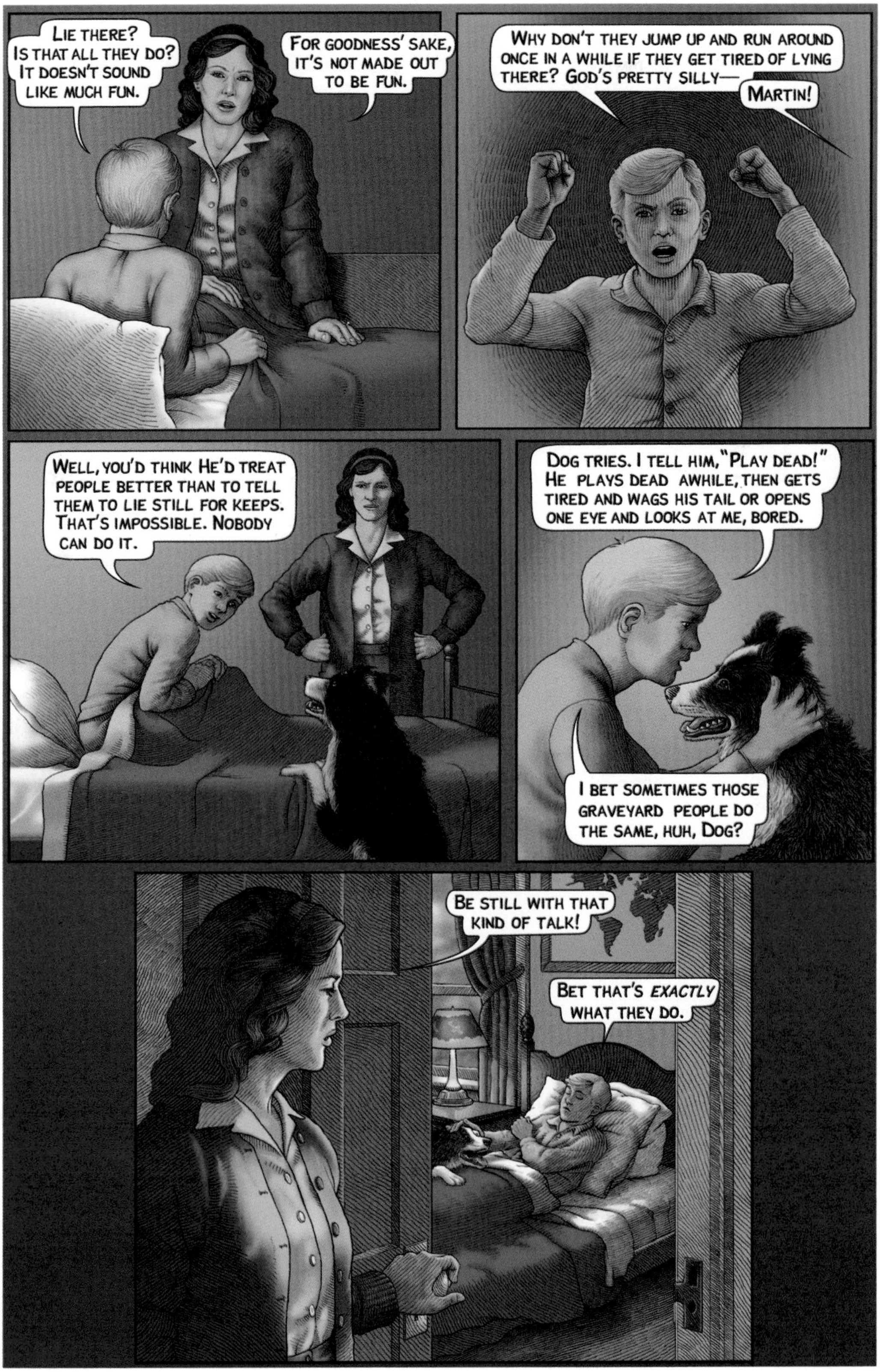
LIE THERE? IS THAT ALL THEY DO? IT DOESN'T SOUND LIKE MUCH FUN.
FOR GOODNESS' SAKE, IT'S NOT MADE OUT TO BE FUN.
WHY DON'T THEY JUMP UP AND RUN AROUND ONCE IN A WHILE IF THEY GET TIRED OF LYING THERE? GOD'S PRETTY SILLY—
MARTIN!
WELL, YOU'D THINK HE'D TREAT PEOPLE BETTER THAN TO TELL THEM TO LIE STILL FOR KEEPS. THAT'S IMPOSSIBLE. NOBODY CAN DO IT.
DOG TRIES. I TELL HIM, "PLAY DEAD!" HE PLAYS DEAD AWHILE, THEN GETS TIRED AND WAGS HIS TAIL OR OPENS ONE EYE AND LOOKS AT ME, BORED.
I BET SOMETIMES THOSE GRAVEYARD PEOPLE DO THE SAME, HUH, DOG?
BE STILL WITH THAT KIND OF TALK!
BET THAT'S *EXACTLY* WHAT THEY DO.

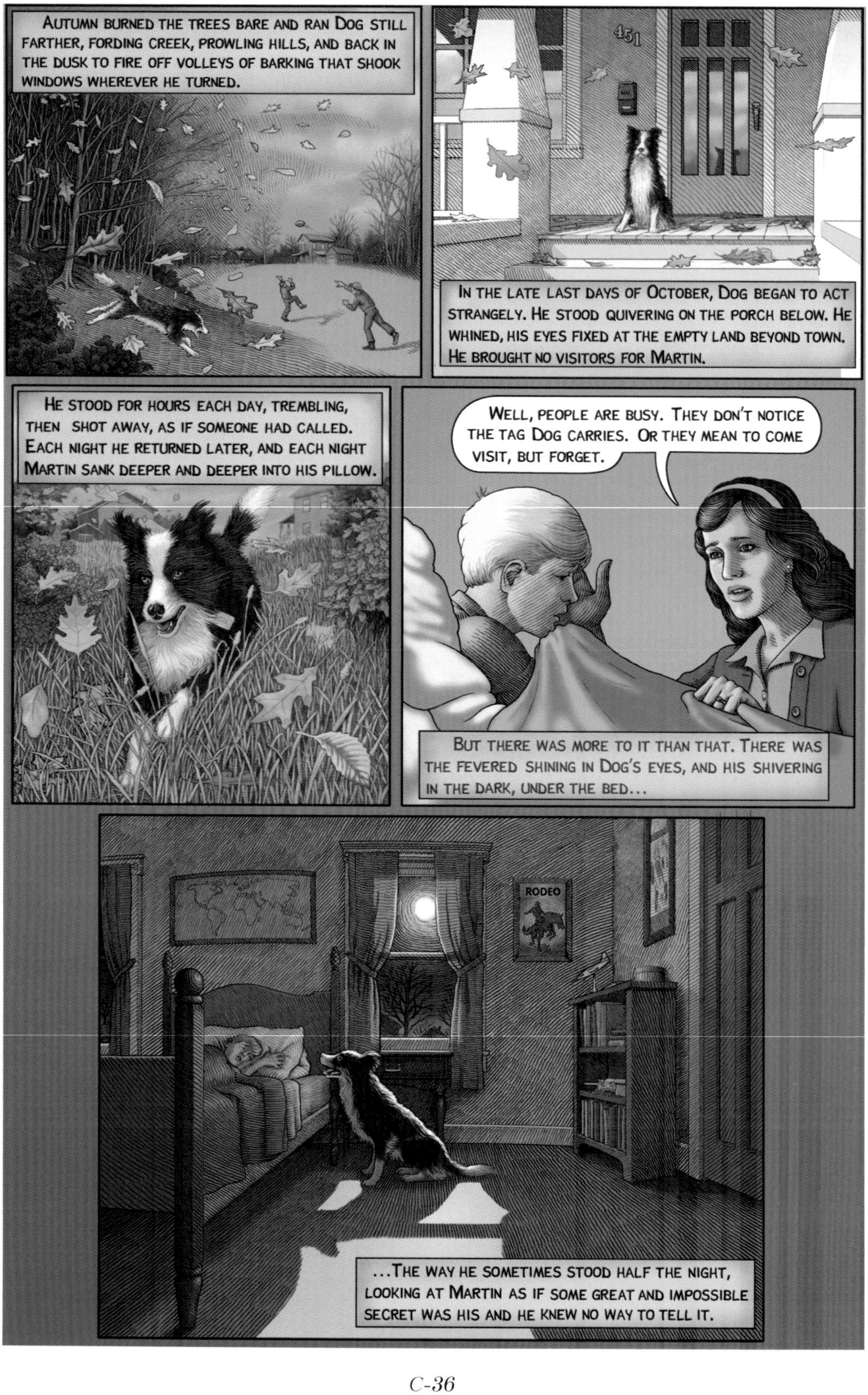
AUTUMN BURNED THE TREES BARE AND RAN DOG STILL FARTHER, FORDING CREEK, PROWLING HILLS, AND BACK IN THE DUSK TO FIRE OFF VOLLEYS OF BARKING THAT SHOOK WINDOWS WHEREVER HE TURNED.
451
IN THE LATE LAST DAYS OF OCTOBER, DOG BEGAN TO ACT STRANGELY. HE STOOD QUIVERING ON THE PORCH BELOW. HE WHINED, HIS EYES FIXED AT THE EMPTY LAND BEYOND TOWN. HE BROUGHT NO VISITORS FOR MARTIN.
HE STOOD FOR HOURS EACH DAY, TREMBLING, THEN SHOT AWAY, AS IF SOMEONE HAD CALLED. EACH NIGHT HE RETURNED LATER, AND EACH NIGHT MARTIN SANK DEEPER AND DEEPER INTO HIS PILLOW.
WELL, PEOPLE ARE BUSY. THEY DON'T NOTICE THE TAG DOG CARRIES. OR THEY MEAN TO COME VISIT, BUT FORGET.
BUT THERE WAS MORE TO IT THAN THAT. THERE WAS THE FEVERED SHINING IN DOG'S EYES, AND HIS SHIVERING IN THE DARK, UNDER THE BED...
RODEO
...THE WAY HE SOMETIMES STOOD HALF THE NIGHT, LOOKING AT MARTIN AS IF SOME GREAT AND IMPOSSIBLE SECRET WAS HIS AND HE KNEW NO WAY TO TELL IT.

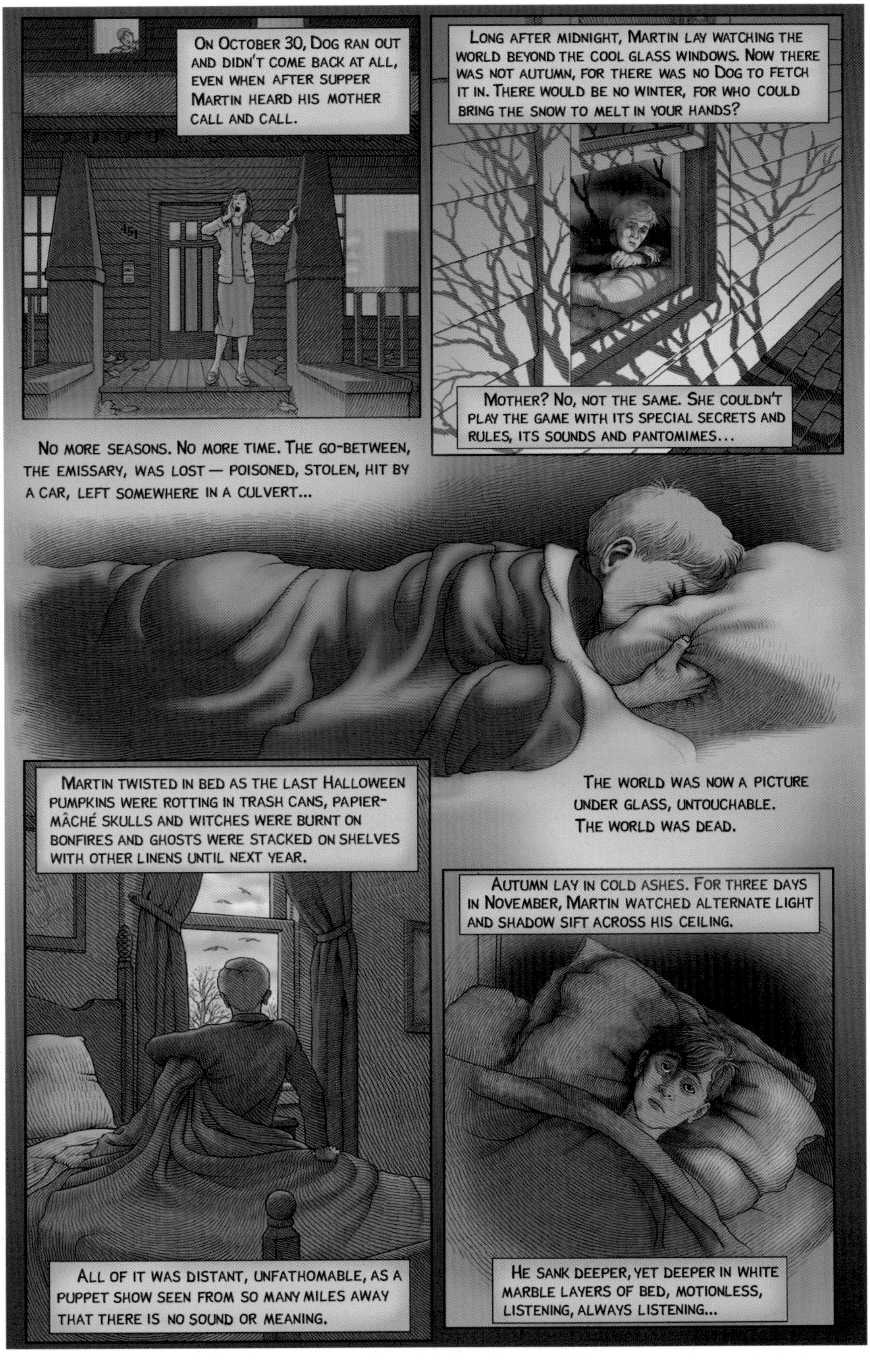

On October 30, Dog ran out and didn't come back at all, even when after supper Martin heard his mother call and call.
Long after midnight, Martin lay watching the world beyond the cool glass windows. Now there was not autumn, for there was no Dog to fetch it in. There would be no winter, for who could bring the snow to melt in your hands?
Mother? No, not the same. She couldn't play the game with its special secrets and rules, its sounds and pantomimes...
No more seasons. No more time. The go-between, the emissary, was lost — poisoned, stolen, hit by a car, left somewhere in a culvert...
The world was now a picture under glass, untouchable. The world was dead.
Martin twisted in bed as the last Halloween pumpkins were rotting in trash cans, papier-mâché skulls and witches were burnt on bonfires and ghosts were stacked on shelves with other linens until next year.
All of it was distant, unfathomable, as a puppet show seen from so many miles away that there is no sound or meaning.
Autumn lay in cold ashes. For three days in November, Martin watched alternate light and shadow sift across his ceiling.
He sank deeper, yet deeper in white marble layers of bed, motionless, listening, always listening...

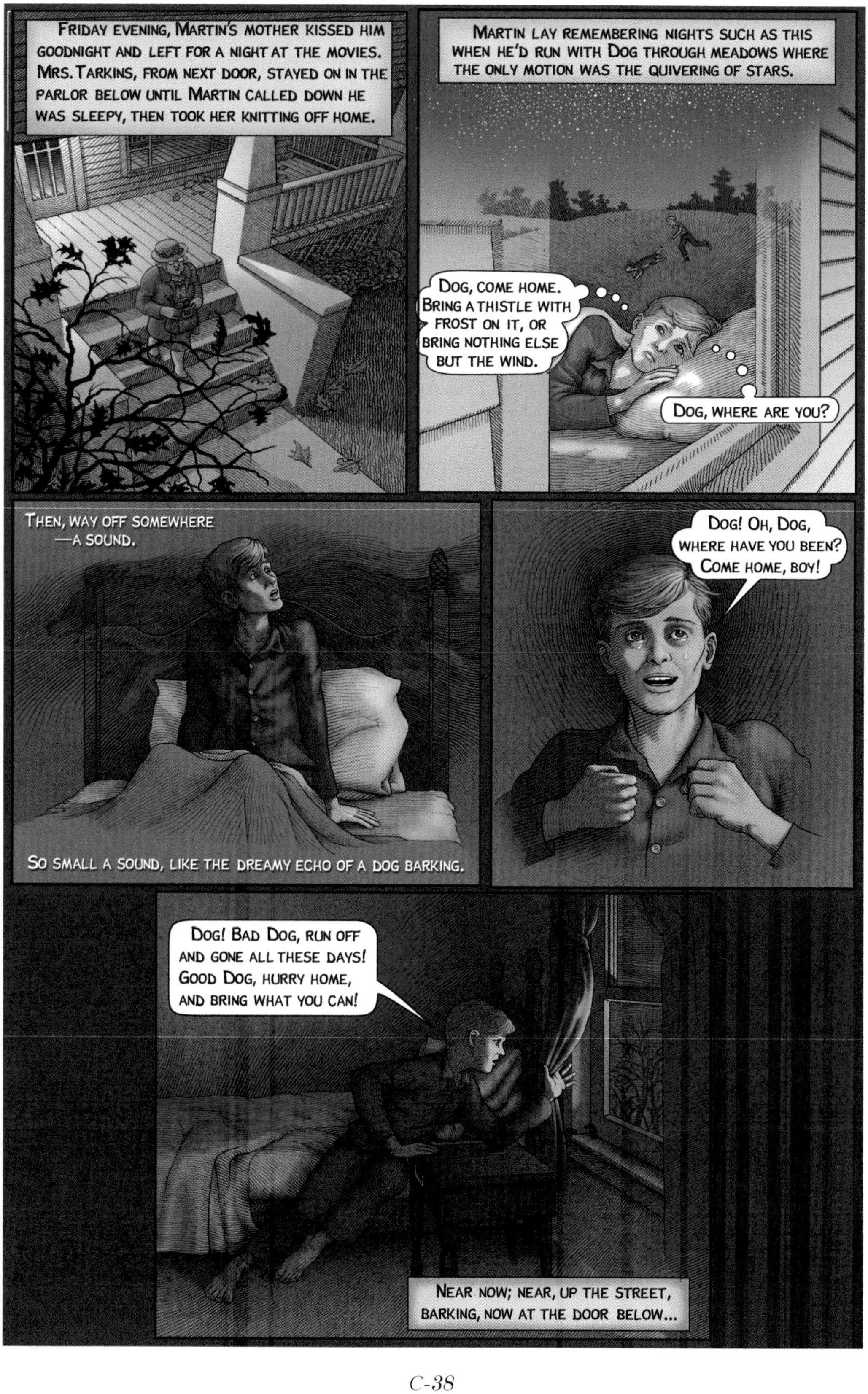
FRIDAY EVENING, MARTIN'S MOTHER KISSED HIM GOODNIGHT AND LEFT FOR A NIGHT AT THE MOVIES. MRS. TARKINS, FROM NEXT DOOR, STAYED ON IN THE PARLOR BELOW UNTIL MARTIN CALLED DOWN HE WAS SLEEPY, THEN TOOK HER KNITTING OFF HOME.
MARTIN LAY REMEMBERING NIGHTS SUCH AS THIS WHEN HE'D RUN WITH DOG THROUGH MEADOWS WHERE THE ONLY MOTION WAS THE QUIVERING OF STARS.
DOG, COME HOME. BRING A THISTLE WITH FROST ON IT, OR BRING NOTHING ELSE BUT THE WIND.
DOG, WHERE ARE YOU?
THEN, WAY OFF SOMEWHERE —A SOUND.
SO SMALL A SOUND, LIKE THE DREAMY ECHO OF A DOG BARKING.
DOG! OH, DOG, WHERE HAVE YOU BEEN? COME HOME, BOY!
DOG! BAD DOG, RUN OFF AND GONE ALL THESE DAYS! GOOD DOG, HURRY HOME, AND BRING WHAT YOU CAN!
NEAR NOW; NEAR, UP THE STREET, BARKING, NOW AT THE DOOR BELOW...

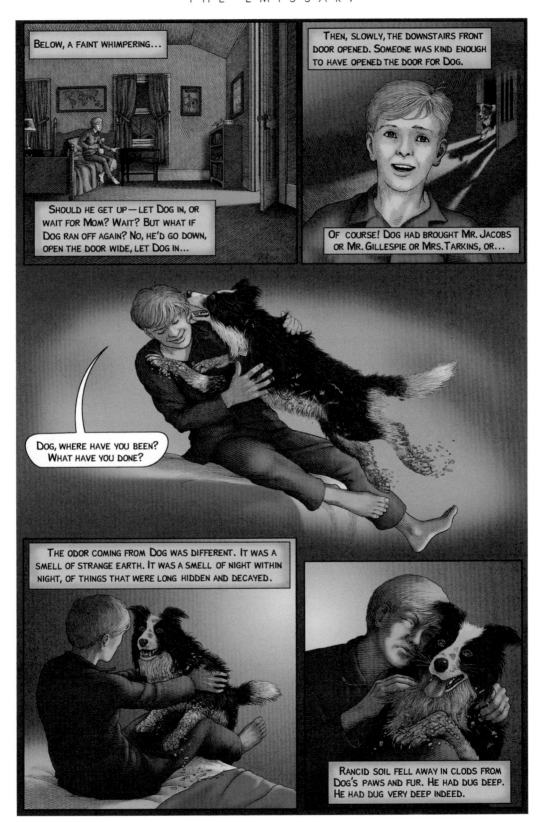

BELOW, A FAINT WHIMPERING...

SHOULD HE GET UP—LET DOG IN, OR WAIT FOR MOM? WAIT? BUT WHAT IF DOG RAN OFF AGAIN? NO, HE'D GO DOWN, OPEN THE DOOR WIDE, LET DOG IN...

THEN, SLOWLY, THE DOWNSTAIRS FRONT DOOR OPENED. SOMEONE WAS KIND ENOUGH TO HAVE OPENED THE DOOR FOR DOG.

OF COURSE! DOG HAD BROUGHT MR. JACOBS OR MR. GILLESPIE OR MRS. TARKINS, OR...

DOG, WHERE HAVE YOU BEEN? WHAT HAVE YOU DONE?

THE ODOR COMING FROM DOG WAS DIFFERENT. IT WAS A SMELL OF STRANGE EARTH. IT WAS A SMELL OF NIGHT WITHIN NIGHT, OF THINGS THAT WERE LONG HIDDEN AND DECAYED.

RANCID SOIL FELL AWAY IN CLODS FROM DOG'S PAWS AND FUR. HE HAD DUG DEEP. HE HAD DUG VERY DEEP INDEED.

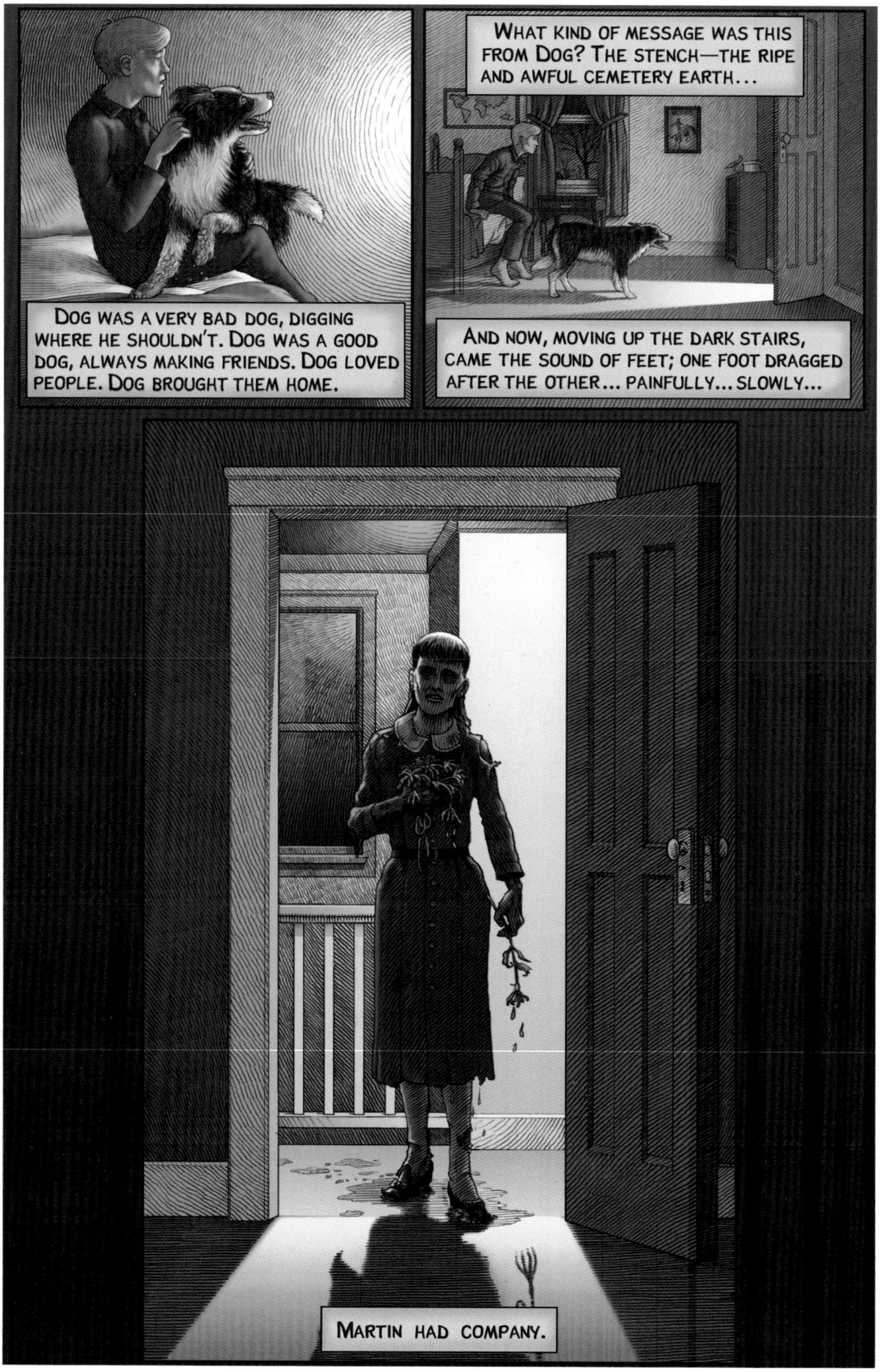
DOG WAS A VERY BAD DOG, DIGGING WHERE HE SHOULDN'T. DOG WAS A GOOD DOG, ALWAYS MAKING FRIENDS. DOG LOVED PEOPLE. DOG BROUGHT THEM HOME.
WHAT KIND OF MESSAGE WAS THIS FROM DOG? THE STENCH—THE RIPE AND AWFUL CEMETERY EARTH...
AND NOW, MOVING UP THE DARK STAIRS, CAME THE SOUND OF FEET; ONE FOOT DRAGGED AFTER THE OTHER... PAINFULLY... SLOWLY...
MARTIN HAD COMPANY.

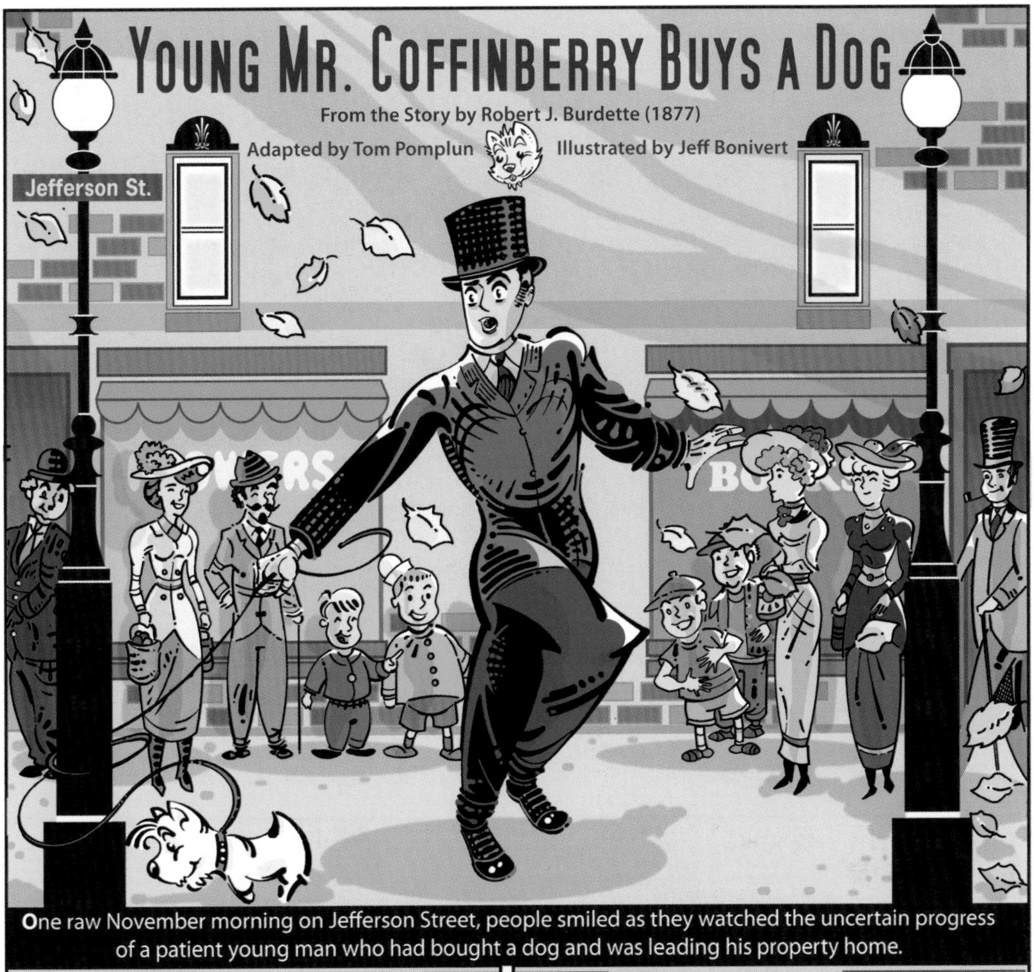
Young Mr. Coffinberry Buys a Dog
From the Story by Robert J. Burdette (1877)
Adapted by Tom Pomplun
Illustrated by Jeff Bonivert
Jefferson St.
One raw November morning on Jefferson Street, people smiled as they watched the uncertain progress of a patient young man who had bought a dog and was leading his property home.

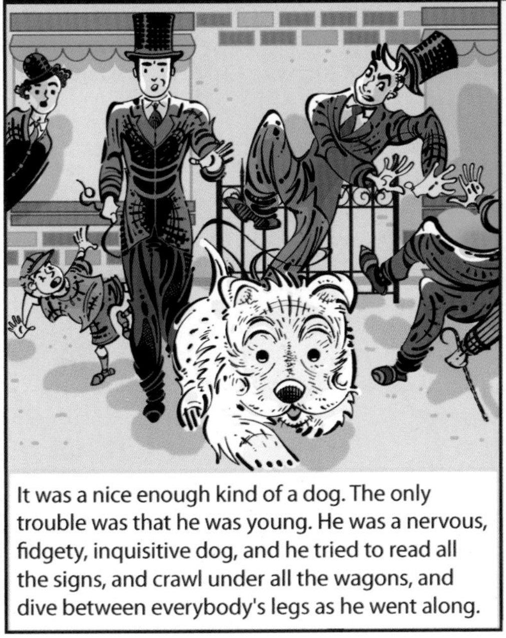
It was a nice enough kind of a dog. The only trouble was that he was young. He was a nervous, fidgety, inquisitive dog, and he tried to read all the signs, and crawl under all the wagons, and dive between everybody's legs as he went along.

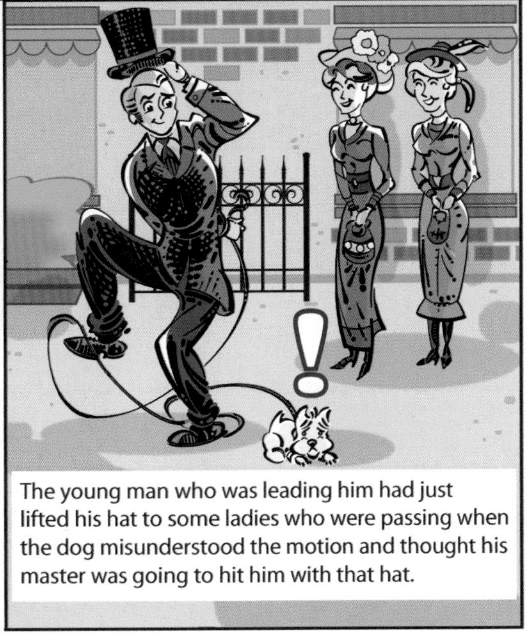
The young man who was leading him had just lifted his hat to some ladies who were passing when the dog misunderstood the motion and thought his master was going to hit him with that hat.

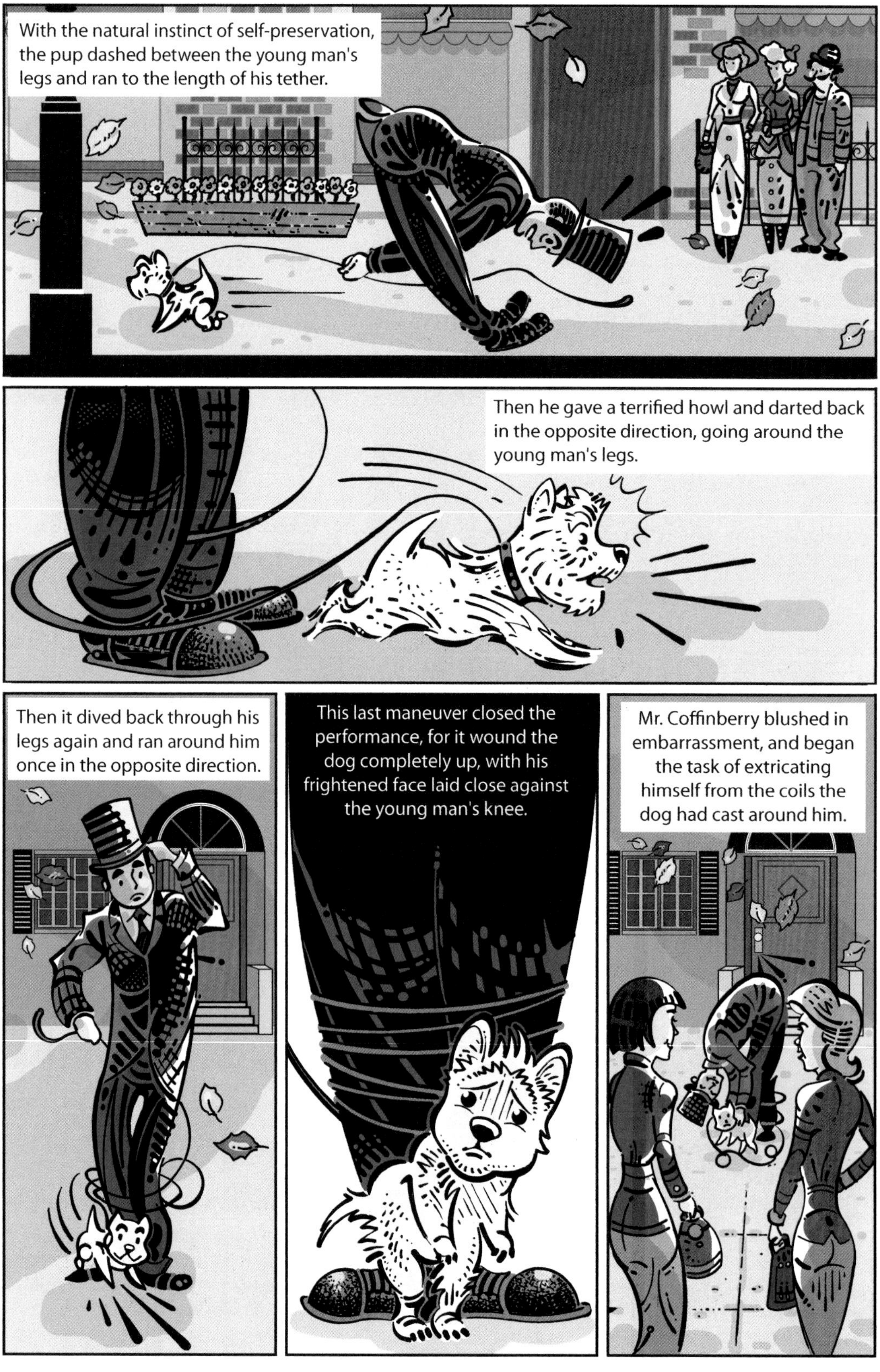
With the natural instinct of self-preservation, the pup dashed between the young man's legs and ran to the length of his tether.
Then he gave a terrified howl and darted back in the opposite direction, going around the young man's legs.
Then it dived back through his legs again and ran around him once in the opposite direction.
This last maneuver closed the performance, for it wound the dog completely up, with his frightened face laid close against the young man's knee.
Mr. Coffinberry blushed in embarrassment, and began the task of extricating himself from the coils the dog had cast around him.

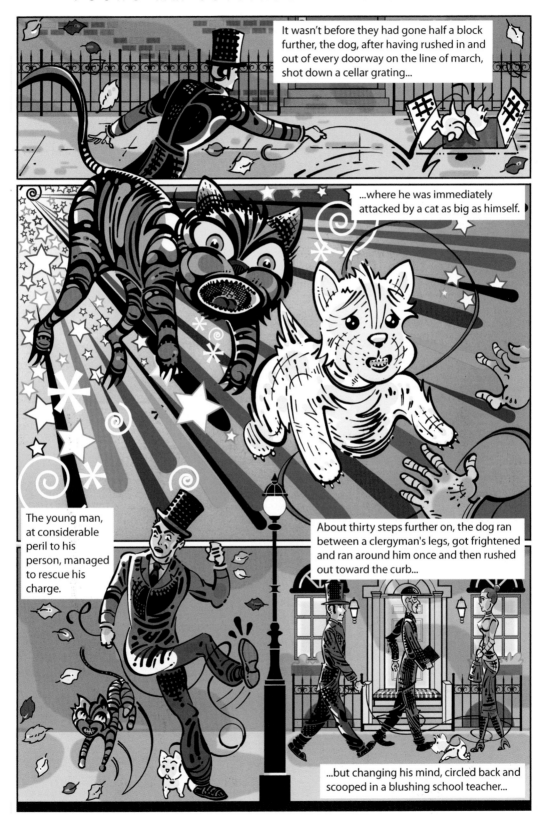

It wasn't before they had gone half a block further, the dog, after having rushed in and out of every doorway on the line of march, shot down a cellar grating...

...where he was immediately attacked by a cat as big as himself.

The young man, at considerable peril to his person, managed to rescue his charge.

About thirty steps further on, the dog ran between a clergyman's legs, got frightened and ran around him once and then rushed out toward the curb...

...but changing his mind, circled back and scooped in a blushing school teacher...

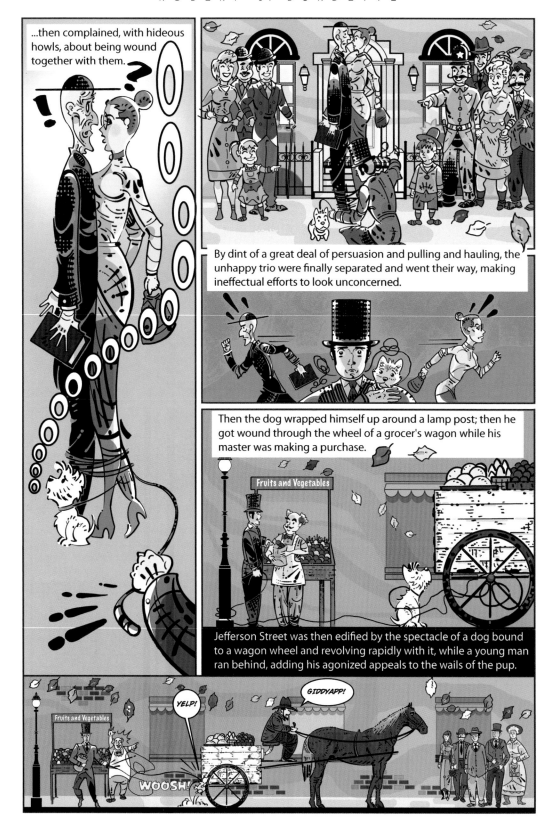

...then complained, with hideous howls, about being wound together with them.

By dint of a great deal of persuasion and pulling and hauling, the unhappy trio were finally separated and went their way, making ineffectual efforts to look unconcerned.

Then the dog wrapped himself up around a lamp post; then he got wound through the wheel of a grocer's wagon while his master was making a purchase.

Fruits and Vegetables

Jefferson Street was then edified by the spectacle of a dog bound to a wagon wheel and revolving rapidly with it, while a young man ran behind, adding his agonized appeals to the wails of the pup.

Fruits and Vegetables

YELP!

GIDDYAPP!

WOOSH!

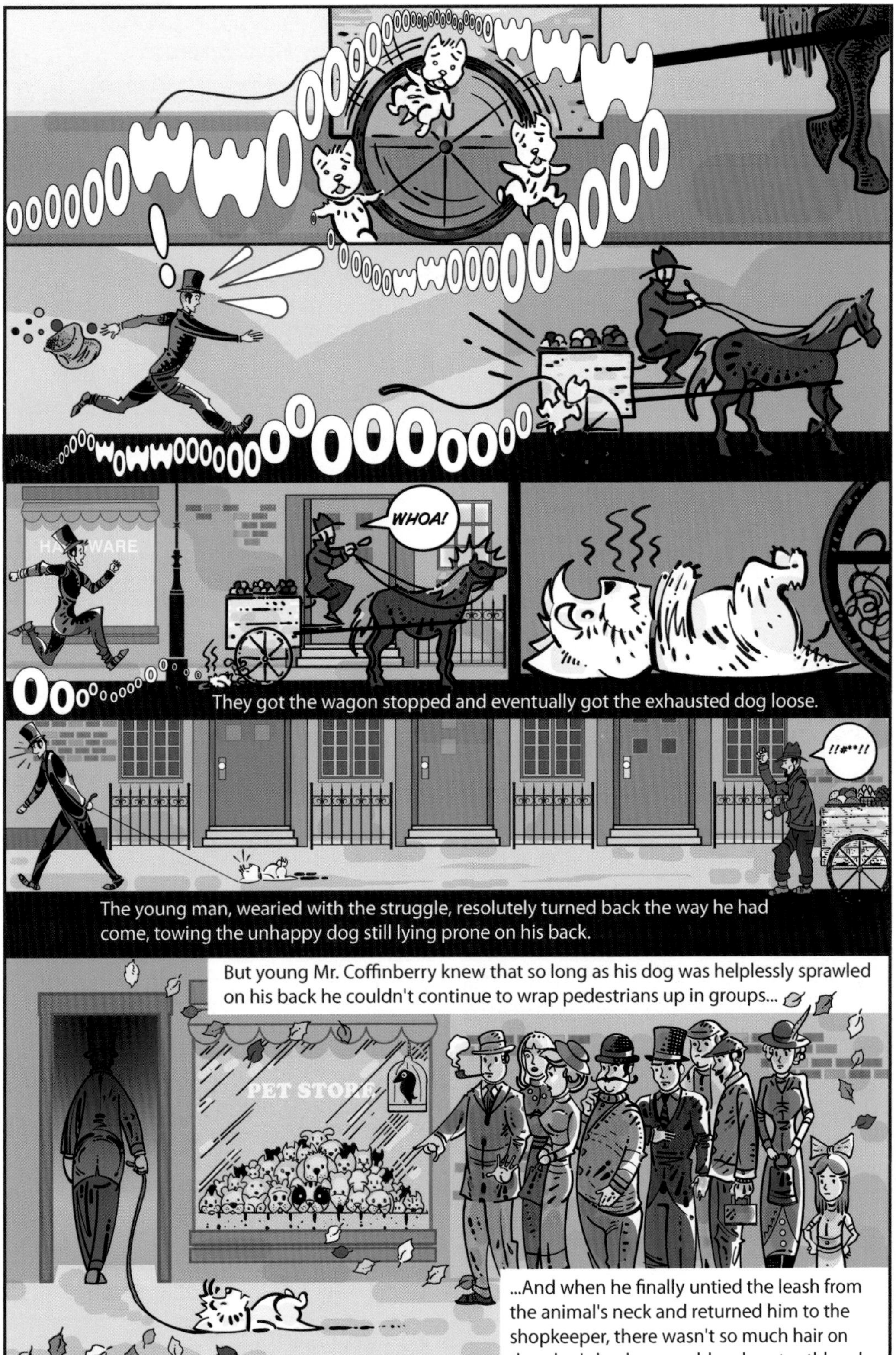
WHOA!
They got the wagon stopped and eventually got the exhausted dog loose.
!!#**!!
The young man, wearied with the struggle, resolutely turned back the way he had come, towing the unhappy dog still lying prone on his back.
But young Mr. Coffinberry knew that so long as his dog was helplessly sprawled on his back he couldn't continue to wrap pedestrians up in groups...
PET STORE
...And when he finally untied the leash from the animal's neck and returned him to the shopkeeper, there wasn't so much hair on that dog's back as would make a toothbrush.
Dedicated to Bailey the Bulldog

AN ELEGY ON THE DEATH OF A MAD DOG

by **Oliver Goldsmith** (1766) / illustrated by **Hunt Emerson**

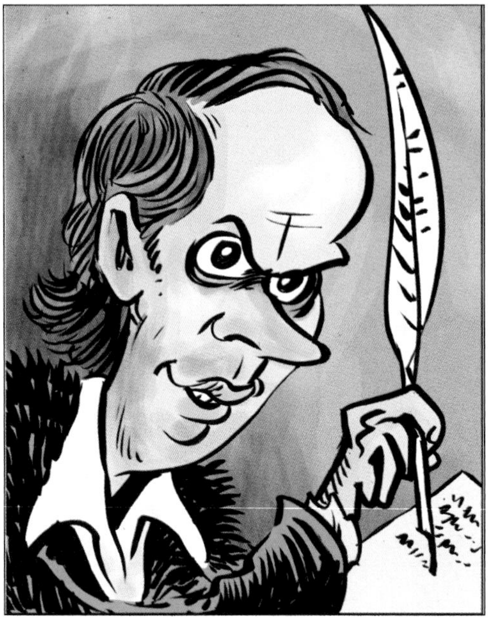

Good people all, of every sort,
  Give ear unto my song,
And if you find it wond'rous short,
  It cannot hold you long.

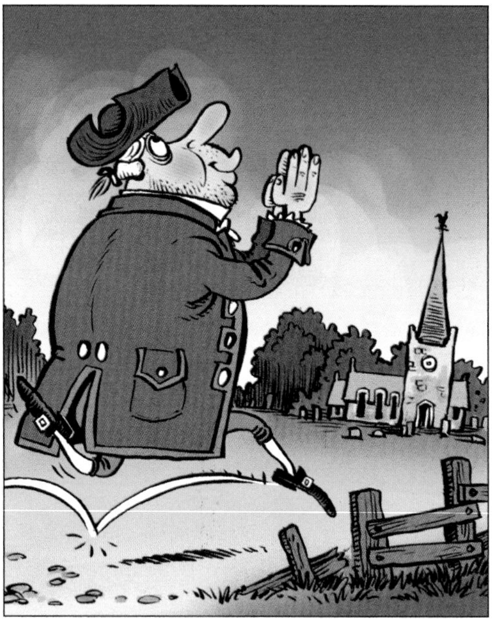

In Islington there was a man
  Of whom the world might say
That still a godly race he ran
  Whene'er he went to pray.

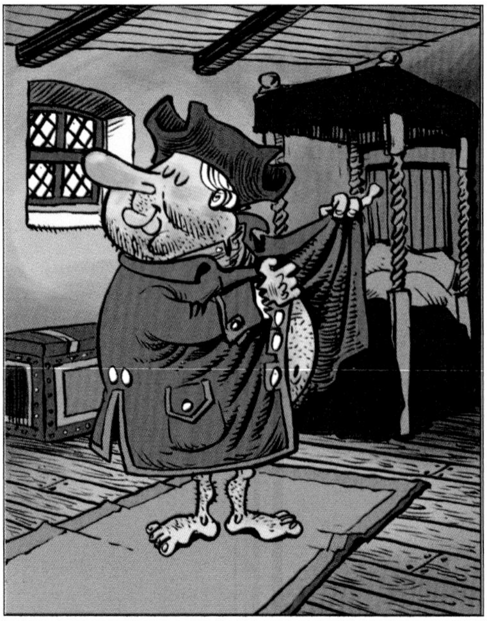

A kind and gentle heart he had,
  To comfort friends and foes;
The naked every day he clad
  When he put on his clothes.

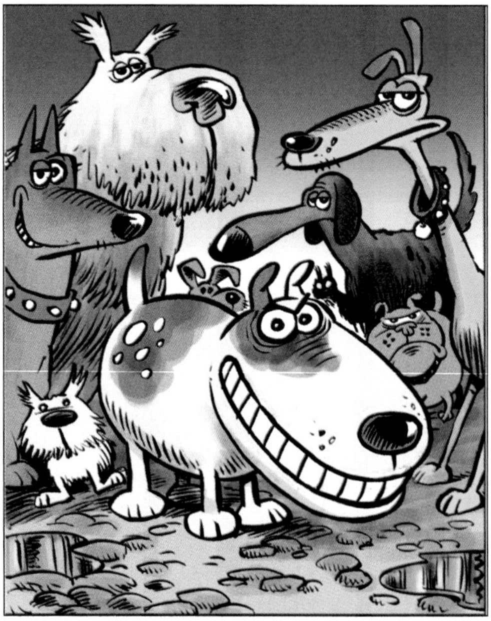

And in that town a dog was found,
  As many dogs there be,
Both mongrel, puppy, whelp and hound,
  And curs of low degree.

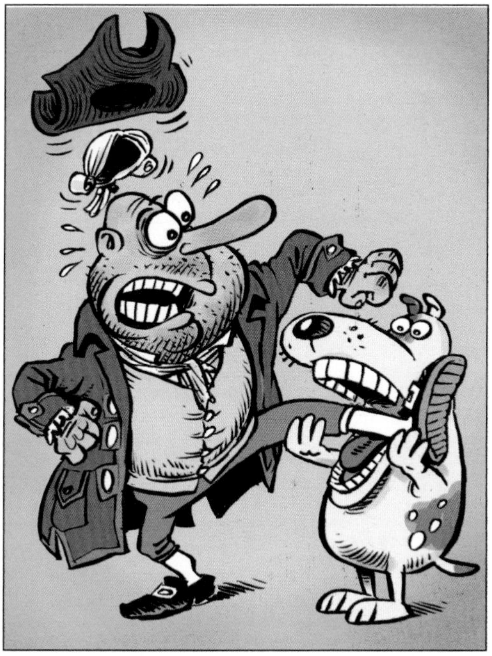

The dog and man at first were friends,
  But when a pique began,
The dog, to gain some private ends,
  Went mad, and bit the man.

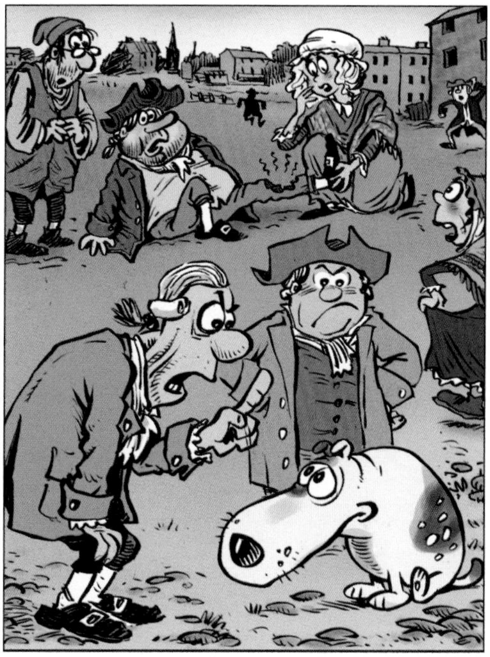

Around from all the neighboring streets
  The wondering neighbors ran,
And swore the dog had lost his wits,
  To bite so good a man.

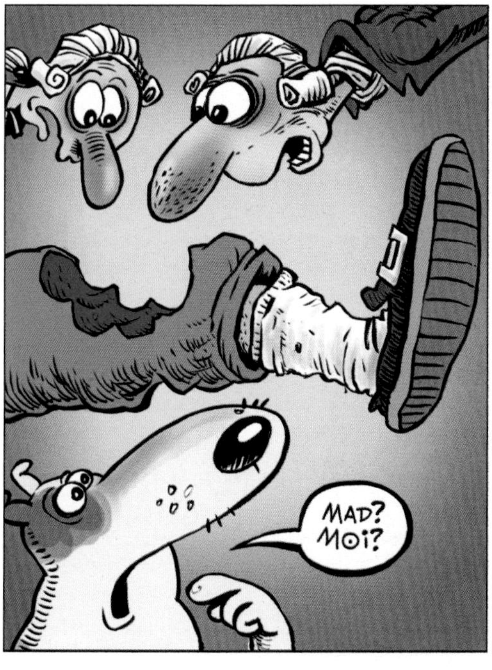
MAD? MOI?

The wound it seem'd both sore and sad
  To every Christian eye;
And while they swore the dog was mad,
  They swore the man would die.

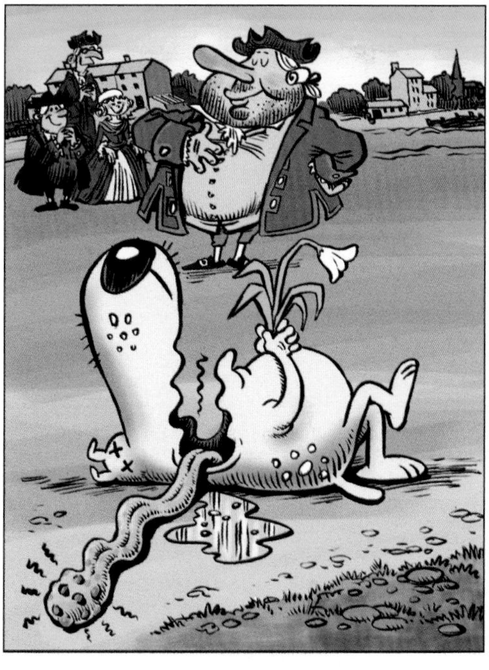

But soon a wonder came to light,
  That showed the rogues they lied;
The man recover'd of the bite,
  The dog it was that died.

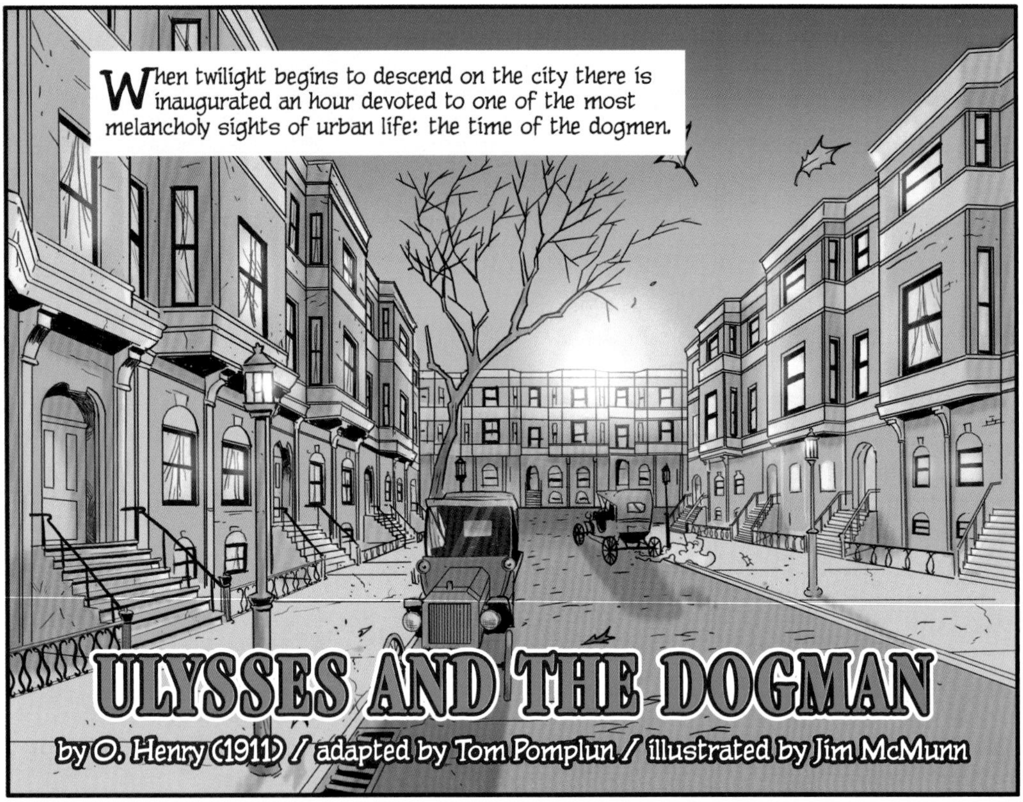
When twilight begins to descend on the city there is inaugurated an hour devoted to one of the most melancholy sights of urban life: the time of the dogmen.
ULYSSES AND THE DOGMAN
by O. Henry (1911) / adapted by Tom Pomplun / illustrated by Jim McMunn

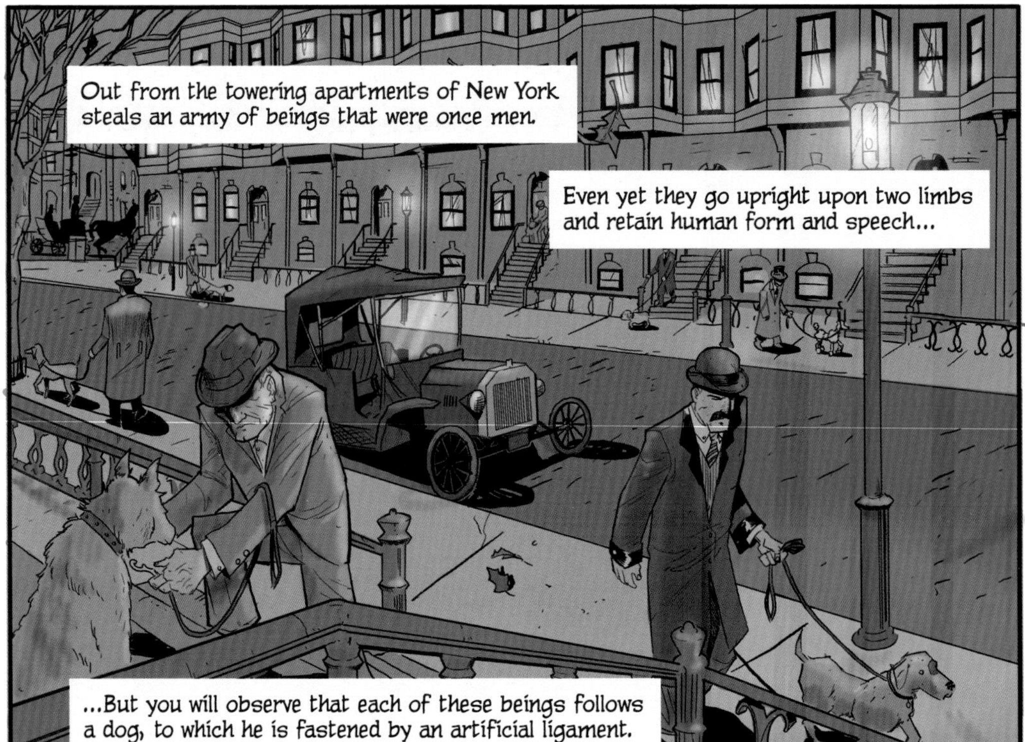
Out from the towering apartments of New York steals an army of beings that were once men.
Even yet they go upright upon two limbs and retain human form and speech...
...But you will observe that each of these beings follows a dog, to which he is fastened by an artificial ligament.

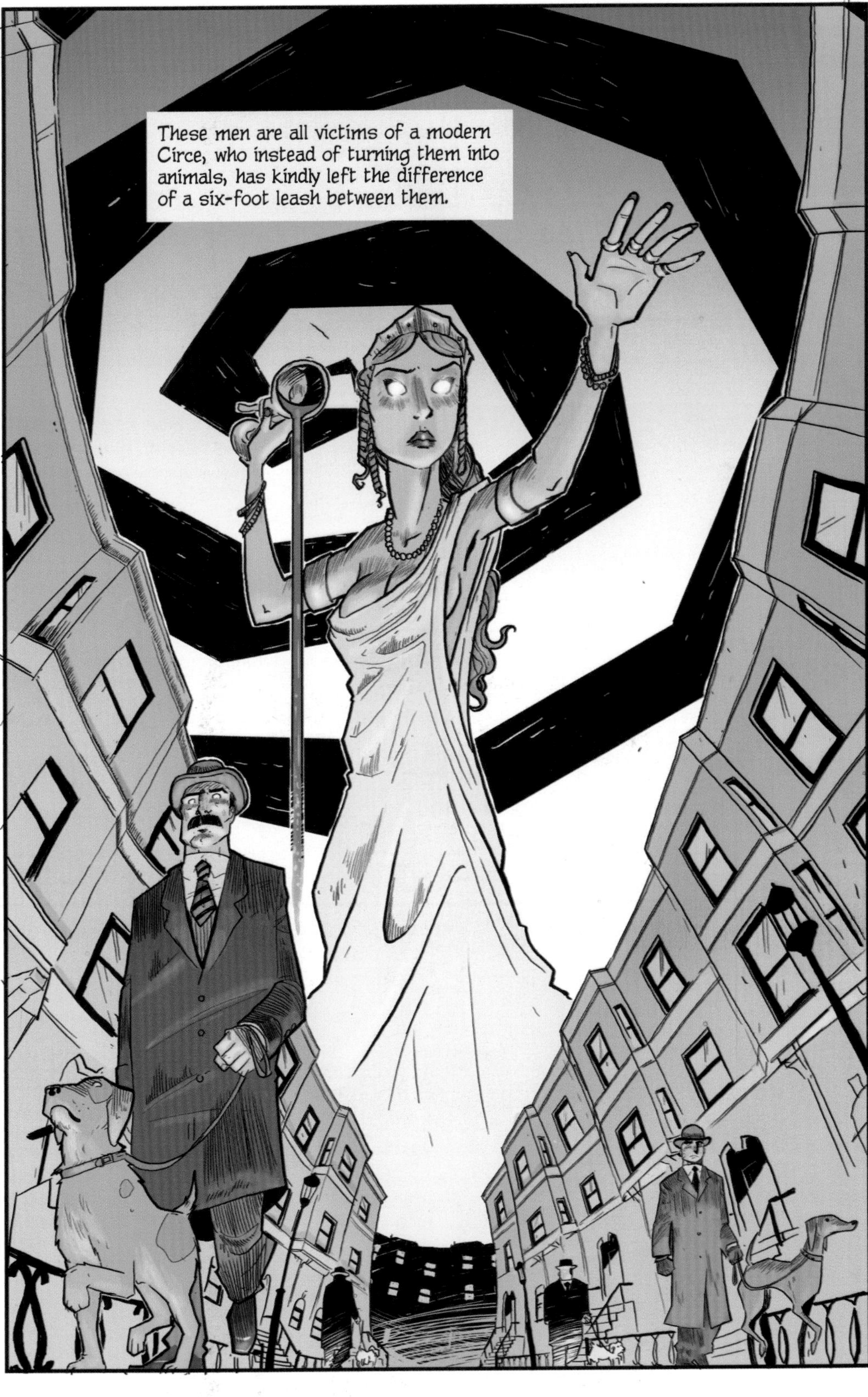
These men are all victims of a modern Circe, who instead of turning them into animals, has kindly left the difference of a six-foot leash between them.

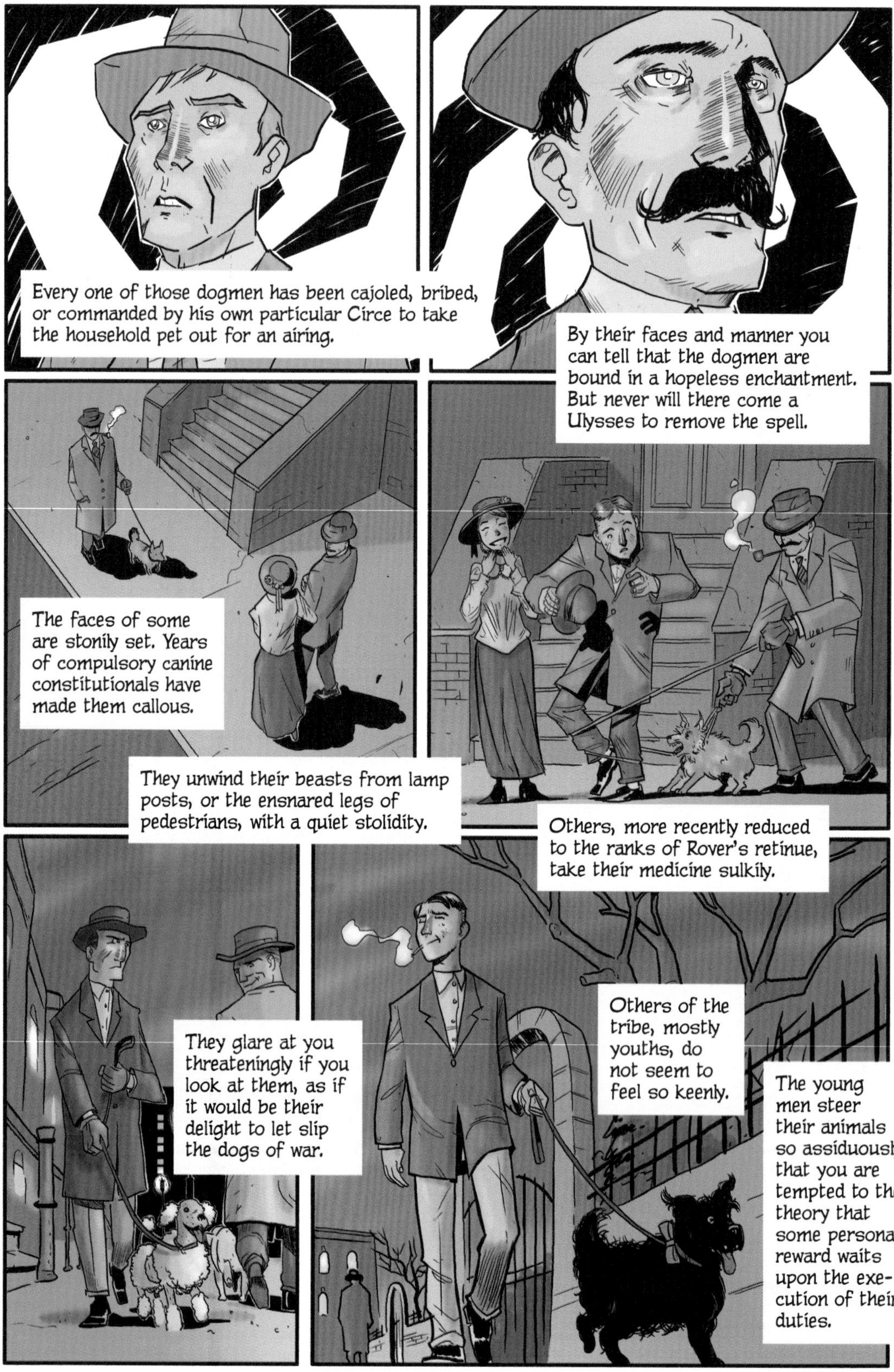
Every one of those dogmen has been cajoled, bribed, or commanded by his own particular Circe to take the household pet out for an airing.
By their faces and manner you can tell that the dogmen are bound in a hopeless enchantment. But never will there come a Ulysses to remove the spell.
The faces of some are stonily set. Years of compulsory canine constitutionals have made them callous.
They unwind their beasts from lamp posts, or the ensnared legs of pedestrians, with a quiet stolidity.
Others, more recently reduced to the ranks of Rover's retinue, take their medicine sulkily.
They glare at you threateningly if you look at them, as if it would be their delight to let slip the dogs of war.
Others of the tribe, mostly youths, do not seem to feel so keenly.
The young men steer their animals so assiduously that you are tempted to the theory that some personal reward waits upon the execution of their duties.

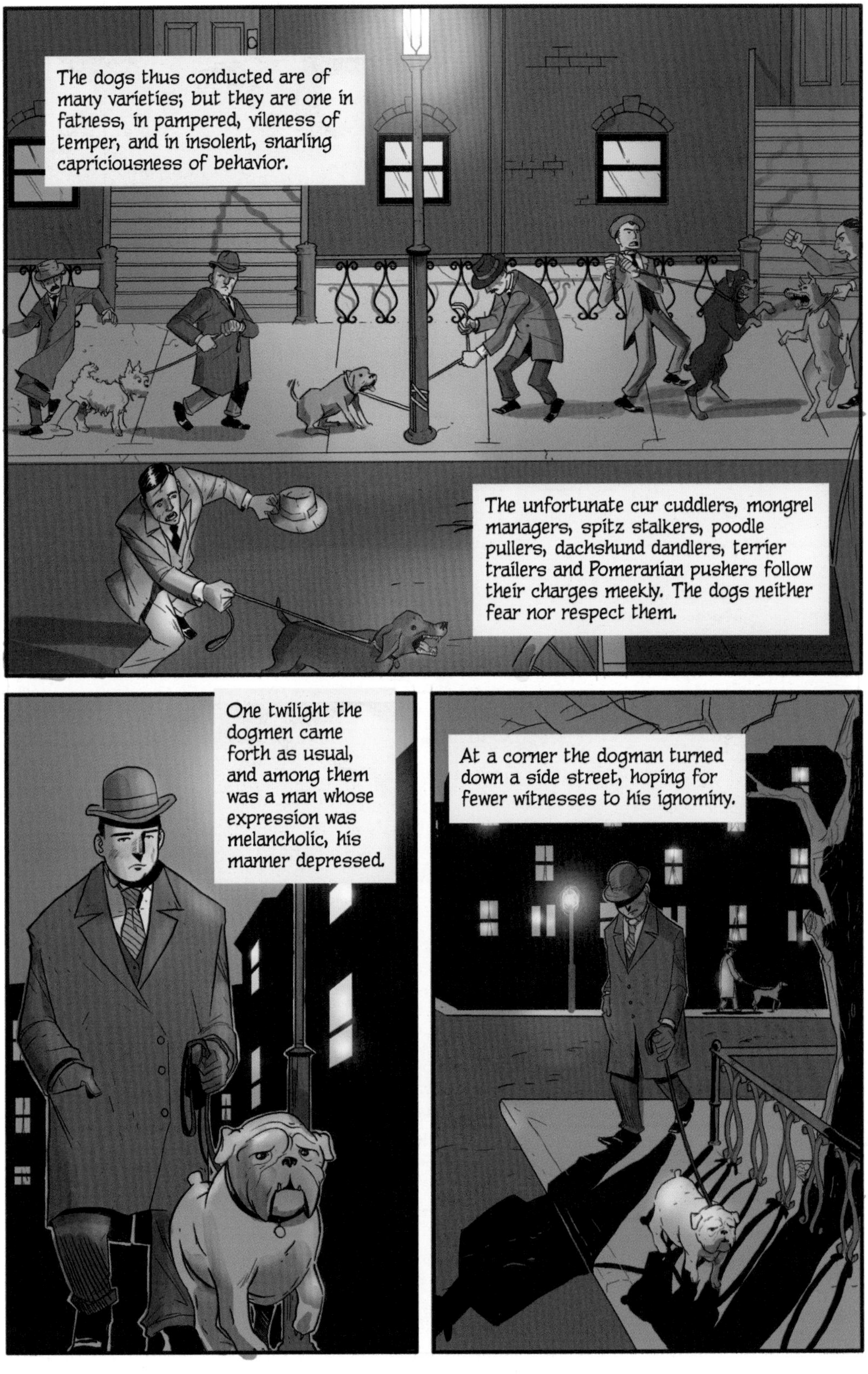
The dogs thus conducted are of many varieties; but they are one in fatness, in pampered, vileness of temper, and in insolent, snarling capriciousness of behavior.
The unfortunate cur cuddlers, mongrel managers, spitz stalkers, poodle pullers, dachshund dandlers, terrier trailers and Pomeranian pushers follow their charges meekly. The dogs neither fear nor respect them.
One twilight the dogmen came forth as usual, and among them was a man whose expression was melancholic, his manner depressed.
At a corner the dogman turned down a side street, hoping for fewer witnesses to his ignominy.

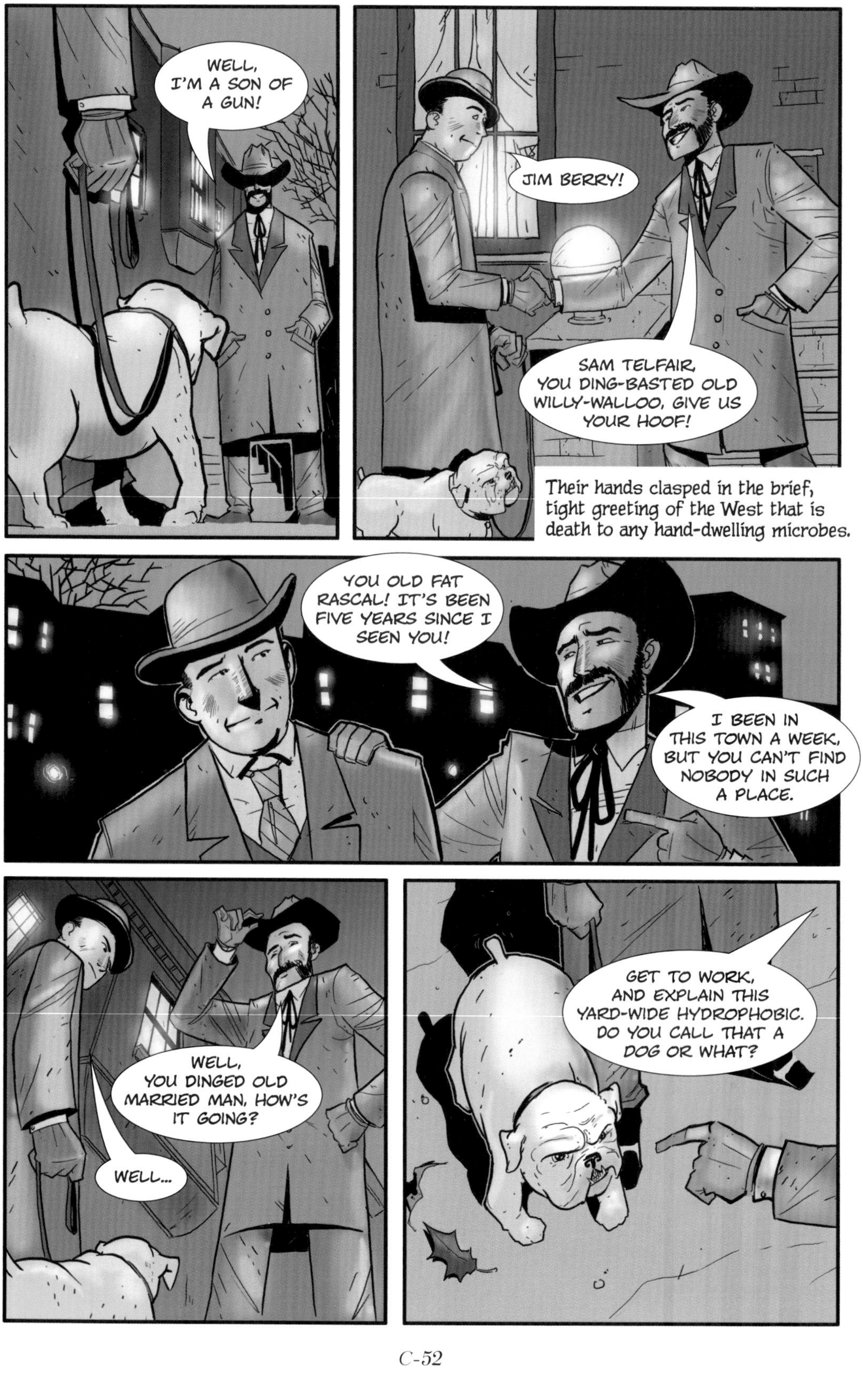
WELL, I'M A SON OF A GUN!
JIM BERRY!
SAM TELFAIR, YOU DING-BASTED OLD WILLY-WALLOO, GIVE US YOUR HOOF!
Their hands clasped in the brief, tight greeting of the West that is death to any hand-dwelling microbes.
YOU OLD FAT RASCAL! IT'S BEEN FIVE YEARS SINCE I SEEN YOU!
I BEEN IN THIS TOWN A WEEK, BUT YOU CAN'T FIND NOBODY IN SUCH A PLACE.
WELL, YOU DINGED OLD MARRIED MAN, HOW'S IT GOING?
WELL...
GET TO WORK, AND EXPLAIN THIS YARD-WIDE HYDROPHOBIC. DO YOU CALL THAT A DOG OR WHAT?

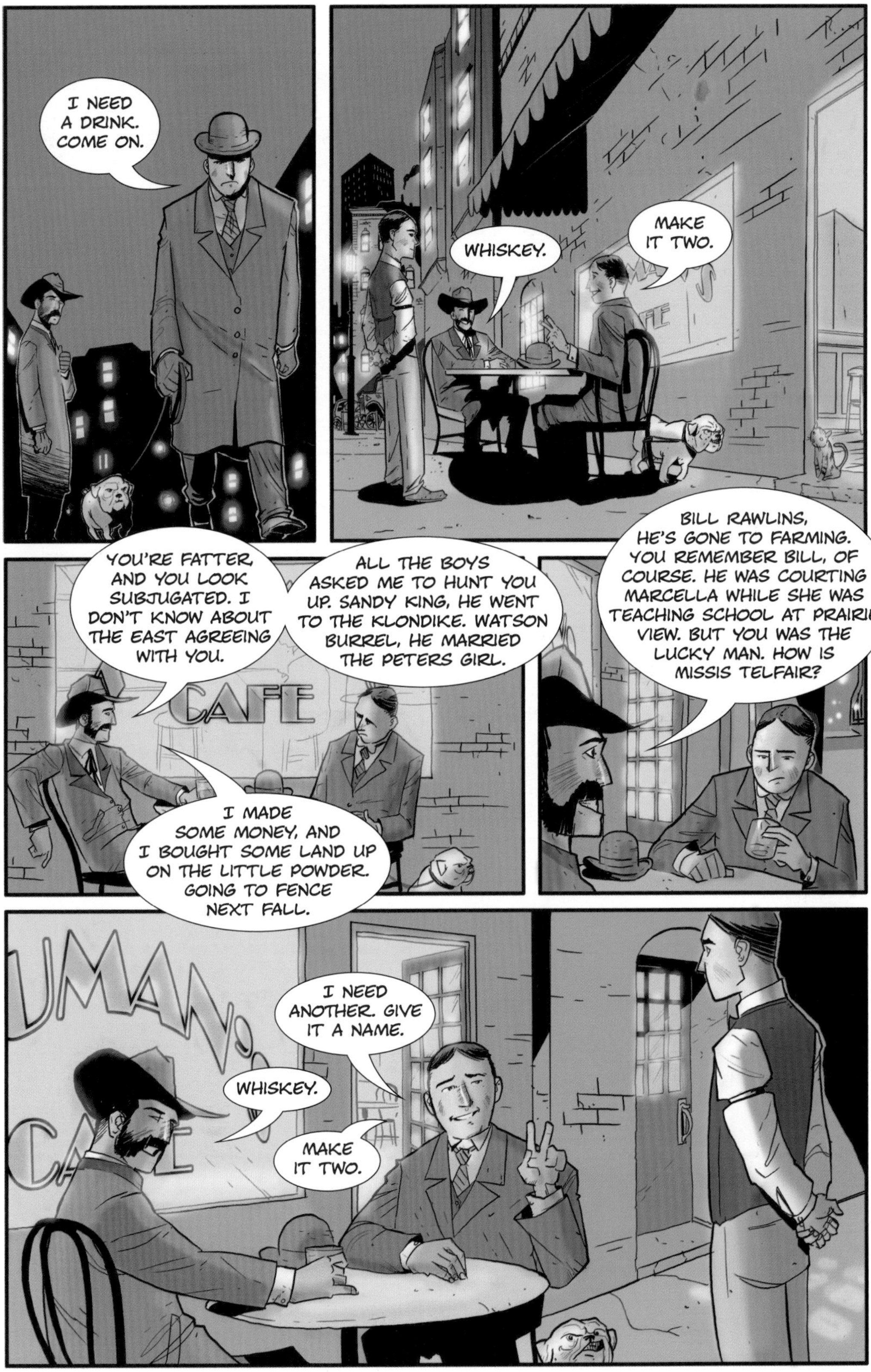
I NEED A DRINK. COME ON.
WHISKEY.
MAKE IT TWO.
YOU'RE FATTER, AND YOU LOOK SUBJUGATED. I DON'T KNOW ABOUT THE EAST AGREEING WITH YOU.
ALL THE BOYS ASKED ME TO HUNT YOU UP. SANDY KING, HE WENT TO THE KLONDIKE. WATSON BURREL, HE MARRIED THE PETERS GIRL.
CAFE
I MADE SOME MONEY, AND I BOUGHT SOME LAND UP ON THE LITTLE POWDER. GOING TO FENCE NEXT FALL.
BILL RAWLINS, HE'S GONE TO FARMING. YOU REMEMBER BILL, OF COURSE. HE WAS COURTING MARCELLA WHILE SHE WAS TEACHING SCHOOL AT PRAIRIE VIEW. BUT YOU WAS THE LUCKY MAN. HOW IS MISSIS TELFAIR?
I NEED ANOTHER. GIVE IT A NAME.
WHISKEY.
MAKE IT TWO.

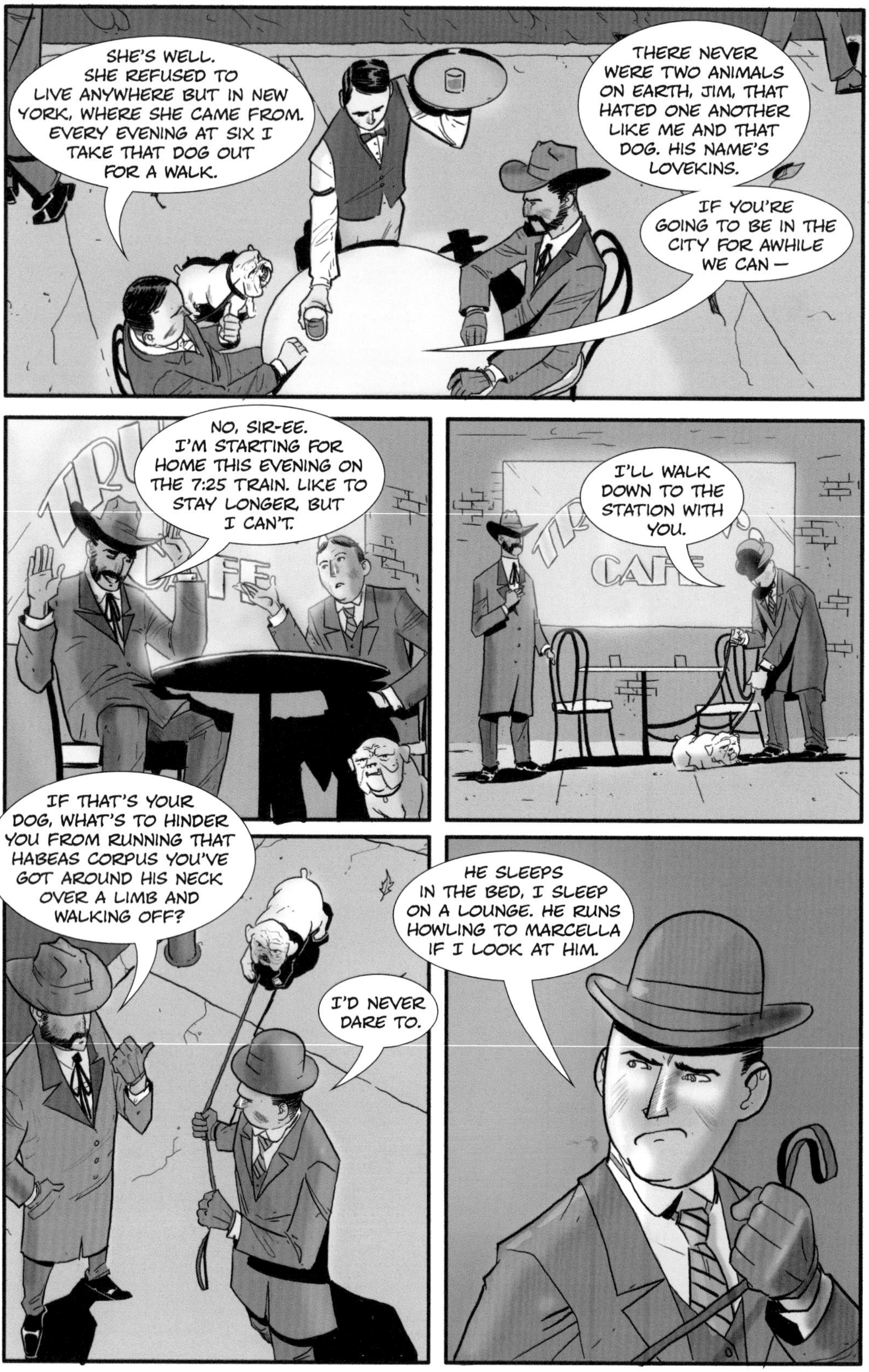
SHE'S WELL. SHE REFUSED TO LIVE ANYWHERE BUT IN NEW YORK, WHERE SHE CAME FROM. EVERY EVENING AT SIX I TAKE THAT DOG OUT FOR A WALK.
THERE NEVER WERE TWO ANIMALS ON EARTH, JIM, THAT HATED ONE ANOTHER LIKE ME AND THAT DOG. HIS NAME'S LOVEKINS.
IF YOU'RE GOING TO BE IN THE CITY FOR AWHILE WE CAN—
NO, SIR-EE. I'M STARTING FOR HOME THIS EVENING ON THE 7:25 TRAIN. LIKE TO STAY LONGER, BUT I CAN'T.
I'LL WALK DOWN TO THE STATION WITH YOU.
IF THAT'S YOUR DOG, WHAT'S TO HINDER YOU FROM RUNNING THAT HABEAS CORPUS YOU'VE GOT AROUND HIS NECK OVER A LIMB AND WALKING OFF?
I'D NEVER DARE TO.
HE SLEEPS IN THE BED, I SLEEP ON A LOUNGE. HE RUNS HOWLING TO MARCELLA IF I LOOK AT HIM.

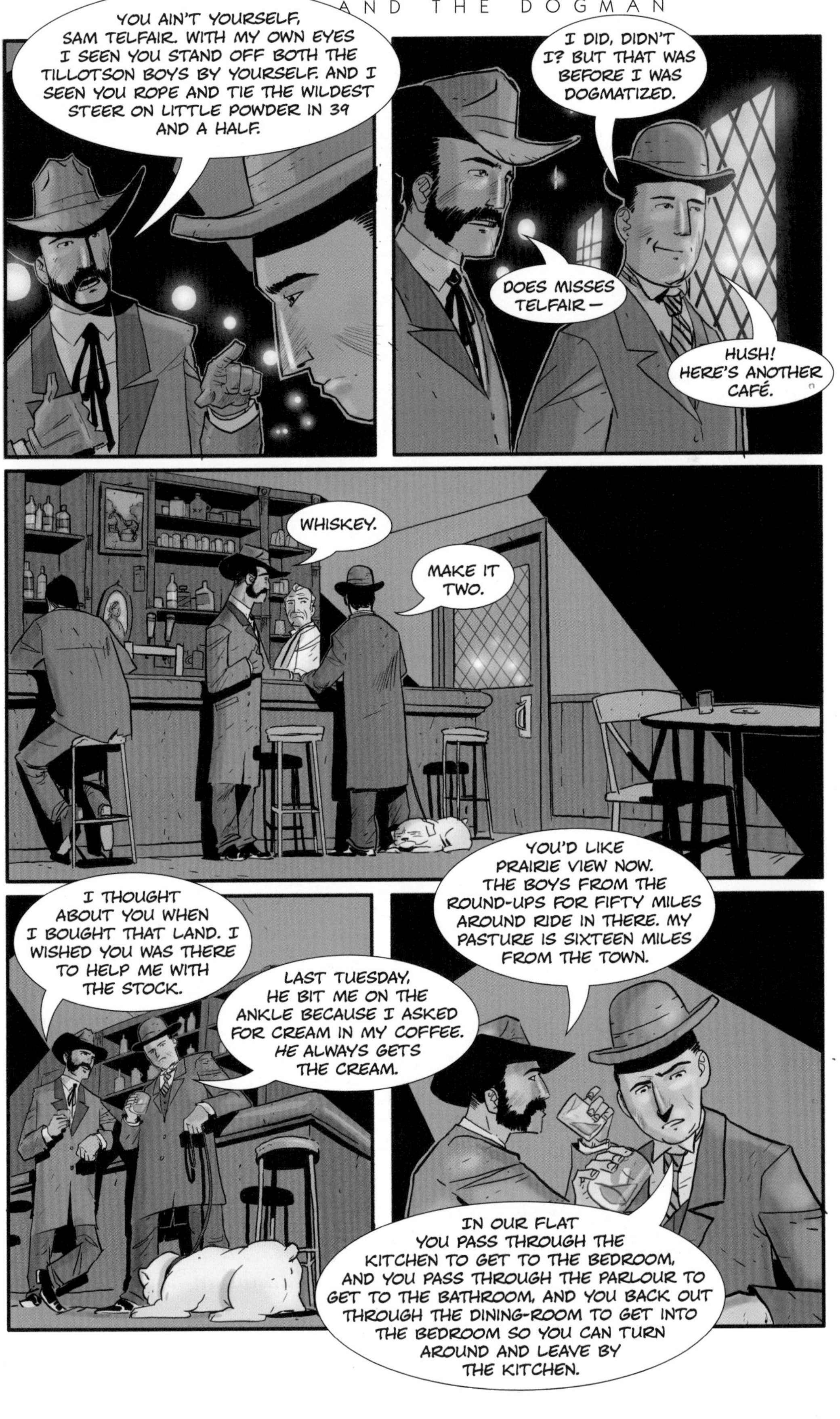
YOU AIN'T YOURSELF, SAM TELFAIR. WITH MY OWN EYES I SEEN YOU STAND OFF BOTH THE TILLOTSON BOYS BY YOURSELF. AND I SEEN YOU ROPE AND TIE THE WILDEST STEER ON LITTLE POWDER IN 39 AND A HALF.
I DID, DIDN'T I? BUT THAT WAS BEFORE I WAS DOGMATIZED.
DOES MISSES TELFAIR—
HUSH! HERE'S ANOTHER CAFÉ.
WHISKEY.
MAKE IT TWO.
I THOUGHT ABOUT YOU WHEN I BOUGHT THAT LAND. I WISHED YOU WAS THERE TO HELP ME WITH THE STOCK.
LAST TUESDAY, HE BIT ME ON THE ANKLE BECAUSE I ASKED FOR CREAM IN MY COFFEE. HE ALWAYS GETS THE CREAM.
YOU'D LIKE PRAIRIE VIEW NOW. THE BOYS FROM THE ROUND-UPS FOR FIFTY MILES AROUND RIDE IN THERE. MY PASTURE IS SIXTEEN MILES FROM THE TOWN.
IN OUR FLAT YOU PASS THROUGH THE KITCHEN TO GET TO THE BEDROOM, AND YOU PASS THROUGH THE PARLOUR TO GET TO THE BATHROOM, AND YOU BACK OUT THROUGH THE DINING-ROOM TO GET INTO THE BEDROOM SO YOU CAN TURN AROUND AND LEAVE BY THE KITCHEN.

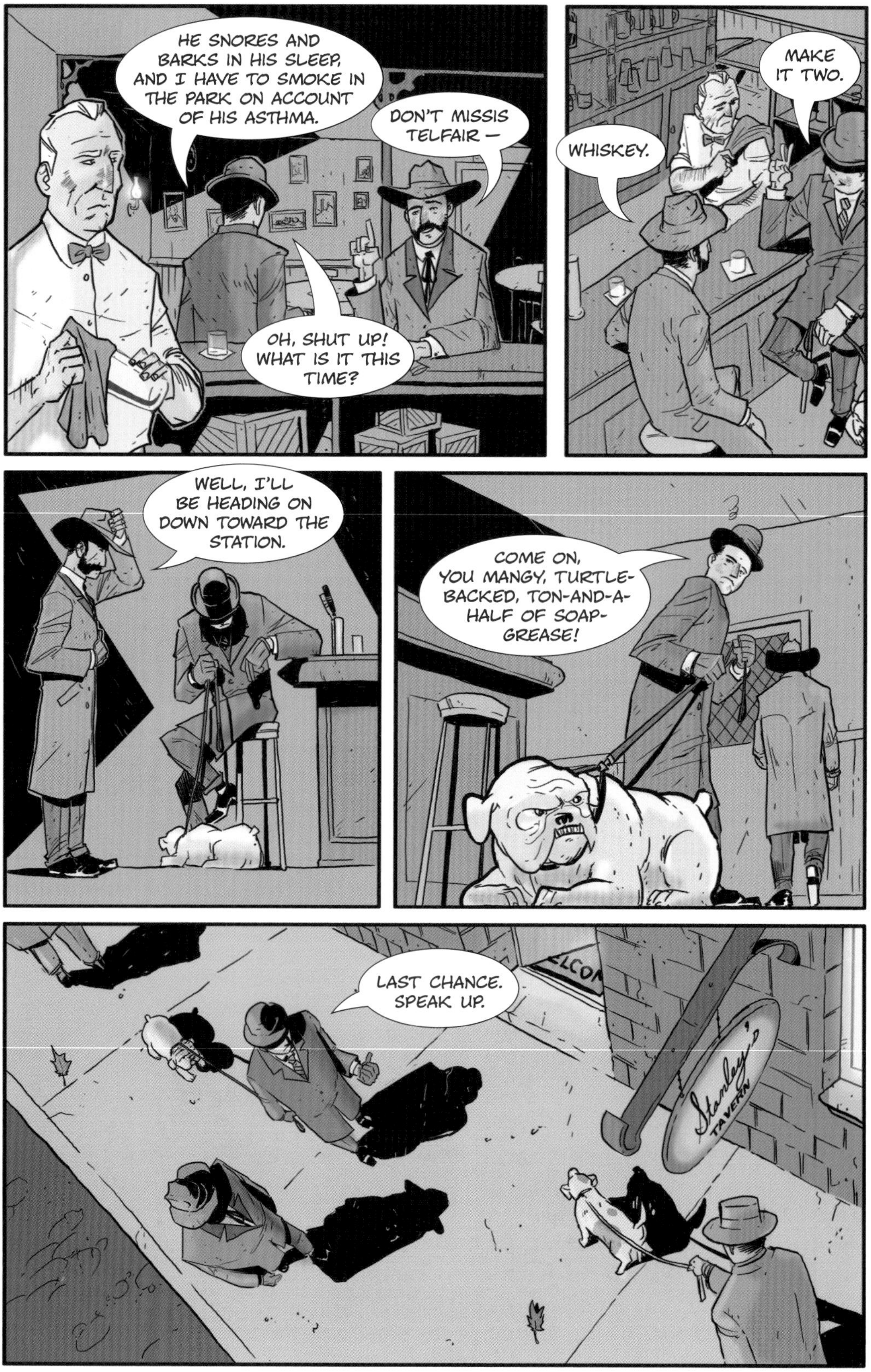
HE SNORES AND BARKS IN HIS SLEEP, AND I HAVE TO SMOKE IN THE PARK ON ACCOUNT OF HIS ASTHMA.
DON'T MISSIS TELFAIR —
OH, SHUT UP! WHAT IS IT THIS TIME?
WHISKEY.
MAKE IT TWO.
WELL, I'LL BE HEADING ON DOWN TOWARD THE STATION.
COME ON, YOU MANGY, TURTLE-BACKED, TON-AND-A-HALF OF SOAP-GREASE!
LAST CHANCE. SPEAK UP.
Stanley's TAVERN

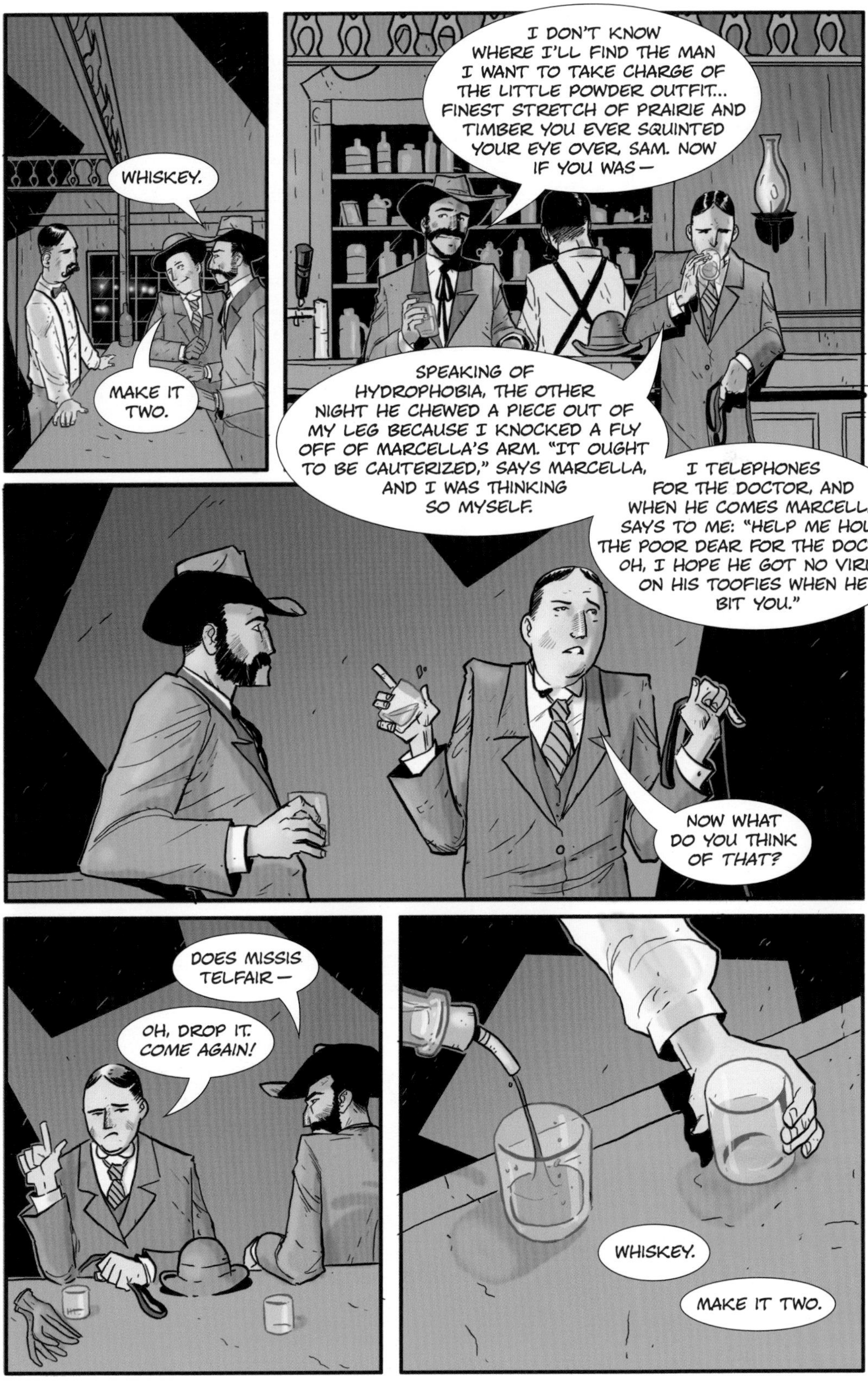
WHISKEY.
MAKE IT TWO.
I DON'T KNOW WHERE I'LL FIND THE MAN I WANT TO TAKE CHARGE OF THE LITTLE POWDER OUTFIT... FINEST STRETCH OF PRAIRIE AND TIMBER YOU EVER SQUINTED YOUR EYE OVER, SAM. NOW IF YOU WAS—
SPEAKING OF HYDROPHOBIA, THE OTHER NIGHT HE CHEWED A PIECE OUT OF MY LEG BECAUSE I KNOCKED A FLY OFF OF MARCELLA'S ARM. "IT OUGHT TO BE CAUTERIZED," SAYS MARCELLA, AND I WAS THINKING SO MYSELF.
I TELEPHONES FOR THE DOCTOR, AND WHEN HE COMES MARCELLA SAYS TO ME: "HELP ME HOLD THE POOR DEAR FOR THE DOCTOR. OH, I HOPE HE GOT NO VIRUS ON HIS TOOFIES WHEN HE BIT YOU."
NOW WHAT DO YOU THINK OF THAT?
DOES MISSIS TELFAIR—
OH, DROP IT. COME AGAIN!
WHISKEY.
MAKE IT TWO.

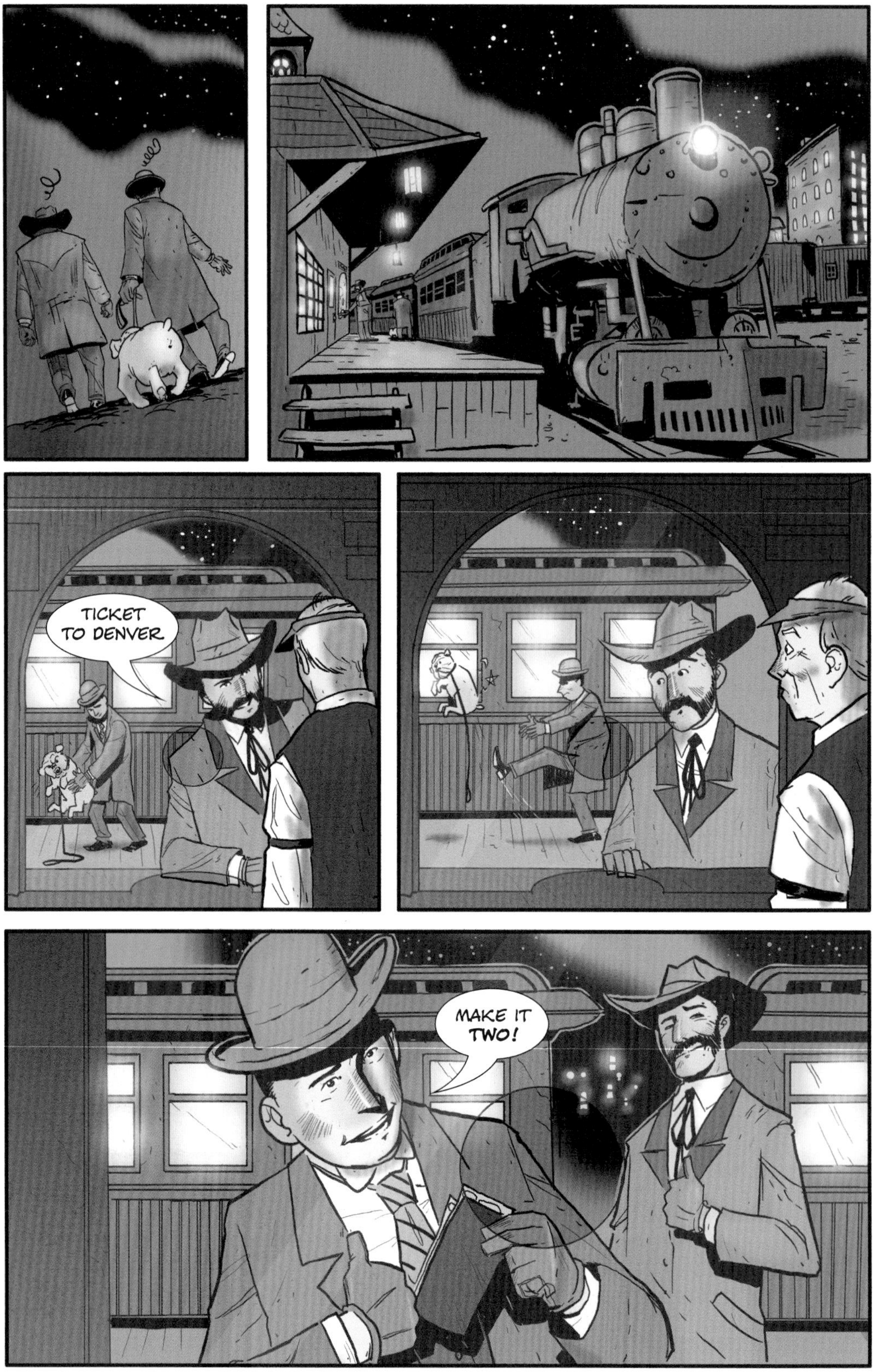
TICKET TO DENVER
MAKE IT TWO!

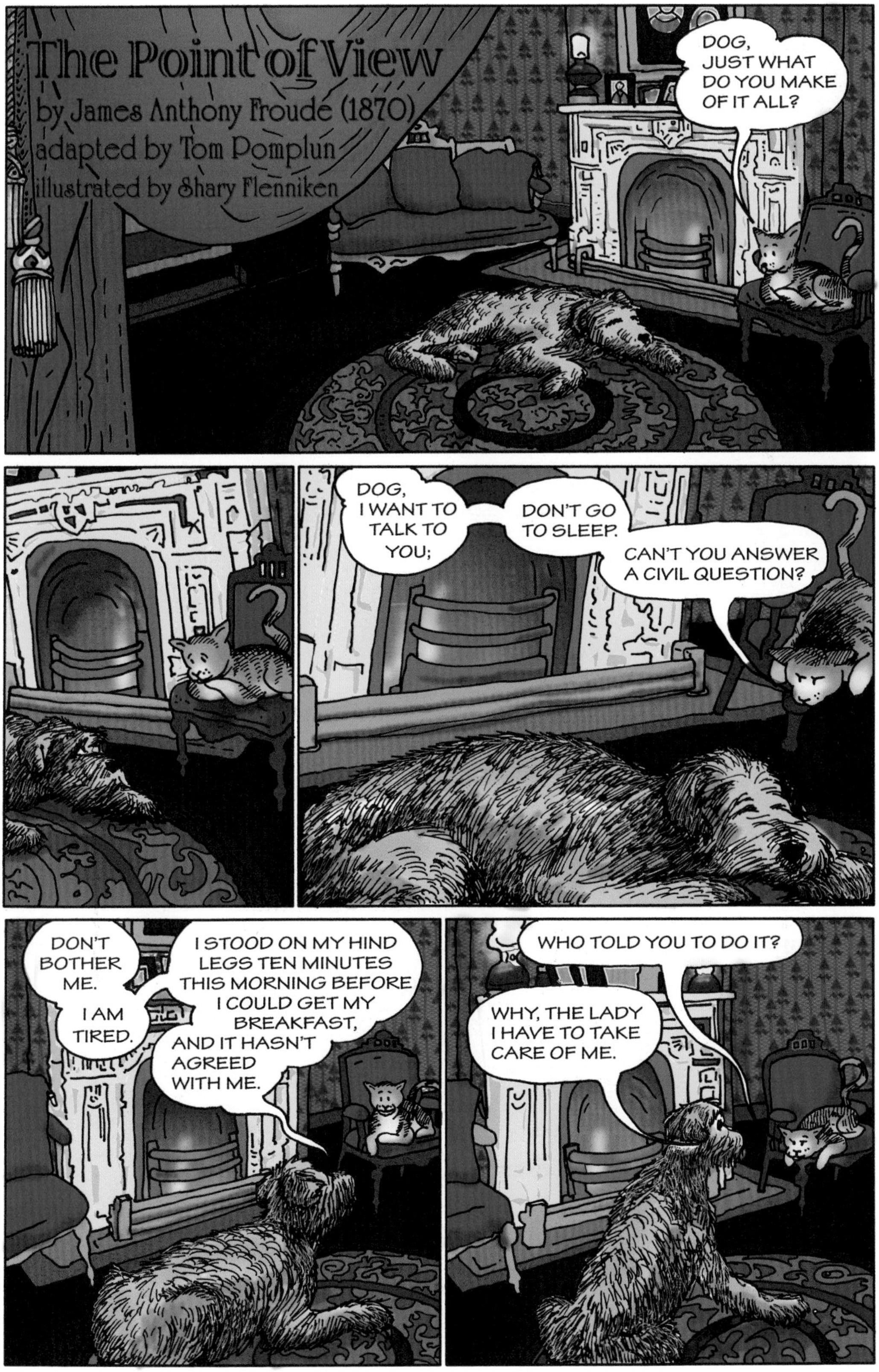
The Point of View
by James Anthony Froude (1870)
adapted by Tom Pomplun
illustrated by Shary Flenniken
DOG, JUST WHAT DO YOU MAKE OF IT ALL?
DOG, I WANT TO TALK TO YOU;
DON'T GO TO SLEEP.
CAN'T YOU ANSWER A CIVIL QUESTION?
DON'T BOTHER ME.
I AM TIRED.
I STOOD ON MY HIND LEGS TEN MINUTES THIS MORNING BEFORE I COULD GET MY BREAKFAST,
AND IT HASN'T AGREED WITH ME.
WHO TOLD YOU TO DO IT?
WHY, THE LADY I HAVE TO TAKE CARE OF ME.

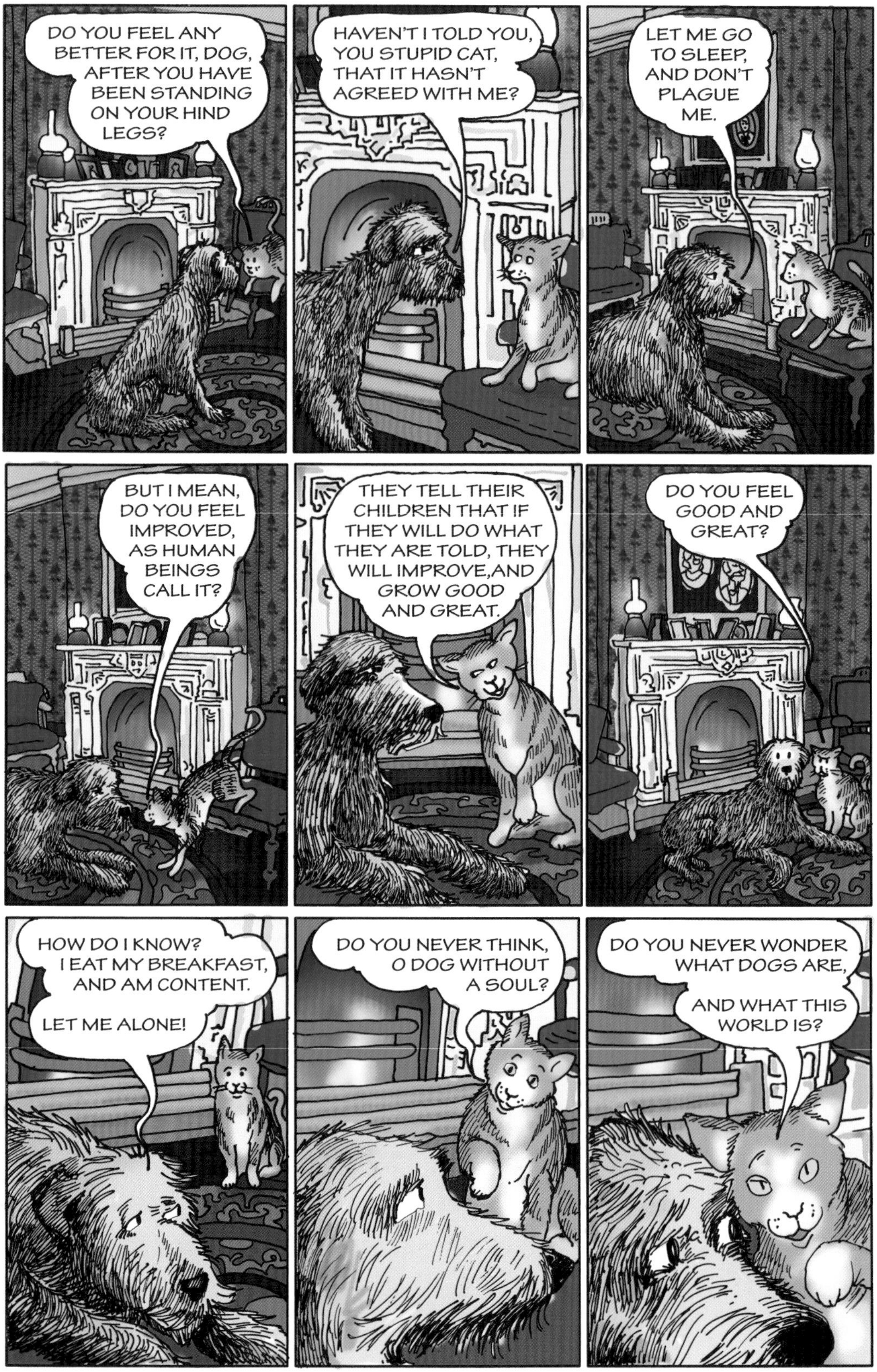
DO YOU FEEL ANY BETTER FOR IT, DOG, AFTER YOU HAVE BEEN STANDING ON YOUR HIND LEGS?
HAVEN'T I TOLD YOU, YOU STUPID CAT, THAT IT HASN'T AGREED WITH ME?
LET ME GO TO SLEEP, AND DON'T PLAGUE ME.
BUT I MEAN, DO YOU FEEL IMPROVED, AS HUMAN BEINGS CALL IT?
THEY TELL THEIR CHILDREN THAT IF THEY WILL DO WHAT THEY ARE TOLD, THEY WILL IMPROVE,AND GROW GOOD AND GREAT.
DO YOU FEEL GOOD AND GREAT?
HOW DO I KNOW? I EAT MY BREAKFAST, AND AM CONTENT.
LET ME ALONE!
DO YOU NEVER THINK, O DOG WITHOUT A SOUL?
DO YOU NEVER WONDER WHAT DOGS ARE,
AND WHAT THIS WORLD IS?

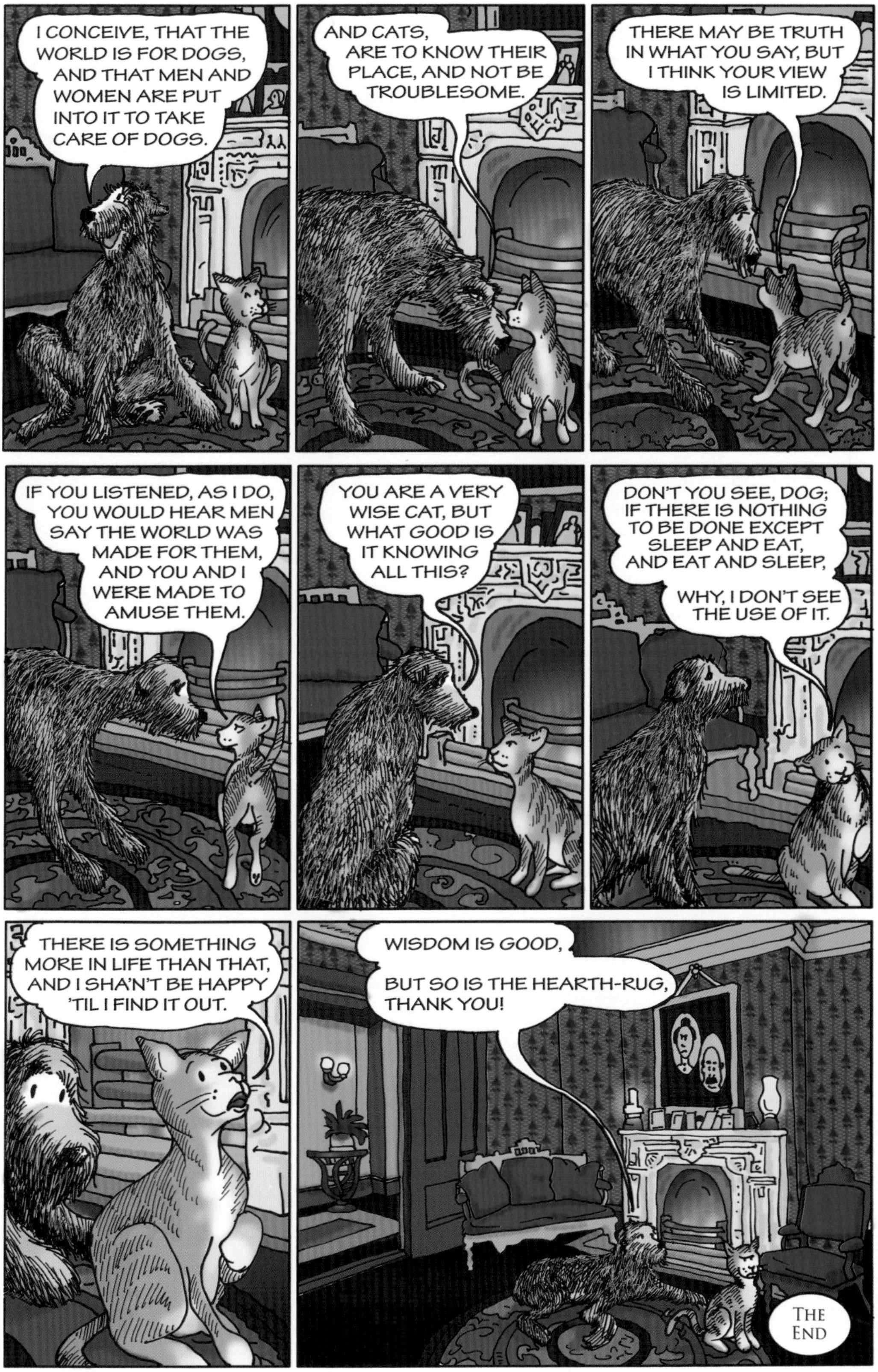
I CONCEIVE, THAT THE WORLD IS FOR DOGS, AND THAT MEN AND WOMEN ARE PUT INTO IT TO TAKE CARE OF DOGS.
AND CATS, ARE TO KNOW THEIR PLACE, AND NOT BE TROUBLESOME.
THERE MAY BE TRUTH IN WHAT YOU SAY, BUT I THINK YOUR VIEW IS LIMITED.
IF YOU LISTENED, AS I DO, YOU WOULD HEAR MEN SAY THE WORLD WAS MADE FOR THEM, AND YOU AND I WERE MADE TO AMUSE THEM.
YOU ARE A VERY WISE CAT, BUT WHAT *GOOD* IS IT KNOWING ALL THIS?
DON'T YOU SEE, DOG; IF THERE IS NOTHING TO BE DONE EXCEPT SLEEP AND EAT, AND EAT AND SLEEP,
WHY, I DON'T SEE THE USE OF IT.
THERE IS SOMETHING MORE IN LIFE THAN THAT, AND I SHA'N'T BE HAPPY 'TIL I FIND IT OUT.
WISDOM IS *GOOD*,
BUT SO IS THE HEARTH-RUG, THANK YOU!
THE END

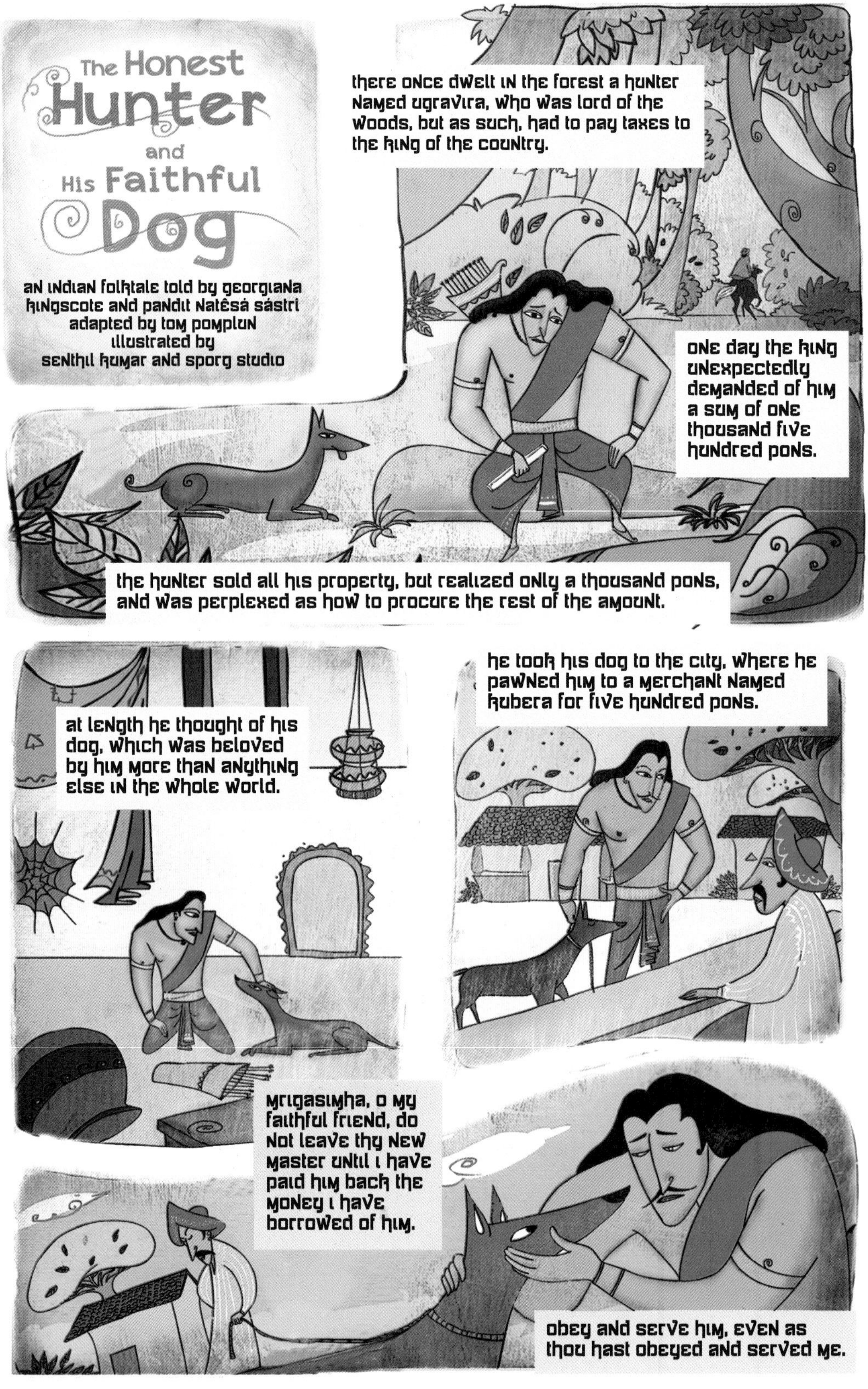
The Honest Hunter and His Faithful Dog
an indian folktale told by georgiana kingscote and pandit natêsá sástri
adapted by tom pomplun
illustrated by
senthil kumar and sporg studio
there once dwelt in the forest a hunter named ugravira, who was lord of the woods, but as such, had to pay taxes to the king of the country.
one day the king unexpectedly demanded of him a sum of one thousand five hundred pons.
the hunter sold all his property, but realized only a thousand pons, and was perplexed as how to procure the rest of the amount.
at length he thought of his dog, which was beloved by him more than anything else in the whole world.
he took his dog to the city, where he pawned him to a merchant named kubera for five hundred pons.
mrigasimha, o my faithful friend, do not leave thy new master until i have paid him back the money i have borrowed of him.
obey and serve him, even as thou hast obeyed and served me.

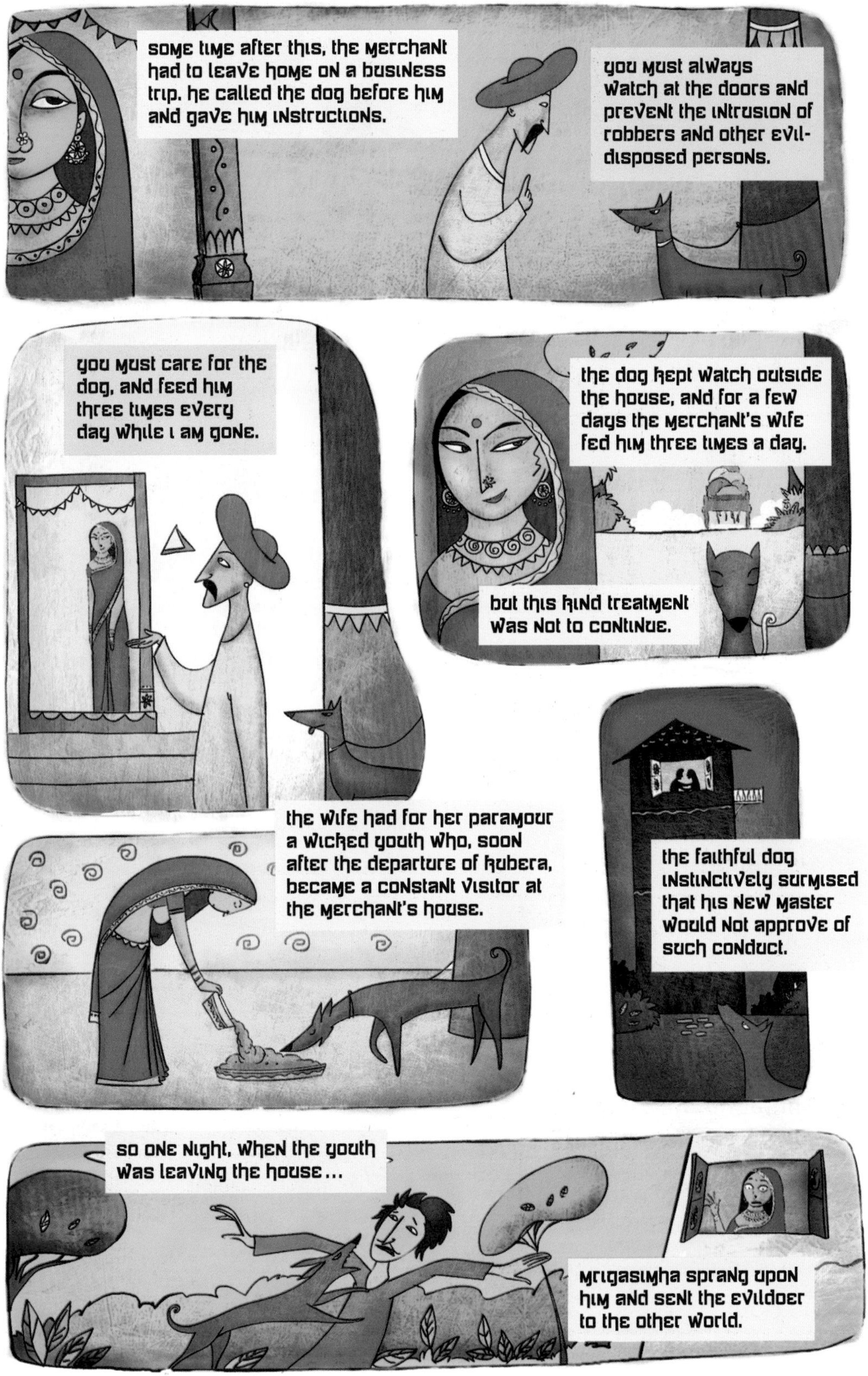
some time after this, the merchant had to leave home on a business trip. he called the dog before him and gave him instructions.
you must always watch at the doors and prevent the intrusion of robbers and other evil-disposed persons.
you must care for the dog, and feed him three times every day while i am gone.
the dog kept watch outside the house, and for a few days the merchant's wife fed him three times a day.
but this kind treatment was not to continue.
the wife had for her paramour a wicked youth who, soon after the departure of kubera, became a constant visitor at the merchant's house.
the faithful dog instinctively surmised that his new master would not approve of such conduct.
so one night, when the youth was leaving the house...
mrigasimha sprang upon him and sent the evildoer to the other world.

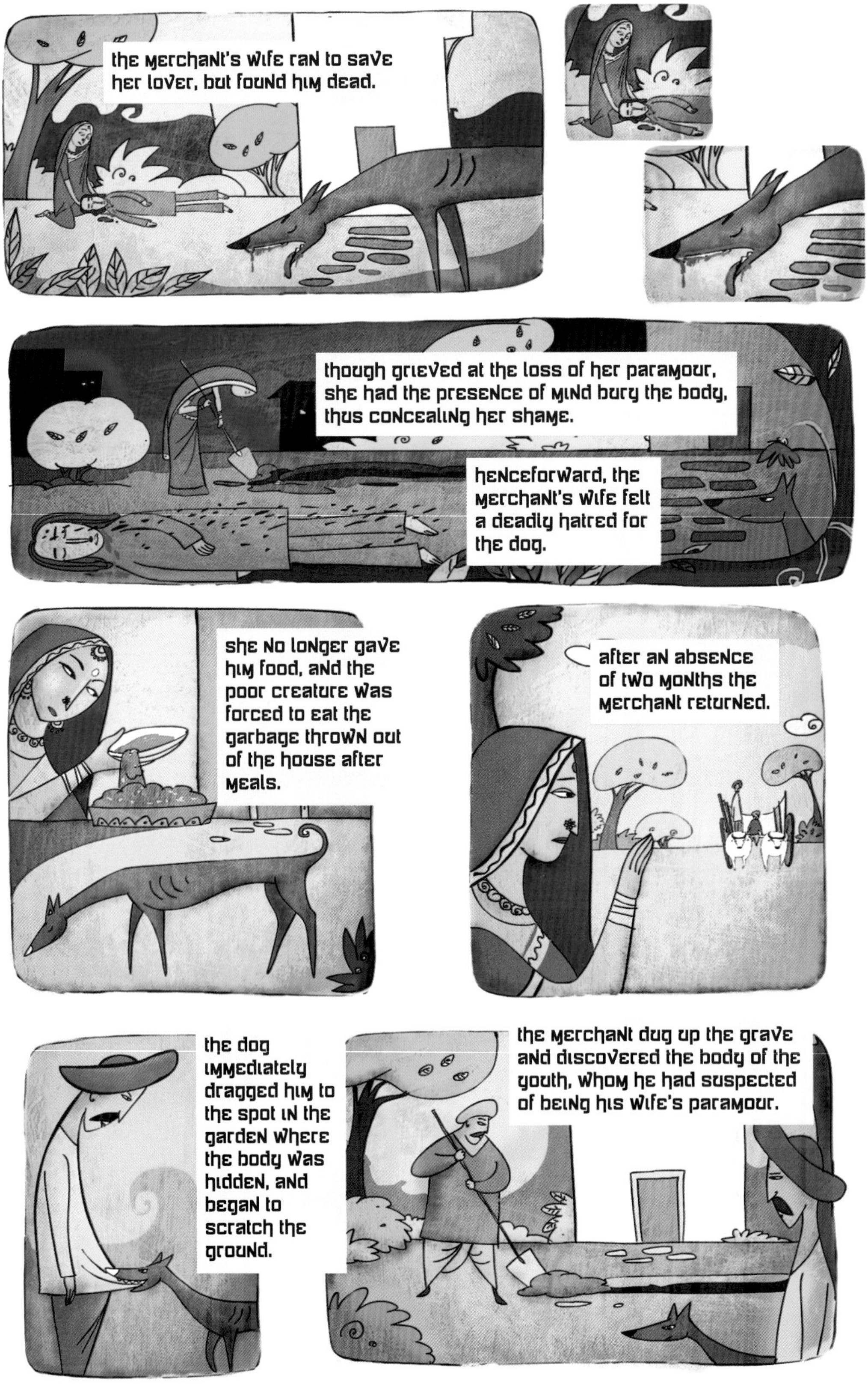
the merchant's wife ran to save her lover, but found him dead.
though grieved at the loss of her paramour, she had the presence of mind bury the body, thus concealing her shame.
henceforward, the merchant's wife felt a deadly hatred for the dog.
she no longer gave him food, and the poor creature was forced to eat the garbage thrown out of the house after meals.
after an absence of two months the merchant returned.
the dog immediately dragged him to the spot in the garden where the body was hidden, and began to scratch the ground.
the merchant dug up the grave and discovered the body of the youth, whom he had suspected of being his wife's paramour.

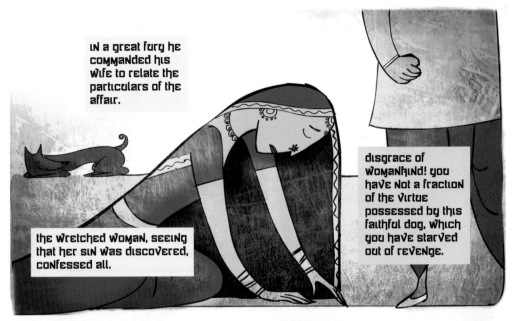

IN a great fury he commanded his wife to relate the particulars of the affair.

the wretched woman, seeing that her sin was discovered, confessed all.

disgrace of womankind! you have not a fraction of the virtue possessed by this faithful dog, which you have starved out of revenge.

depart this house, and let me see thy face no more!

thou trusty friend, the five hundred pons which I lent the hunter are as nothing compared with thy services to me.

I consider the debt as more than paid, and I now give thee leave to return to thy old master.

Now by this time the hunter had managed to save up the five hundred pons, and with the money he was traveling to the merchant to reclaim his dog.

to his great surprise he met Mrigasimha on the way.

but the hunter concluded that the poor brute had run away from the merchant.

this dishonored both of them, and he determined he must put the dog to death.

the faithful creature, who was expecting nothing but kindness from his old master, was by him most cruelly hanged.

the hunter then continued his journey to the merchant's house.

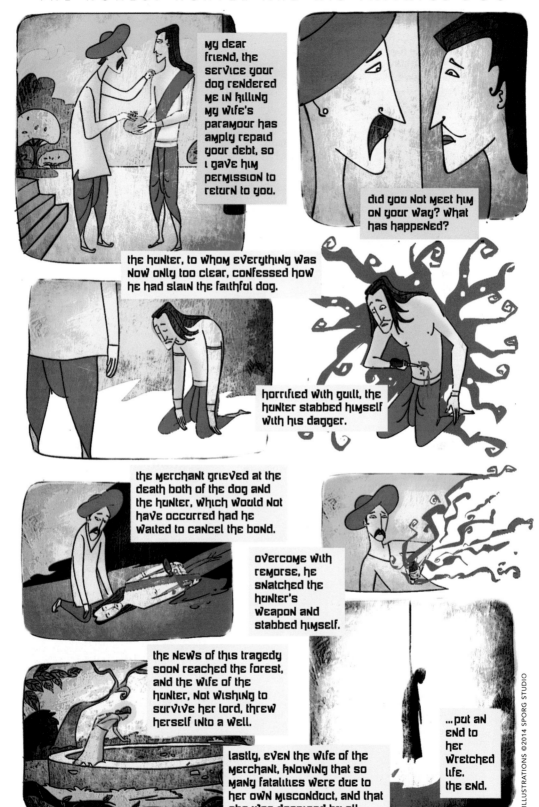

My dear friend, the service your dog rendered me in killing my wife's paramour has amply repaid your debt, so I gave him permission to return to you.

did you not meet him on your way? what has happened?

the hunter, to whom everything was now only too clear, confessed how he had slain the faithful dog.

horrified with guilt, the hunter stabbed himself with his dagger.

the merchant grieved at the death both of the dog and the hunter, which would not have occurred had he waited to cancel the bond.

overcome with remorse, he snatched the hunter's weapon and stabbed himself.

the news of this tragedy soon reached the forest, and the wife of the hunter, not wishing to survive her lord, threw herself into a well.

lastly, even the wife of the merchant, knowing that so many fatalities were due to her own misconduct, and that she was despised by all....

...put an end to her wretched life. the end.

ILLUSTRATIONS ©2014 SPORG STUDIO

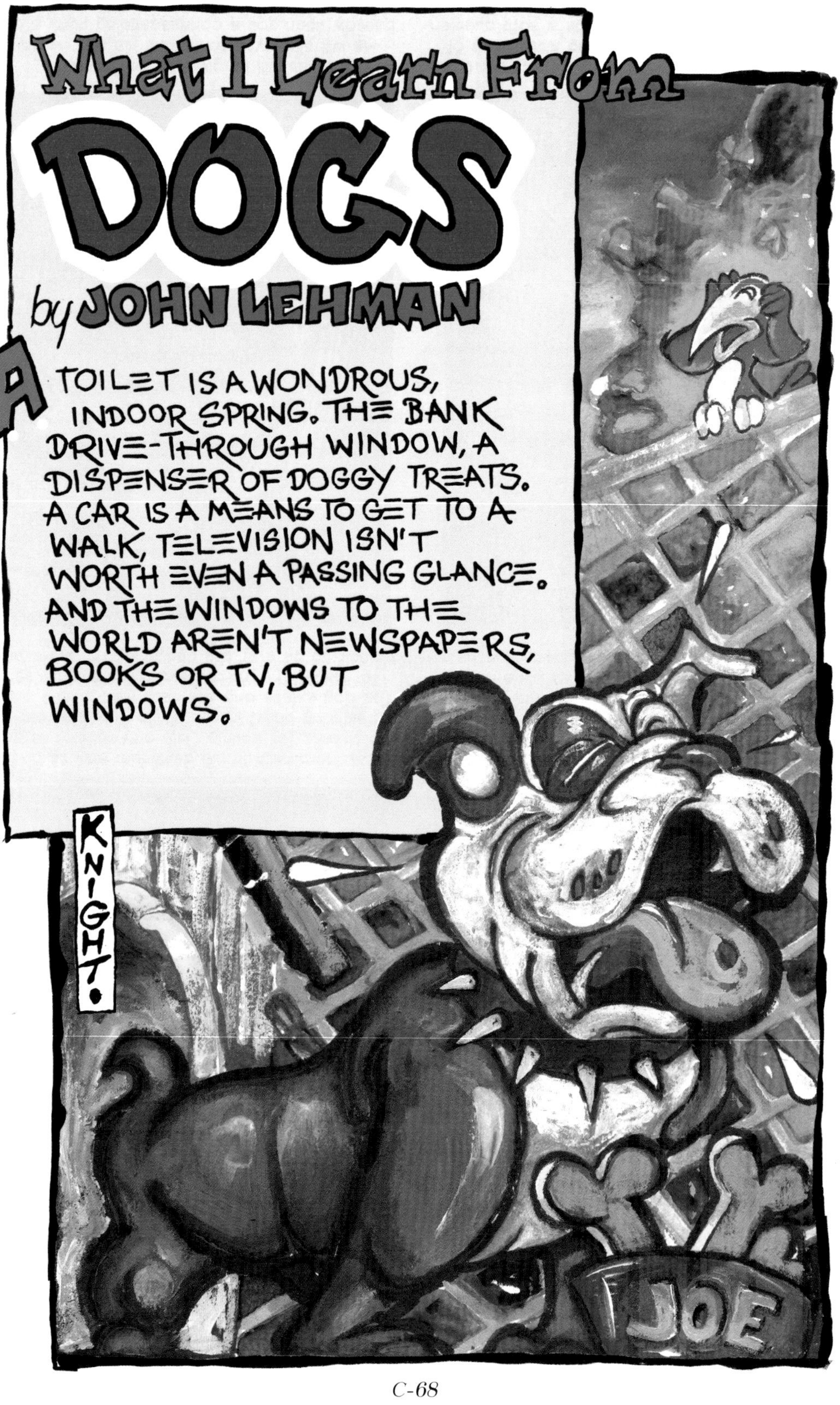
What I Learn From
DOGS
by JOHN LEHMAN
A TOILET IS A WONDROUS, INDOOR SPRING. THE BANK DRIVE-THROUGH WINDOW, A DISPENSER OF DOGGY TREATS. A CAR IS A MEANS TO GET TO A WALK, TELEVISION ISN'T WORTH EVEN A PASSING GLANCE. AND THE WINDOWS TO THE WORLD AREN'T NEWSPAPERS, BOOKS OR TV, BUT WINDOWS.
KNIGHT.
JOE

FELINE CLASSICS

Graphic Classics® Volume Twenty-Five
2014

Edited by Tom Pomplun

Associate Editor
John Lehman

EUREKA PRODUCTIONS

8778 Oak Grove Road, Mount Horeb, Wisconsin 53572
www.graphicclassics.com

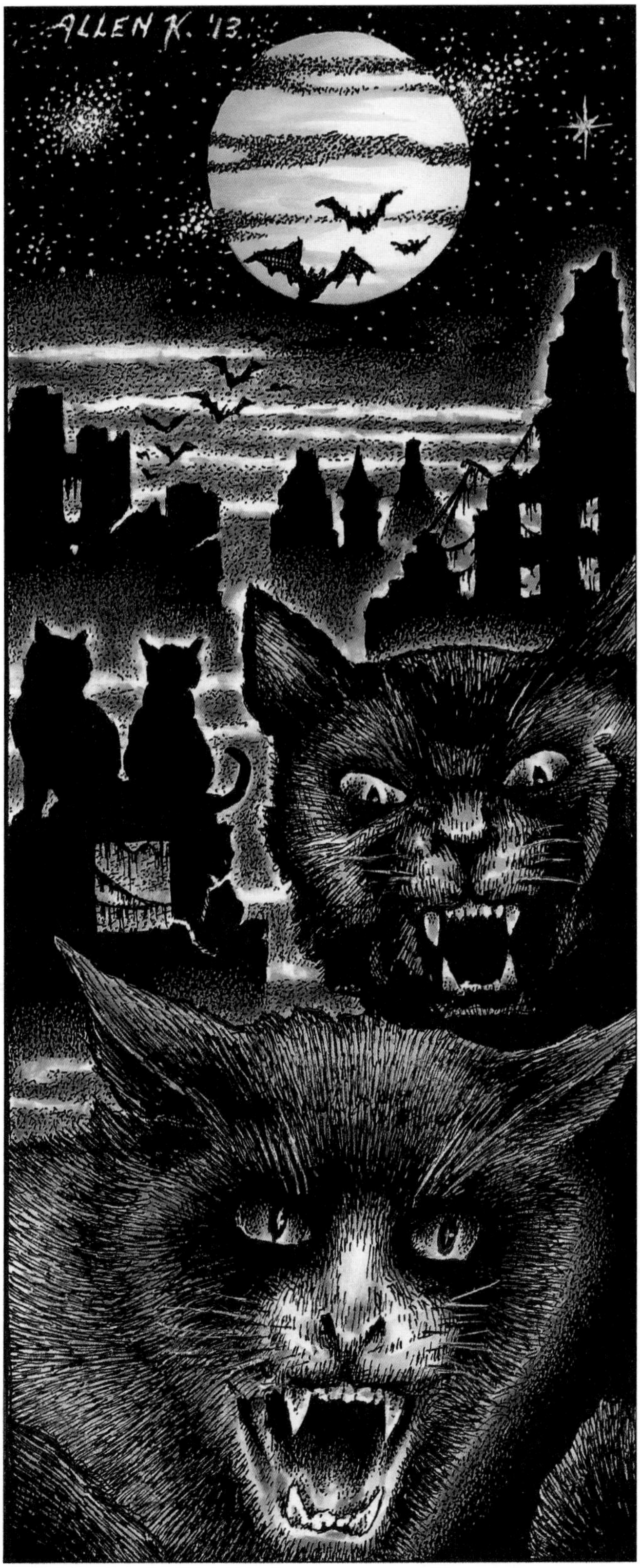
ALLEN K. '13

The Cats

by **H. P. LOVECRAFT**
illustrated by **ALLEN KOSZOWSKI**

Babels of blocks to the high heavens tow'ring,
Flames of futility swirling below;
Poisonous fungi in brick and stone flow'ring,
Lanterns that shudder and death-lights that glow.

Black monstrous bridges across oily rivers,
Cobwebs of cable by nameless things spun;
Catacomb deeps whose dank chaos delivers
Streams of live foetor, that rots in the sun.

Colour and splendour, disease and decaying,
Shrieking and ringing and scrambling insane,
Rabbles exotic to stranger-gods praying,
Jumbles of odour that stifle the brain.

Legions of cats from the alleys nocturnal,
Howling and lean in the glare of the moon,
Screaming the future with mouthings infernal,
Yelling the burden of Pluto's red rune.

Tall tow'rs and pyramids ivy'd and crumbling,
Bats that swoop low in the weed-cumber'd streets;
Bleak broken bridges o'er rivers whose rumbling
Joins with no voice as the thick tide retreats.

Belfries that blackly against the moon totter,
Caverns whose mouths are by mosses effac'd,
And living to answer the wind and the water,
Only the lean cats that howl in the waste!

FELINE CLASSICS

Graphic Classics® Volume 25

ILLUSTRATION ©2014 DRAGAN KOVACEVIC

Cover illustrations by Toni Pawlowsky
Page F-1 illustration by Evert Geradts
Page F-3 illustration
KittyLand by Dragan Kovacevic

Canine/Feline Classics: Graphic Classics Volume 25, ISBN 978-0-9825630-8-3 is published by Eureka Productions. Price US $19.95, CAN $21.95. Available from Eureka Productions, 8778 Oak Grove Road, Mount Horeb, WI 53572. Tom Pomplun, designer and publisher, tom@graphicclassics.com. John Lehman, associate editor. Lisa Nielsen Agnew, editorial assistant. Permission to print H.P. Lovecraft's *The Cats* in this volume has been granted by Lovecraft Holdings, LLC. Permission to adapt *The Emissary* ©1947 by Arkham House, renewed 1975 by Ray Bradbury, has been granted by Don Congdon Associates, Inc. Permission to adapt Joe R. Lansdale's *Dog, Cat, and Baby* ©1987 Joe R. Lansdale, has been granted by the author. *What I Learn from Cats* ©2014 John Lehman and *What I Learn from Dogs* ©1998 John Lehman printed by permission of the author. *The Beast from the Abyss* ©1971 Robert E. Howard Properties Inc. ROBERT E. HOWARD and related names, logos, characters and distinctive likenesses thereof are trademarks or registered trademarks of Robert E. Howard Properties Inc. Graphic Classics is a registered trademark of Eureka Productions. For ordering information and previews of upcoming volumes please visit the Graphic Classics website at http://www.graphicclassics.com. Printed in USA.

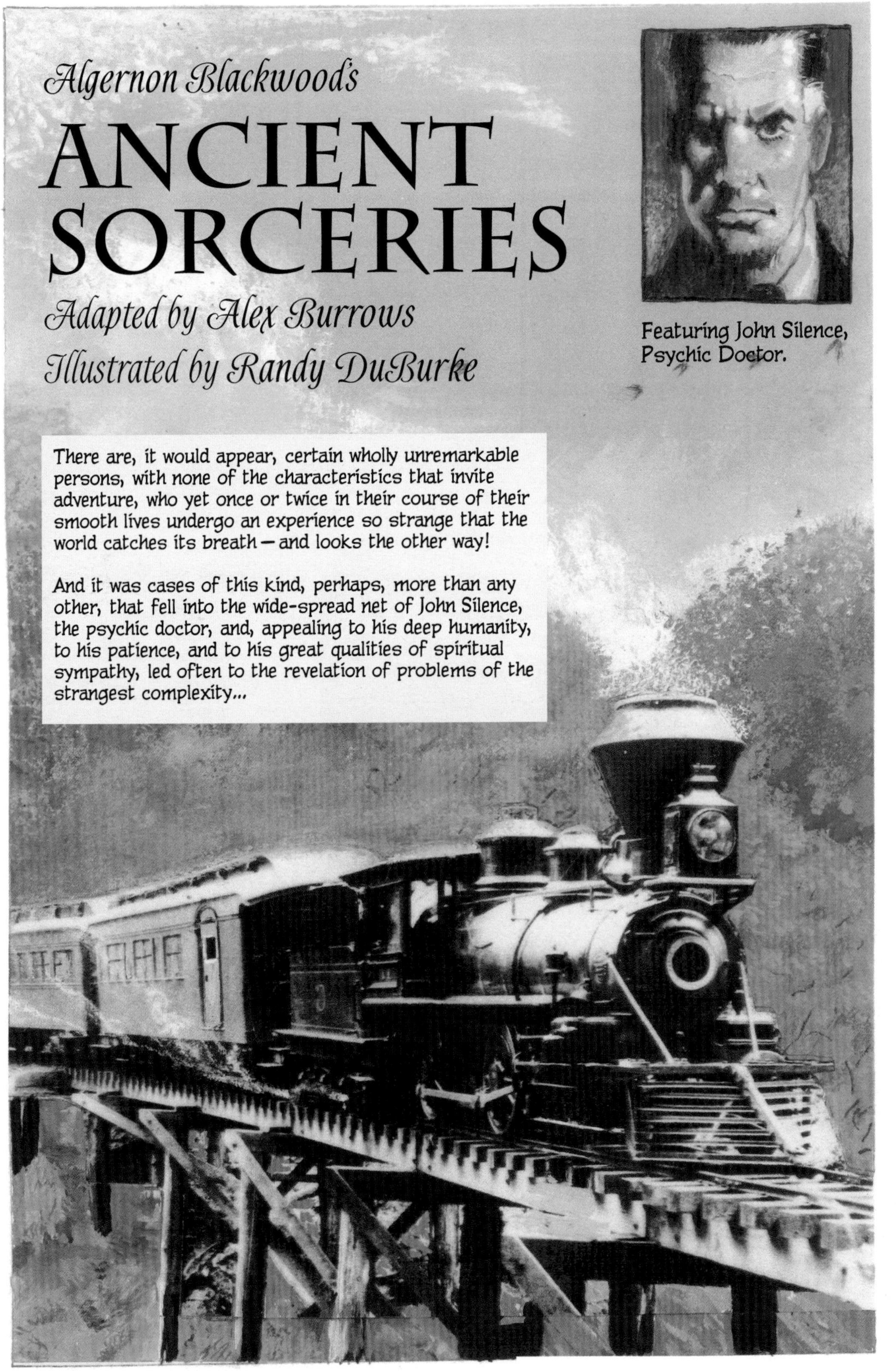
Algernon Blackwood's
ANCIENT SORCERIES
Adapted by Alex Burrows
Illustrated by Randy DuBurke
Featuring John Silence, Psychic Doctor.
There are, it would appear, certain wholly unremarkable persons, with none of the characteristics that invite adventure, who yet once or twice in their course of their smooth lives undergo an experience so strange that the world catches its breath — and looks the other way!
And it was cases of this kind, perhaps, more than any other, that fell into the wide-spread net of John Silence, the psychic doctor, and, appealing to his deep humanity, to his patience, and to his great qualities of spiritual sympathy, led often to the revelation of problems of the strangest complexity...

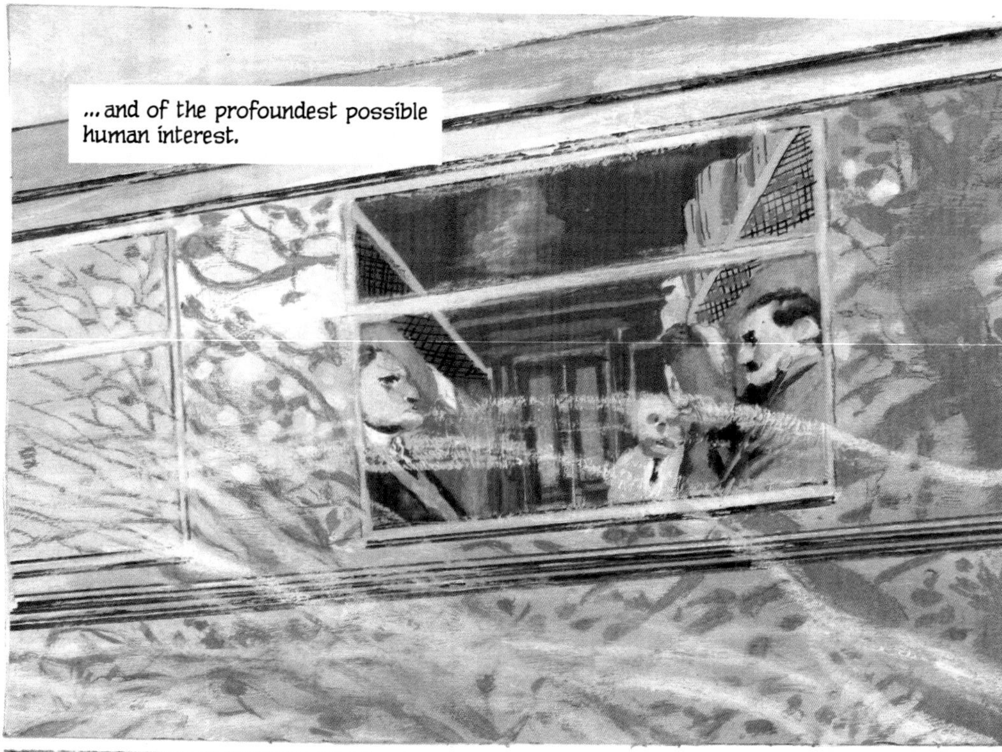
...and of the profoundest possible human interest.

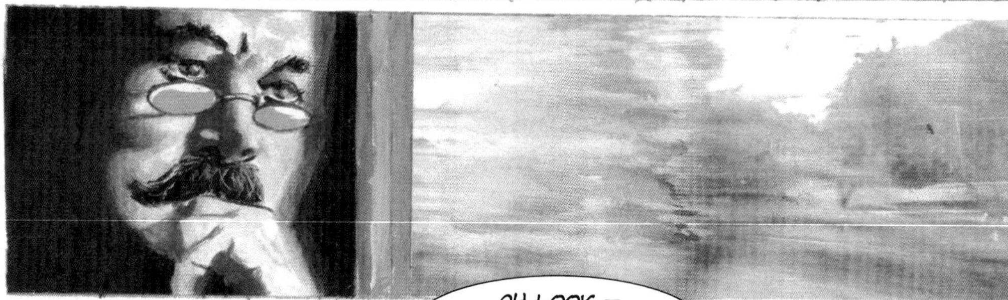

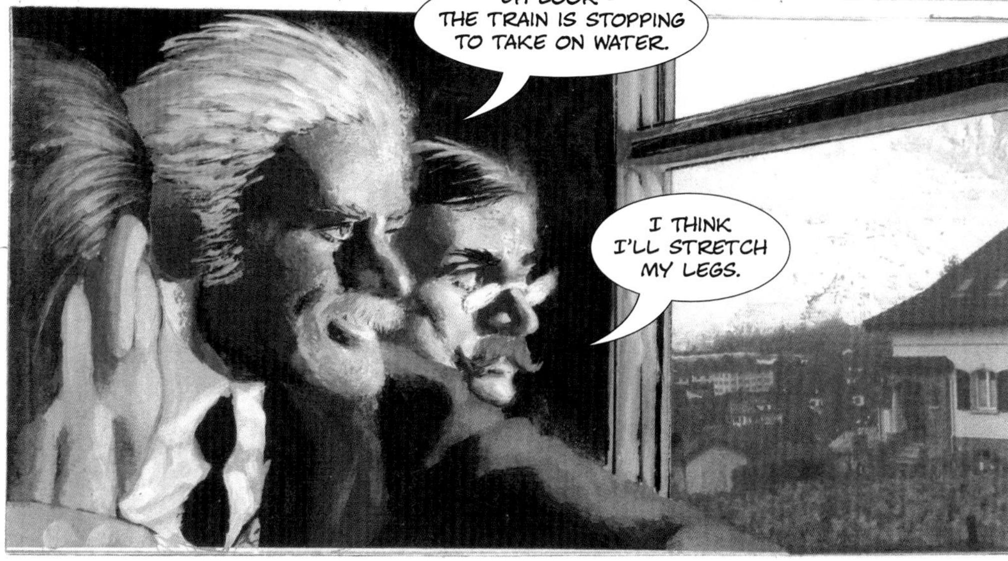
OH LOOK – THE TRAIN IS STOPPING TO TAKE ON WATER.
I THINK I'LL STRETCH MY LEGS.

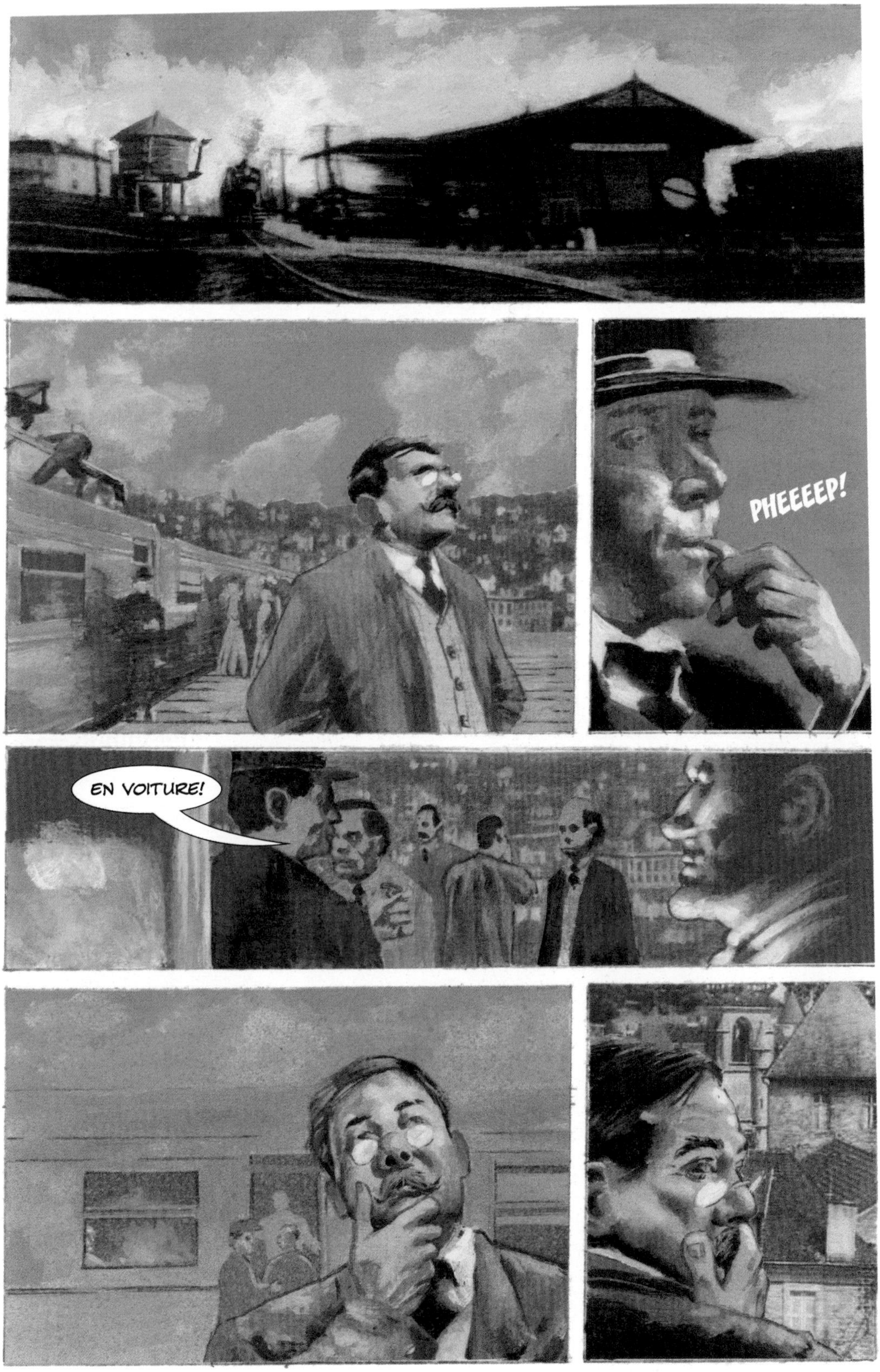
PHEEEEP!
EN VOITURE!

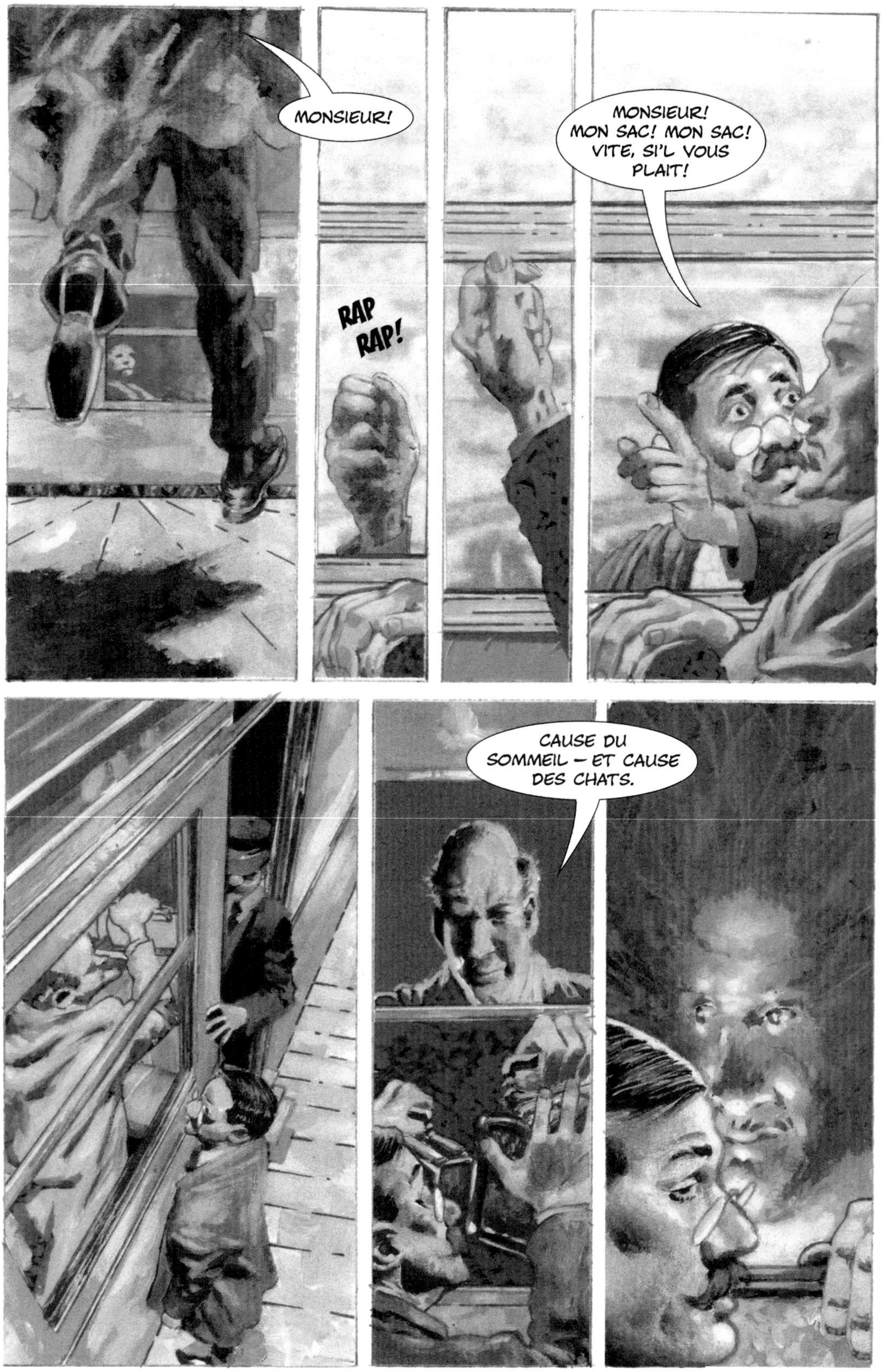
MONSIEUR!
RAP RAP!
MONSIEUR! MON SAC! MON SAC! VITE, SI'L VOUS PLAIT!
CAUSE DU SOMMEIL – ET CAUSE DES CHATS.

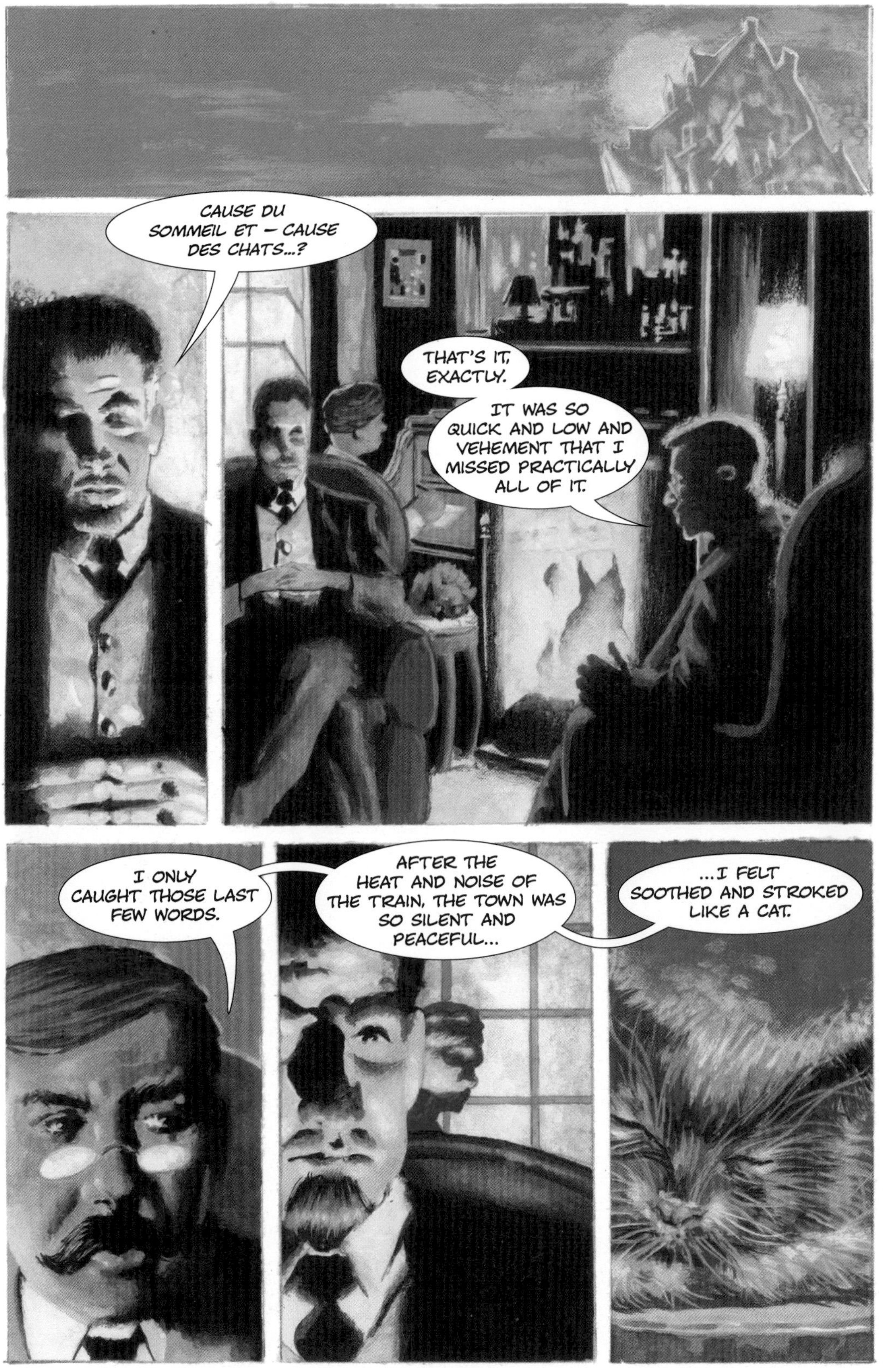
CAUSE DU SOMMEIL ET – CAUSE DES CHATS...?
THAT'S IT, EXACTLY.
IT WAS SO QUICK AND LOW AND VEHEMENT THAT I MISSED PRACTICALLY ALL OF IT.
I ONLY CAUGHT THOSE LAST FEW WORDS.
AFTER THE HEAT AND NOISE OF THE TRAIN, THE TOWN WAS SO SILENT AND PEACEFUL...
...I FELT SOOTHED AND STROKED LIKE A CAT.

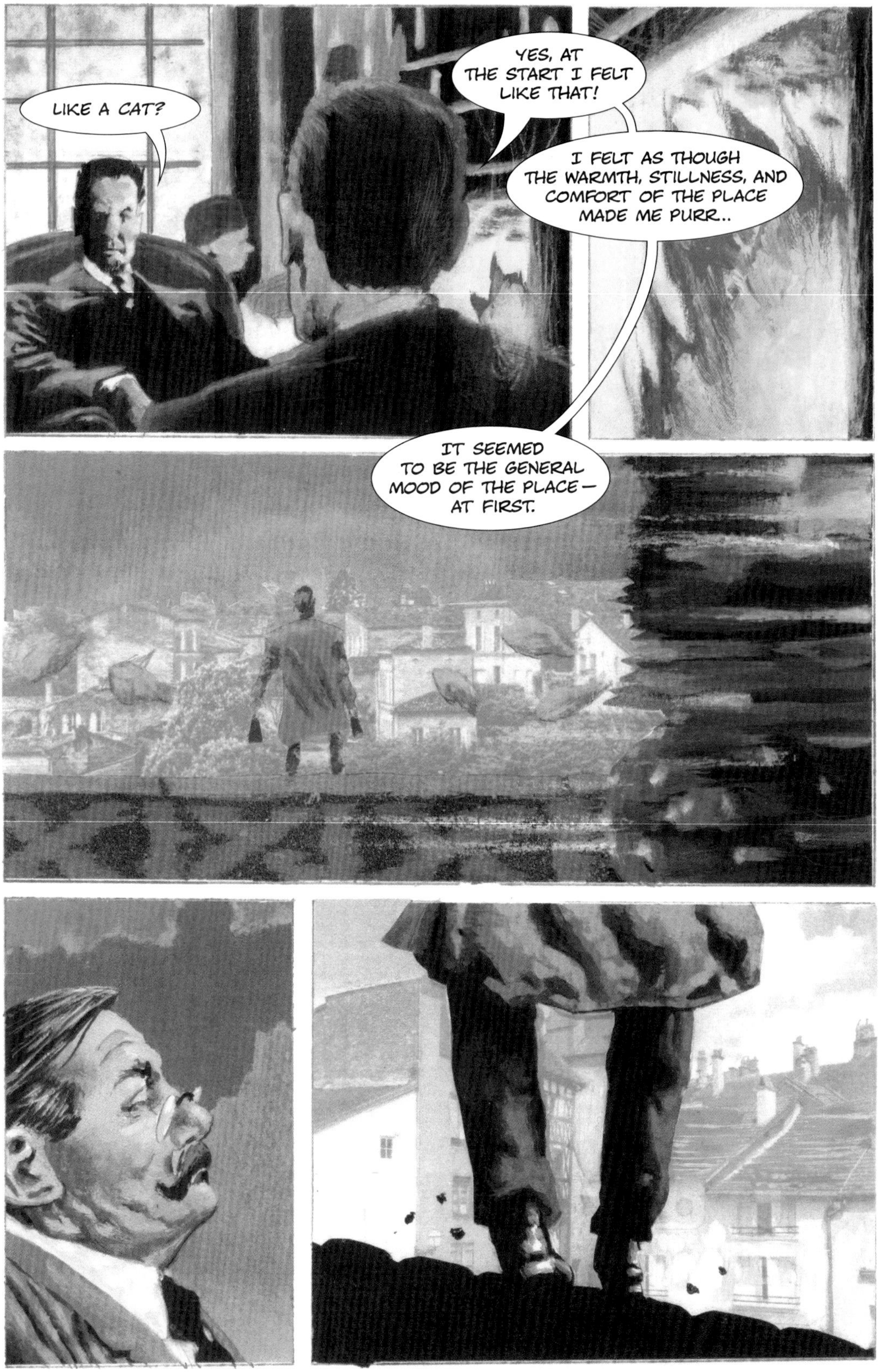
LIKE A CAT?
YES, AT THE START I FELT LIKE THAT!
I FELT AS THOUGH THE WARMTH, STILLNESS, AND COMFORT OF THE PLACE MADE ME PURR..
IT SEEMED TO BE THE GENERAL MOOD OF THE PLACE— AT FIRST.

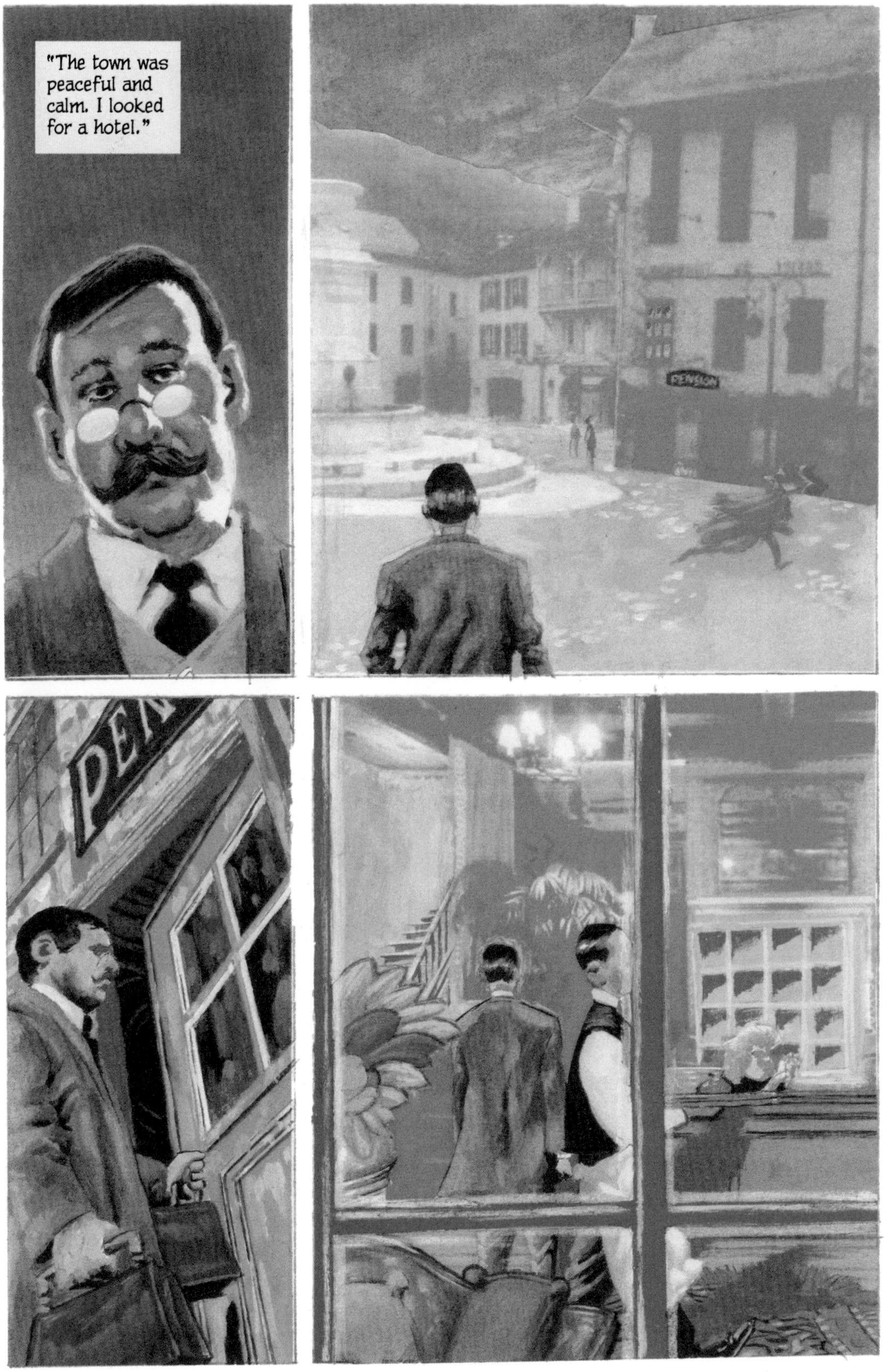
"The town was peaceful and calm. I looked for a hotel."
PENSION
PEN

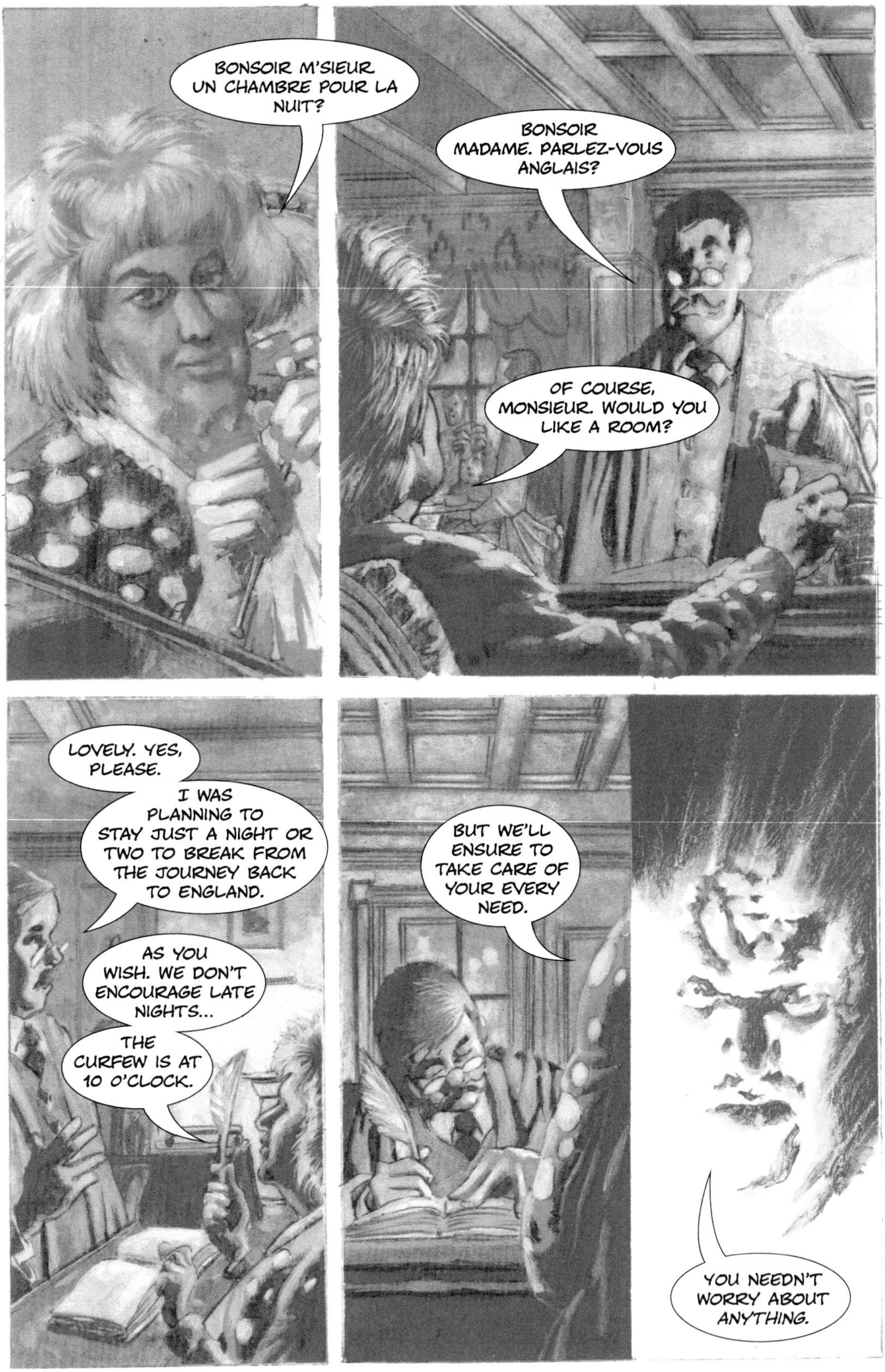
BONSOIR M'SIEUR UN CHAMBRE POUR LA NUIT?
BONSOIR MADAME. PARLEZ-VOUS ANGLAIS?
OF COURSE, MONSIEUR. WOULD YOU LIKE A ROOM?
LOVELY. YES, PLEASE.
I WAS PLANNING TO STAY JUST A NIGHT OR TWO TO BREAK FROM THE JOURNEY BACK TO ENGLAND.
AS YOU WISH. WE DON'T ENCOURAGE LATE NIGHTS...
THE CURFEW IS AT 10 O'CLOCK.
BUT WE'LL ENSURE TO TAKE CARE OF YOUR EVERY NEED.
YOU NEEDN'T WORRY ABOUT ANYTHING.

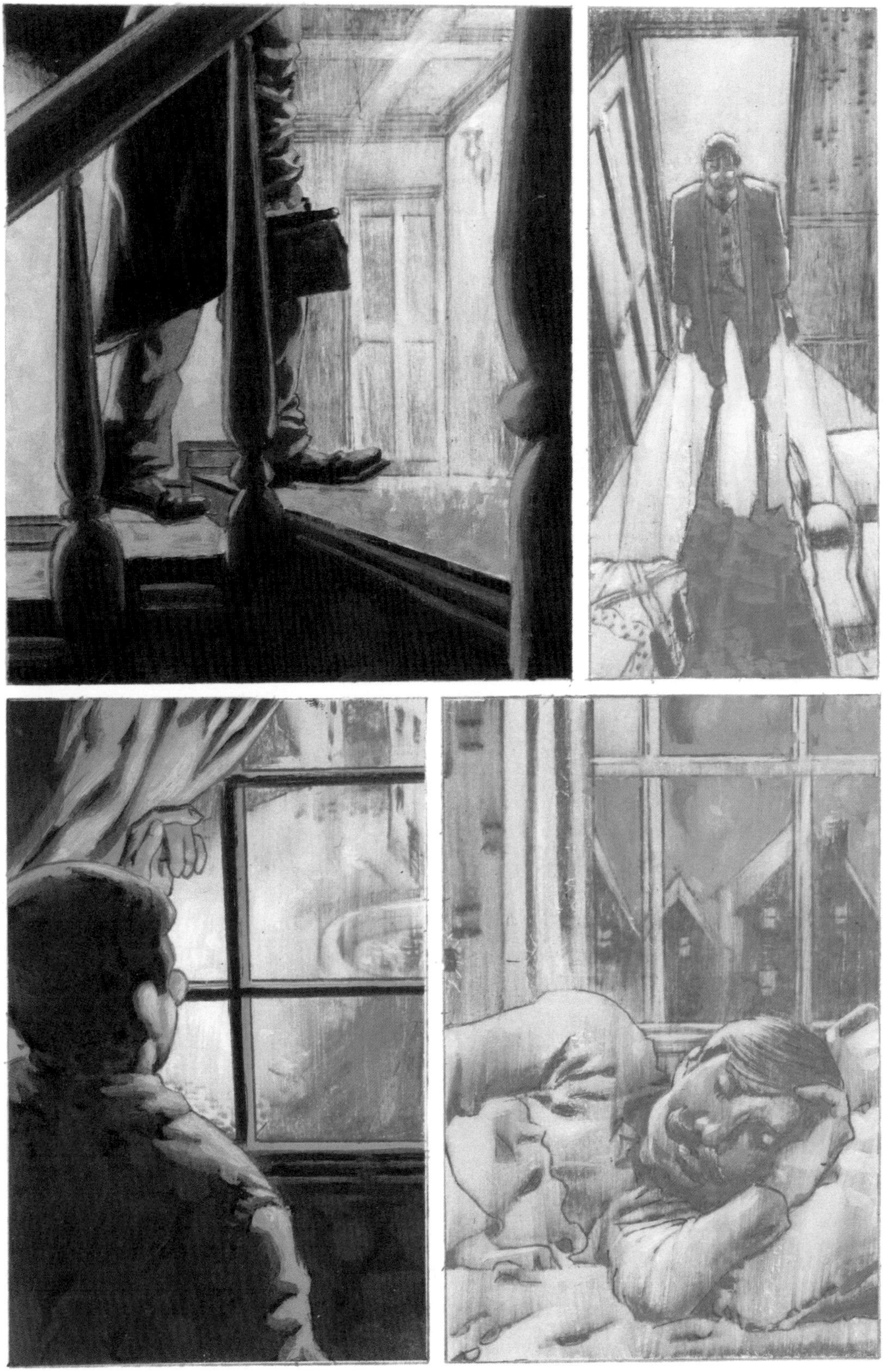

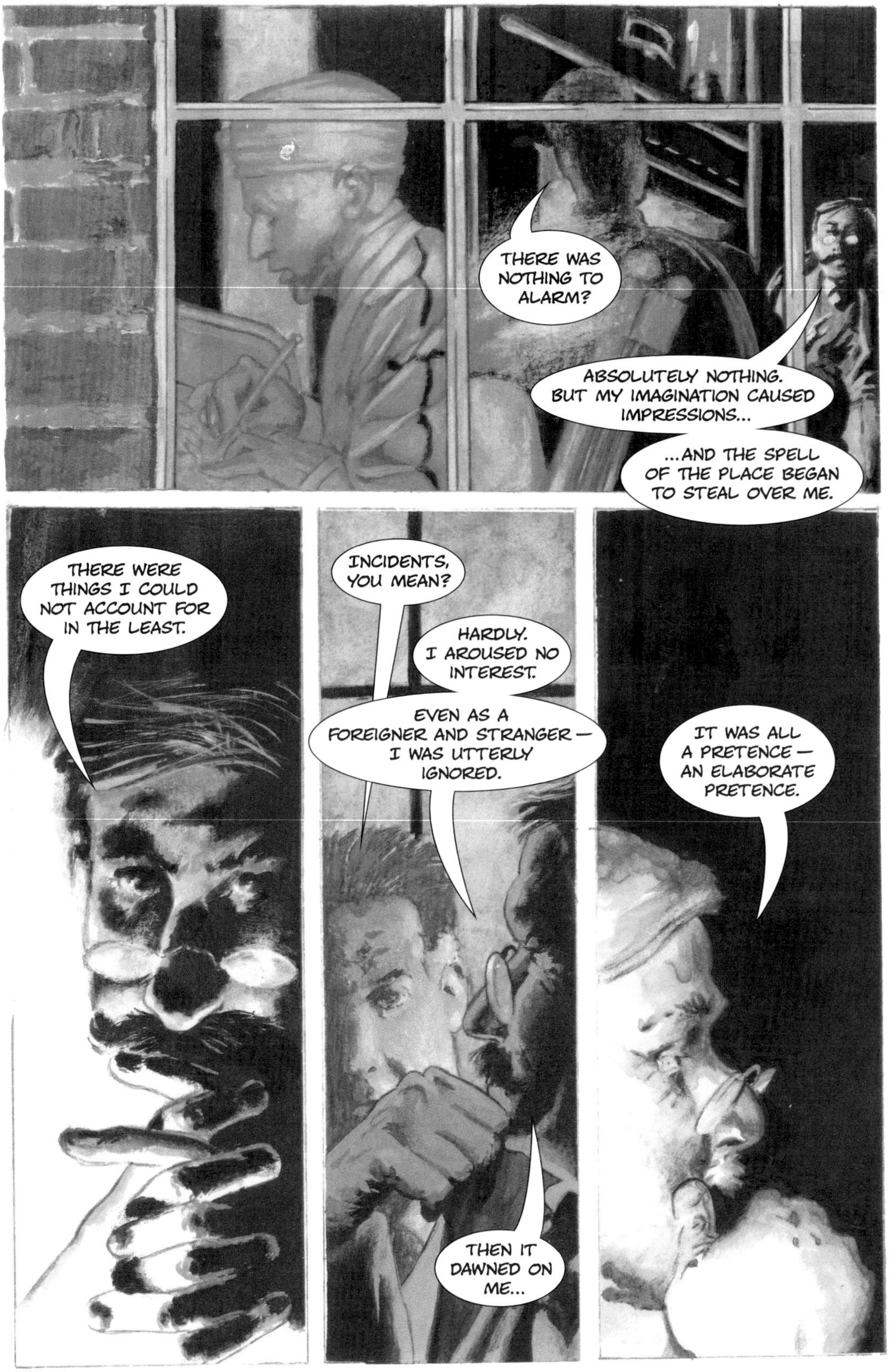
THERE WAS NOTHING TO ALARM?
ABSOLUTELY NOTHING. BUT MY IMAGINATION CAUSED IMPRESSIONS...
...AND THE SPELL OF THE PLACE BEGAN TO STEAL OVER ME.
THERE WERE THINGS I COULD NOT ACCOUNT FOR IN THE LEAST.
INCIDENTS, YOU MEAN?
HARDLY. I AROUSED NO INTEREST.
EVEN AS A FOREIGNER AND STRANGER — I WAS UTTERLY IGNORED.
THEN IT DAWNED ON ME...
IT WAS ALL A PRETENCE — AN ELABORATE PRETENCE.

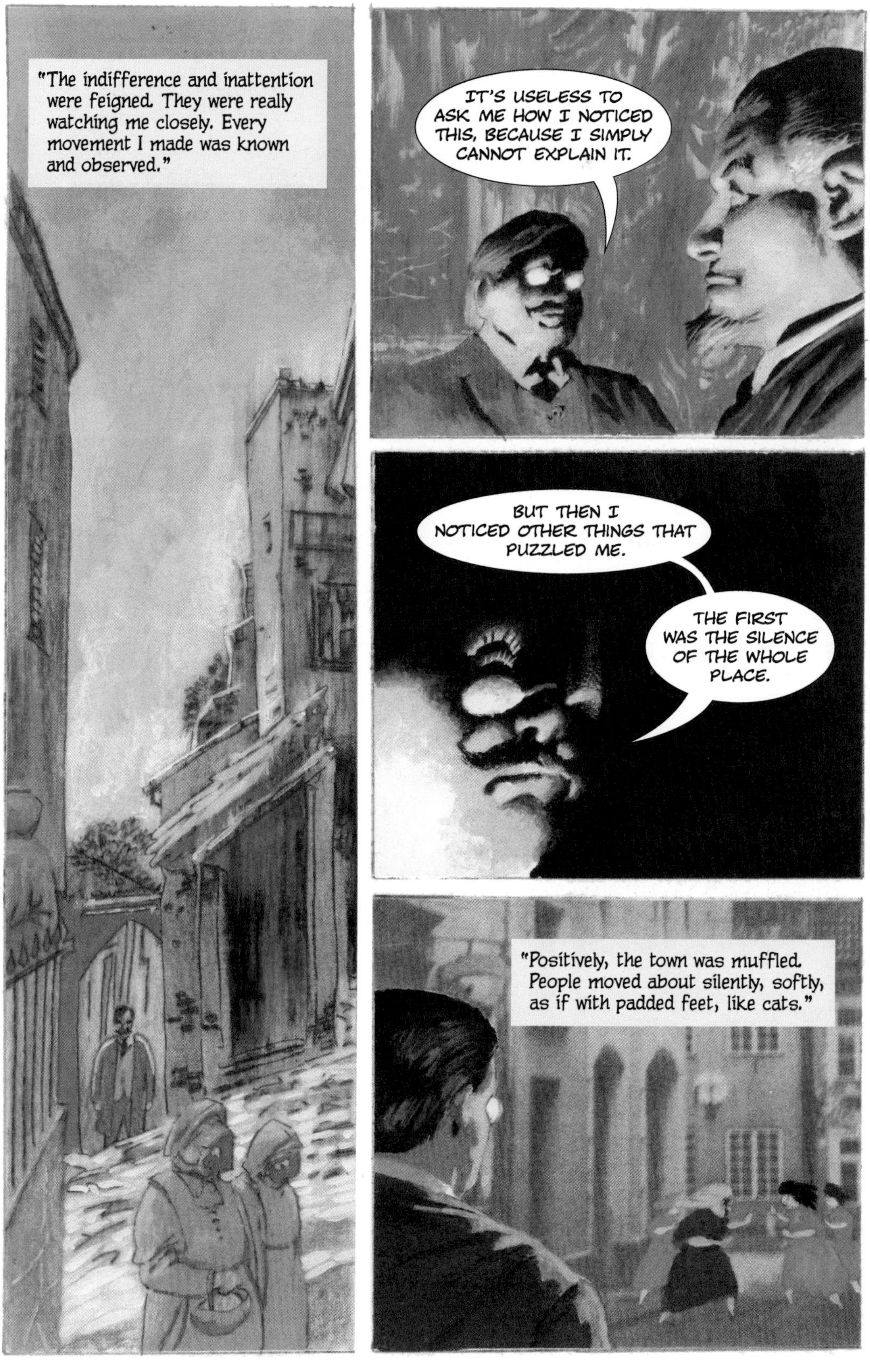
"The indifference and inattention were feigned. They were really watching me closely. Every movement I made was known and observed."
IT'S USELESS TO ASK ME HOW I NOTICED THIS, BECAUSE I SIMPLY CANNOT EXPLAIN IT.
BUT THEN I NOTICED OTHER THINGS THAT PUZZLED ME.
THE FIRST WAS THE SILENCE OF THE WHOLE PLACE.
"Positively, the town was muffled. People moved about silently, softly, as if with padded feet, like cats."

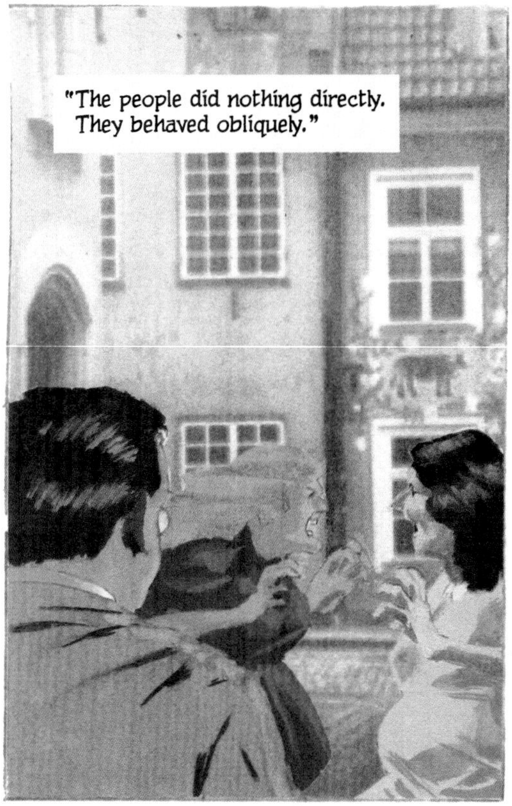
"The people did nothing directly.
They behaved obliquely."

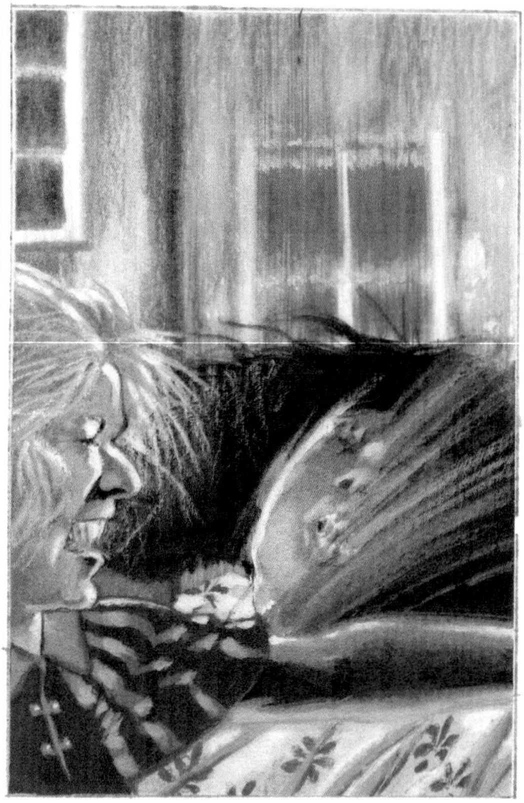

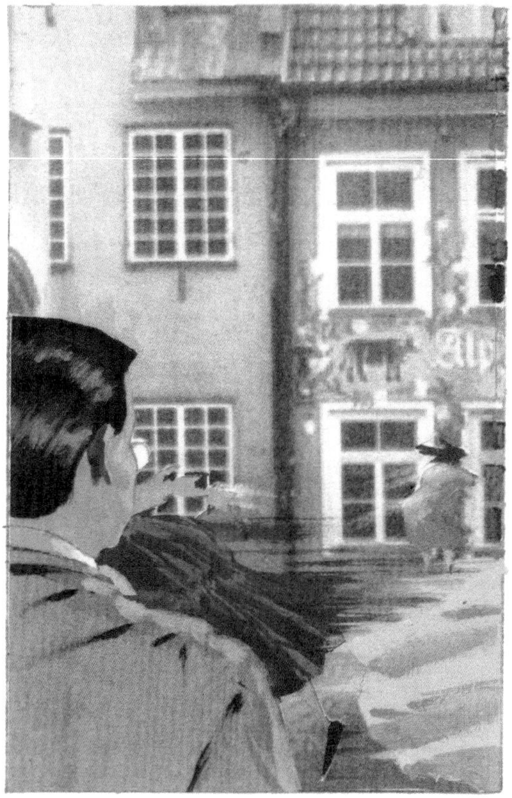

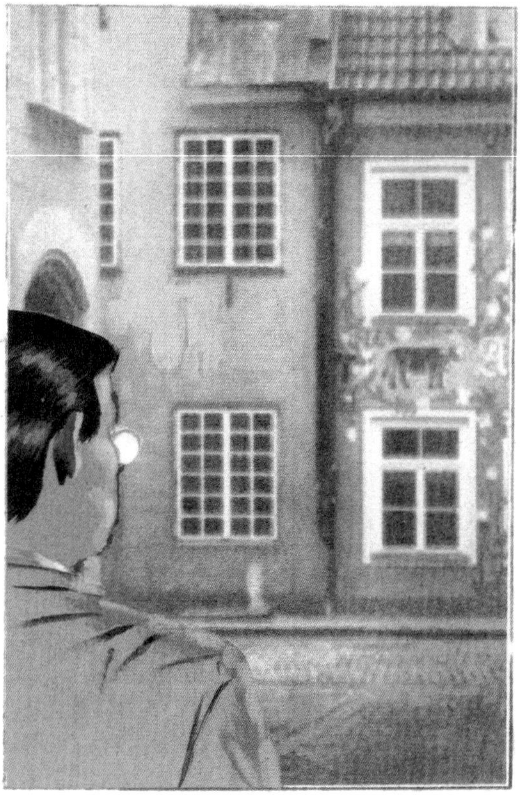

"The whole spirit of the town evaded me."

"But it felt like the inhabitants were waiting..."

"...waiting for me to declare something. But *what?*"

CAUSE DU SOMMEIL —ET CAUSE DES CHATS.

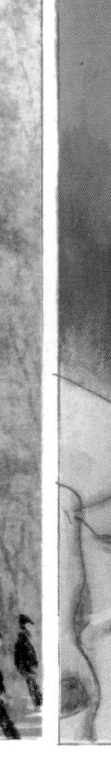

"I remembered the words of the man on the train. And something made me sleep like the dead."

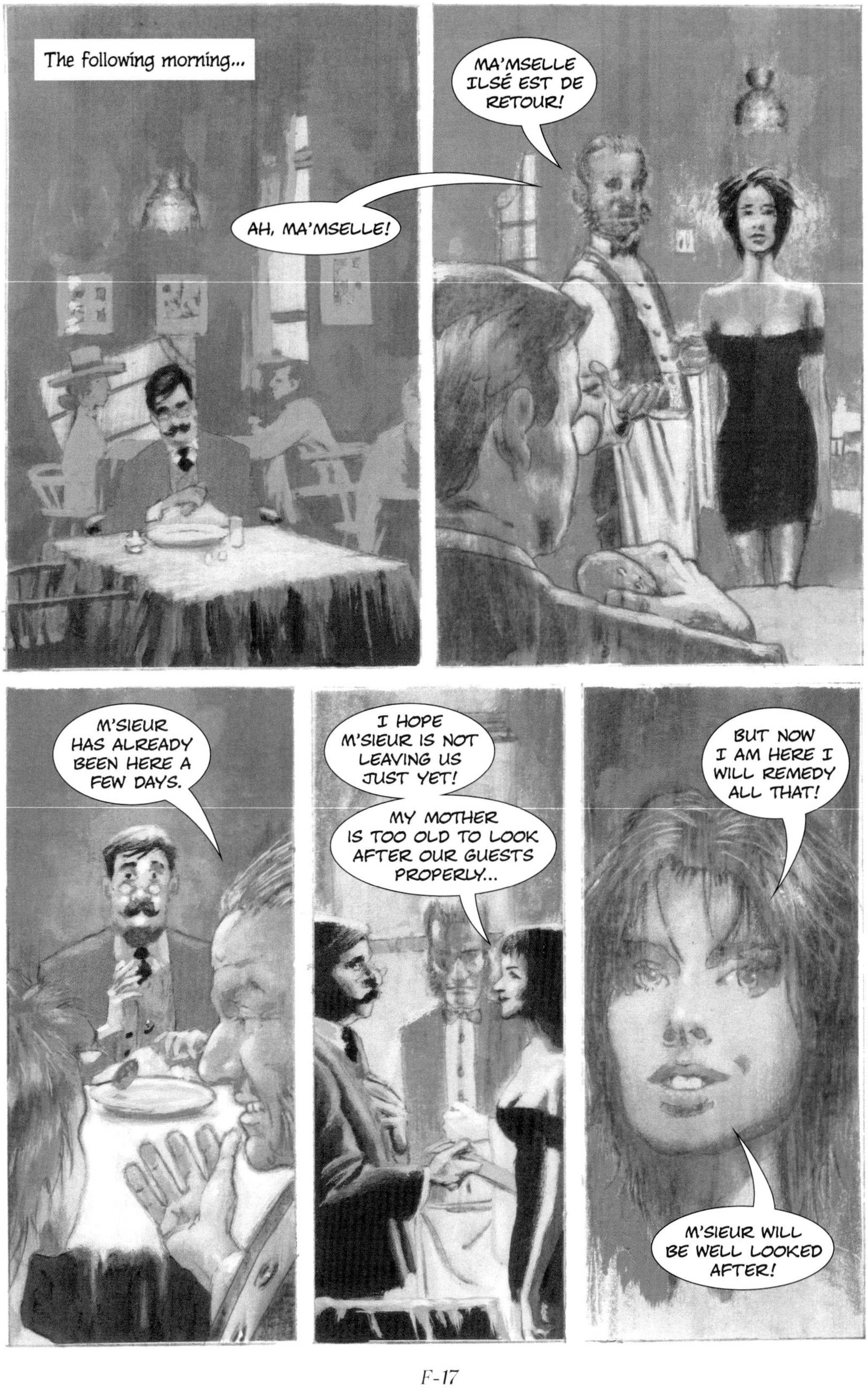
The following morning...
AH, MA'MSELLE!
MA'MSELLE ILSÉ EST DE RETOUR!
M'SIEUR HAS ALREADY BEEN HERE A FEW DAYS.
I HOPE M'SIEUR IS NOT LEAVING US JUST YET!
MY MOTHER IS TOO OLD TO LOOK AFTER OUR GUESTS PROPERLY...
BUT NOW I AM HERE I WILL REMEDY ALL THAT!
M'SIEUR WILL BE WELL LOOKED AFTER!

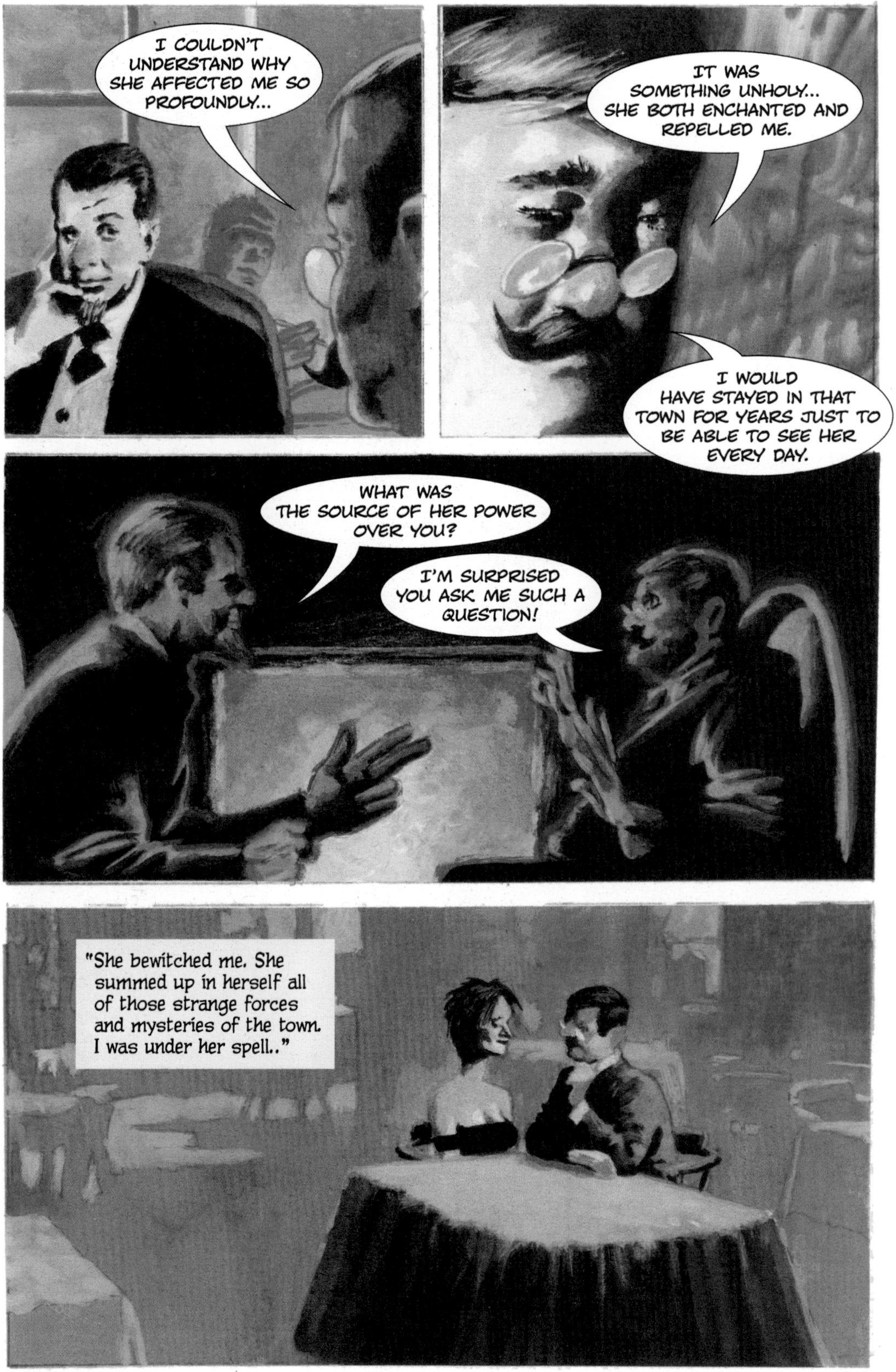
I COULDN'T UNDERSTAND WHY SHE AFFECTED ME SO PROFOUNDLY...
IT WAS SOMETHING UNHOLY... SHE BOTH ENCHANTED AND REPELLED ME.
I WOULD HAVE STAYED IN THAT TOWN FOR YEARS JUST TO BE ABLE TO SEE HER EVERY DAY.
WHAT WAS THE SOURCE OF HER POWER OVER YOU?
I'M SURPRISED YOU ASK ME SUCH A QUESTION!
"She bewitched me. She summed up in herself all of those strange forces and mysteries of the town. I was under her spell.."

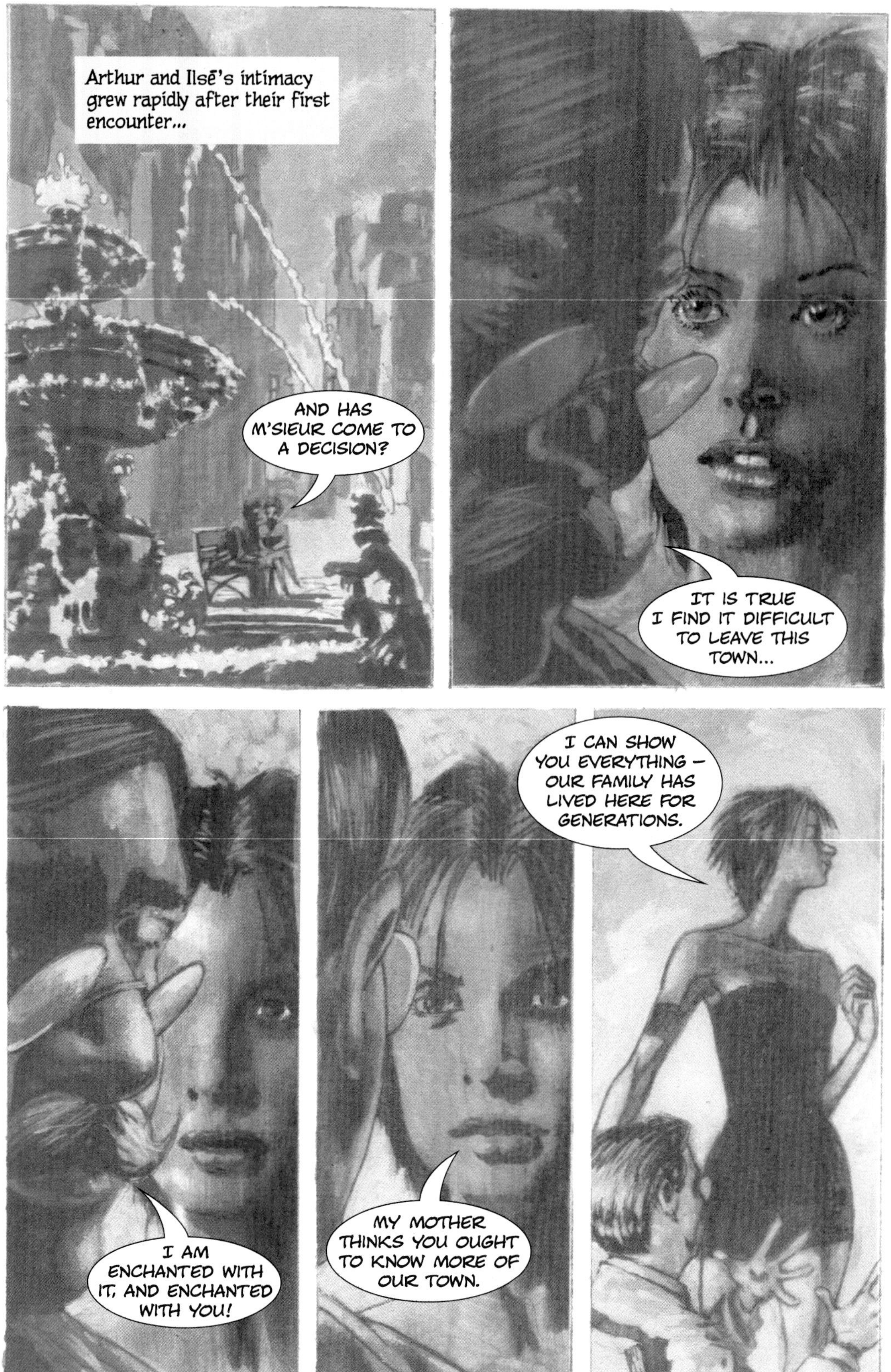
Arthur and Ilsē's intimacy grew rapidly after their first encounter...
AND HAS M'SIEUR COME TO A DECISION?
IT IS TRUE I FIND IT DIFFICULT TO LEAVE THIS TOWN...
I AM ENCHANTED WITH IT, AND ENCHANTED WITH YOU!
MY MOTHER THINKS YOU OUGHT TO KNOW MORE OF OUR TOWN.
I CAN SHOW YOU EVERYTHING – OUR FAMILY HAS LIVED HERE FOR GENERATIONS.

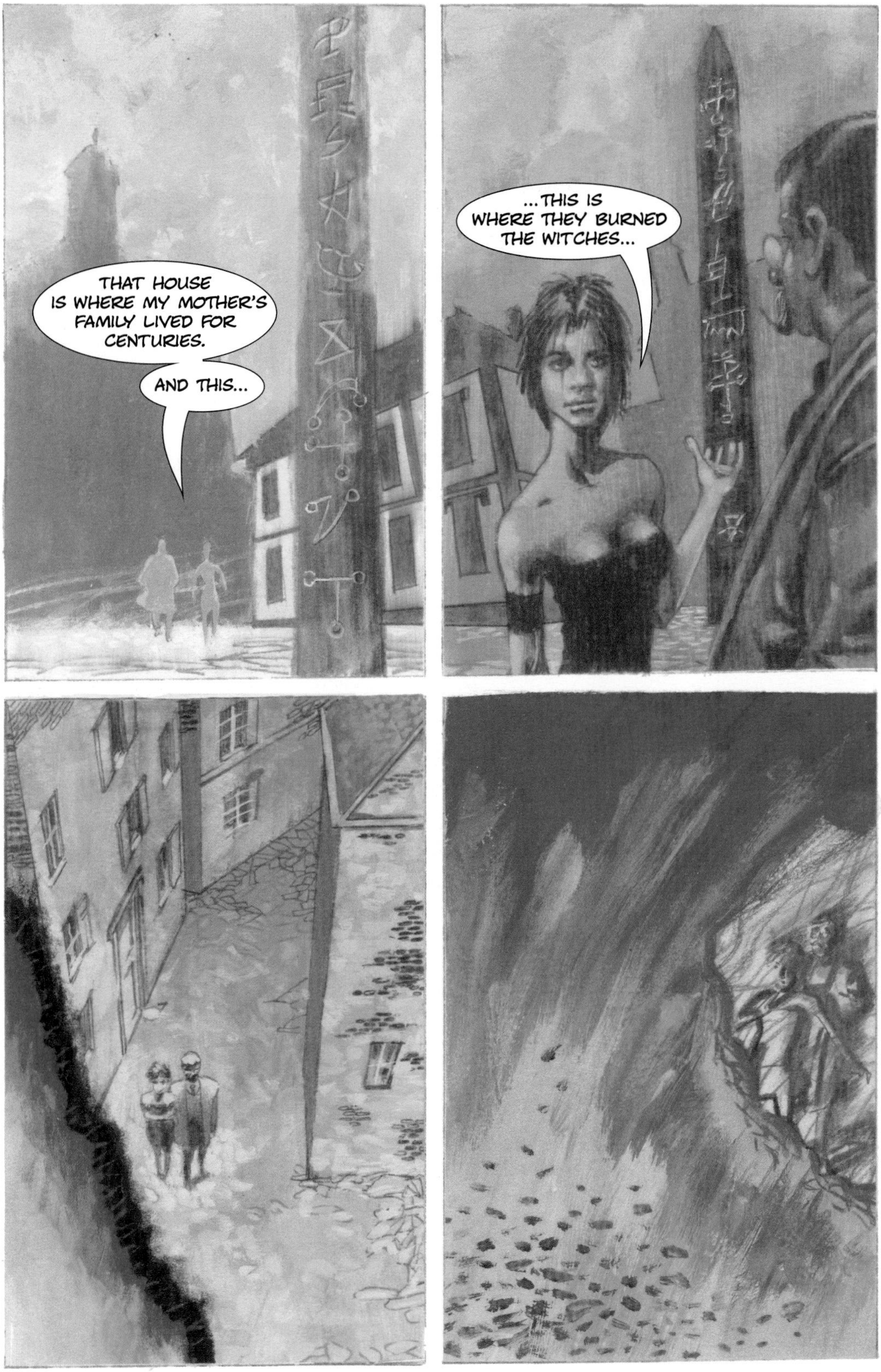
THAT HOUSE IS WHERE MY MOTHER'S FAMILY LIVED FOR CENTURIES.
AND THIS...
...THIS IS WHERE THEY BURNED THE WITCHES...

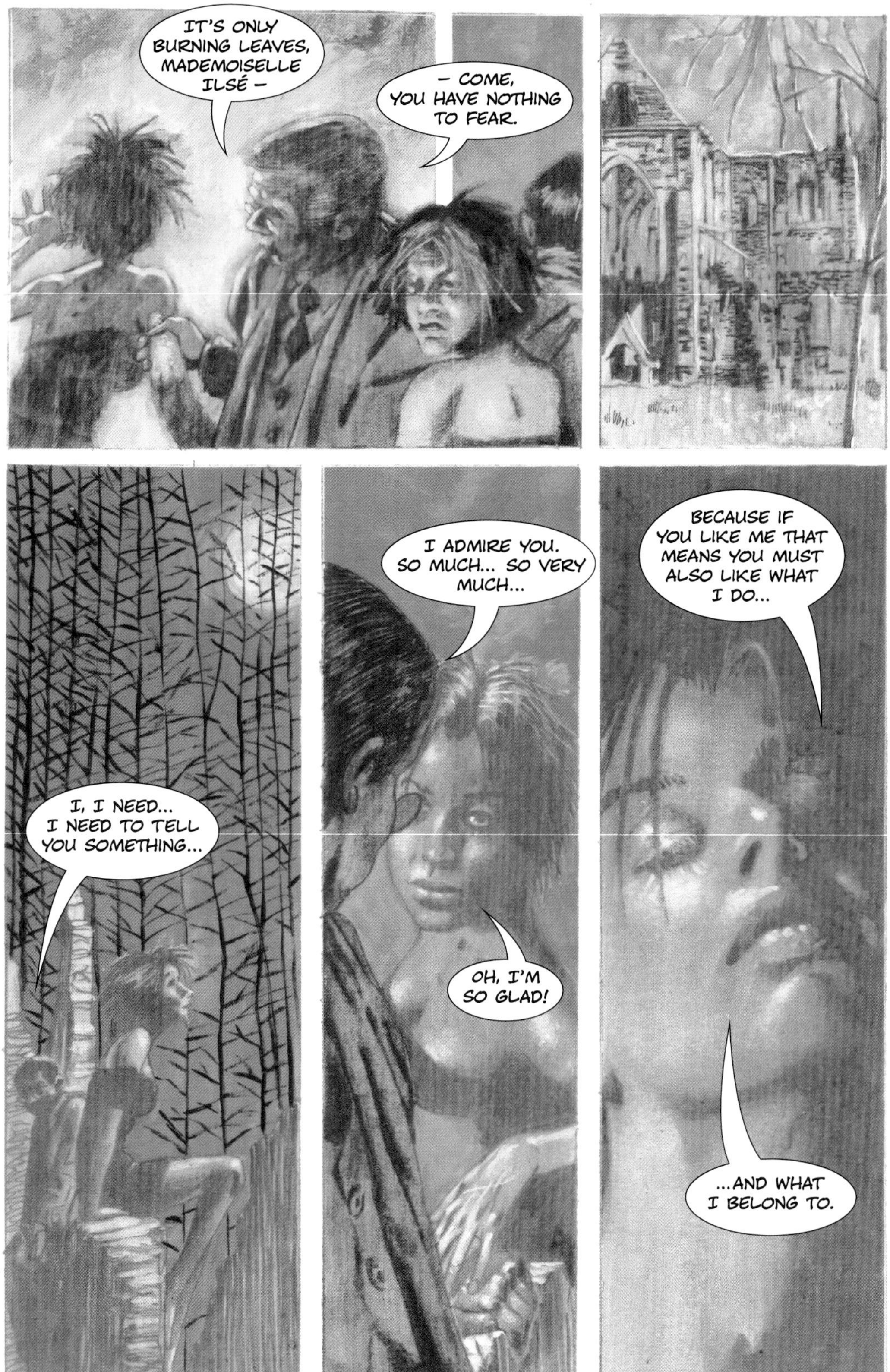
IT'S ONLY BURNING LEAVES, MADEMOISELLE ILSÉ –
– COME, YOU HAVE NOTHING TO FEAR.
I, I NEED... I NEED TO TELL YOU SOMETHING...
I ADMIRE YOU. SO MUCH... SO VERY MUCH...
OH, I'M SO GLAD!
BECAUSE IF YOU LIKE ME THAT MEANS YOU MUST ALSO LIKE WHAT I DO...
...AND WHAT I BELONG TO.

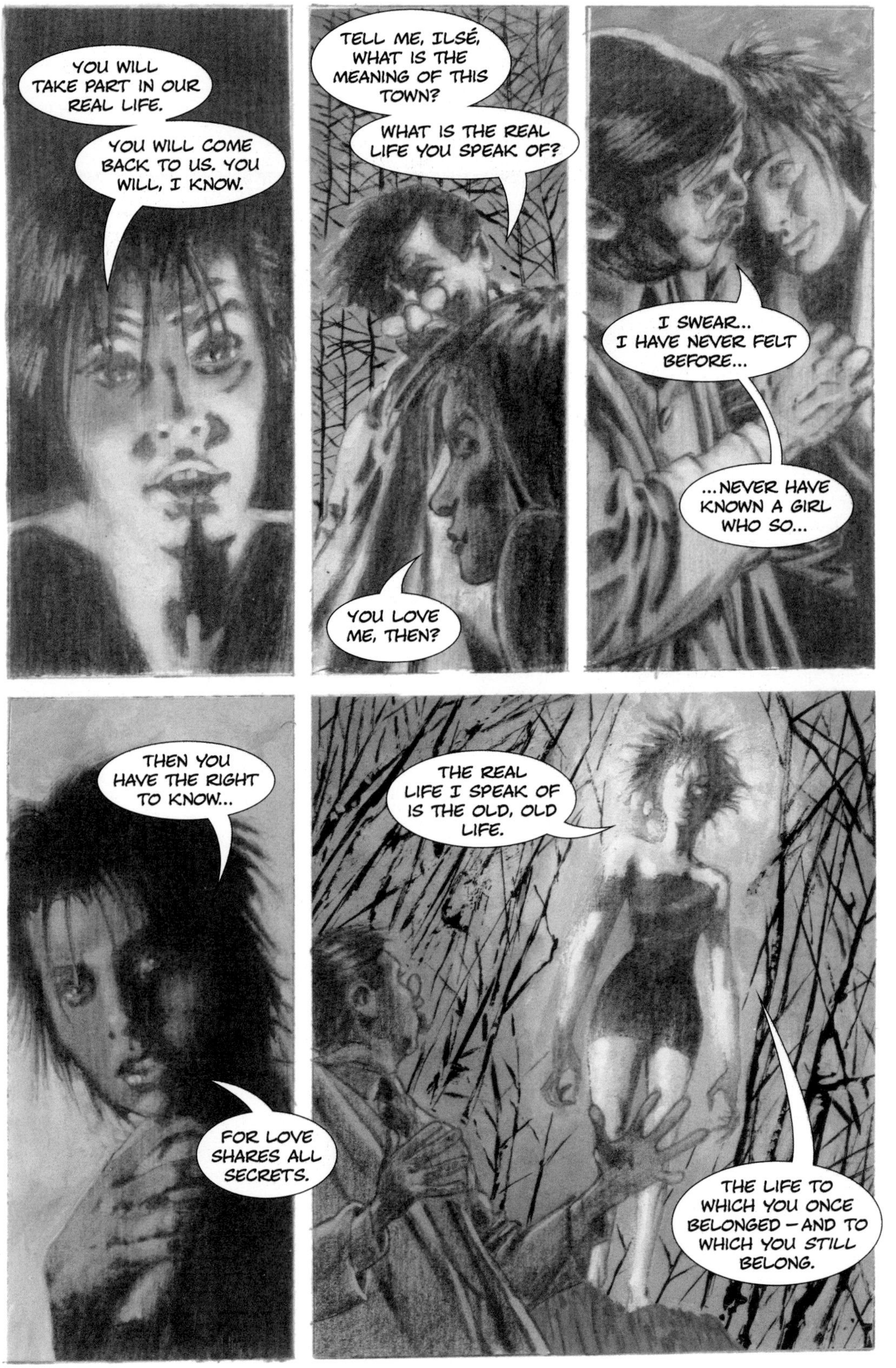
YOU WILL TAKE PART IN OUR REAL LIFE.
YOU WILL COME BACK TO US. YOU WILL, I KNOW.
TELL ME, ILSÉ, WHAT IS THE MEANING OF THIS TOWN?
WHAT IS THE REAL LIFE YOU SPEAK OF?
YOU LOVE ME, THEN?
I SWEAR.. I HAVE NEVER FELT BEFORE...
...NEVER HAVE KNOWN A GIRL WHO SO...
THEN YOU HAVE THE RIGHT TO KNOW...
FOR LOVE SHARES ALL SECRETS.
THE REAL LIFE I SPEAK OF IS THE OLD, OLD LIFE.
THE LIFE TO WHICH YOU ONCE BELONGED—AND TO WHICH YOU STILL BELONG.

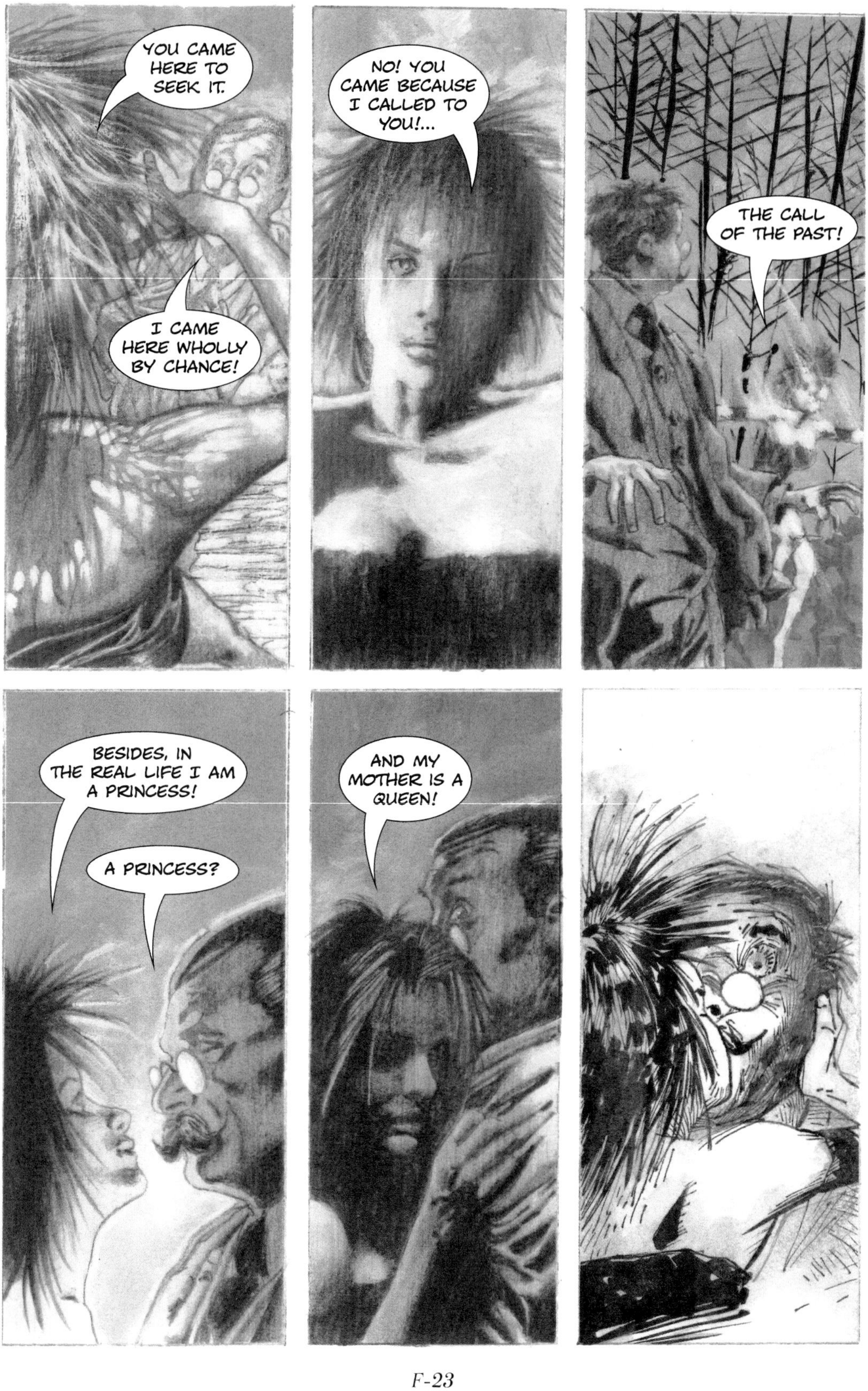
YOU CAME HERE TO SEEK IT.
I CAME HERE WHOLLY BY CHANCE!
NO! YOU CAME BECAUSE I CALLED TO YOU!...
THE CALL OF THE PAST!
BESIDES, IN THE REAL LIFE I AM A PRINCESS!
A PRINCESS?
AND MY MOTHER IS A QUEEN!

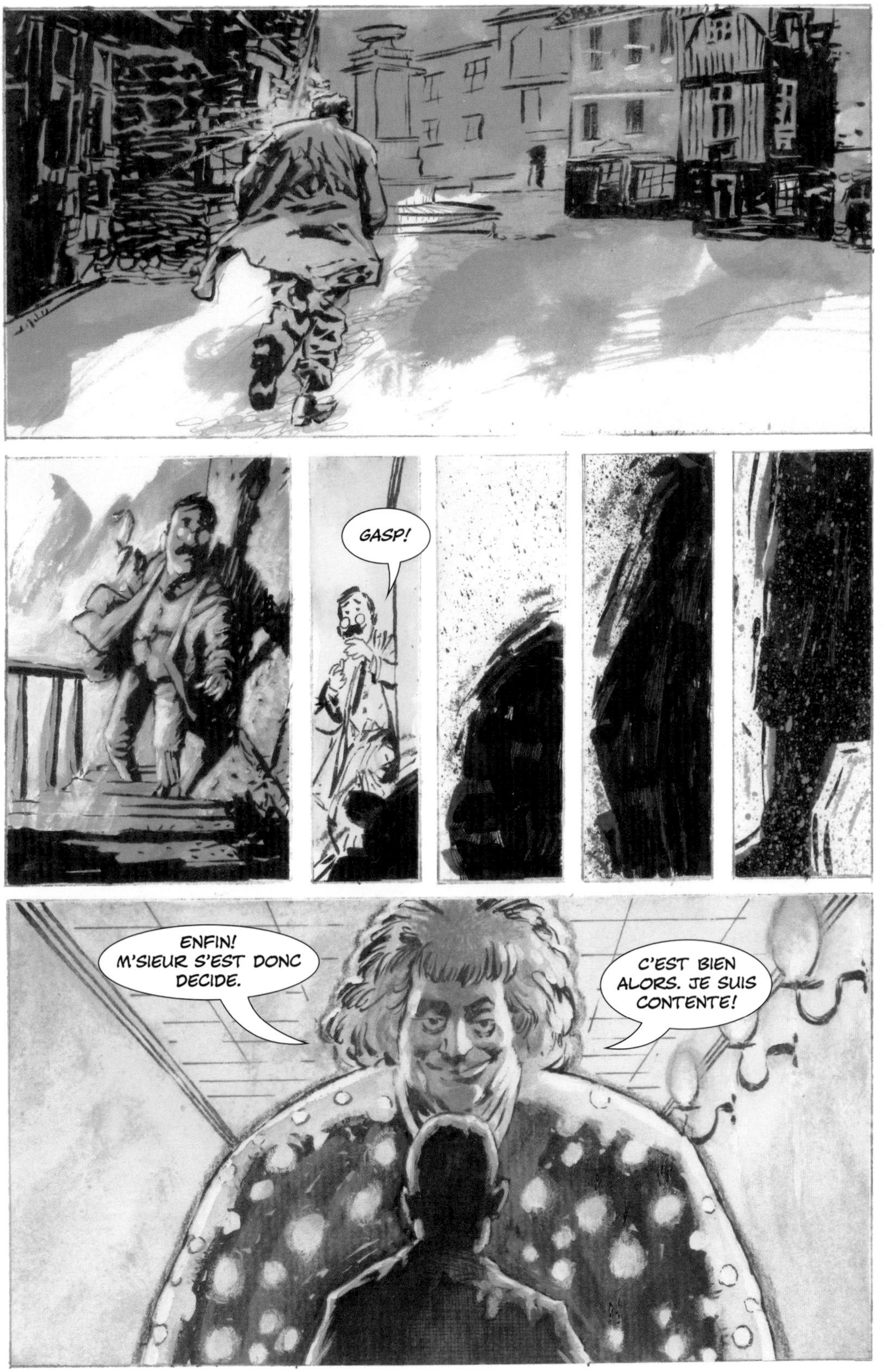
GASP!
ENFIN! M'SIEUR S'EST DONC DECIDE.
C'EST BIEN ALORS. JE SUIS CONTENTE!

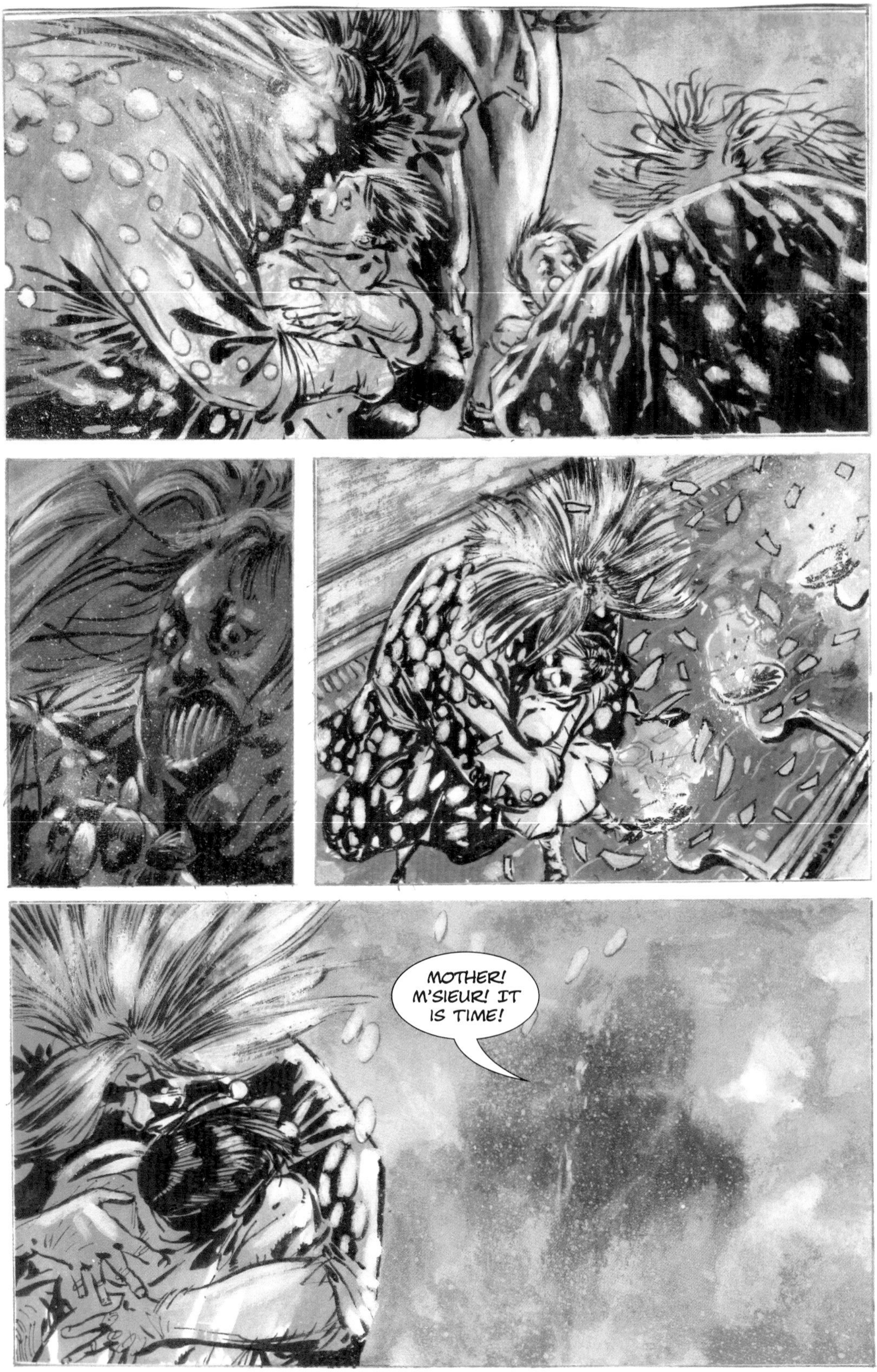
MOTHER! M'SIEUR! IT IS TIME!

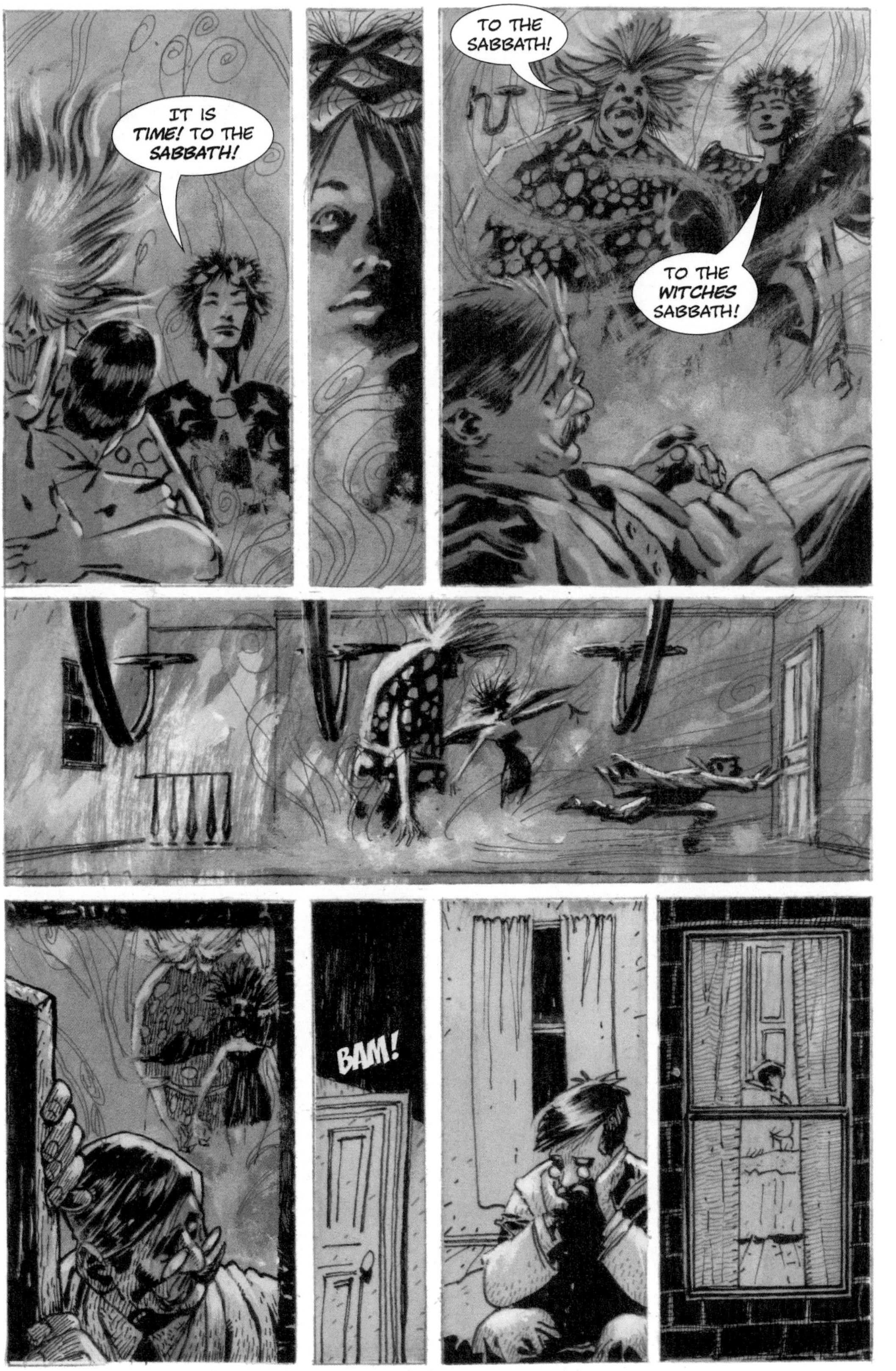
IT IS TIME! TO THE SABBATH!
TO THE SABBATH!
TO THE WITCHES SABBATH!
BAM!

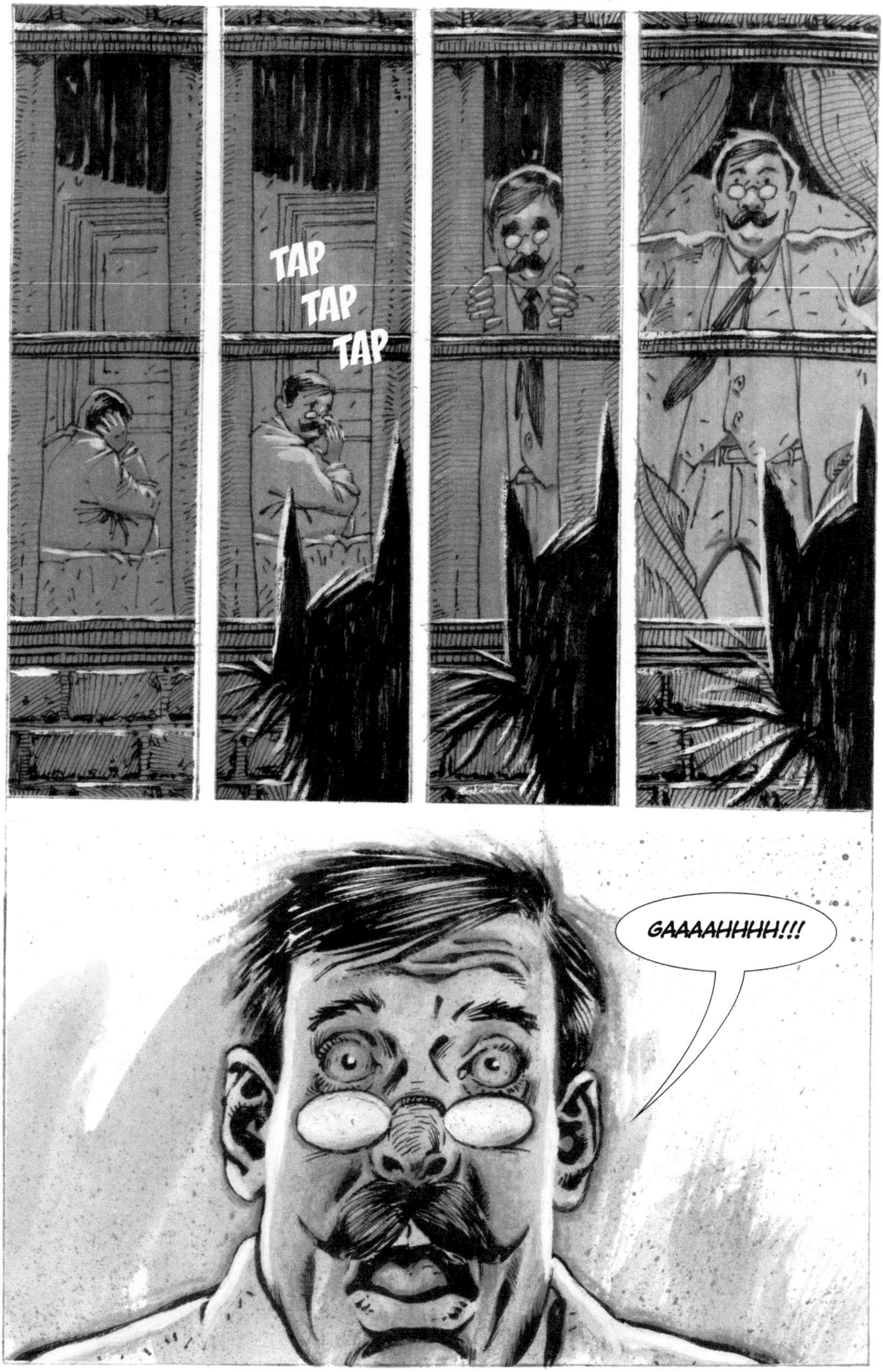
TAP
TAP
TAP
GAAAAHHHH!!!

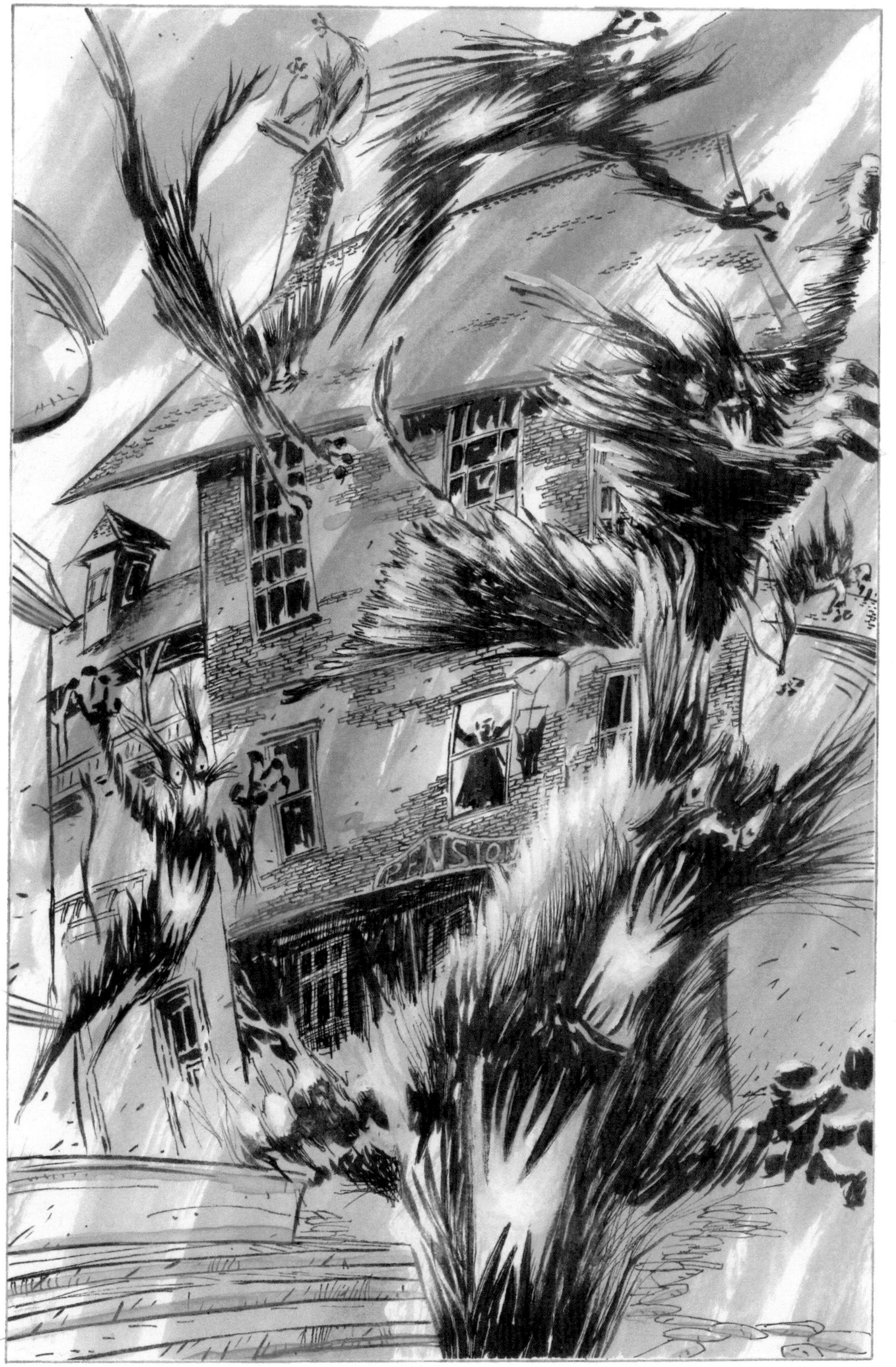
PENSION

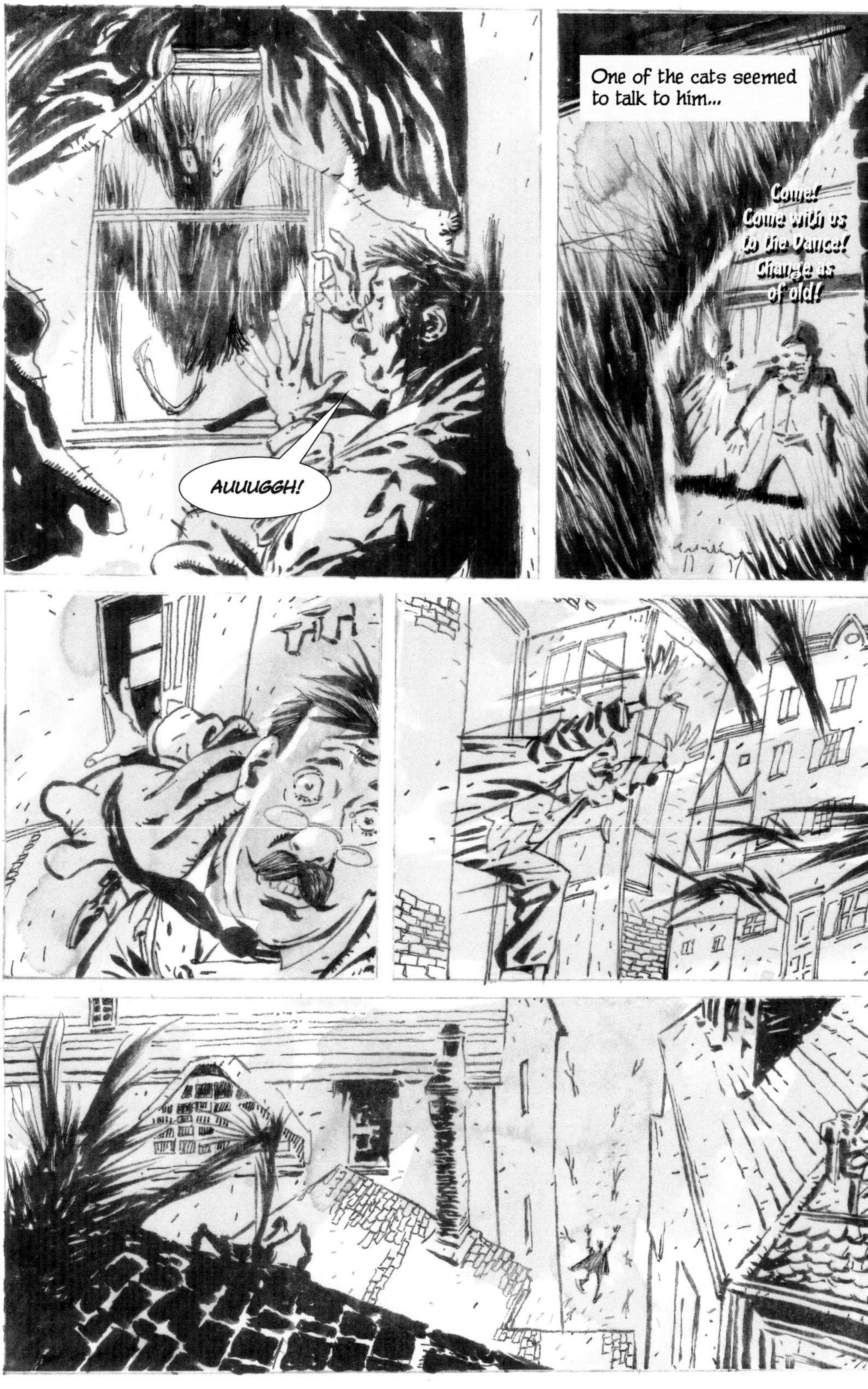
AUUUGGH!
One of the cats seemed to talk to him...
Come! Come with us to the Dance! Change as of old!

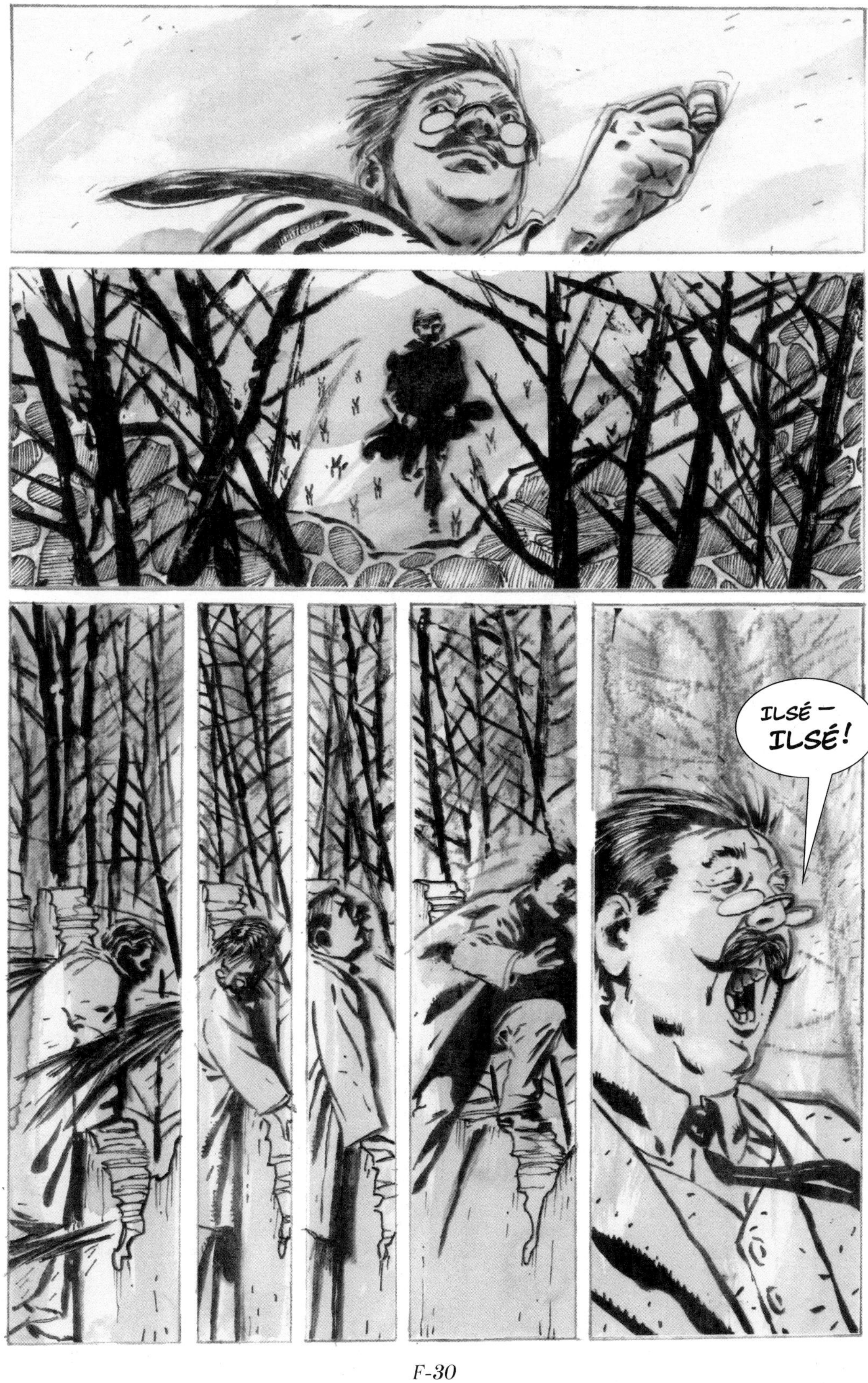
ILSÉ — ILSÉ!

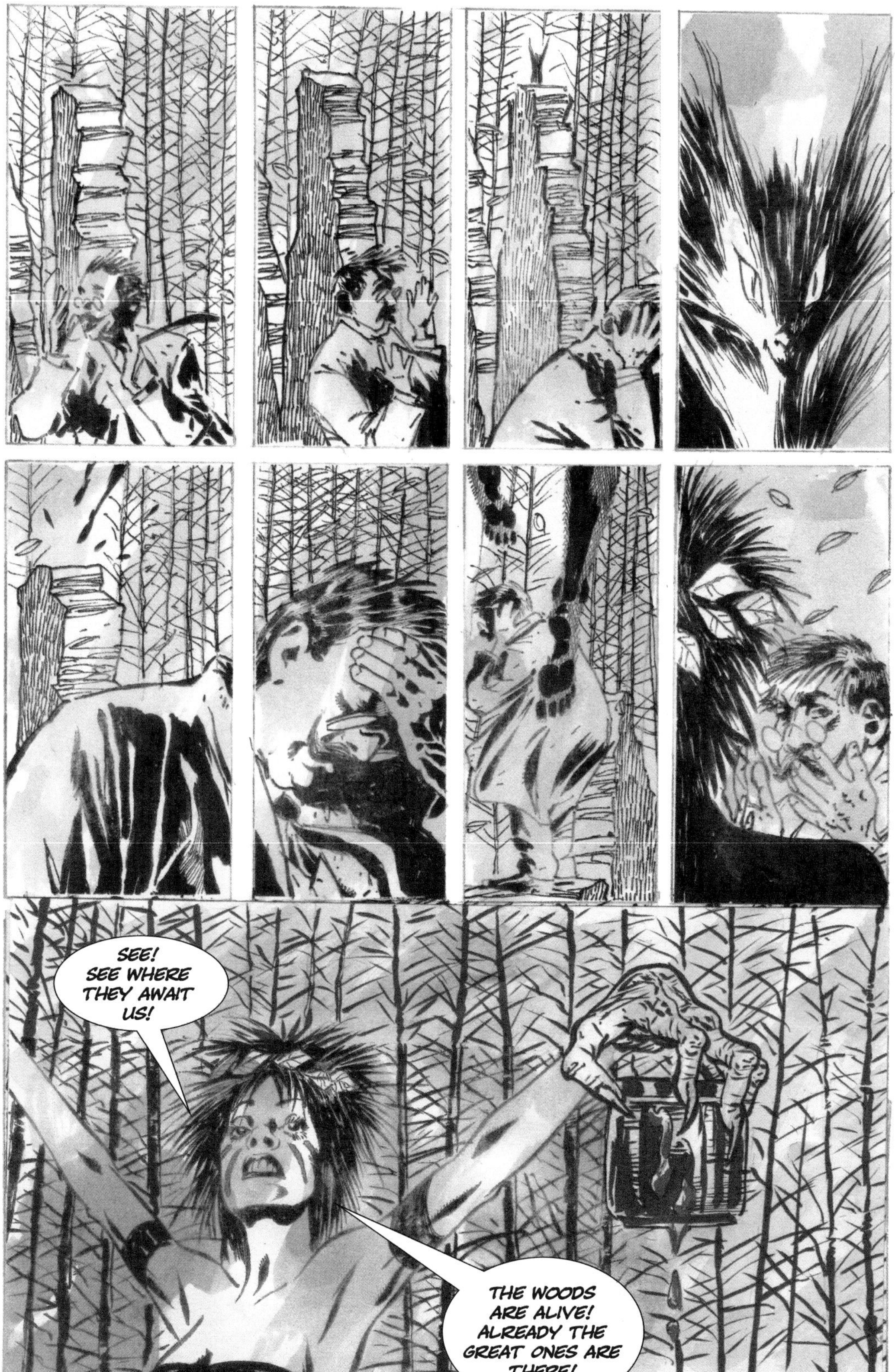
SEE! SEE WHERE THEY AWAIT US!
THE WOODS ARE ALIVE! ALREADY THE GREAT ONES ARE THERE!

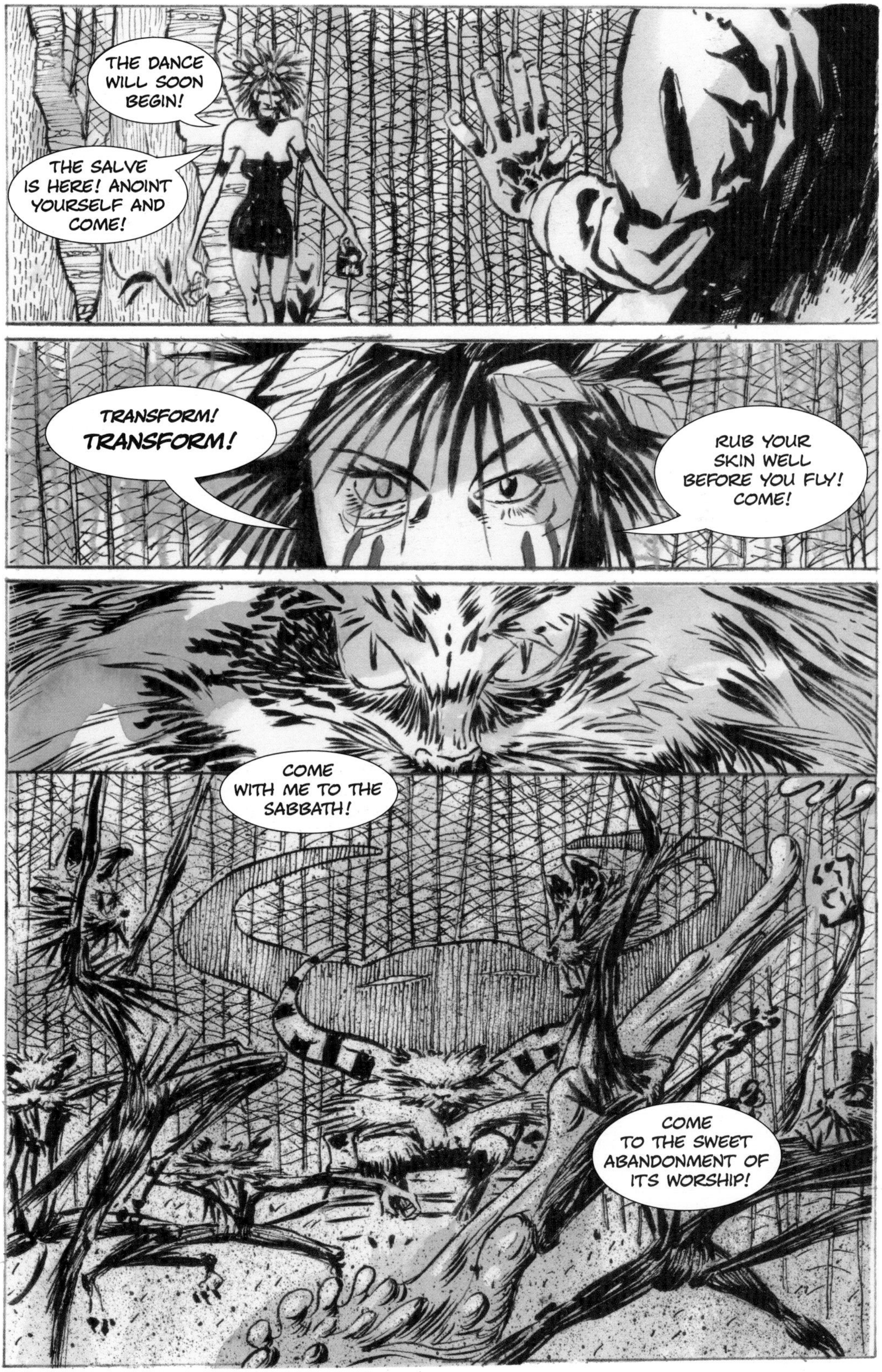
THE DANCE WILL SOON BEGIN!
THE SALVE IS HERE! ANOINT YOURSELF AND COME!
TRANSFORM! TRANSFORM!
RUB YOUR SKIN WELL BEFORE YOU FLY! COME!
COME WITH ME TO THE SABBATH!
COME TO THE SWEET ABANDONMENT OF ITS WORSHIP!

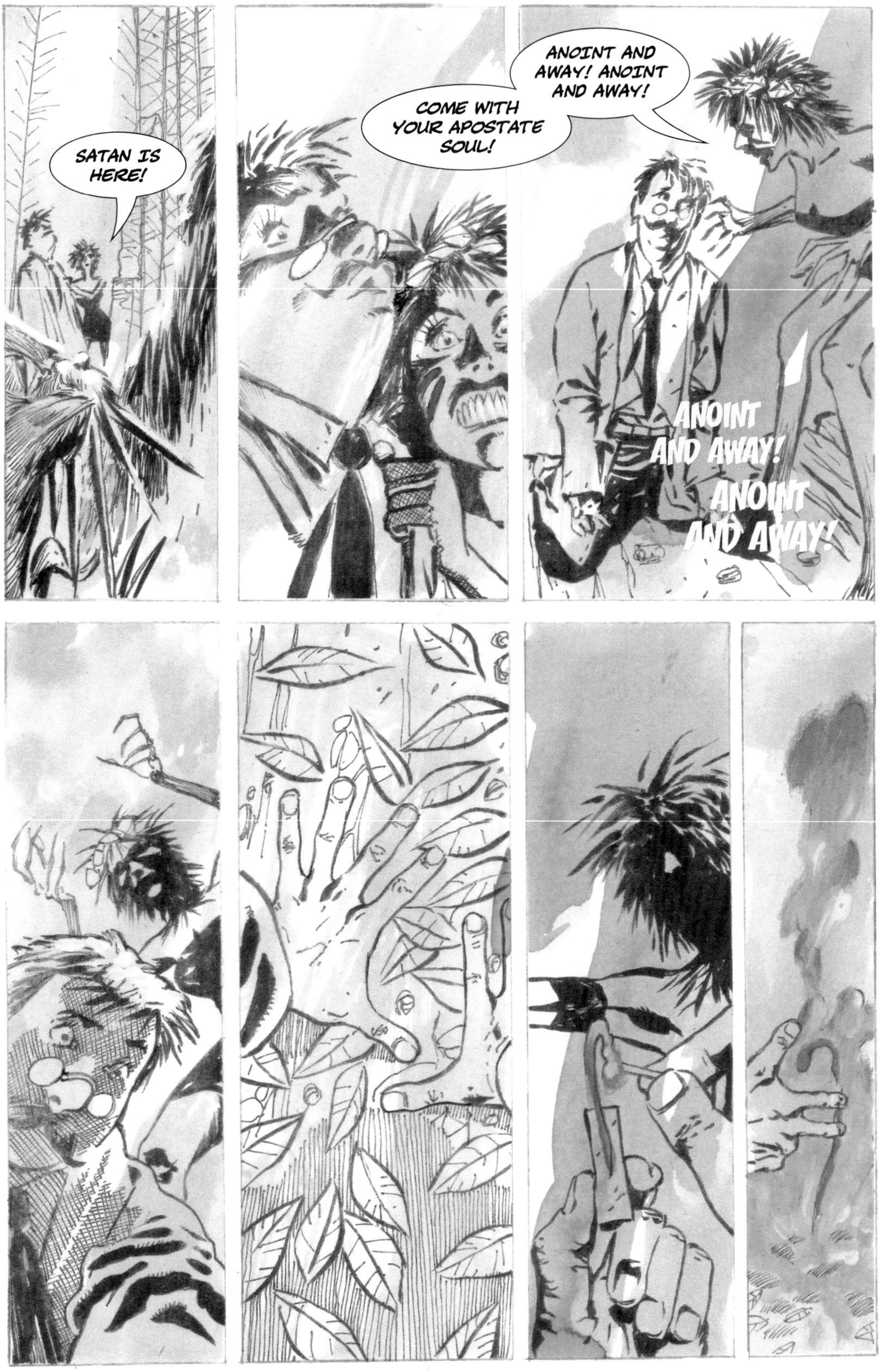
SATAN IS HERE!
COME WITH YOUR APOSTATE SOUL!
ANOINT AND AWAY! ANOINT AND AWAY!
ANOINT AND AWAY!
ANOINT AND AWAY!

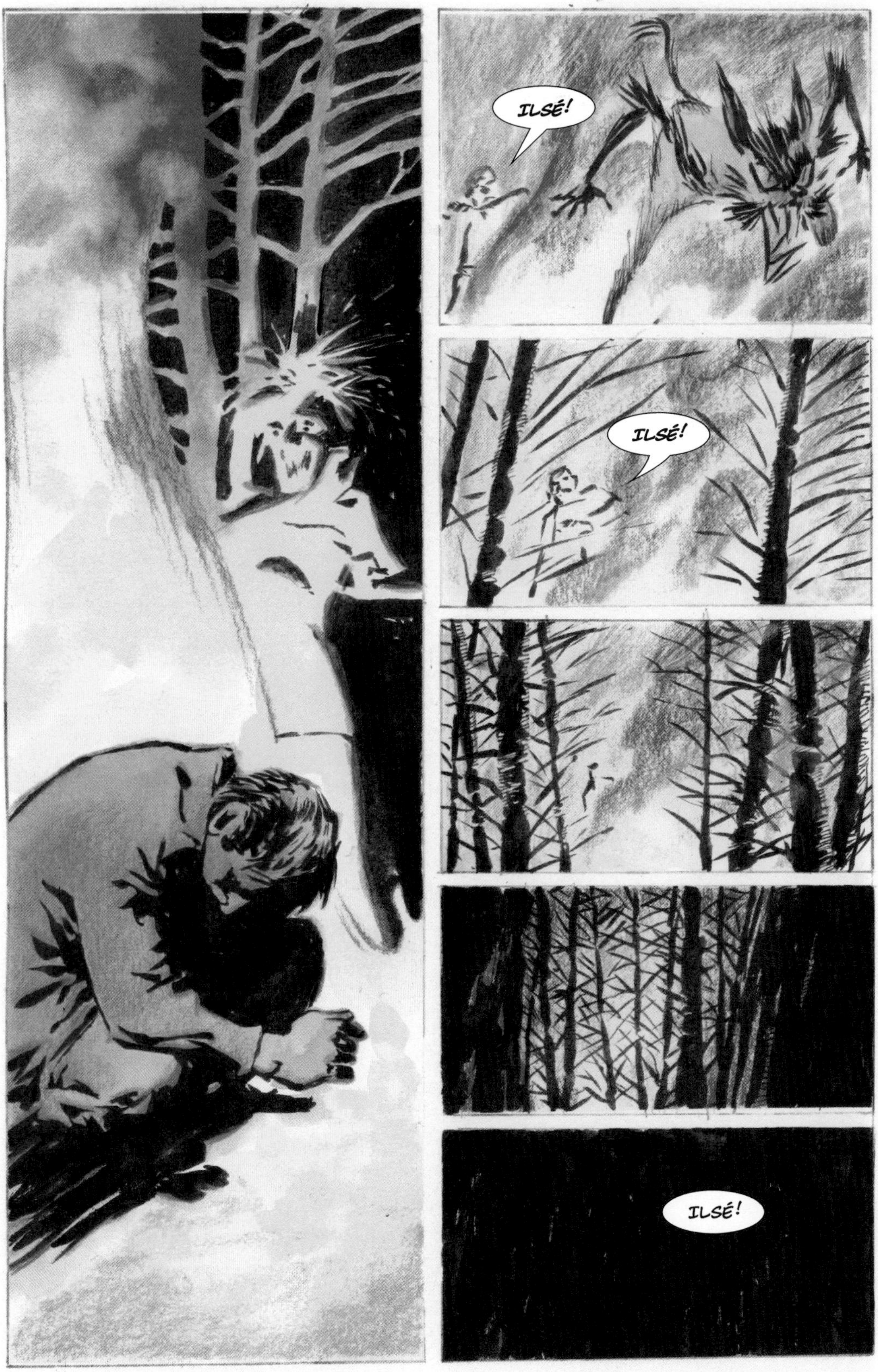
ILSÉ!
ILSÉ!
ILSÉ!

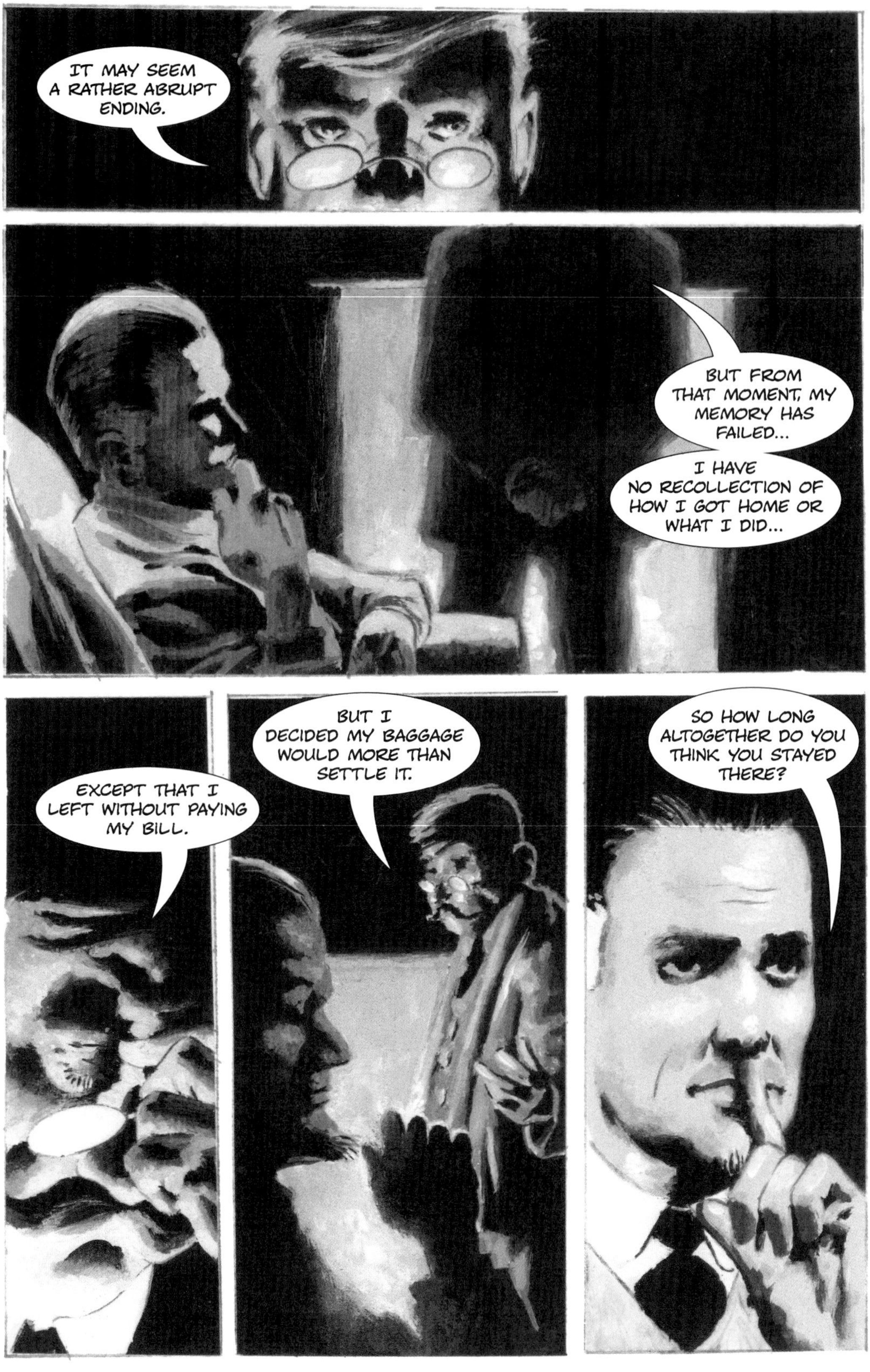
IT MAY SEEM A RATHER ABRUPT ENDING.
BUT FROM THAT MOMENT, MY MEMORY HAS FAILED...
I HAVE NO RECOLLECTION OF HOW I GOT HOME OR WHAT I DID...
EXCEPT THAT I LEFT WITHOUT PAYING MY BILL.
BUT I DECIDED MY BAGGAGE WOULD MORE THAN SETTLE IT.
SO HOW LONG ALTOGETHER DO YOU THINK YOU STAYED THERE?

I WAS COMING TO THAT...
ON ARRIVAL IN LONDON I FOUND I WAS A WHOLE WEEK OUT...
IT OUGHT TO HAVE BEEN SEPTEMBER 15TH BUT IT WAS ONLY THE 10TH.
I COULD HAVE SWORN I STAYED AT LEAST A WEEK IN THE TOWN.
SO IN REALITY YOU ONLY STAYED A NIGHT OR TWO?
I CAN'T EXPLAIN IT. BUT LOOK...
...THAT NIGHT ON THE RAMPARTS.

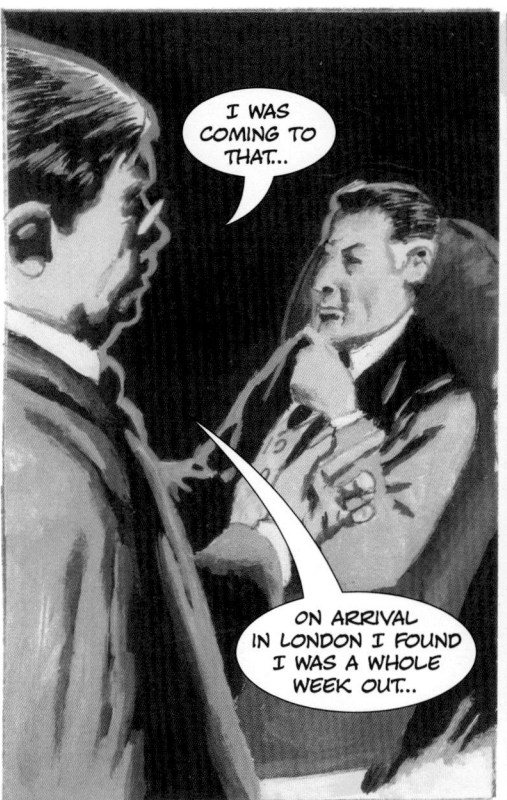

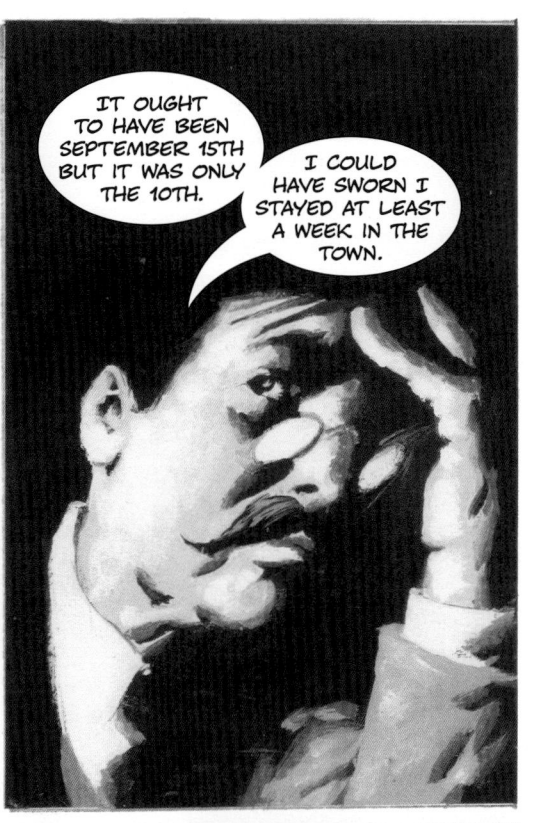

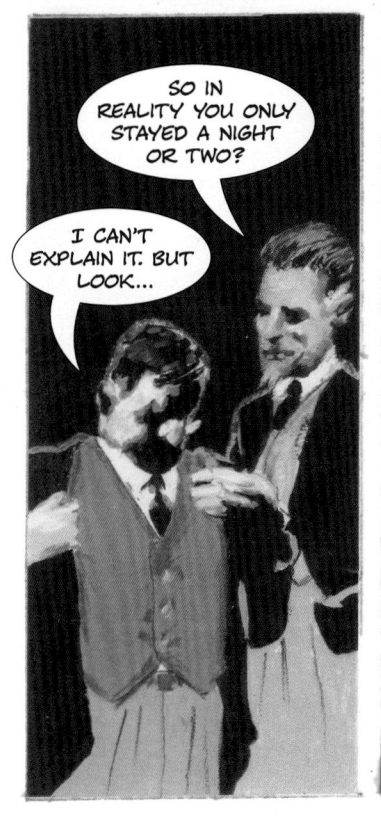

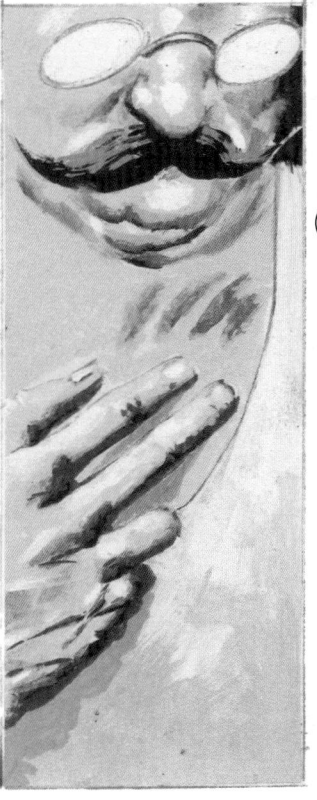

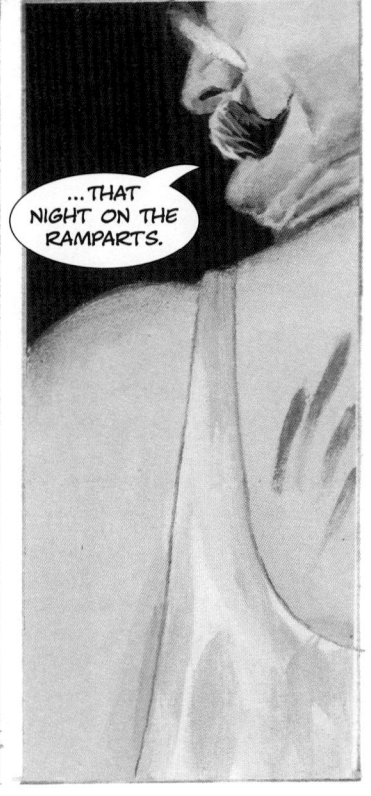

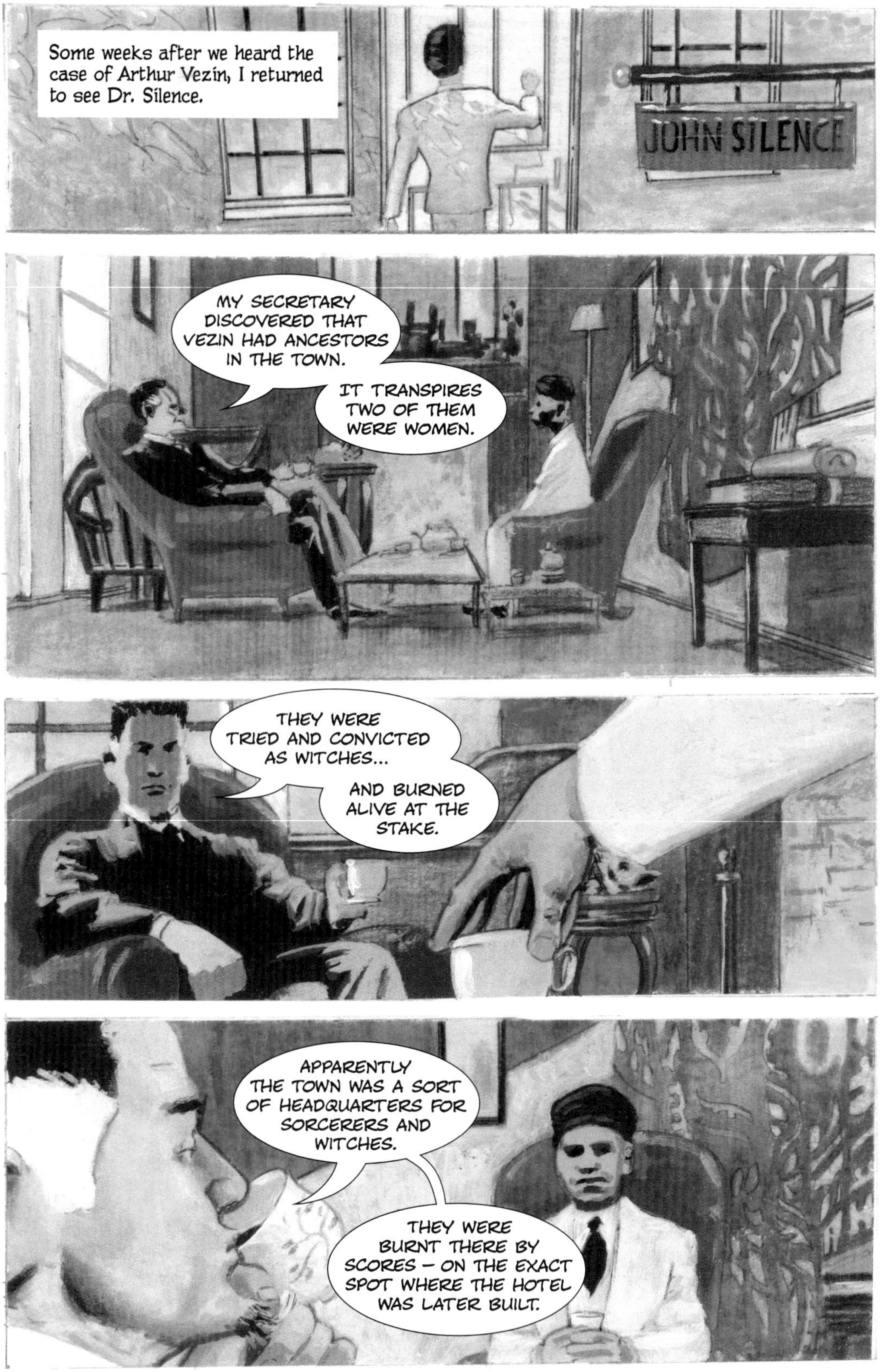
Some weeks after we heard the case of Arthur Vezin, I returned to see Dr. Silence.
JOHN SILENCE
MY SECRETARY DISCOVERED THAT VEZIN HAD ANCESTORS IN THE TOWN.
IT TRANSPIRES TWO OF THEM WERE WOMEN.
THEY WERE TRIED AND CONVICTED AS WITCHES...
AND BURNED ALIVE AT THE STAKE.
APPARENTLY THE TOWN WAS A SORT OF HEADQUARTERS FOR SORCERERS AND WITCHES.
THEY WERE BURNT THERE BY SCORES – ON THE EXACT SPOT WHERE THE HOTEL WAS LATER BUILT.

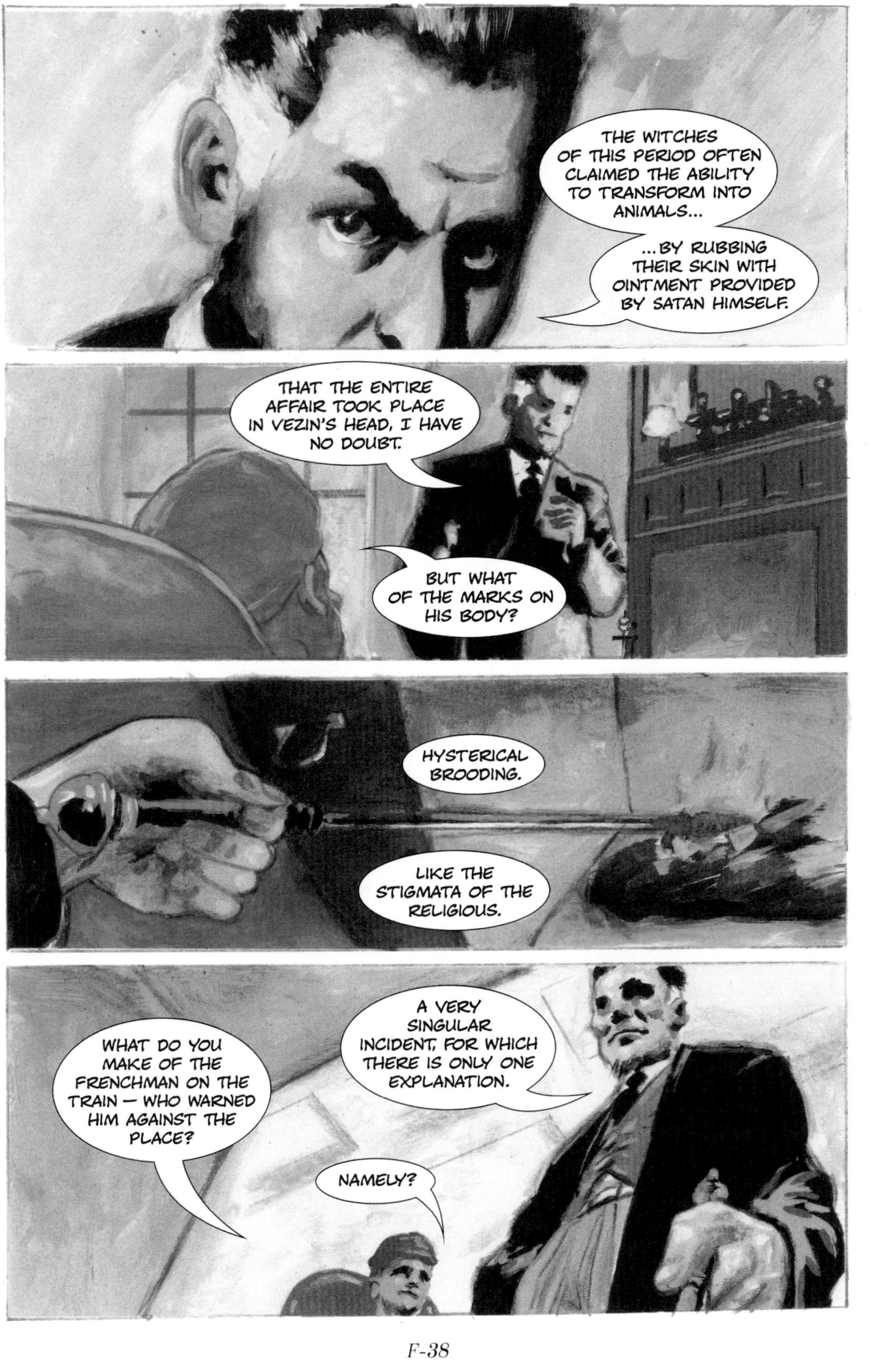
THE WITCHES OF THIS PERIOD OFTEN CLAIMED THE ABILITY TO TRANSFORM INTO ANIMALS...
...BY RUBBING THEIR SKIN WITH OINTMENT PROVIDED BY SATAN HIMSELF.
THAT THE ENTIRE AFFAIR TOOK PLACE IN VEZIN'S HEAD, I HAVE NO DOUBT.
BUT WHAT OF THE MARKS ON HIS BODY?
HYSTERICAL BROODING.
LIKE THE STIGMATA OF THE RELIGIOUS.
WHAT DO YOU MAKE OF THE FRENCHMAN ON THE TRAIN — WHO WARNED HIM AGAINST THE PLACE?
A VERY SINGULAR INCIDENT, FOR WHICH THERE IS ONLY ONE EXPLANATION.
NAMELY?

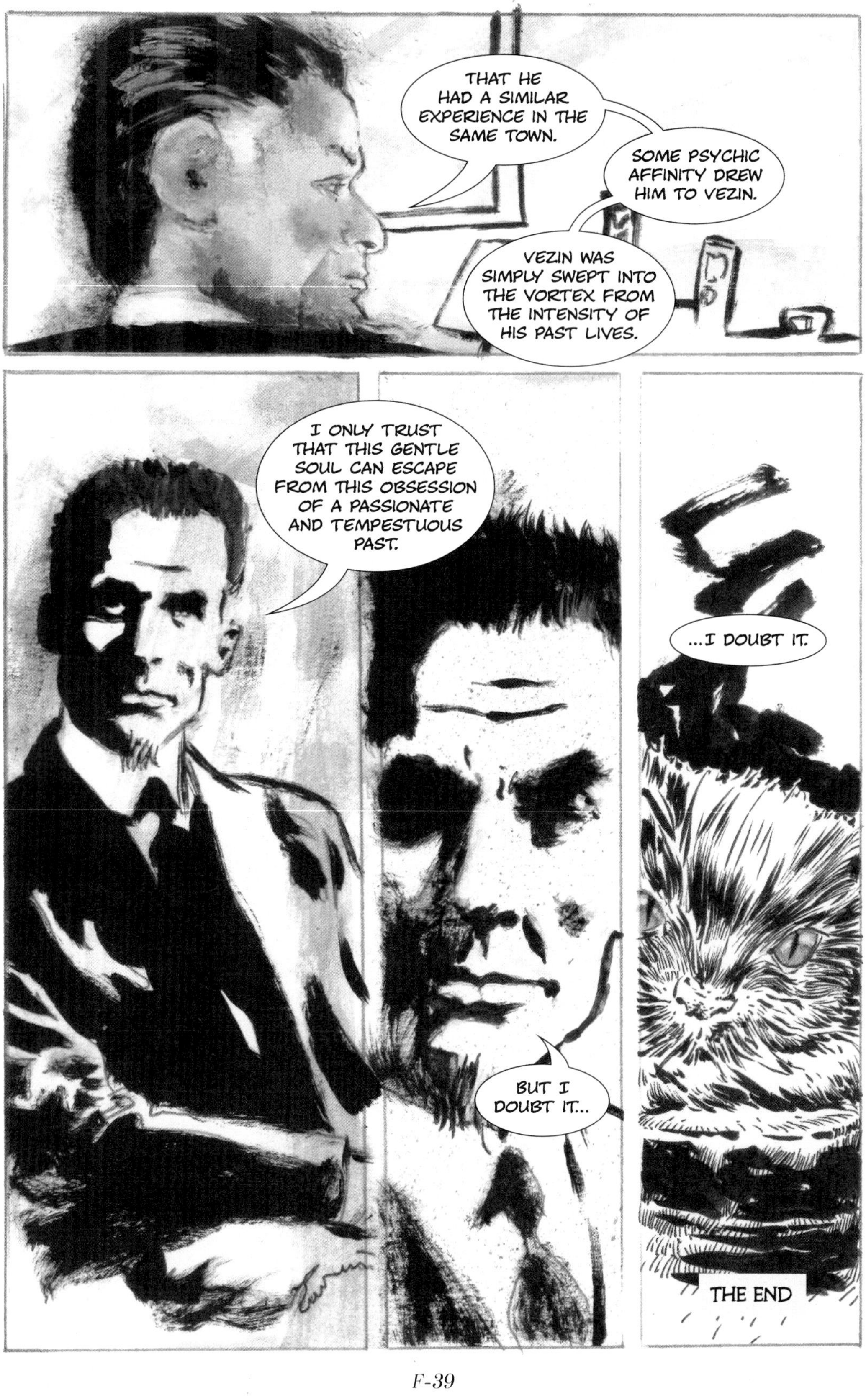
THAT HE HAD A SIMILAR EXPERIENCE IN THE SAME TOWN.
SOME PSYCHIC AFFINITY DREW HIM TO VEZIN.
VEZIN WAS SIMPLY SWEPT INTO THE VORTEX FROM THE INTENSITY OF HIS PAST LIVES.
I ONLY TRUST THAT THIS GENTLE SOUL CAN ESCAPE FROM THIS OBSESSION OF A PASSIONATE AND TEMPESTUOUS PAST.
BUT I DOUBT IT...
...I DOUBT IT.
THE END

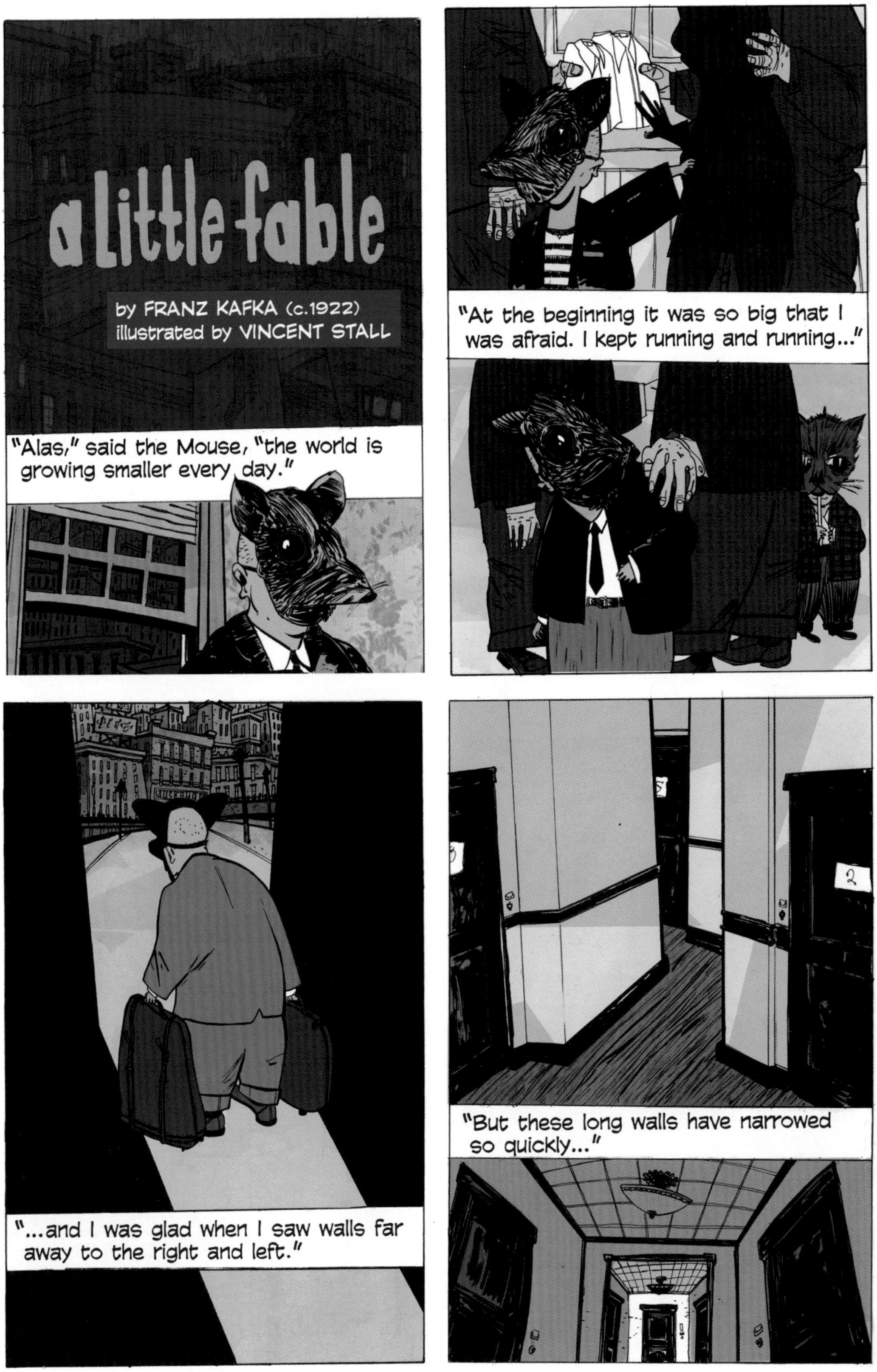
a little fable
by FRANZ KAFKA (c.1922)
illustrated by VINCENT STALL
"Alas," said the Mouse, "the world is growing smaller every day."
"At the beginning it was so big that I was afraid. I kept running and running..."
"...and I was glad when I saw walls far away to the right and left."
"But these long walls have narrowed so quickly..."

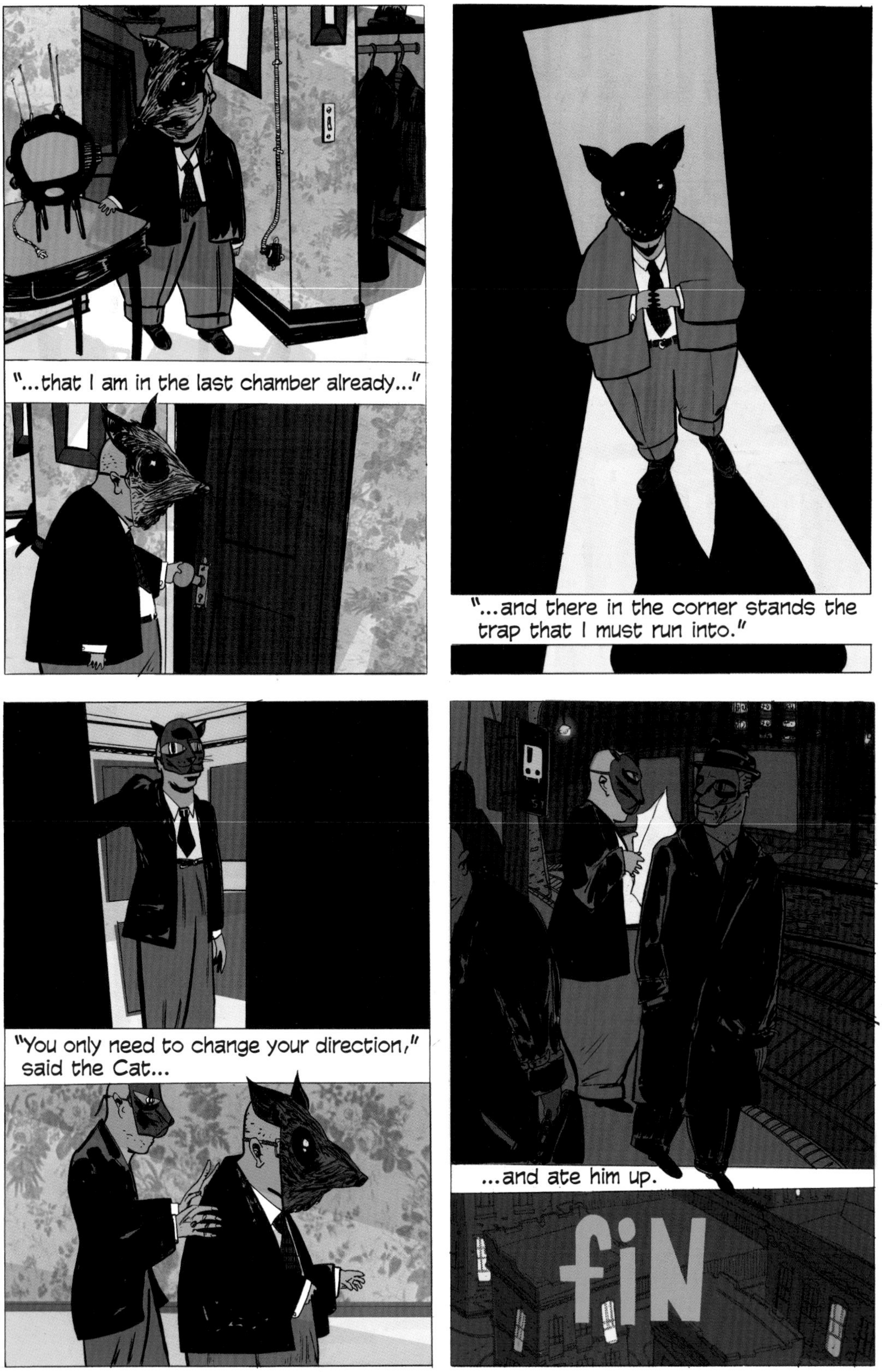
"...that I am in the last chamber already..."
"...and there in the corner stands the trap that I must run into."
"You only need to change your direction," said the Cat...
...and ate him up.
fiN

SAKI

TOBERMORY

by SAKI

Adapted by TRINA ROBBINS

Illustrated by LISA K. WEBER

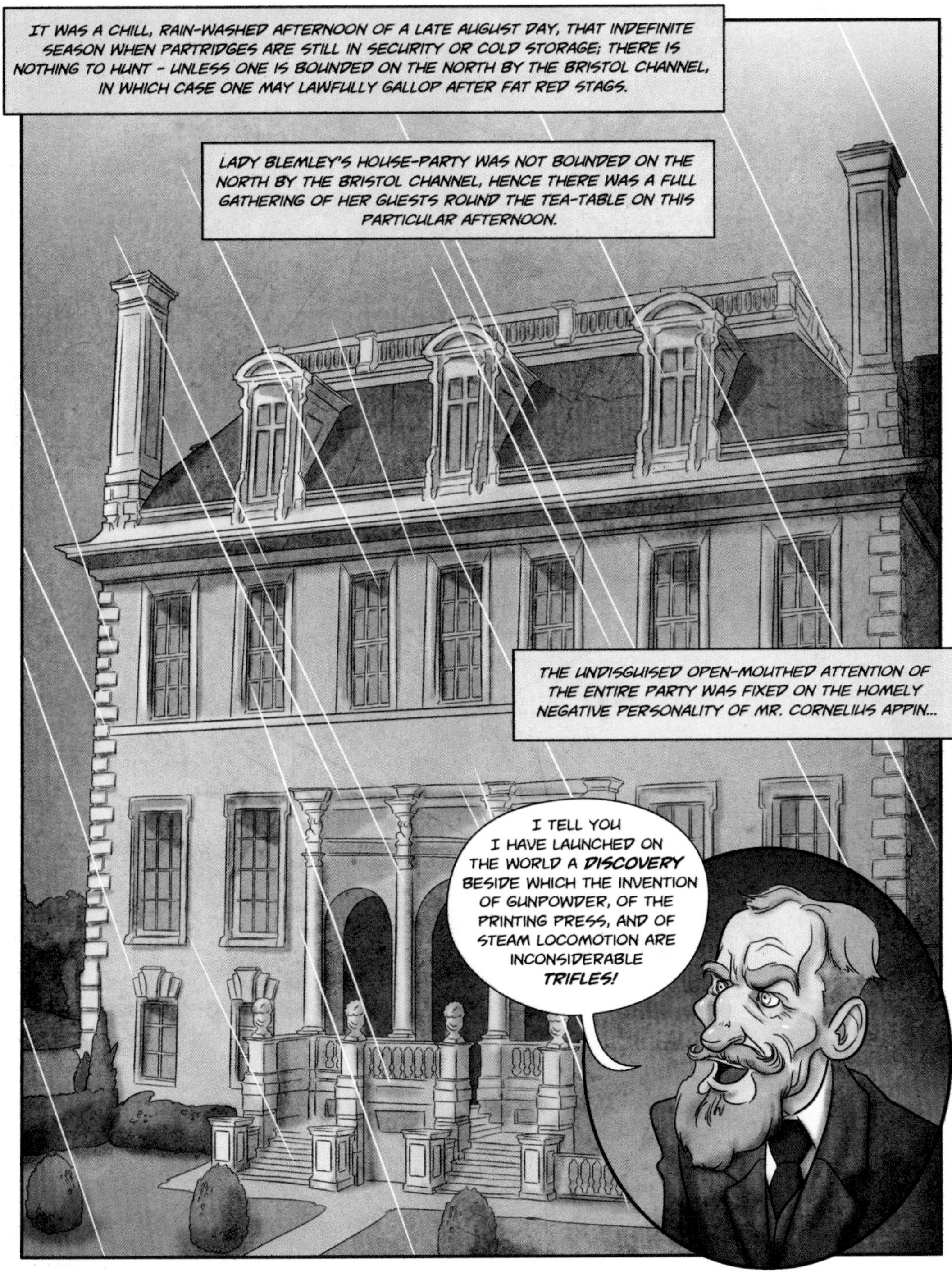
IT WAS A CHILL, RAIN-WASHED AFTERNOON OF A LATE AUGUST DAY, THAT INDEFINITE SEASON WHEN PARTRIDGES ARE STILL IN SECURITY OR COLD STORAGE; THERE IS NOTHING TO HUNT - UNLESS ONE IS BOUNDED ON THE NORTH BY THE BRISTOL CHANNEL, IN WHICH CASE ONE MAY LAWFULLY GALLOP AFTER FAT RED STAGS.
LADY BLEMLEY'S HOUSE-PARTY WAS NOT BOUNDED ON THE NORTH BY THE BRISTOL CHANNEL, HENCE THERE WAS A FULL GATHERING OF HER GUESTS ROUND THE TEA-TABLE ON THIS PARTICULAR AFTERNOON.
THE UNDISGUISED OPEN-MOUTHED ATTENTION OF THE ENTIRE PARTY WAS FIXED ON THE HOMELY NEGATIVE PERSONALITY OF MR. CORNELIUS APPIN...
I TELL YOU I HAVE LAUNCHED ON THE WORLD A DISCOVERY BESIDE WHICH THE INVENTION OF GUNPOWDER, OF THE PRINTING PRESS, AND OF STEAM LOCOMOTION ARE INCONSIDERABLE TRIFLES!

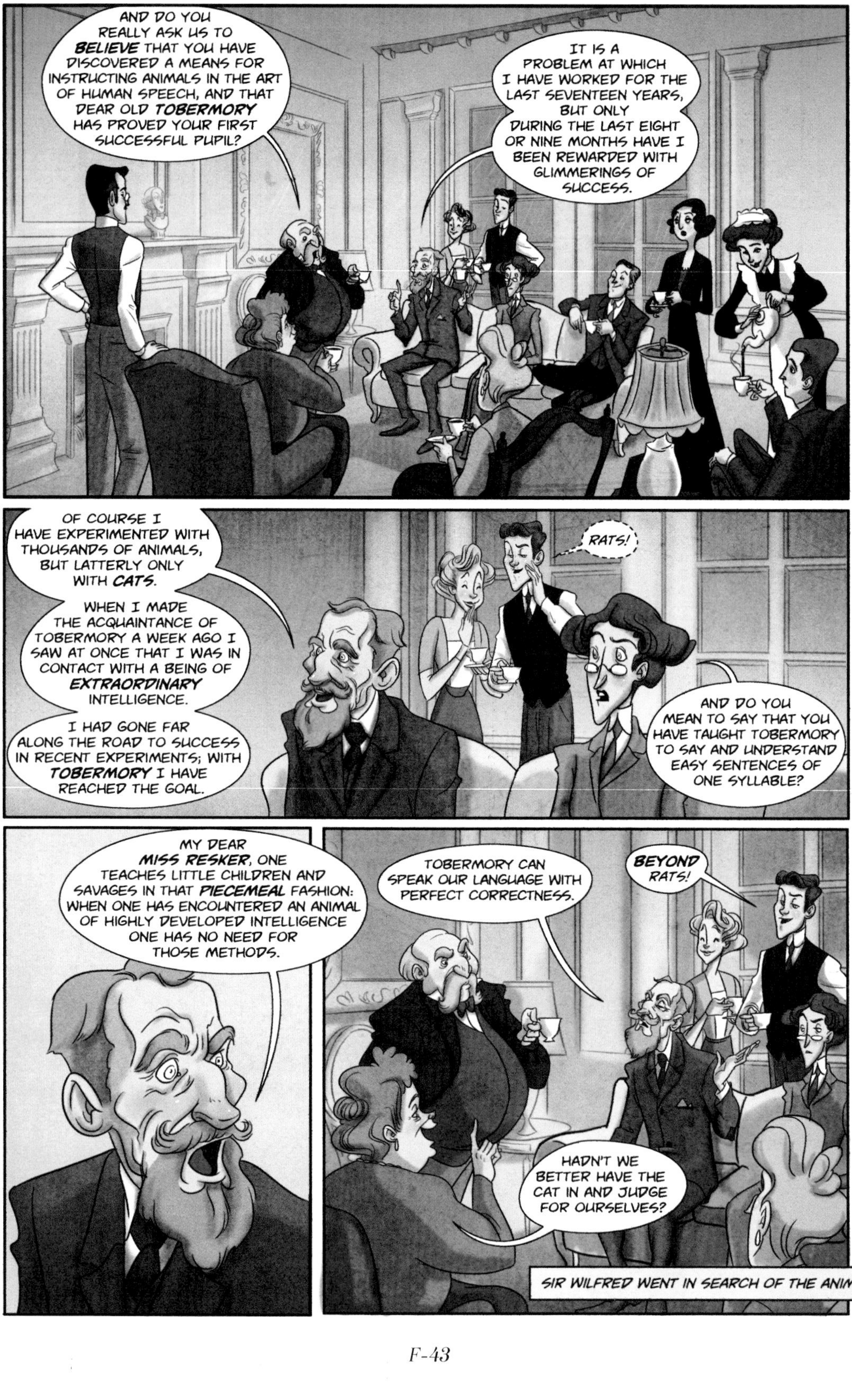
AND DO YOU REALLY ASK US TO **BELIEVE** THAT YOU HAVE DISCOVERED A MEANS FOR INSTRUCTING ANIMALS IN THE ART OF HUMAN SPEECH, AND THAT DEAR OLD **TOBERMORY** HAS PROVED YOUR FIRST SUCCESSFUL PUPIL?
IT IS A PROBLEM AT WHICH I HAVE WORKED FOR THE LAST SEVENTEEN YEARS, BUT ONLY DURING THE LAST EIGHT OR NINE MONTHS HAVE I BEEN REWARDED WITH GLIMMERINGS OF SUCCESS.
OF COURSE I HAVE EXPERIMENTED WITH THOUSANDS OF ANIMALS, BUT LATTERLY ONLY WITH **CATS**.
WHEN I MADE THE ACQUAINTANCE OF TOBERMORY A WEEK AGO I SAW AT ONCE THAT I WAS IN CONTACT WITH A BEING OF **EXTRAORDINARY** INTELLIGENCE.
I HAD GONE FAR ALONG THE ROAD TO SUCCESS IN RECENT EXPERIMENTS; WITH **TOBERMORY** I HAVE REACHED THE GOAL.
RATS!
AND DO YOU MEAN TO SAY THAT YOU HAVE TAUGHT TOBERMORY TO SAY AND UNDERSTAND EASY SENTENCES OF ONE SYLLABLE?
MY DEAR **MISS RESKER**, ONE TEACHES LITTLE CHILDREN AND SAVAGES IN THAT **PIECEMEAL** FASHION: WHEN ONE HAS ENCOUNTERED AN ANIMAL OF HIGHLY DEVELOPED INTELLIGENCE ONE HAS NO NEED FOR THOSE METHODS.
TOBERMORY CAN SPEAK OUR LANGUAGE WITH PERFECT CORRECTNESS.
BEYOND RATS!
HADN'T WE BETTER HAVE THE CAT IN AND JUDGE FOR OURSELVES?
SIR WILFRED WENT IN SEARCH OF THE ANIMAL.

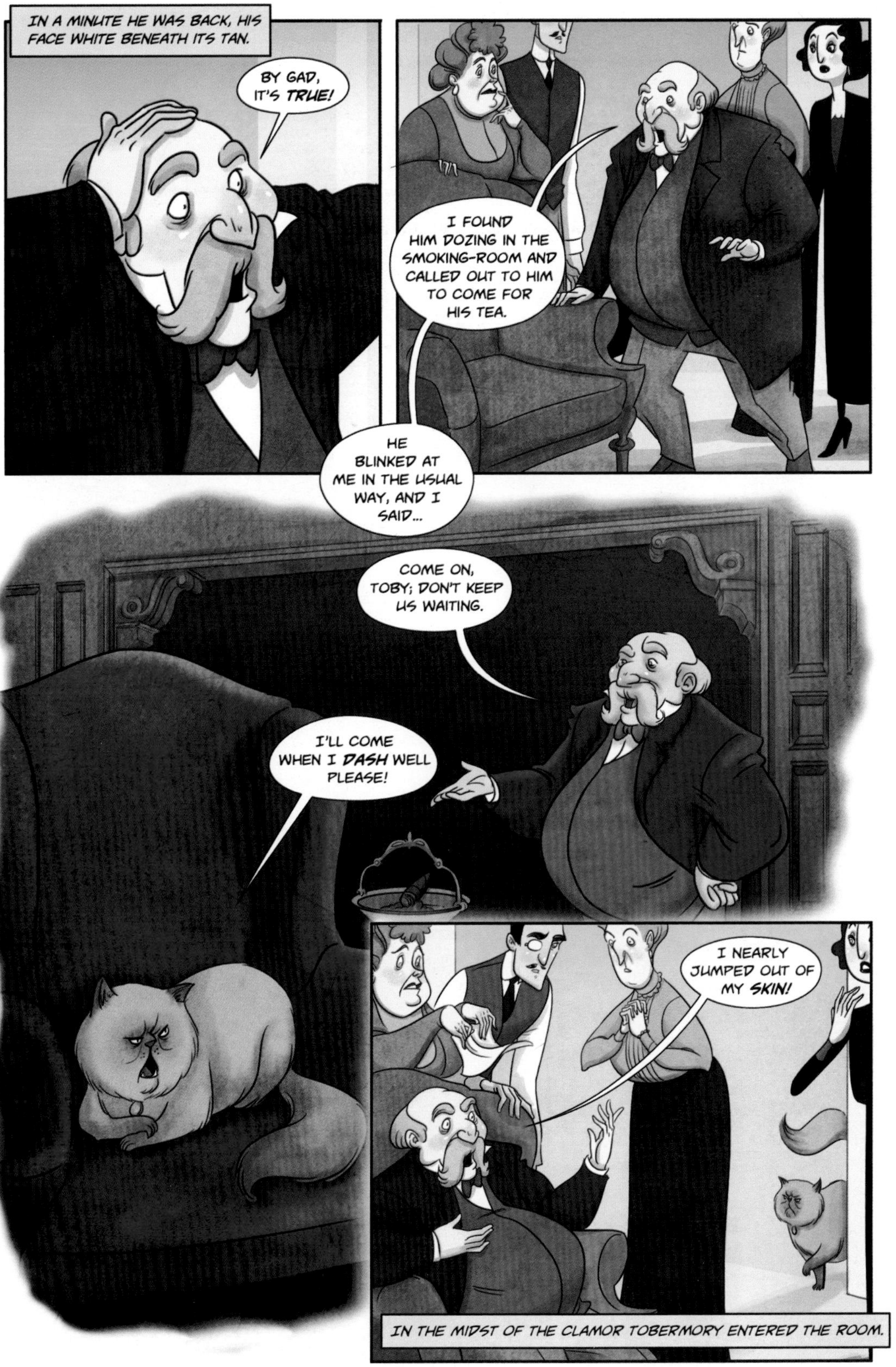
IN A MINUTE HE WAS BACK, HIS FACE WHITE BENEATH ITS TAN.
BY GAD, IT'S TRUE!
I FOUND HIM DOZING IN THE SMOKING-ROOM AND CALLED OUT TO HIM TO COME FOR HIS TEA.
HE BLINKED AT ME IN THE USUAL WAY, AND I SAID...
COME ON, TOBY; DON'T KEEP US WAITING.
I'LL COME WHEN I DASH WELL PLEASE!
I NEARLY JUMPED OUT OF MY SKIN!
IN THE MIDST OF THE CLAMOR TOBERMORY ENTERED THE ROOM.

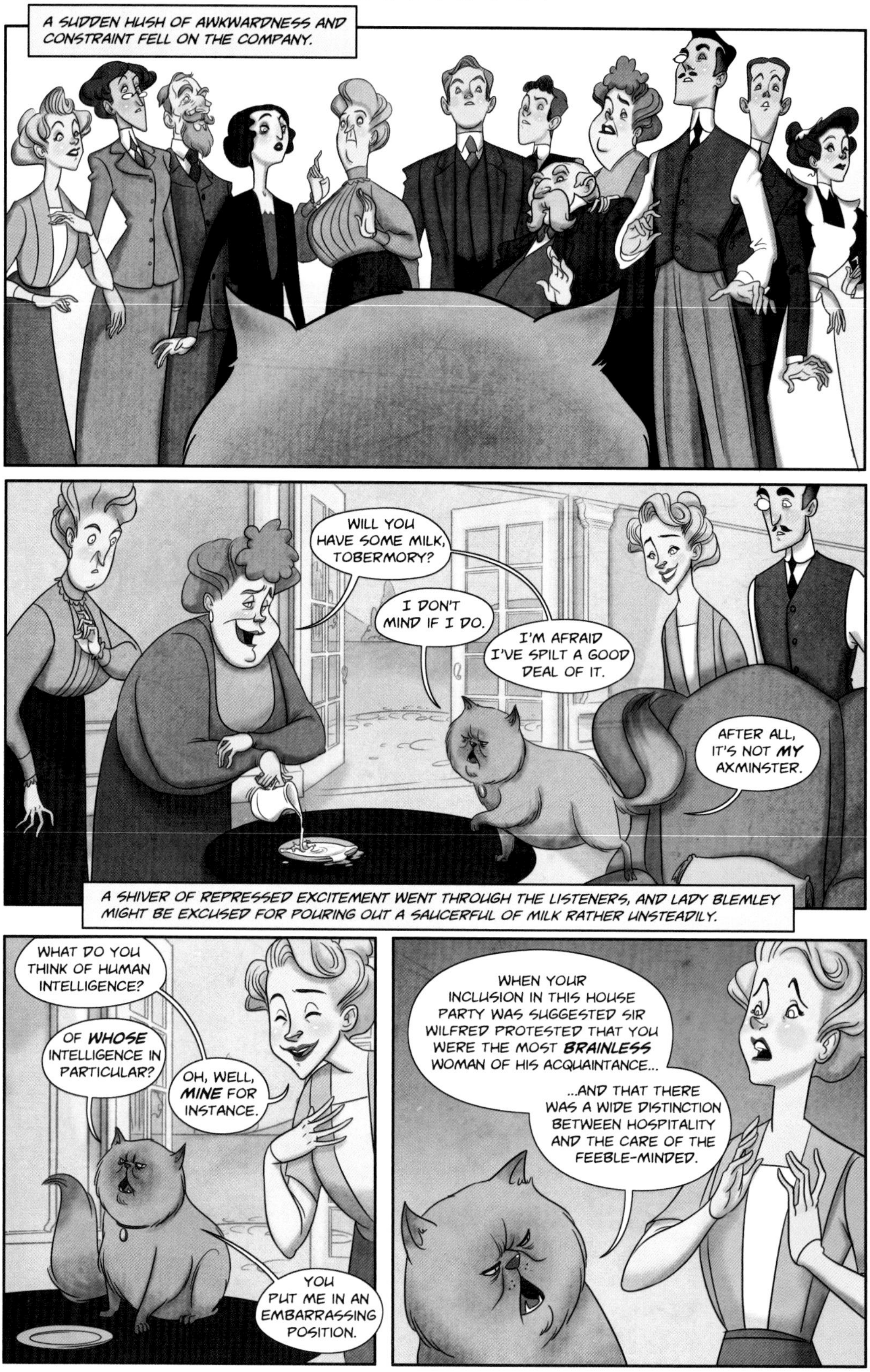
A SUDDEN HUSH OF AWKWARDNESS AND CONSTRAINT FELL ON THE COMPANY.
WILL YOU HAVE SOME MILK, TOBERMORY?
I DON'T MIND IF I DO.
I'M AFRAID I'VE SPILT A GOOD DEAL OF IT.
AFTER ALL, IT'S NOT **MY** AXMINSTER.
A SHIVER OF REPRESSED EXCITEMENT WENT THROUGH THE LISTENERS, AND LADY BLEMLEY MIGHT BE EXCUSED FOR POURING OUT A SAUCERFUL OF MILK RATHER UNSTEADILY.
WHAT DO YOU THINK OF HUMAN INTELLIGENCE?
OF **WHOSE** INTELLIGENCE IN PARTICULAR?
OH, WELL, **MINE** FOR INSTANCE.
YOU PUT ME IN AN EMBARRASSING POSITION.
WHEN YOUR INCLUSION IN THIS HOUSE PARTY WAS SUGGESTED SIR WILFRED PROTESTED THAT YOU WERE THE MOST **BRAINLESS** WOMAN OF HIS ACQUAINTANCE...
...AND THAT THERE WAS A WIDE DISTINCTION BETWEEN HOSPITALITY AND THE CARE OF THE FEEBLE-MINDED.

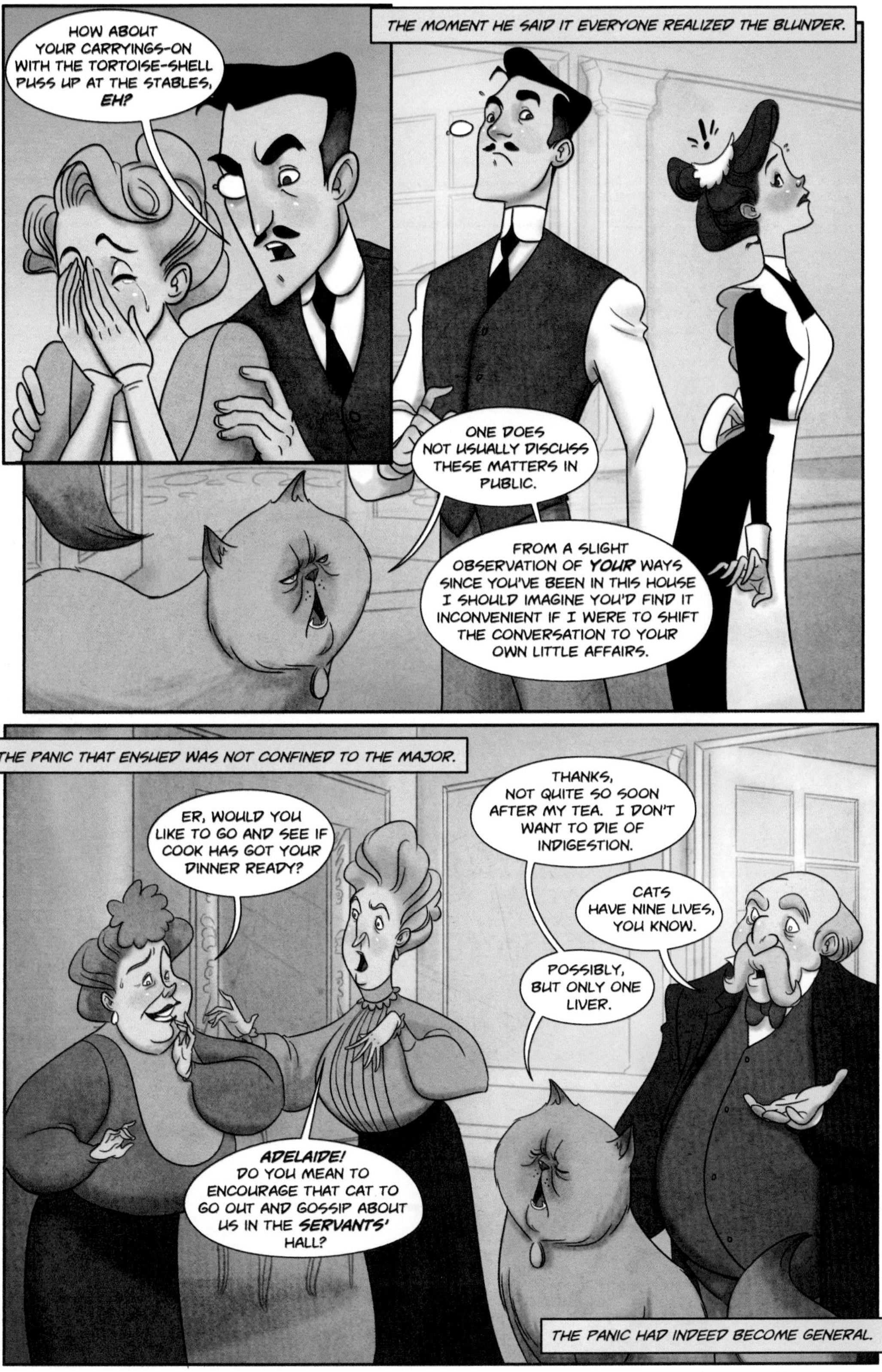
HOW ABOUT YOUR CARRYINGS-ON WITH THE TORTOISE-SHELL PUSS UP AT THE STABLES, EH?
THE MOMENT HE SAID IT EVERYONE REALIZED THE BLUNDER.
ONE DOES NOT USUALLY DISCUSS THESE MATTERS IN PUBLIC.
FROM A SLIGHT OBSERVATION OF YOUR WAYS SINCE YOU'VE BEEN IN THIS HOUSE I SHOULD IMAGINE YOU'D FIND IT INCONVENIENT IF I WERE TO SHIFT THE CONVERSATION TO YOUR OWN LITTLE AFFAIRS.
THE PANIC THAT ENSUED WAS NOT CONFINED TO THE MAJOR.
ER, WOULD YOU LIKE TO GO AND SEE IF COOK HAS GOT YOUR DINNER READY?
THANKS, NOT QUITE SO SOON AFTER MY TEA. I DON'T WANT TO DIE OF INDIGESTION.
CATS HAVE NINE LIVES, YOU KNOW.
POSSIBLY, BUT ONLY ONE LIVER.
ADELAIDE! DO YOU MEAN TO ENCOURAGE THAT CAT TO GO OUT AND GOSSIP ABOUT US IN THE SERVANTS' HALL?
THE PANIC HAD INDEED BECOME GENERAL.

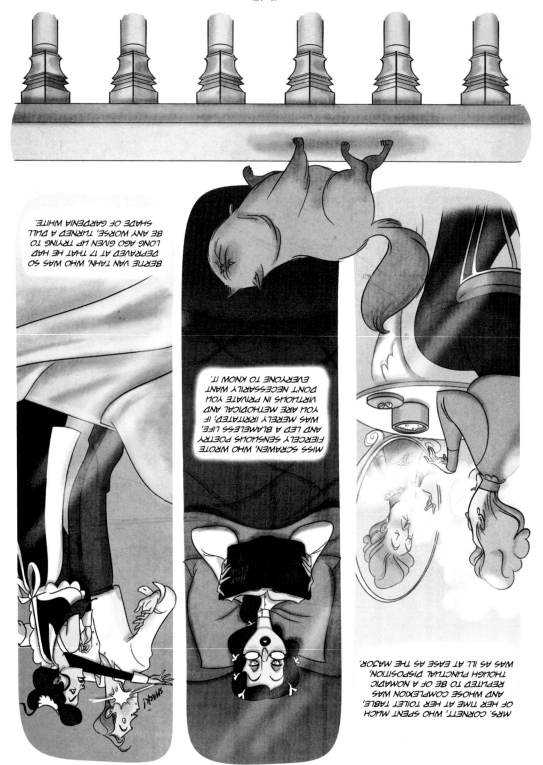

TOBERMORY

A NARROW ORNAMENTAL BALLISTRADE RAN IN FRONT OF MOST OF THE BEDROOM WINDOWS AT THE TOWERS, AND IT WAS RECALLED WITH DISMAY THAT THIS HAD FORMED A FAVORITE PROMENADE FOR TOBERMORY AT ALL HOURS WHENCE HE COULD WATCH THE PIGEONS -- AND HEAVEN KNEW WHAT ELSE BESIDES.

MRS. CORNETT, WHO SPENT MUCH OF HER TIME AT HER TOILET TABLE, AND WHOSE COMPLEXION WAS REPUTED TO BE OF A NOMADIC THOUGH PUNCTUAL DISPOSITION, WAS AS ILL AT EASE AS THE MAJOR.

MISS SCRAWEN, WHO WROTE FIERCELY SENSUOUS POETRY AND LED A BLAMELESS LIFE, WAS MERELY IRRITATED; IF YOU ARE METHODICAL AND VIRTUOUS IN PRIVATE YOU DON'T NECESSARILY WANT EVERYONE TO KNOW IT.

BERTIE VAN TAHN, WHO WAS SO DEPRAVED AT 17 THAT HE HAD LONG AGO GIVEN UP TRYING TO BE ANY WORSE, TURNED A DULL SHADE OF GARDENIA WHITE.

SMACK!

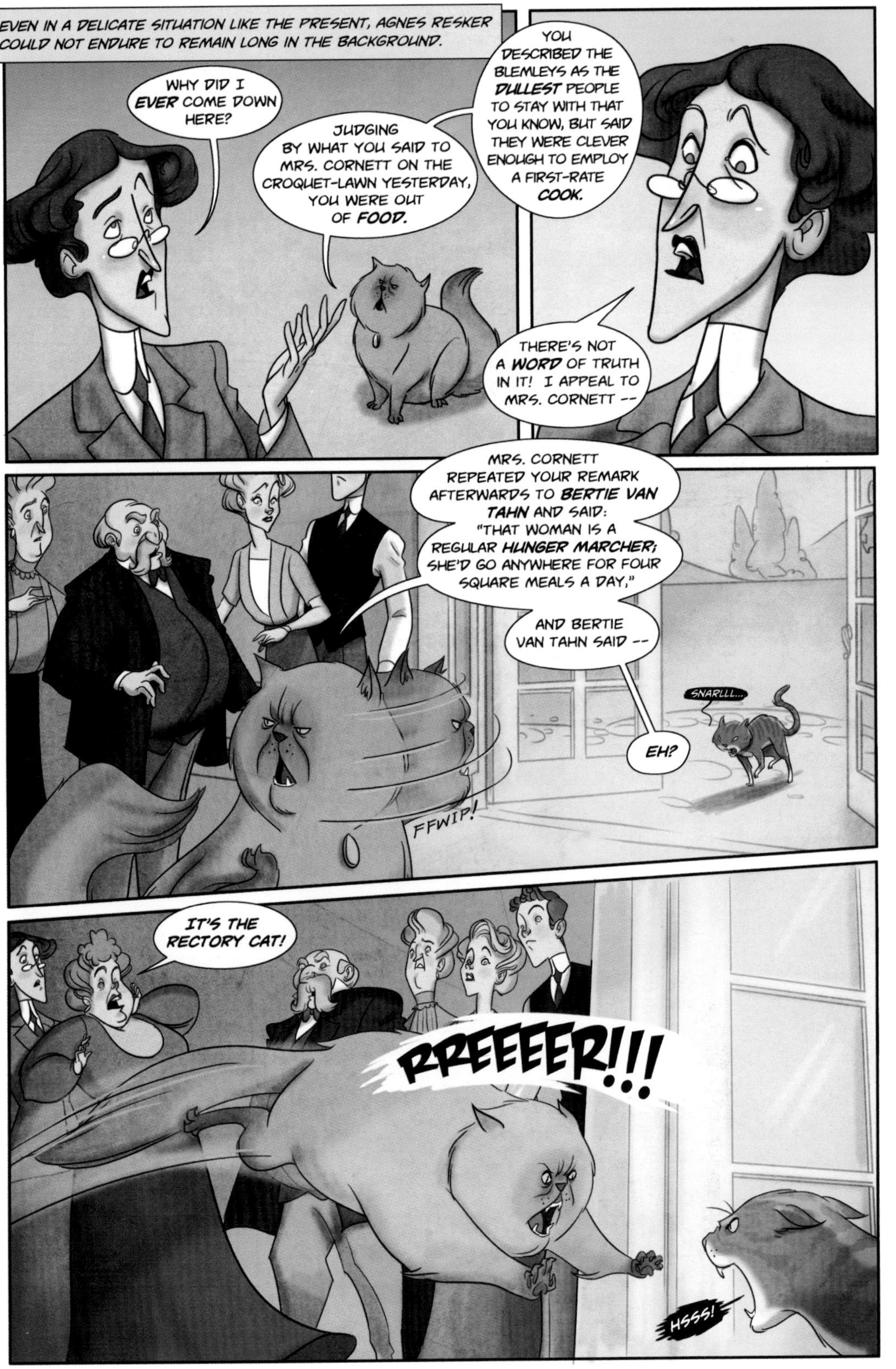
EVEN IN A DELICATE SITUATION LIKE THE PRESENT, AGNES RESKER COULD NOT ENDURE TO REMAIN LONG IN THE BACKGROUND.
WHY DID I **EVER** COME DOWN HERE?
JUDGING BY WHAT YOU SAID TO MRS. CORNETT ON THE CROQUET-LAWN YESTERDAY, YOU WERE OUT OF **FOOD.**
YOU DESCRIBED THE BLEMLEYS AS THE **DULLEST** PEOPLE TO STAY WITH THAT YOU KNOW, BUT SAID THEY WERE CLEVER ENOUGH TO EMPLOY A FIRST-RATE **COOK.**
THERE'S NOT A **WORD** OF TRUTH IN IT! I APPEAL TO MRS. CORNETT --
MRS. CORNETT REPEATED YOUR REMARK AFTERWARDS TO **BERTIE VAN TAHN** AND SAID: "THAT WOMAN IS A REGULAR **HUNGER MARCHER;** SHE'D GO ANYWHERE FOR FOUR SQUARE MEALS A DAY,"
AND BERTIE VAN TAHN SAID --
SNARLLL...
EH?
FFWIP!
IT'S THE RECTORY CAT!
RREEEEER!!!
HSSS!

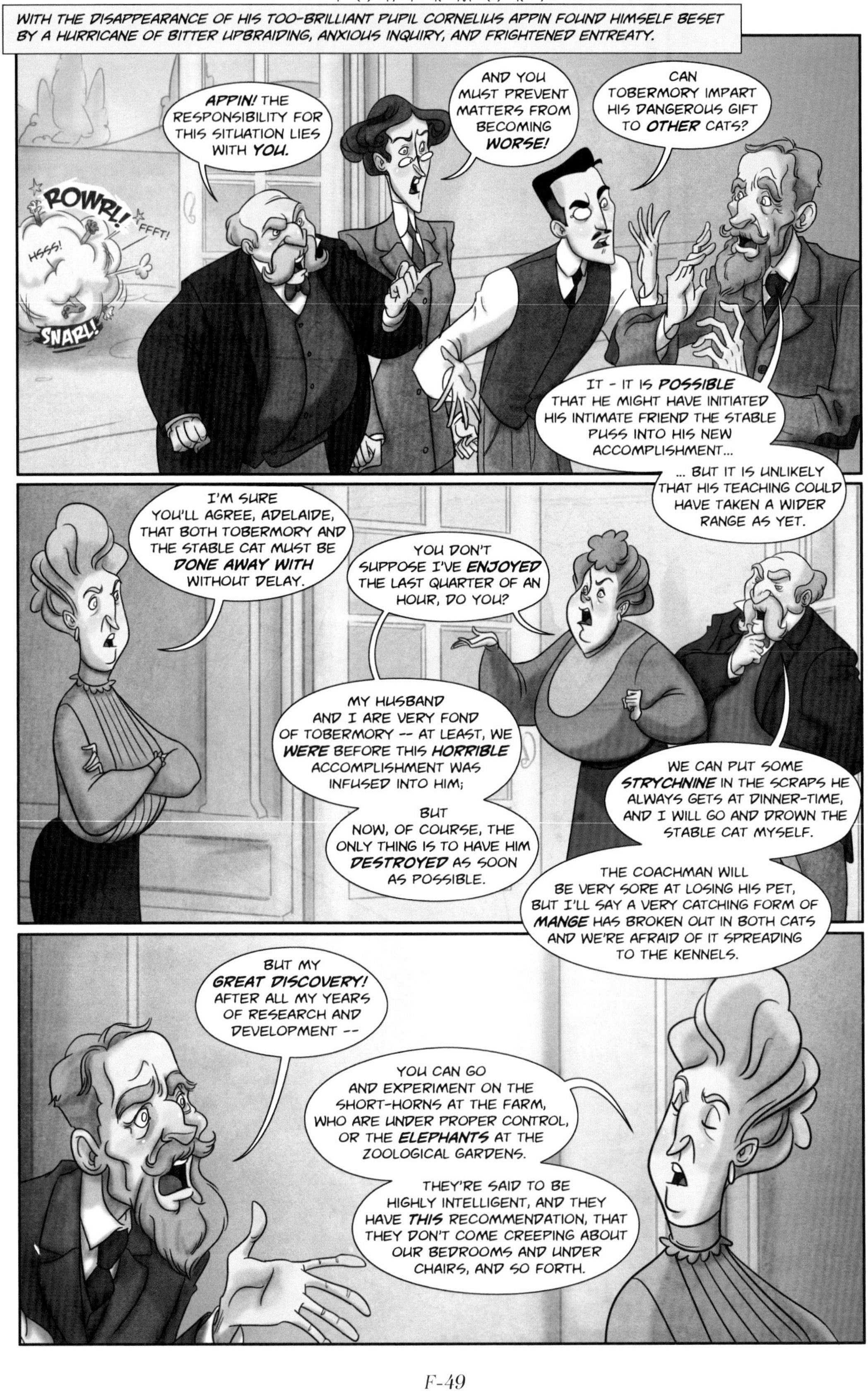
WITH THE DISAPPEARANCE OF HIS TOO-BRILLIANT PUPIL CORNELIUS APPIN FOUND HIMSELF BESET BY A HURRICANE OF BITTER UPBRAIDING, ANXIOUS INQUIRY, AND FRIGHTENED ENTREATY.
ROWR!! FFFT! HSSS! SNARL!
APPIN! THE RESPONSIBILITY FOR THIS SITUATION LIES WITH YOU.
AND YOU MUST PREVENT MATTERS FROM BECOMING WORSE!
CAN TOBERMORY IMPART HIS DANGEROUS GIFT TO OTHER CATS?
IT - IT IS POSSIBLE THAT HE MIGHT HAVE INITIATED HIS INTIMATE FRIEND THE STABLE PUSS INTO HIS NEW ACCOMPLISHMENT...
... BUT IT IS UNLIKELY THAT HIS TEACHING COULD HAVE TAKEN A WIDER RANGE AS YET.
I'M SURE YOU'LL AGREE, ADELAIDE, THAT BOTH TOBERMORY AND THE STABLE CAT MUST BE DONE AWAY WITH WITHOUT DELAY.
YOU DON'T SUPPOSE I'VE ENJOYED THE LAST QUARTER OF AN HOUR, DO YOU?
MY HUSBAND AND I ARE VERY FOND OF TOBERMORY -- AT LEAST, WE WERE BEFORE THIS HORRIBLE ACCOMPLISHMENT WAS INFUSED INTO HIM;
BUT NOW, OF COURSE, THE ONLY THING IS TO HAVE HIM DESTROYED AS SOON AS POSSIBLE.
WE CAN PUT SOME STRYCHNINE IN THE SCRAPS HE ALWAYS GETS AT DINNER-TIME, AND I WILL GO AND DROWN THE STABLE CAT MYSELF.
THE COACHMAN WILL BE VERY SORE AT LOSING HIS PET, BUT I'LL SAY A VERY CATCHING FORM OF MANGE HAS BROKEN OUT IN BOTH CATS AND WE'RE AFRAID OF IT SPREADING TO THE KENNELS.
BUT MY GREAT DISCOVERY! AFTER ALL MY YEARS OF RESEARCH AND DEVELOPMENT --
YOU CAN GO AND EXPERIMENT ON THE SHORT-HORNS AT THE FARM, WHO ARE UNDER PROPER CONTROL, OR THE ELEPHANTS AT THE ZOOLOGICAL GARDENS.
THEY'RE SAID TO BE HIGHLY INTELLIGENT, AND THEY HAVE THIS RECOMMENDATION, THAT THEY DON'T COME CREEPING ABOUT OUR BEDROOMS AND UNDER CHAIRS, AND SO FORTH.

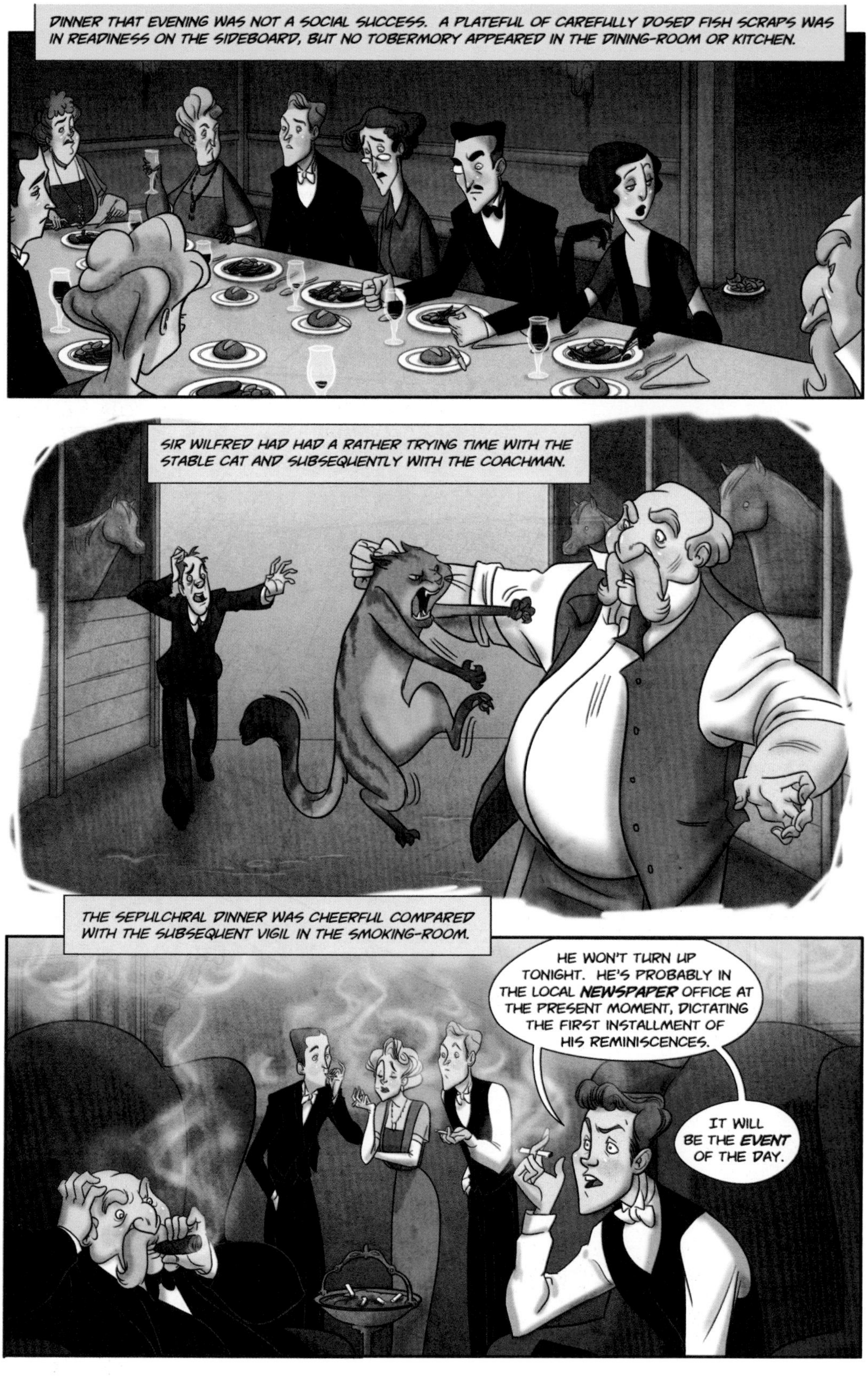
DINNER THAT EVENING WAS NOT A SOCIAL SUCCESS. A PLATEFUL OF CAREFULLY DOSED FISH SCRAPS WAS IN READINESS ON THE SIDEBOARD, BUT NO TOBERMORY APPEARED IN THE DINING-ROOM OR KITCHEN.
SIR WILFRED HAD HAD A RATHER TRYING TIME WITH THE STABLE CAT AND SUBSEQUENTLY WITH THE COACHMAN.
THE SEPULCHRAL DINNER WAS CHEERFUL COMPARED WITH THE SUBSEQUENT VIGIL IN THE SMOKING-ROOM.
HE WON'T TURN UP TONIGHT. HE'S PROBABLY IN THE LOCAL NEWSPAPER OFFICE AT THE PRESENT MOMENT, DICTATING THE FIRST INSTALLMENT OF HIS REMINISCENCES.
IT WILL BE THE EVENT OF THE DAY.

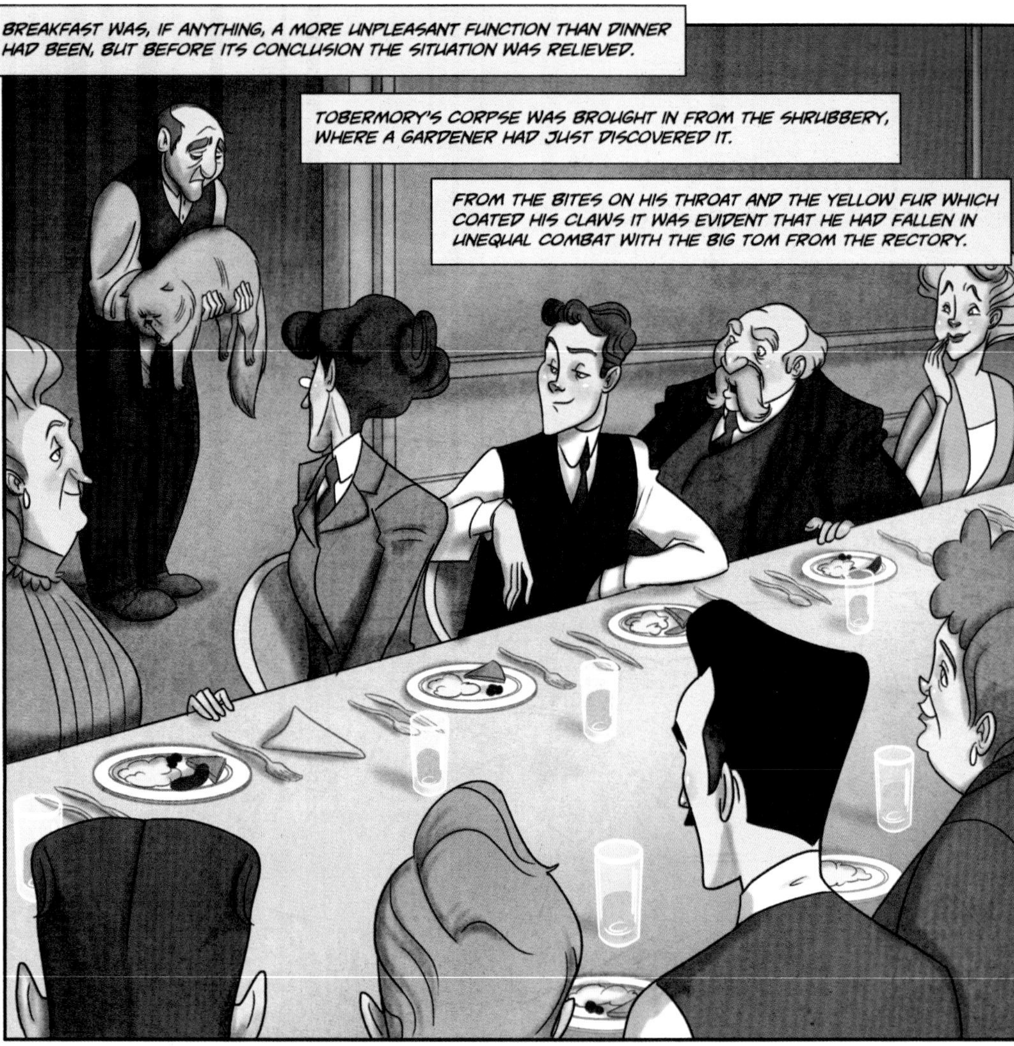
BREAKFAST WAS, IF ANYTHING, A MORE UNPLEASANT FUNCTION THAN DINNER HAD BEEN, BUT BEFORE ITS CONCLUSION THE SITUATION WAS RELIEVED.
TOBERMORY'S CORPSE WAS BROUGHT IN FROM THE SHRUBBERY, WHERE A GARDENER HAD JUST DISCOVERED IT.
FROM THE BITES ON HIS THROAT AND THE YELLOW FUR WHICH COATED HIS CLAWS IT WAS EVIDENT THAT HE HAD FALLEN IN UNEQUAL COMBAT WITH THE BIG TOM FROM THE RECTORY.

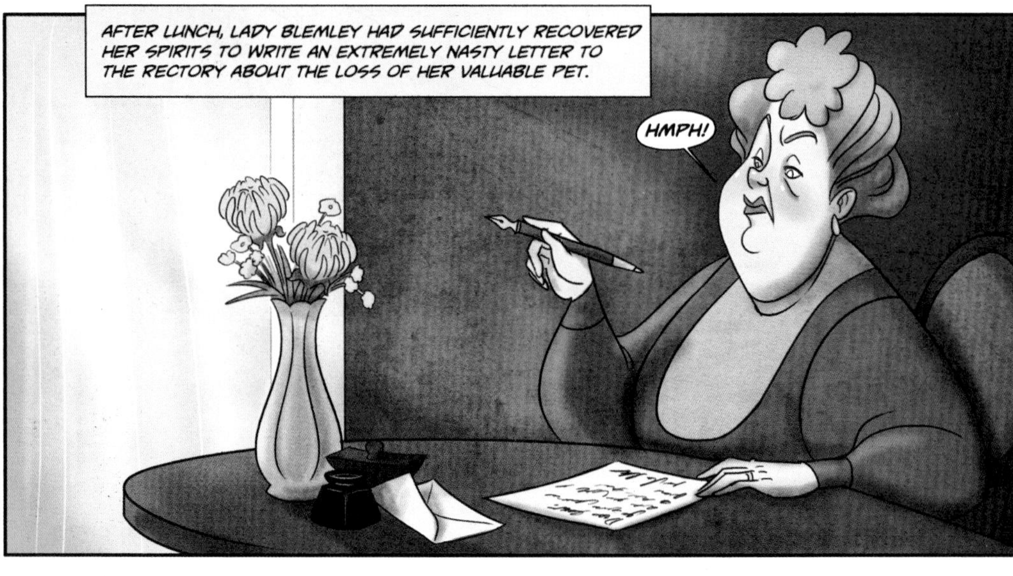
AFTER LUNCH, LADY BLEMLEY HAD SUFFICIENTLY RECOVERED HER SPIRITS TO WRITE AN EXTREMELY NASTY LETTER TO THE RECTORY ABOUT THE LOSS OF HER VALUABLE PET.
HMPH!

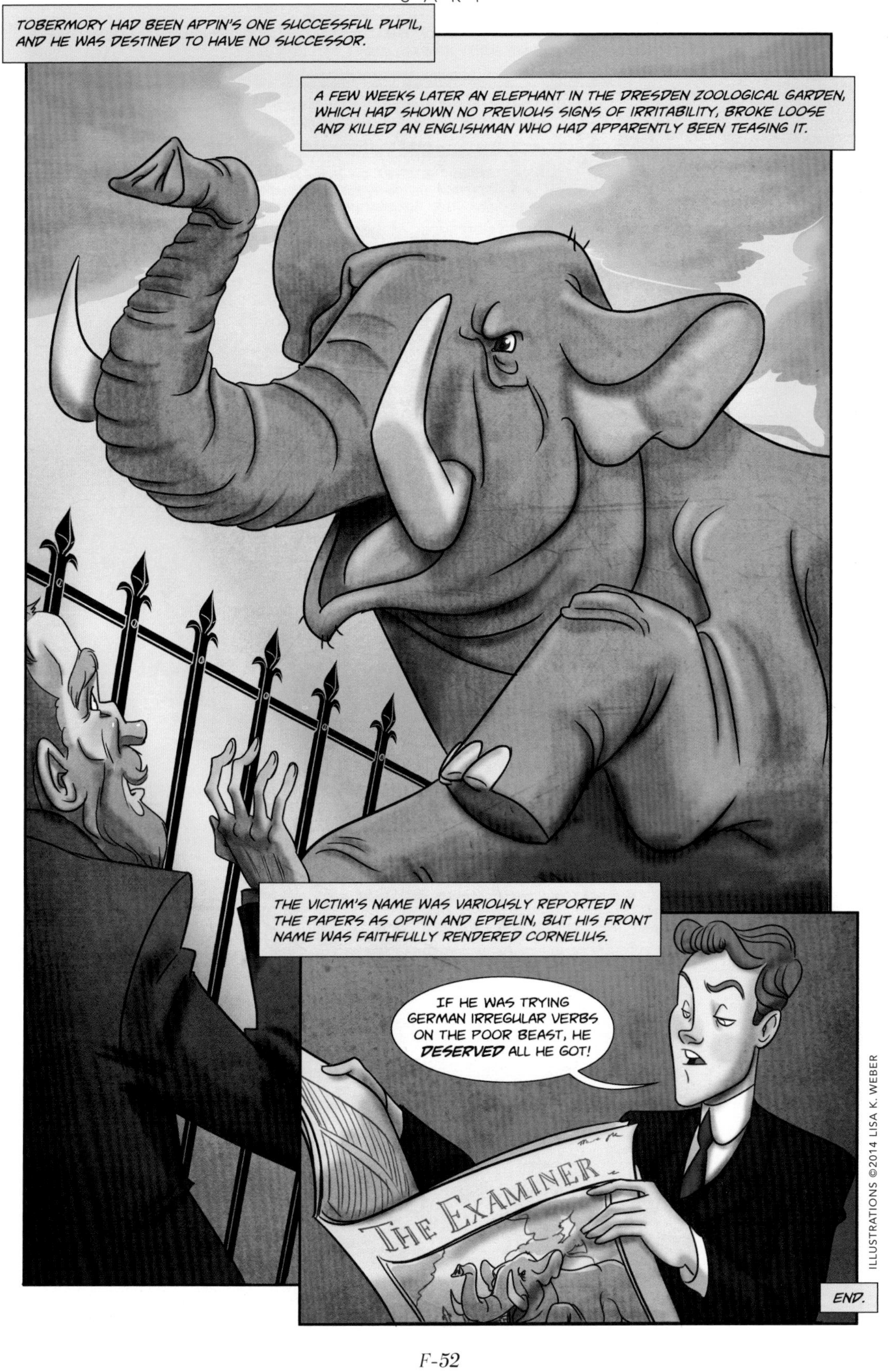
TOBERMORY HAD BEEN APPIN'S ONE SUCCESSFUL PUPIL, AND HE WAS DESTINED TO HAVE NO SUCCESSOR.
A FEW WEEKS LATER AN ELEPHANT IN THE DRESDEN ZOOLOGICAL GARDEN, WHICH HAD SHOWN NO PREVIOUS SIGNS OF IRRITABILITY, BROKE LOOSE AND KILLED AN ENGLISHMAN WHO HAD APPARENTLY BEEN TEASING IT.
THE VICTIM'S NAME WAS VARIOUSLY REPORTED IN THE PAPERS AS OPPIN AND EPPELIN, BUT HIS FRONT NAME WAS FAITHFULLY RENDERED CORNELIUS.
IF HE WAS TRYING GERMAN IRREGULAR VERBS ON THE POOR BEAST, HE **DESERVED** ALL HE GOT!
THE EXAMINER
END.

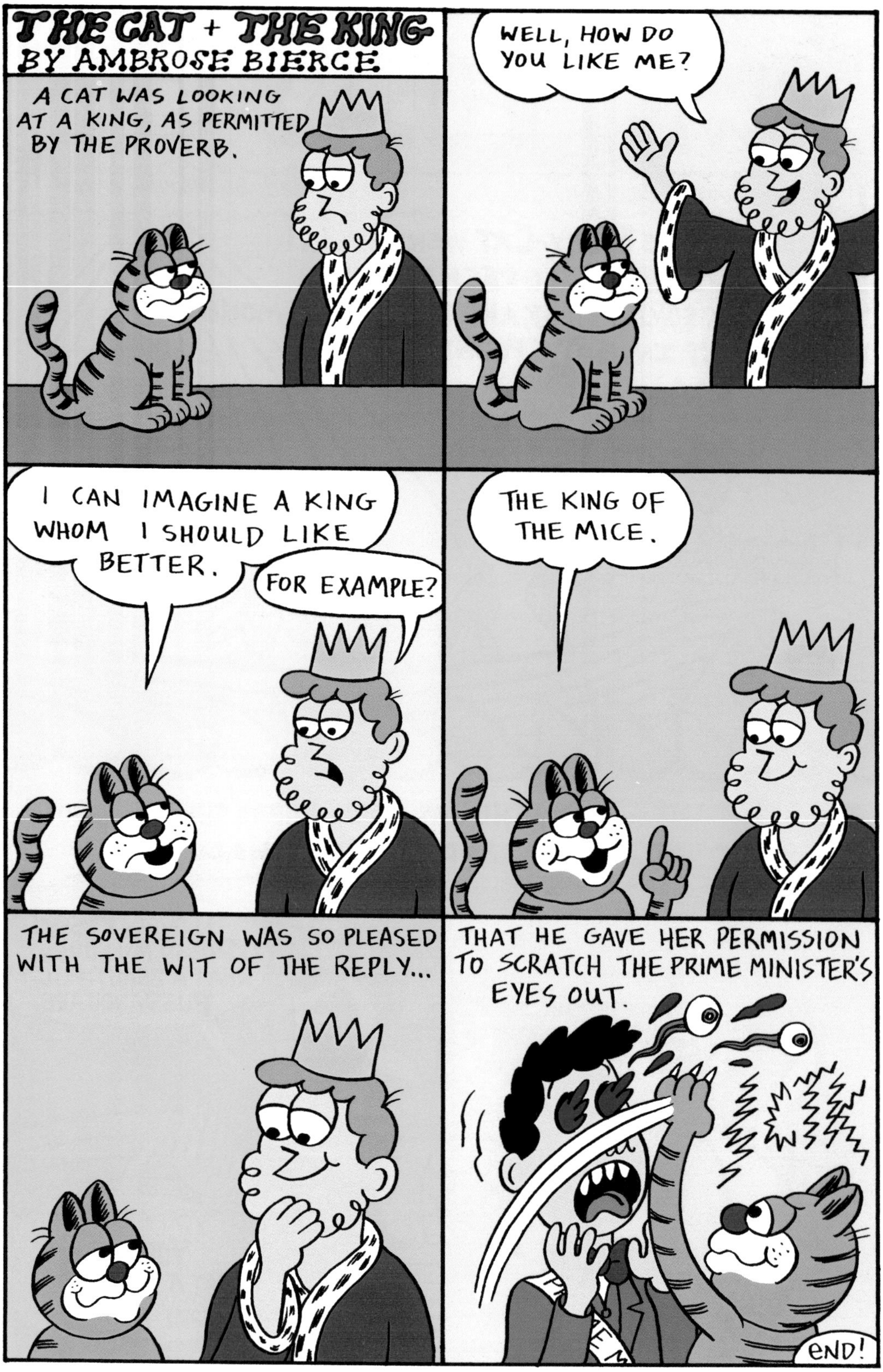
THE CAT + THE KING
BY AMBROSE BIERCE
A CAT WAS LOOKING AT A KING, AS PERMITTED BY THE PROVERB.
WELL, HOW DO YOU LIKE ME?
I CAN IMAGINE A KING WHOM I SHOULD LIKE BETTER.
FOR EXAMPLE?
THE KING OF THE MICE.
THE SOVEREIGN WAS SO PLEASED WITH THE WIT OF THE REPLY...
THAT HE GAVE HER PERMISSION TO SCRATCH THE PRIME MINISTER'S EYES OUT.
END!

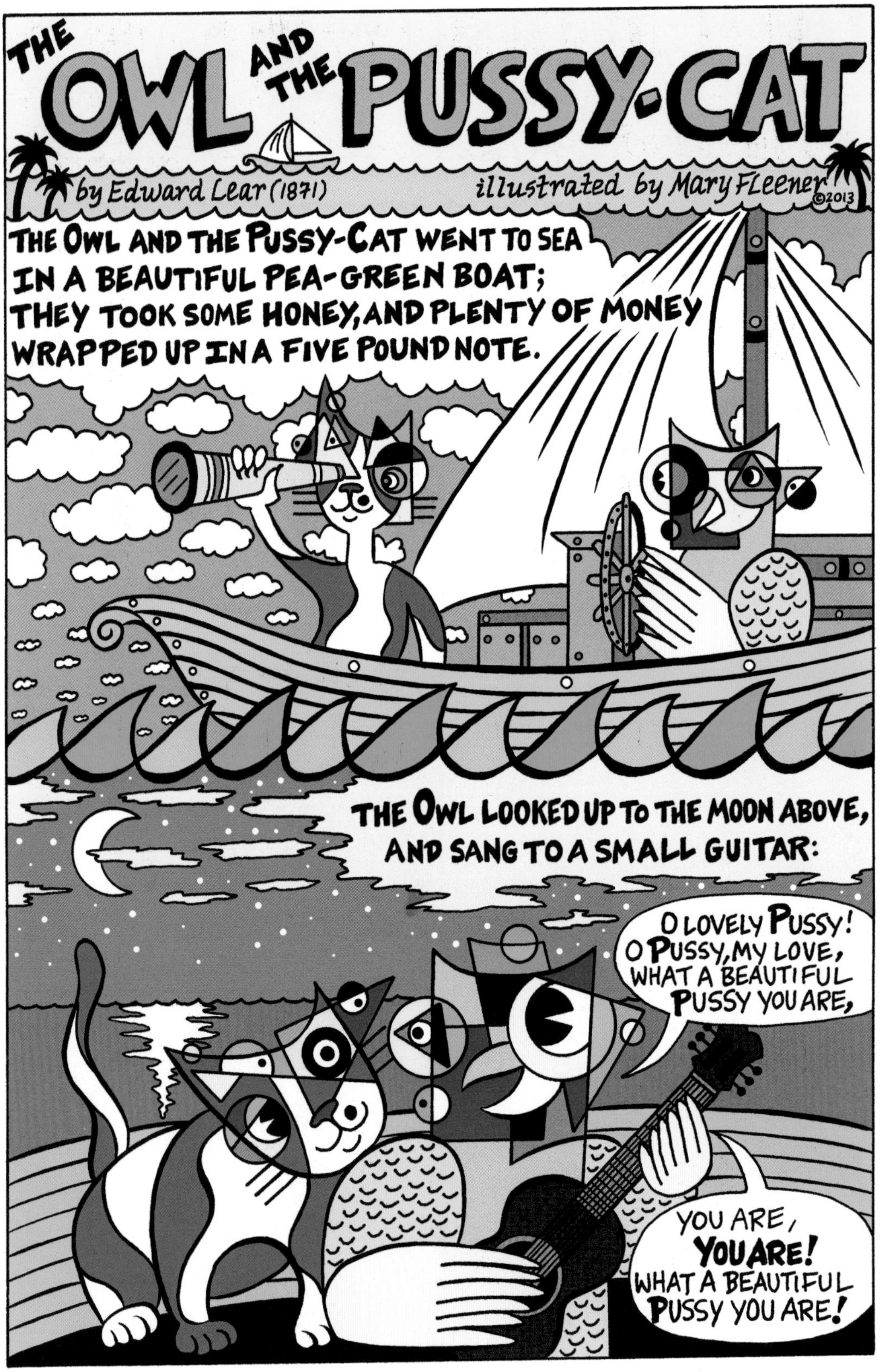
THE OWL AND THE PUSSY-CAT
by Edward Lear (1871)
illustrated by Mary Fleener ©2013
THE OWL AND THE PUSSY-CAT WENT TO SEA
IN A BEAUTIFUL PEA-GREEN BOAT;
THEY TOOK SOME HONEY, AND PLENTY OF MONEY
WRAPPED UP IN A FIVE POUND NOTE.
THE OWL LOOKED UP TO THE MOON ABOVE,
AND SANG TO A SMALL GUITAR:
O LOVELY PUSSY! O PUSSY, MY LOVE, WHAT A BEAUTIFUL PUSSY YOU ARE,
YOU ARE, YOU ARE! WHAT A BEAUTIFUL PUSSY YOU ARE!

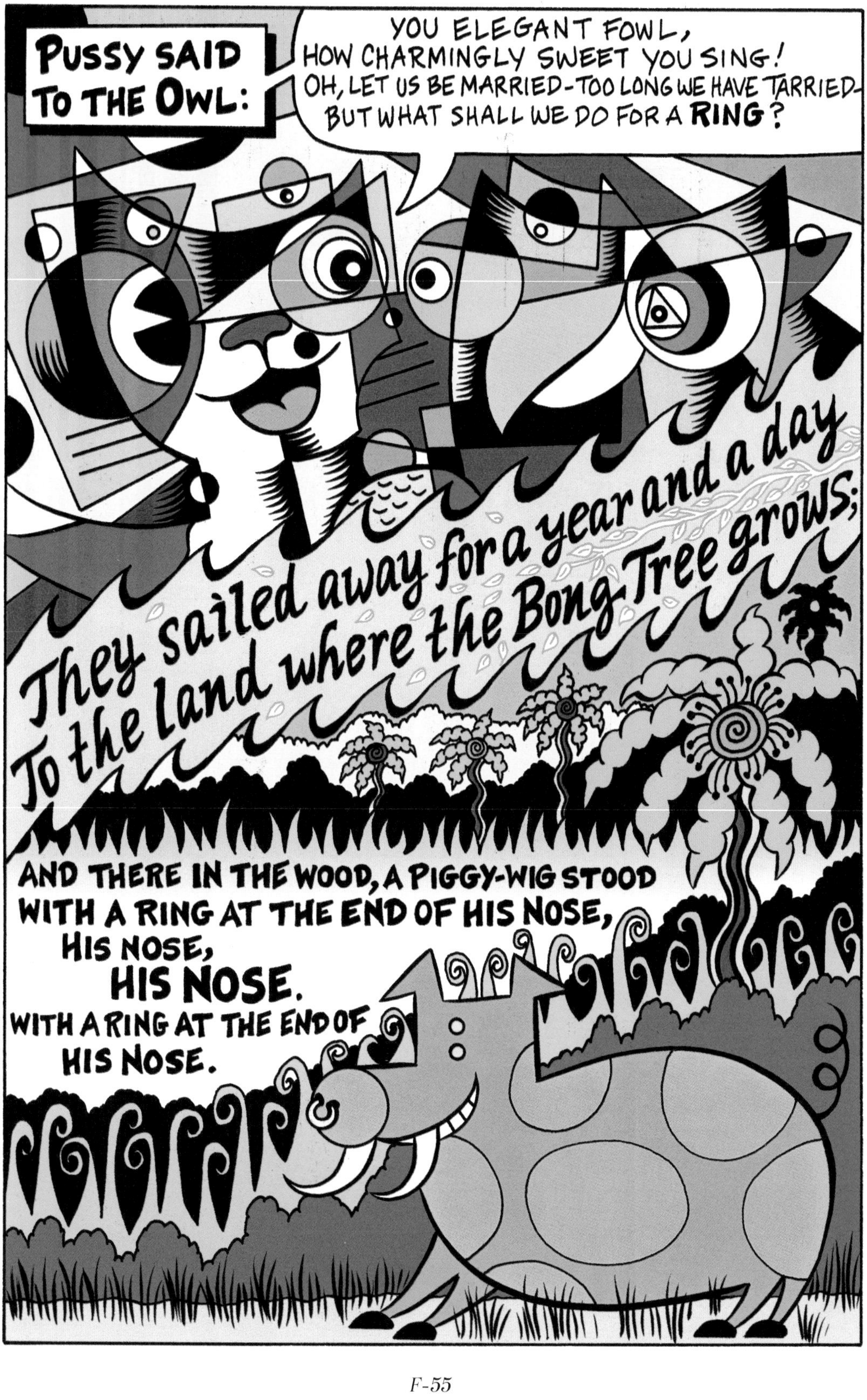
PUSSY SAID TO THE OWL:
YOU ELEGANT FOWL, HOW CHARMINGLY SWEET YOU SING! OH, LET US BE MARRIED-TOO LONG WE HAVE TARRIED- BUT WHAT SHALL WE DO FOR A RING?
They sailed away for a year and a day
To the land where the Bong-Tree grows;
AND THERE IN THE WOOD, A PIGGY-WIG STOOD
WITH A RING AT THE END OF HIS NOSE,
HIS NOSE,
HIS NOSE.
WITH A RING AT THE END OF
HIS NOSE.

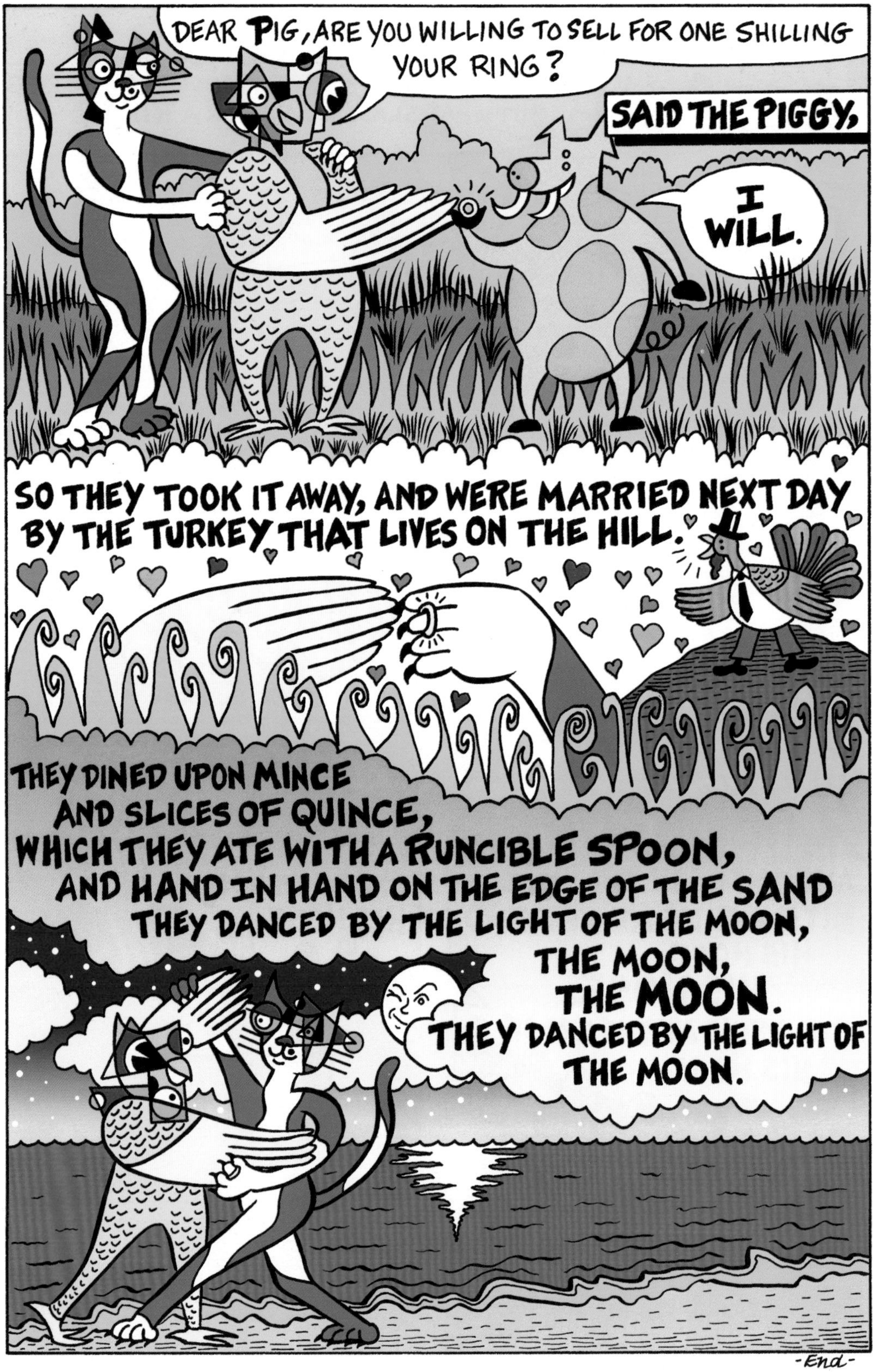
DEAR PIG, ARE YOU WILLING TO SELL FOR ONE SHILLING YOUR RING?
SAID THE PIGGY,
I WILL.
SO THEY TOOK IT AWAY, AND WERE MARRIED NEXT DAY
BY THE TURKEY THAT LIVES ON THE HILL.
THEY DINED UPON MINCE
AND SLICES OF QUINCE,
WHICH THEY ATE WITH A RUNCIBLE SPOON,
AND HAND IN HAND ON THE EDGE OF THE SAND
THEY DANCED BY THE LIGHT OF THE MOON,
THE MOON,
THE MOON.
THEY DANCED BY THE LIGHT OF
THE MOON.
-End-

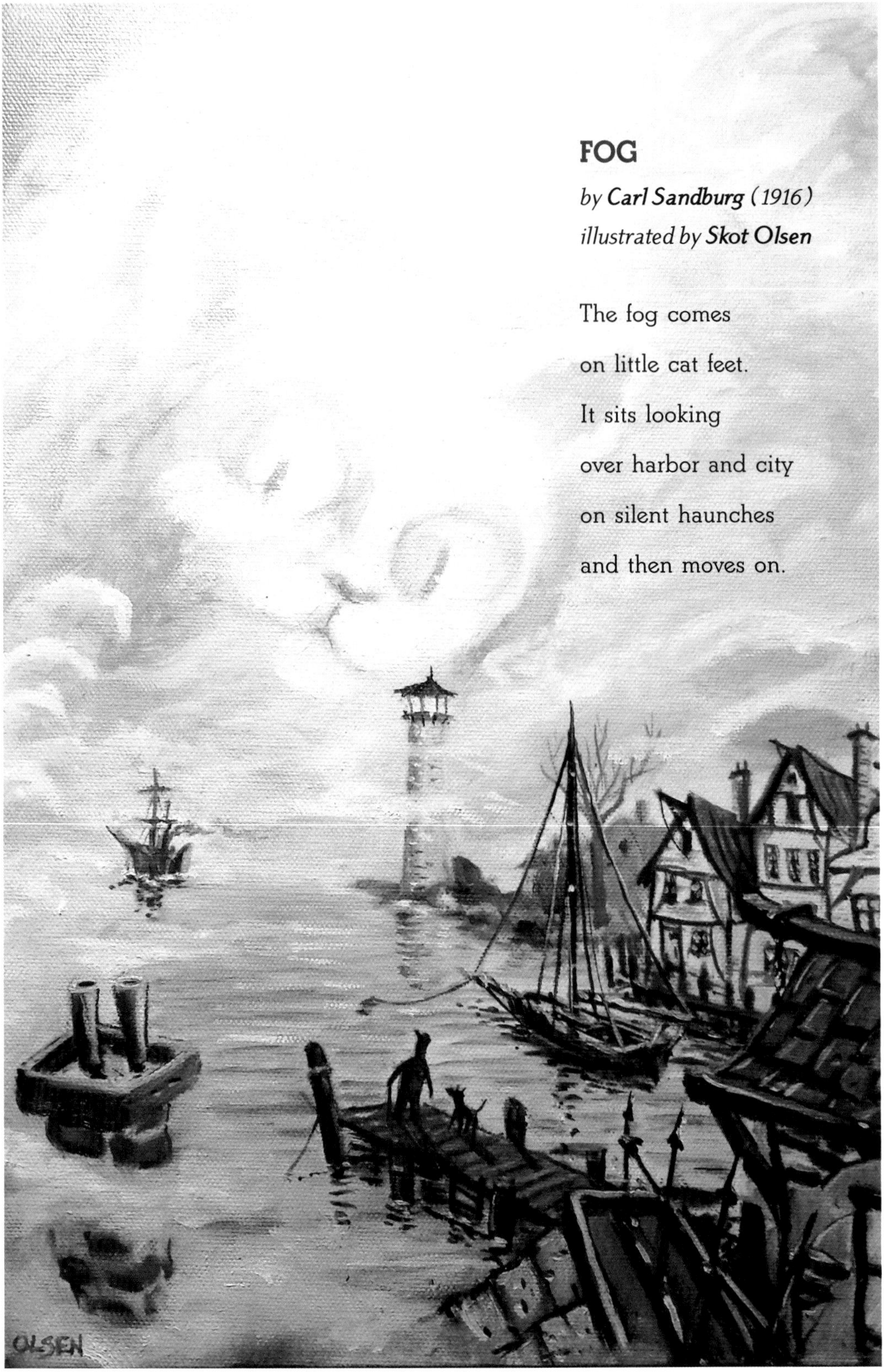
OLSEN

FOG

by ***Carl Sandburg*** *(1916)*
illustrated by ***Skot Olsen***

The fog comes
on little cat feet.
It sits looking
over harbor and city
on silent haunches
and then moves on.

THE BEAST FROM THE ABYSS

from the essay by
Robert E. Howard

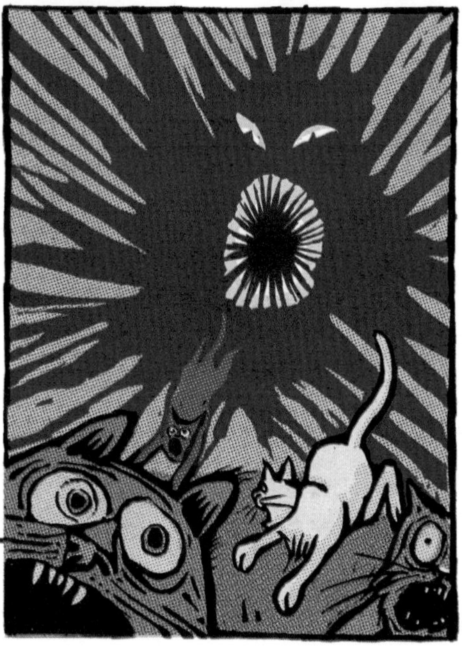

illustrated by
Peter Kuper

Having spent most of my life in oil boom towns, I am not unfamiliar with the sight of torn and mangled humanity. Oftener than I like to remember I have seen men suffering, bleeding and dying from machinery accidents, knife stabs, gunshot wounds, and other mishaps.

Yet I believe the most sickening spectacle of all was that of a crippled cat dragging along a sidewalk, occasionally emitting a low moaning cry that only slightly resembled the ordinary vocal expressions of a feline.

There is something particularly harrowing about the sight of an animal in pain; the desperate despair, undiluted by hope or reason, that makes it, in a way, a more awful and tragic sight than that of an injured human.

In the agony cry of a cat all the blind abysmal anguish of the black cosmic pits seems concentrated. It is a scream from the jungle, the death howl of a Past unspeakably distant, forgotten and denied by humanity, yet which still lies awake at the back of the subconciousness.

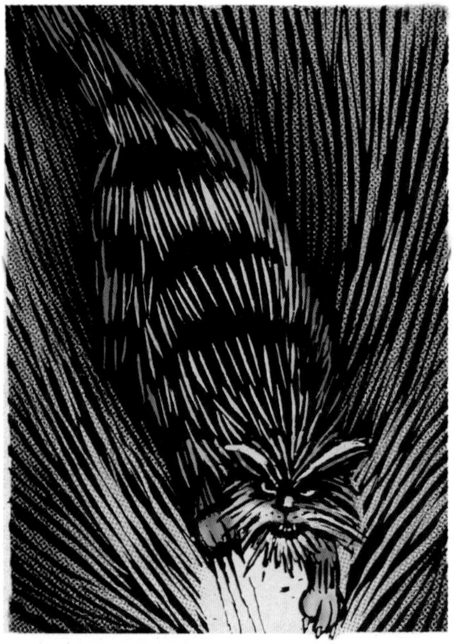

In his anger cries and in his love cries, the gliding course through the grass, the hunger that burns shamelessly from his slitted eyes, in all his movements and actions is advertised his kinship with the wild, his tamelessness, and his contempt for man.

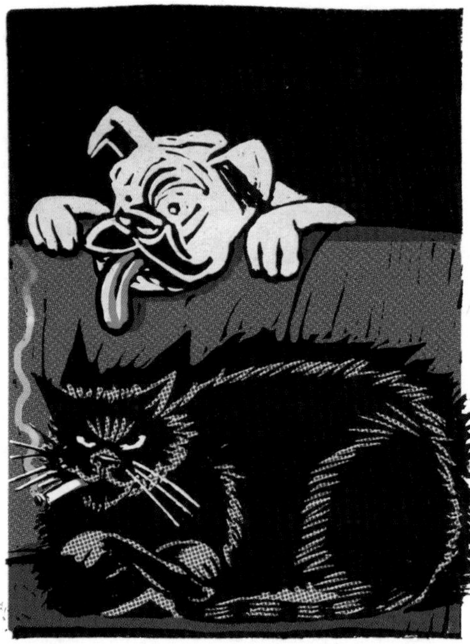

Inferior to the dog the cat is, nevertheless, more like human beings than is the former. For he is vain yet servile, greedy yet fastidious, lazy, lustful and selfish.

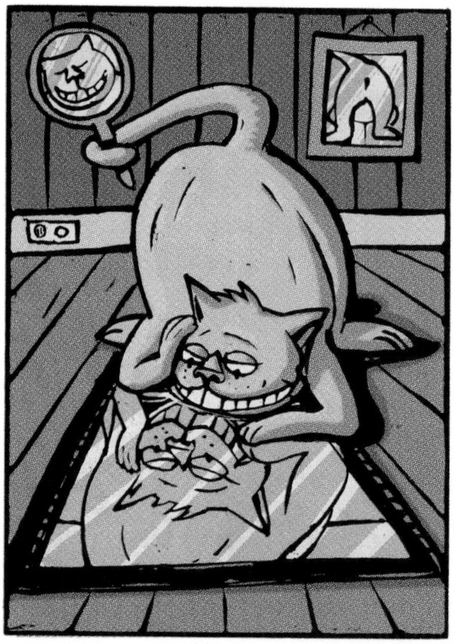

That last characteristic is, indeed, the dominant feline trait. He is monumentally selfish. In his self love he is brazen, candid and unashamed.

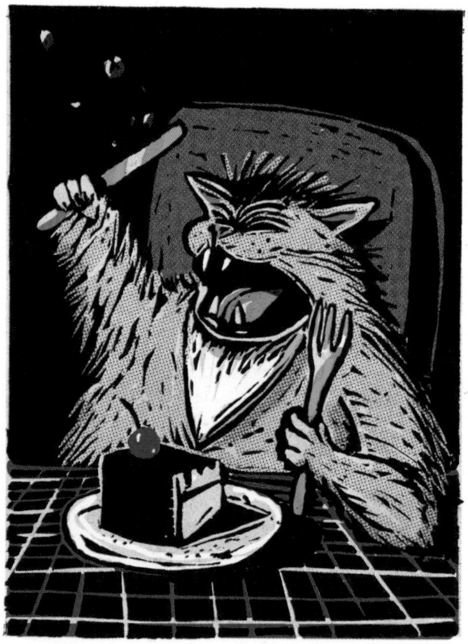

Giving nothing in return, he demands everything — and he demands it in a raspy, hungry, whining squall that seems to tremble with self-pity, and accuse the world at large of perfidy and broken contract.

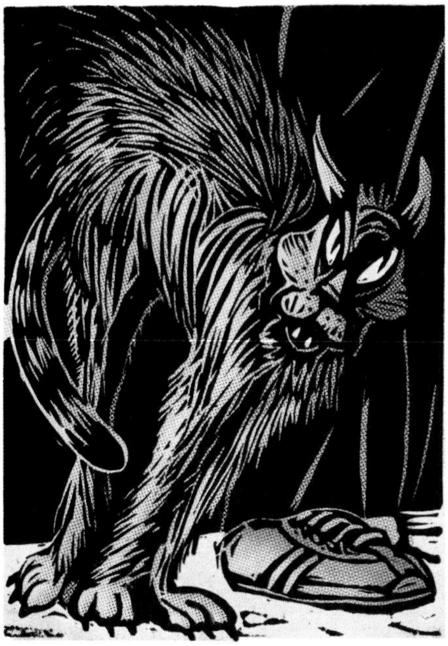

His eyes are suspicious and avaricious. His manner is at once arrogant and debased. He arches his back and rubs himself against humanity's leg, dirging a doleful plea, while his eyes glare threats and his claws slide convulsively in and out of their padded sheaths.

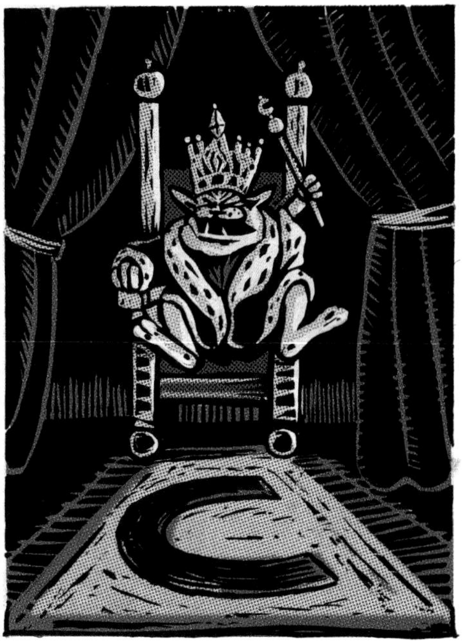

He is inordinate in his demands, and he gives no thanks for bounty. His only religion is an unfaltering belief in the divine rights of cats. The dog exists only for man, man exists only for cats. The introverted feline conceives himself to be ever the center of the universe.

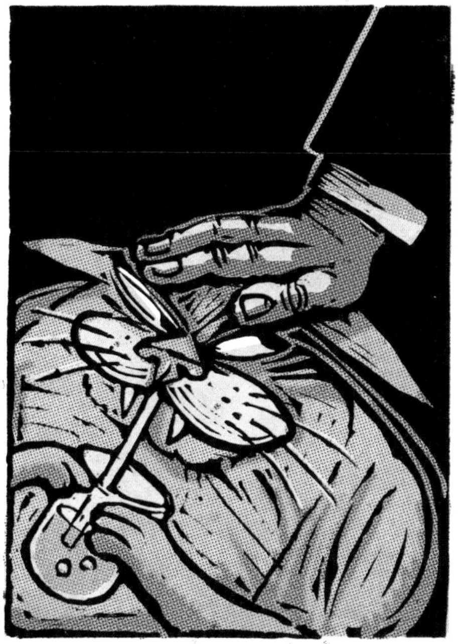

In his narrow skull there is no room for the finer feelings. Pull a drowning kitten out of the gutter and provide him with a soft cushion to sleep upon, and cream as often as he desires. Shelter, pamper and coddle him all his useless and self-centered life.

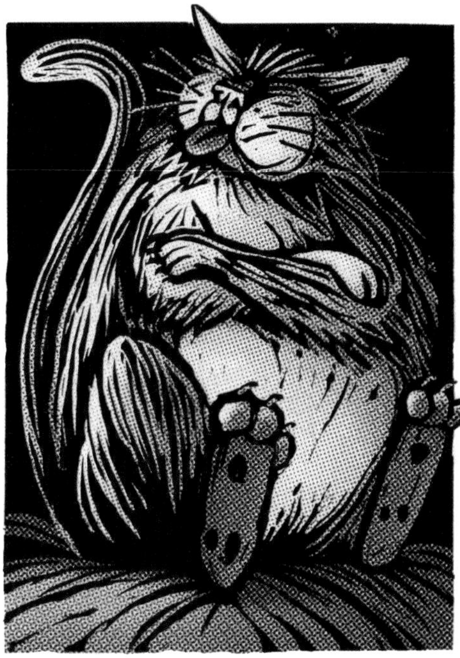

What will he give you in return?
He will allow you to stroke his fur; he will bestow upon you a condescending purr, after the manner of one conferring a great favor. There the evidences of gratitude end.

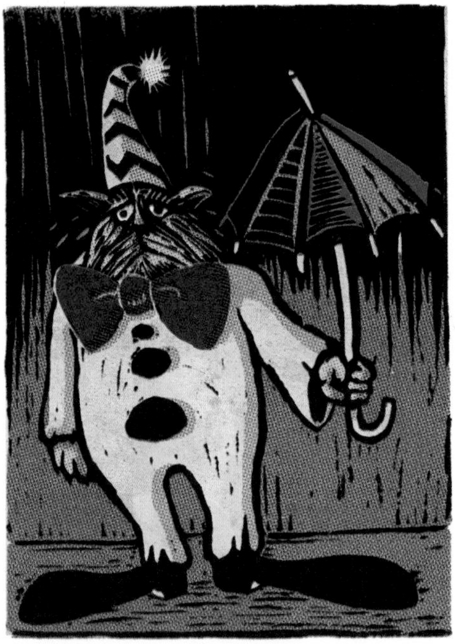

I am not a victim of the peculiar cat-phobia which afflicts some people, neither I am one of those whose fondness for the animals is as inexplicable and tyrannical in its way as the above mentioned repulsion. I can take cats or leave them alone.

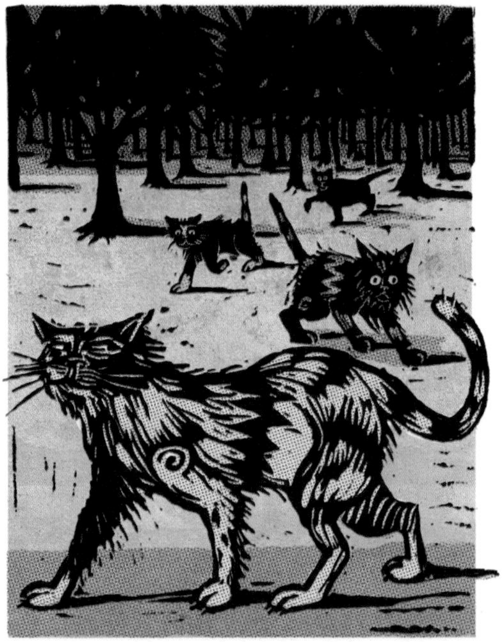

Just now I am uncertain as to the number of cats I possess. I could not prove my ownership of a single cat, but several have taken up their abode in the feed shed and beside the back step, allowed me to feed them, and at times bestowed upon me the favor of a purr.

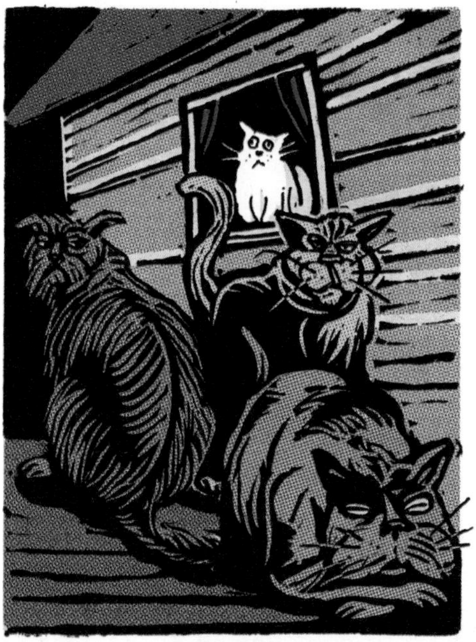

So long as no one claims them, I suppose I can look on them as my property. I am uncertain as to their numbers, because there has been an addition to the community, and I do not know how many.

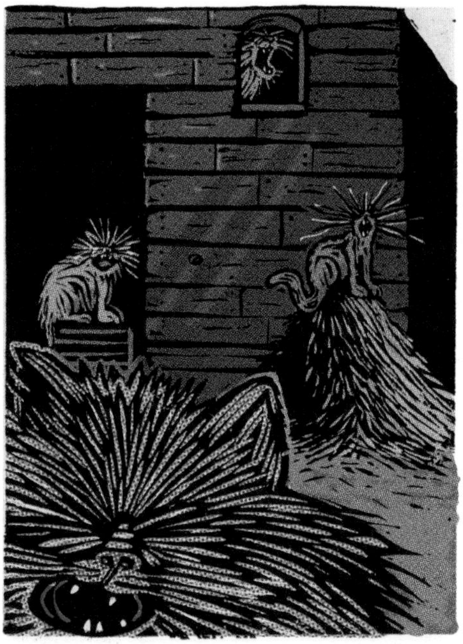

I hear them squalling among the hay bales, but I have not had an opportunity to count them. I know only that they are the offspring of a stocky, lazy gray cat, whose democratic mongrel blood is diluted with some sort of thoroughbred stock.

The life of a cat is not numbered by nine.
Usually it is short, violent and tragic.
He suffers, and makes others suffer if he can.
He is primitive, bestially selfish.

He is, in short, a creature of awful and terrible
potentialities, a crystalization of primordial
self-love, a materialization of the blackness
and squalor of the abyss.

He is a green-eyed, steel-thewed, fur-clad
block of darkness hewed from the Pits which
know not light, nor sympathy, nor dreams, nor
hope, nor beauty, nor anything except hunger
and the satiating of hunger.

But he has dwelt with man since the
beginning, and when the last man lies down
and dies, a cat will watch his throes, and
likelier than not, will gorge its abysmal hunger
on his cooling flesh.

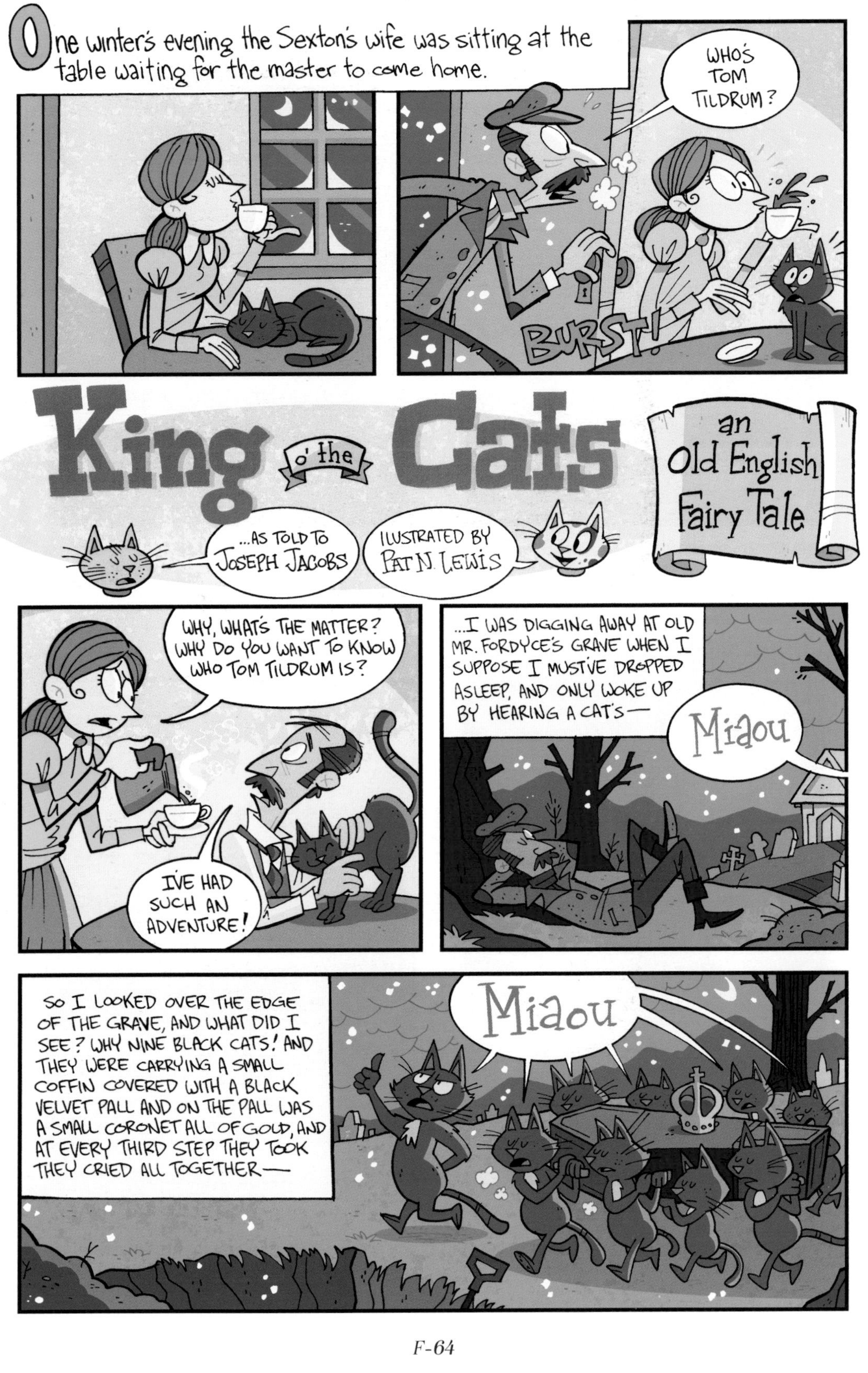
One winter's evening the Sexton's wife was sitting at the table waiting for the master to come home.
WHO'S TOM TILDRUM?
BURST!
King o' the Cats
an Old English Fairy Tale
...AS TOLD TO JOSEPH JACOBS
ILLUSTRATED BY PAT N. LEWIS
WHY, WHAT'S THE MATTER? WHY DO YOU WANT TO KNOW WHO TOM TILDRUM IS?
I'VE HAD SUCH AN ADVENTURE!
...I WAS DIGGING AWAY AT OLD MR. FORDYCE'S GRAVE WHEN I SUPPOSE I MUST'VE DROPPED ASLEEP, AND ONLY WOKE UP BY HEARING A CAT'S—
Miaou
SO I LOOKED OVER THE EDGE OF THE GRAVE, AND WHAT DID I SEE? WHY NINE BLACK CATS! AND THEY WERE CARRYING A SMALL COFFIN COVERED WITH A BLACK VELVET PALL AND ON THE PALL WAS A SMALL CORONET ALL OF GOLD, AND AT EVERY THIRD STEP THEY TOOK THEY CRIED ALL TOGETHER—
Miaou

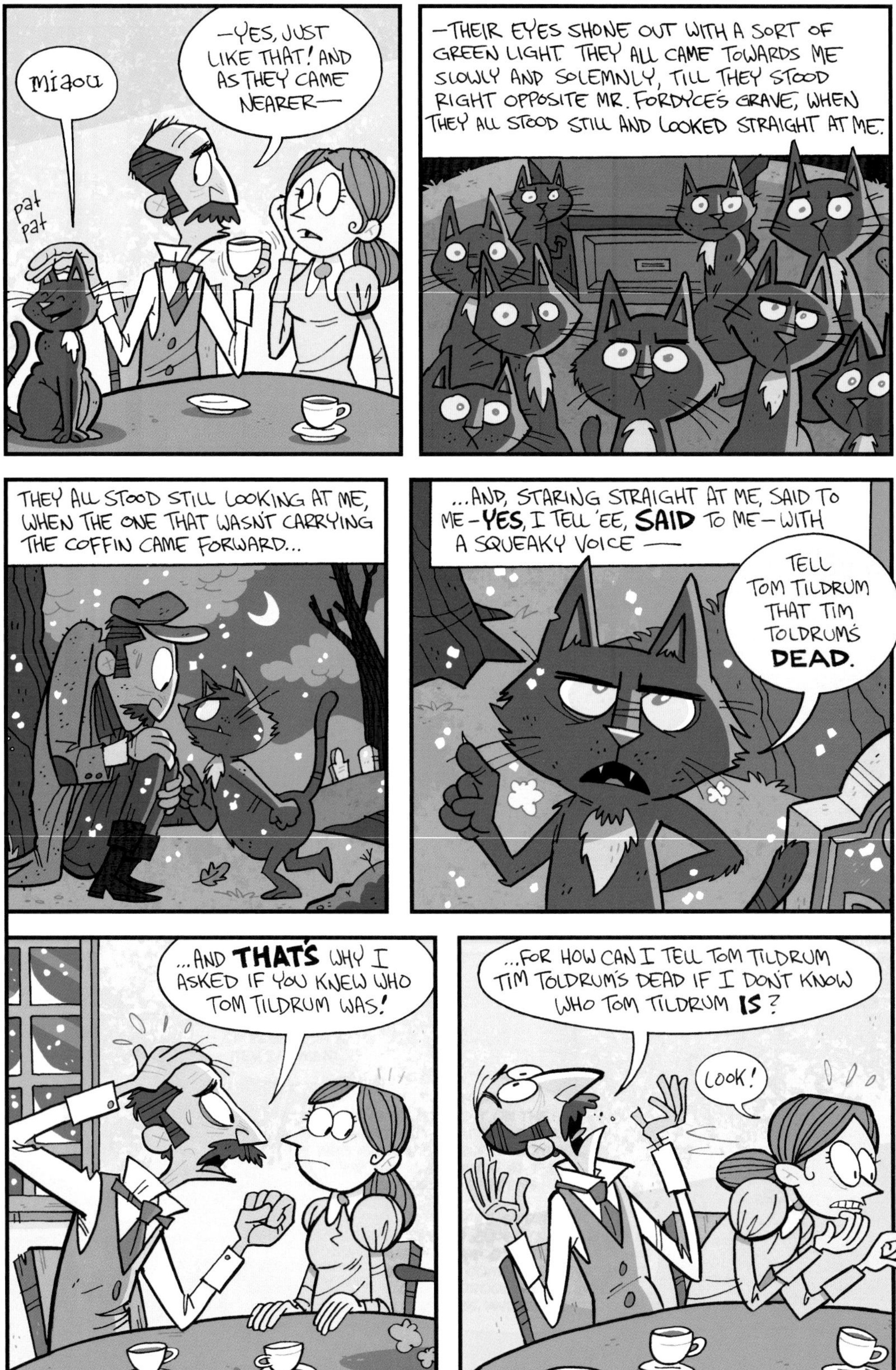
Miaou
—YES, JUST LIKE THAT! AND AS THEY CAME NEARER—
pat pat
—THEIR EYES SHONE OUT WITH A SORT OF GREEN LIGHT. THEY ALL CAME TOWARDS ME SLOWLY AND SOLEMNLY, TILL THEY STOOD RIGHT OPPOSITE MR. FORDYCE'S GRAVE, WHEN THEY ALL STOOD STILL AND LOOKED STRAIGHT AT ME.
THEY ALL STOOD STILL LOOKING AT ME, WHEN THE ONE THAT WASN'T CARRYING THE COFFIN CAME FORWARD...
...AND, STARING STRAIGHT AT ME, SAID TO ME—YES, I TELL 'EE, SAID TO ME—WITH A SQUEAKY VOICE —
TELL TOM TILDRUM THAT TIM TOLDRUM'S DEAD.
...AND THAT'S WHY I ASKED IF YOU KNEW WHO TOM TILDRUM WAS!
...FOR HOW CAN I TELL TOM TILDRUM TIM TOLDRUM'S DEAD IF I DON'T KNOW WHO TOM TILDRUM IS?
LOOK!

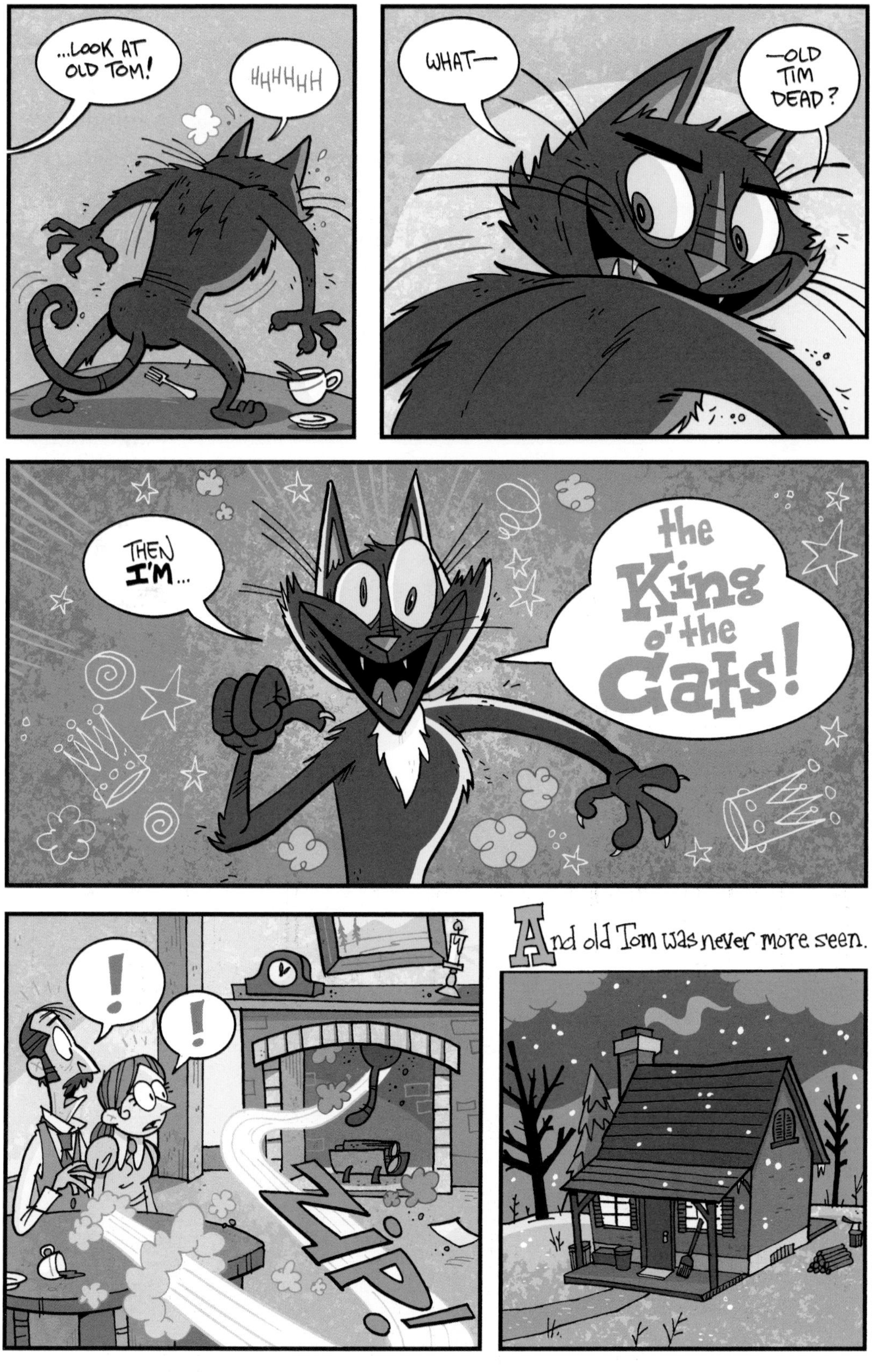
...LOOK AT OLD TOM!
HHHHHH
WHAT—
—OLD TIM DEAD?
THEN I'M...
the King o' the Cats!
!
!
ZIP!
And old Tom was never more seen.

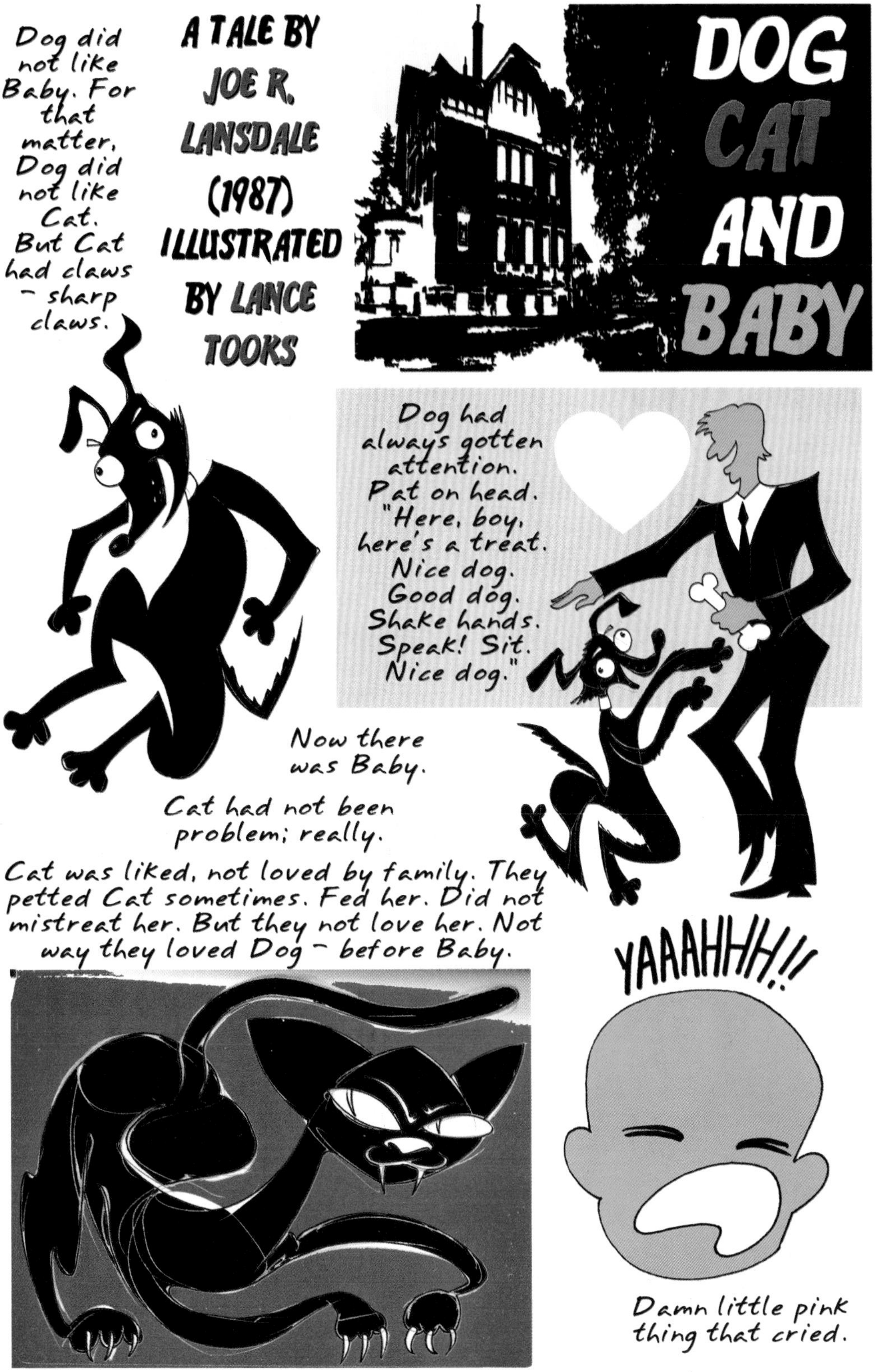
Dog did not like Baby. For that matter, Dog did not like Cat. But Cat had claws – sharp claws.
A TALE BY JOE R. LANSDALE (1987) ILLUSTRATED BY LANCE TOOKS
DOG CAT AND BABY
Dog had always gotten attention. Pat on head. "Here, boy, here's a treat. Nice dog. Good dog. Shake hands. Speak! Sit. Nice dog."
Now there was Baby.
Cat had not been problem; really.
Cat was liked, not loved by family. They petted Cat sometimes. Fed her. Did not mistreat her. But they not love her. Not way they loved Dog – before Baby.
YAAAHHH!!
Damn little pink thing that cried.

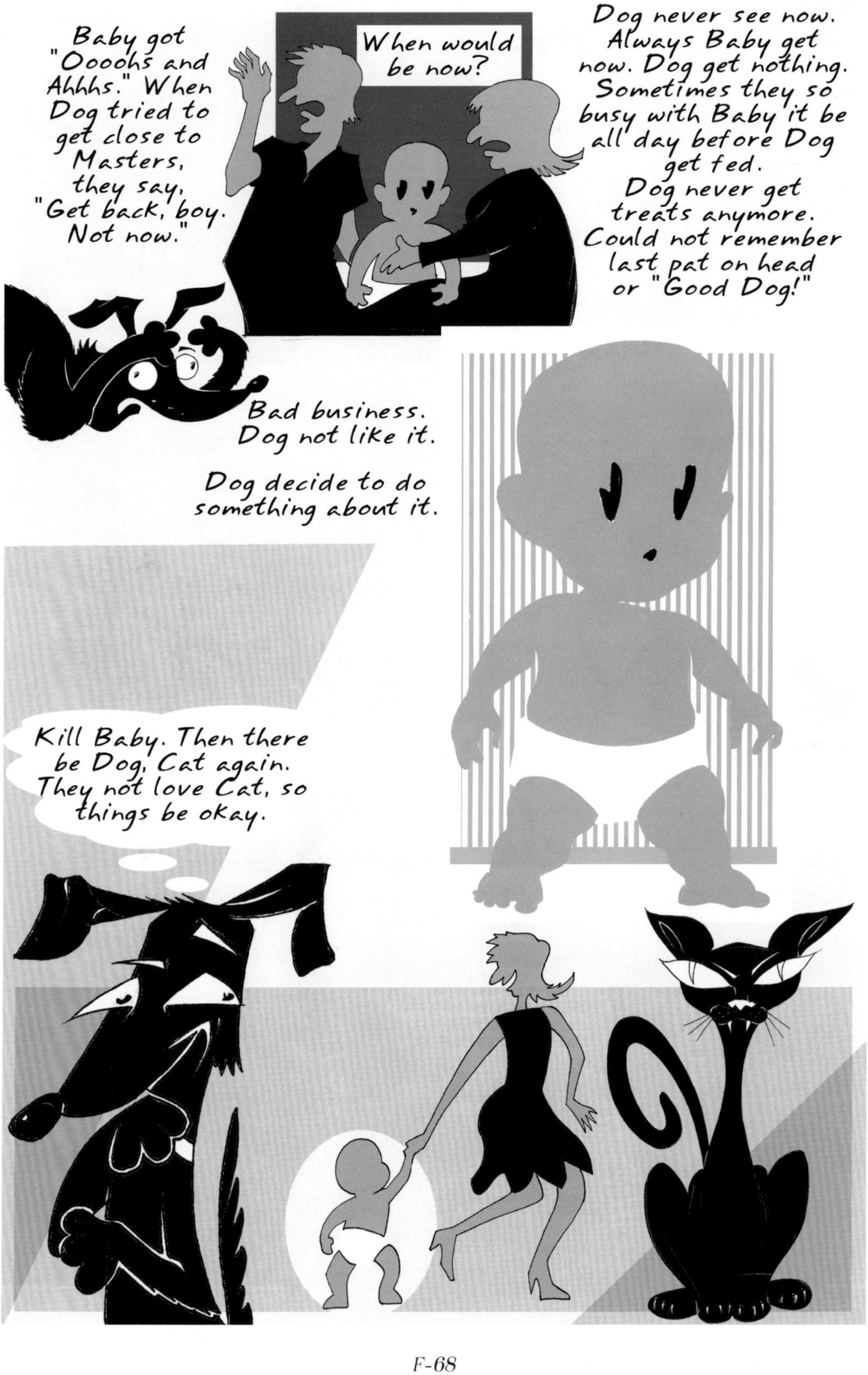
Baby got "Ooochs and Ahhhs." When Dog tried to get close to Masters, they say, "Get back, boy. Not now."
When would be now?
Dog never see now. Always Baby get now. Dog get nothing. Sometimes they so busy with Baby it be all day before Dog get fed. Dog never get treats anymore. Could not remember last pat on head or "Good Dog!"
Bad business. Dog not like it.
Dog decide to do something about it.
Kill Baby. Then there be Dog, Cat again. They not love Cat, so things be okay.

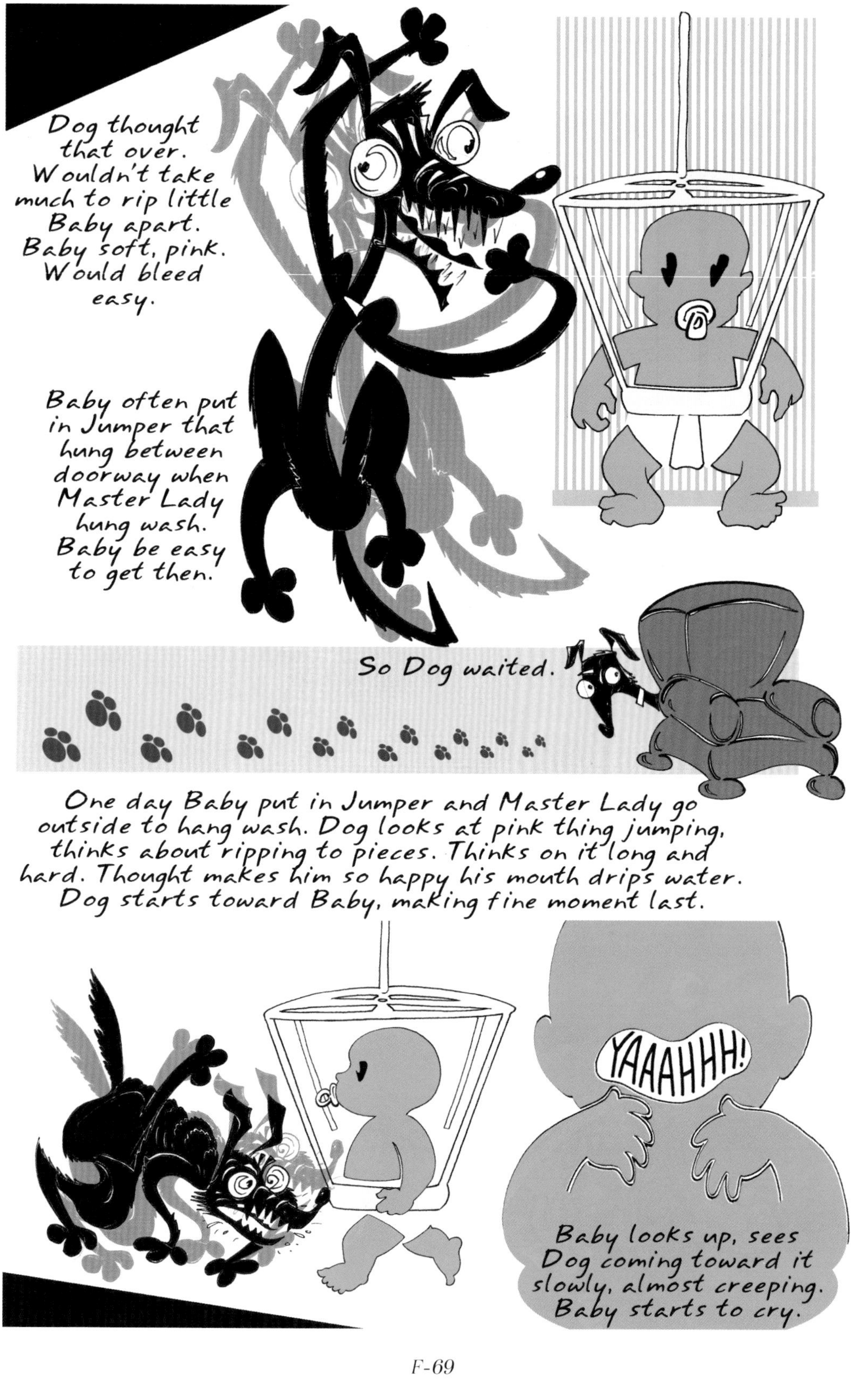
Dog thought that over. Wouldn't take much to rip little Baby apart. Baby soft, pink. Would bleed easy.
Baby often put in Jumper that hung between doorway when Master Lady hung wash. Baby be easy to get then.
So Dog waited.
One day Baby put in Jumper and Master Lady go outside to hang wash. Dog looks at pink thing jumping, thinks about ripping to pieces. Thinks on it long and hard. Thought makes him so happy his mouth drips water. Dog starts toward Baby, making fine moment last.
YAAAHHH!
Baby looks up, sees Dog coming toward it slowly, almost creeping. Baby starts to cry.

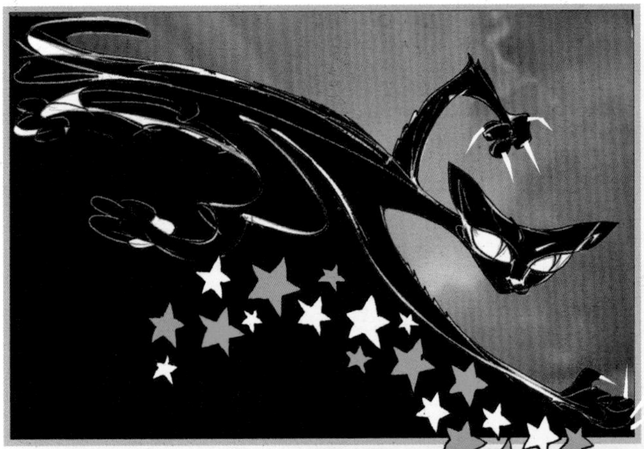

But before Dog can reach Baby, Cat jumps.

Cat been hiding behind couch.

Cat goes after Dog, tears Dog's face with teeth, with claws. Dog bleeds, tries to run. Cat goes after him.

Dog turns to bite.

Cat hangs claw in Dog's eye.

Dog yelps, runs.

Cat jumps on Dog's back, biting Dog on top of head.

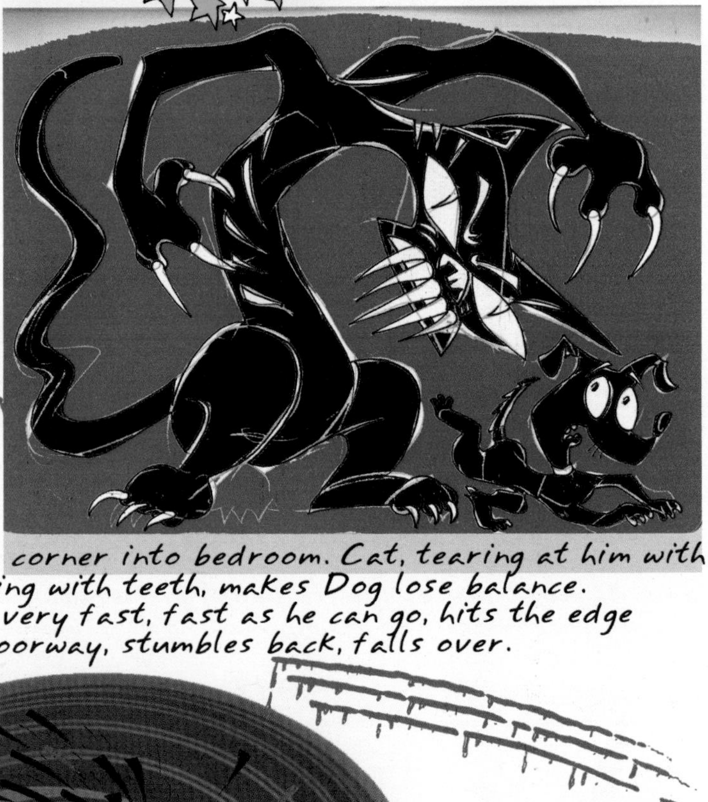

Dog tries to turn corner into bedroom. Cat, tearing at him with claws biting with teeth, makes Dog lose balance. Dog running very fast, fast as he can go, hits the edge of doorway, stumbles back, falls over.

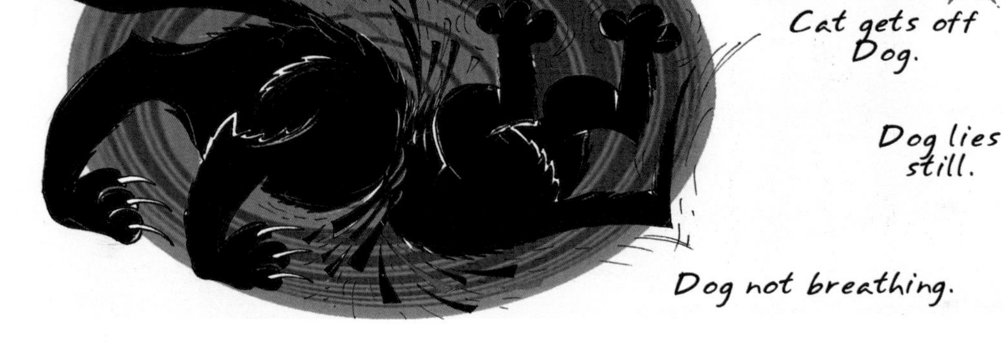

Cat gets off Dog.

Dog lies still.

Dog not breathing.

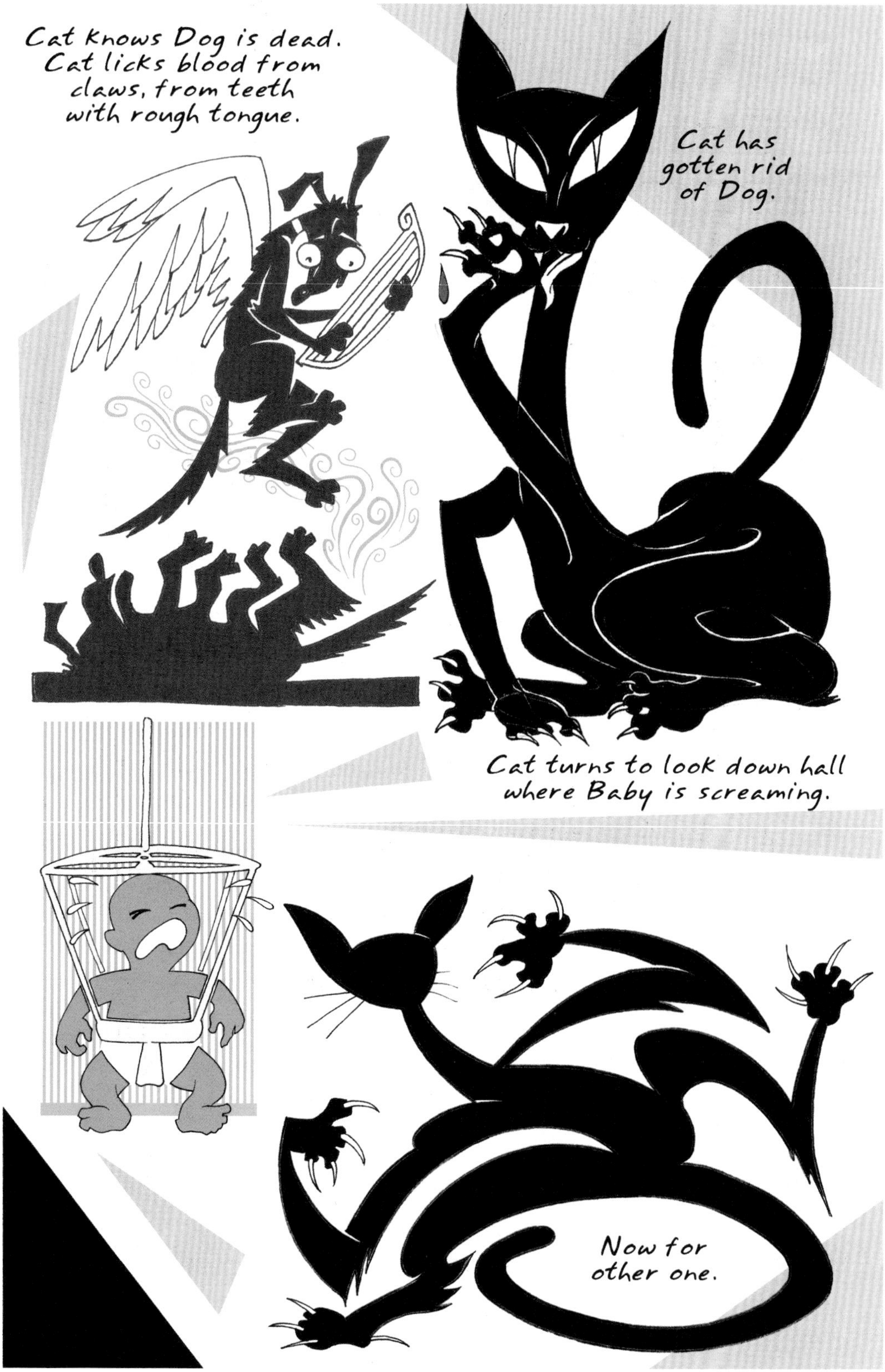
Cat knows Dog is dead. Cat licks blood from claws, from teeth with rough tongue.
Cat has gotten rid of Dog.
Cat turns to look down hall where Baby is screaming.
Now for other one.

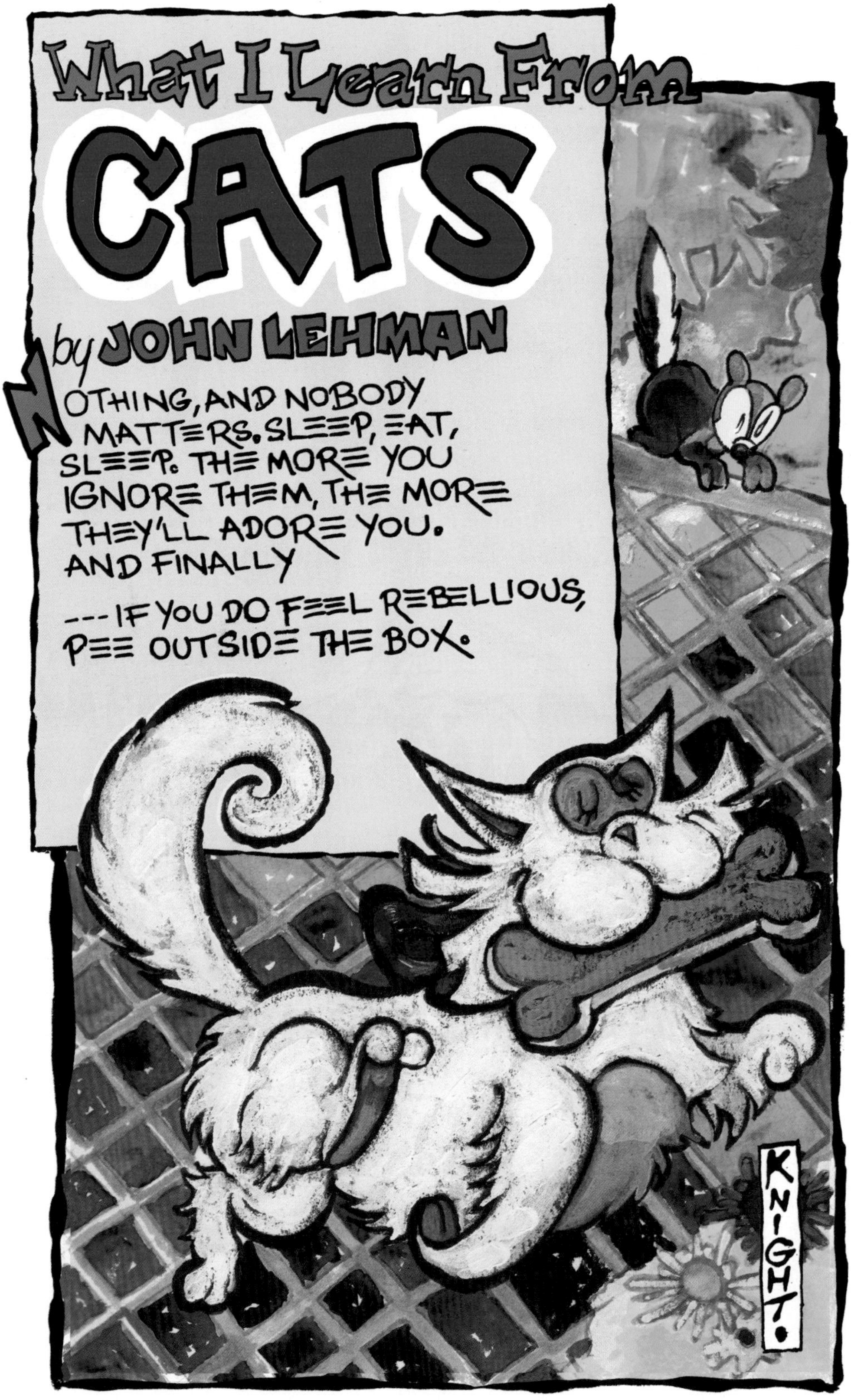
What I Learn From
CATS
by JOHN LEHMAN
NOTHING, AND NOBODY MATTERS. SLEEP, EAT, SLEEP. THE MORE YOU IGNORE THEM, THE MORE THEY'LL ADORE YOU. AND FINALLY
---IF YOU DO FEEL REBELLIOUS, PEE OUTSIDE THE BOX.
KNIGHT.

TONI PAWLOWSKY *(covers)*
Toni is both an exhibiting fine artist and a commercial illustrator. She shows her watercolors at the Fanny Garver Gallery in Madison, WI, and is also represented by Langley and Associates in Chicago. Her commercial work includes numerous CD covers for the series *Music for Little People*, including two covers for Taj Mahal. She has done work for the Wisconsin Dance Ensemble and Madison Ballet, and was the featured artist in *Rosebud 17*. Her greeting cards are available at www.redoakcards.com, and prints can be purchased at www.artfulhome.com.
Toni's illustrations also appear in:
Graphic Classics: Edgar Allan Poe
Graphic Classics: Mark Twain
Graphic Classics: Louisa May Alcott

EVERT GERADTS *(pages C-1, F-1)*
Evert Geradts is a Dutch comics artist now living in Toulouse, France. One of the founders of the Dutch underground comix scene, he started the influential magazine *Tante Leny Presents*, in which appeared his first *Sailears & Susie* stories. He is a disciple of Carl Barks, whom he names "the Aesop of the 20th century." Over the years Geradts has written about a thousand stories featuring Donald Duck and other Disney characters for Dutch comics. He also writes stories for the popular comic series *Sjors & Sjimmie* and *De Muziekbuurters*. Evert's work can be seen in:
Graphic Classics: Edgar Allan Poe
Graphic Classics: Ambrose Bierce
Graphic Classics: Bram Stoker
Fantasy Classics: Graphic Classics Volume 15
Christmas Classics: Graphic Classics Volume 19

AMBROSE BIERCE *(page C-2)*
Born in rural Ohio in 1842, Bierce became a printer's apprentice for a small Indiana newspaper until 1860, when he enlisted in the Union army and witnessed some of the major battles of the Civil War. Following a short military career, he resigned in disgust over a lack of promotion and instead pursued a successful career in journalism. In his time, Bierce was a celebrity as a satirical columnist, but disappointment over a lack of acceptance of his fiction and a troubled personal life caused him to become increasingly bitter and withdrawn in his later years. In 1913, at the age of 71, he crossed the border into Mexico, "with a pretty definite purpose, which, however, is not at present disclosable." He was never heard from again. You can find more stories and poems by Bierce in:
Graphic Classics: Ambrose Bierce
Horror Classics: Graphic Classics Volume 10
Graphic Classics: Special Edition
Graphic Classics Catalog of Publications

NEALE BLANDEN *(page C-2)*
Neale Blanden teaches visual narrative and theory at a college in Australia & has been cartooning for A LONG TIME! He has been published & had comics in exhibitions in the four corners of the world. Currently Neale is working on short pieces for local small press anthologies. He is also working on a self-published wordless graphic novel. More stories by Neale appear in:
Graphic Classics: Ambrose Bierce
Graphic Classics: Robert Louis Stevenson
Poe's Tales of Mystery: Graphic Classics Volume 21

DRAGAN KOVACEVIC *(pages C-3, F-3)*
Dragan Kovacevic (also known as Hammerson) is a cartoonist, illustrator, comics artist and filmmaker from Split, Croatia. As a comics artist, he has won various awards in his homeland and published an anthology of his works in 2006. As a filmmaker, he has worked on numerous music and promotional videos and various short and feature-length live action independent movies. In 2010, he co-founded Dream Division production company. Samples of his artwork can be found at www.hammersonhoek.daportfolio.com

P.G. WODEHOUSE *(page C-4)*
Sir Pelham Grenville Wodehouse (1881 – 1975) was an English humorist who wrote 96 books in his career. His works include novels, collections of short stories, and musical comedies. Best known today for the Jeeves and Blandings Castle novels and short stories, his Blandings, Jeeves, Ukridge and Mulliner stories have all been adapted for television. Wodehouse was also a playwright and lyricist who was part author and writer of 15 plays and of 250 lyrics for some 30 musical comedies, many of them produced in collaboration with Jerome Kern, Guy Bolton, and Cole Porter. Wodehouse spent the last decades of his life in the United States, becoming an American citizen in 1955, because of controversy that arose after he made five light-hearted broadcasts from Germany during World War II. Although an investigation later cleared him of any crimes, he never returned to England. At the age of ninty-three he received a long-overdue knighthood, only to die on St Valentine's Day some forty-five days later.

ANTONELLA CAPUTO *(page C-4)*
Antonella Caputo was born and raised in Rome, Italy, and now lives in Lancaster, England. She has been an architect, archaeologist, art restorer, photographer, calligrapher, interior designer, theater designer, actress, and theater director. Her first published work was *Casa Montesi*, a fortnightly comic strip which appeared in the national magazine *Il Giornalino*. She has since written comedies for children and scripts for comics and magazines in the U.K., Europe and the U.S. Antonella works with Nick Miller as the writer for Team Sputnik, and has collaborated with Nick and others in:
Graphic Classics: Arthur Conan Doyle
Graphic Classics: H.G. Wells
Graphic Classics: Jack London
Graphic Classics: Ambrose Bierce
Graphic Classics: Mark Twain
Graphic Classics: O. Henry
Graphic Classics: Rafael Sabatini
Graphic Classics: Oscar Wilde
Graphic Classics: Louisa May Alcott
Horror Classics: Graphic Classics Volume 10
Adventure Classics: Graphic Classics Volume 12
Gothic Classics: Graphic Classics Volume 14
Fantasy Classics: Graphic Classics Volume 15
Poe's Tales of Mystery: Graphic Classics Volume 21
Halloween Classics: Graphic Classics Volume 23
Graphic Classics: Special Edition

SHEPHERD HENDRIX *(page C-4)*
Shepherd Hendrix began his comics career in 1991 as an inker on DC Comics' *Swamp Thing*. He also penciled and inked *Restaurant at the End of the Universe* with Steve Leialoha. In the late 1990s, he left the industry and began working as a storyboard artist, background designer, and concept artist, using both traditional and digital mediums, collaborating with LucasArts and EA Games. In 2006, he returned to comics, illustrating the Eisner Award-nominated *Stagger Lee*, written by Derek McCulloch, for Image Comics. You can find pages from *Stagger Lee* in *Black Comix: African American Independent Comics, Art & Culture*, and examples of Shepherd's art at www.shepko.com. You can find more of Shepherd's art in:
African-American Classics: Graphic Classics Volume 22
Halloween Classics: Graphic Classics Volume 23

RAY BRADBURY *(page C-30)*
Ray Bradbury (1920–2012) was a prolific author of hundreds of short stories and close to fifty books, as well as numerous poems, essays, operas, plays, teleplays, and screenplays, Bradbury was one of the most celebrated writers of our time, and many of his works have been adapted into comics, television and films. His groundbreaking works include *Fahrenheit 451*, *The Martian Chronicles*, *The Illustrated Man*, and *Dandelion Wine*. He wrote the screenplay for John Huston's classic film adaptation of *Moby Dick*, and was nominated for an Academy Award. He adapted sixty-five of his stories for television's *The Ray Bradbury Theater*, and won an Emmy for his teleplay of *The Halloween Tree*. *The New York Times'* obituary of Bradbury stated that he was "the writer most responsible for bringing modern science fiction into the literary mainstream." Another Bradbury story will appear in the upcoming *Vampire Classics: Graphic Classics Volume 26.*

JOHN FINDLEY *(page C-30)*
John was raised in Ohio and Florida and graduated from Emory University with a BA in Humanities. He worked in advertising as a TV producer/director, art director, copywriter, and graphic designer for eleven years, after which he left agency work for a career as a freelance illustrator and designer. He is best known for his graphic series *Tex Arcana*, which ran in *Heavy Metal* magazine from 1981 to 1987. The series was collected under one cover as *Tex Arcana: a Saga of the Old West*. John lives with his wife Cindy in Sacramento, California. His work appears in:
Western Classics: Graphic Classics Volume 20
Native American Classics: Graphic Classics Volume 24

ROBERT J. BURDETTE *(page C-41)*
Robert Jones Burdette (1844 – 1914) was an American humorist and clergyman who became noted for his writings in the *Burlington* (Iowa) *Hawkeye*. He delivered his lecture "The Rise and Fall of the Mustache" to packed houses well over three thousand times over the course of thirty years.

J.B. BONIVERT *(page C-41)*
Jeff Bonivert is a Bay Area native who has contributed to independent comics as both artist and writer, in such books as *The Funboys*, *Turtle Soup* and *Mister Monster*. Jeff's biography of artist Murphy Anderson appears in *Spark Generators*, and *Muscle and Faith*, his Casey Jones/Teenage Mutant Ninja Turtles epic, can be seen online at www.flyingcolorscomics.com. J.B. Bonivert's work has also appeared in
Graphic Classics: Edgar Allan Poe
Graphic Classics: Arthur Conan Doyle
Graphic Classics: H.P. Lovecraft
Graphic Classics: Jack London

Graphic Classics: Ambrose Bierce
Graphic Classics: Bram Stoker
Adventure Classics: Graphic Classics Volume Twelve

OLIVER GOLDSMITH *(page C-46)*
Oliver Goldsmith (1730 – 1774) was an Irish novelist, playwright and poet, who is best known for his novel *The Vicar of Wakefield*, his poem *The Deserted Village*, and his plays *The Good-Natur'd Man* and *She Stoops to Conquer*. He also wrote *An History of the Earth* and *Animated Nature*. Perennially in debt and addicted to gambling, Goldsmith produced a massive output for the publishers of London, but his few painstaking works earned him the company of Samuel Johnson, with whom he was a founding member of "The Club". The combination of his literary work and his dissolute lifestyle led Horace Walpole to give him the epithet "inspired idiot".

HUNT EMERSON *(page C-46)*
The dean of British comics artists, Hunt Emerson has drawn cartoons and comic strips since the early 1970s. His work appears in publications as diverse as *Fiesta, Fortean Times*, and *The Wall Street Journal Europe*, and he has also worked widely in advertising. Hunt has published over twenty comic books and albums, including *Lady Chatterley's Lover, The Rime of the Ancient Mariner*, and *Casanova's Last Stand*, and his comics have been translated into ten languages. Hunt was assisted on *The Blue Carbuncle* by Tony McGee, creator of the fantasy series *Outcastes* (truestories.awardspace.com), who did the color work. You can see lots of cartoons, comics, fun and laffs on Hunt's website at www.largecow.demon.co.uk, and find more of his art in:
Graphic Classics: Jack London
Graphic Classics: Robert Louis Stevenson
Graphic Classics: Rafael Sabatini
Adventure Classics: Graphic Classics Volume 10
Science Fiction Classics: Graphic Classics Volume 17
Christmas Classics: Graphic Classics Volume 19

O. HENRY *(page C-48)*
O. Henry is the pen name of William Sydney Porter. The master of the surprise ending was born in 1862 in Greensboro, North Carolina. Porter left school at age fifteen, worked a number of jobs, then moved to Texas in 1882 where he became a ranch hand, then a pharmacist, and a bookkeeper. He married in 1887, and briefly published a humorous weekly, the *Rolling Stone*. When that paper failed, he joined the *Houston Post* as a reporter and columnist. He also worked as, most unfortunately, a bank clerk. He was accused of embezzlement, and fled, first to New Orleans, and then to Honduras to escape trial. While in Honduras he received word that his wife was terminally ill. He returned to Austin, and shortly after her death in 1897 was convicted and sentenced to five years in a federal penitentiary in Ohio. It was while in prison that he adopted the pen name O. Henry (taken from the name of one of his guards) and began to write fiction. He was released from prison after three years and moved to New York City, where he wrote for the *New York World* and other publications. O. Henry was a prolific and extremely popular writer, and before his death in 1910 published over 600 short stories, many of which are adapted to comics in:
Graphic Classics: O. Henry
Christmas Classics: Graphic Classics Volume 19

JIM MCMUNN *(page C-48)*
Jim McMunn is an independent comic artist "fighting the good fight in the indie trenches." His work has appeared in numerous small press publications including *PLB Comics* and *215 ink*. A frequent contributor to anthologies, his most recent work can be seen in *The New York Times* best-seller *FUBAR: European Theatre of the Damned* from Fubar Press and *Once Upon A Time Machine* from Dark Horse comics.
You can see more in:
Native American Classics: Graphic Classics Volume 24

JAMES ANTHONY FROUDE *(page C-59)*
James Anthony Froude (1818 – 1894) was an English historian, novelist, biographer, and editor of *Fraser's Magazine*. Froude intended to become a clergyman, but doubts about the doctrines of the Anglican church, published in his scandalous 1849 novel *The Nemesis of Faith*, drove him to abandon his religious career. Froude turned to writing history, becoming one of the best known historians of his time for his *History of England from the Fall of Wolsey to the Defeat of the Spanish Armada*. Froude continued to be controversial up until his death for his *Life of Carlyle*.

SHARY FLENNIKEN *(page C-59)*
Cartoonist, editor, author and screenwriter Shary Flenniken is the daughter of a Rear Admiral in the United States Navy, and was raised in Alaska, Panama and Seattle. In 1970 she met cartoonist Dan O'Neill at the Sky River Rock Festival, and became a member of the infamous art collective The Air Pirates, which included Bobby London, Ted Richards and Gary Hallgren. The group produced three issues of *Air Pirates Funnies*, Disney parodies for which the corporation sued them in a case that dragged out for nine years. Shary is best known for her irreverent comic strip *Trots & Bonnie*, about precocious preteens, which appeared in various underground comics and in *National Lampoon* magazine from 1972 to 1990. Her graphic stories and comic strips have appeared in *Details, Premiere, Harvey*, and *Mad* magazines, and in the books *When a Man Loves A Walnut, Nice Guys Sleep Alone*, and *Seattle Laughs*. She is currently teaching comedy writing and cartooning while working on a book of fairy tales and a series of novels that she claims are "not even remotely autobiographical."
You can purchase original artwork at www.sharyflenniken.com, and check out Shary's work in:
Graphic Classics: Ambrose Bierce
Graphic Classics: Robert Louis Stevenson
Graphic Classics: Mark Twain
Graphic Classics: O. Henry
Graphic Classics: Louisa May Alcott
Gothic Classics: Graphic Classics Volume 14

GEORGIANA KINGSCOTE *(page C-62)*
Adeline Georgiana Isabel Kingscote (1868 – 1908) was an English novelist, the author of over sixty works including *The Woman Who Wouldn't*. After her marriage to Colonel Howard Kingscote, most of her novels were published under the name Mrs. Howard Kingscote. Earlier books were published under the pseudonym Lucas Cleeve. Best known as a novelist, Kingscote was a traveler and linguist who compiled a book of Indian folklore, *Tales of the Sun, or, Folklore of Southern India*, and a work entitled *The English Baby in India and How to Rear It*.

PANDIT NATESA SASTRI *(page C-62)*
Natesa Sastri Sangendhi Mahalingam (1859 – 1906) was a native of Tiruchirapalli district in Tamil Nadu. His *Folklore in Southern India* contains tales recounted by his stepmother and grandmother and those collected during his service in various parts of South India. He co-wrote *Tales of the Sun* in 1890 with Georgiana Kingscote.

SENTHIL KUMAR *(page C-62)*
Senthil Kumar is a design and communication professional in Chennai, India. Through his SPORG studio (http://www.sporgstudio.in), a network of talented artists across India, he provides quality service in art and digital painting for children's book illustration, comics, animation backgrounds and concept art, flash games, and activity books.

JOHN LEHMAN *(page C-68, F-72)*
John (Jack) Lehman (www.LehmanInfo.com) is the founder of *Rosebud Magazine*. For years he was literary editor of *Wisconsin People & Ideas* and is now editor of *Lit Noir* (a digital magazine) and president/CEO of Zelda Wilde Publishing. A nationally published writer and poet with twenty-five years experience teaching creative writing, and twenty years as a creative director/senior copywriter for advertising agencies, he has presented seminars throughout the country. He lives with his wife, Talia Schorr, and their three dogs and twelve cats in Rockdale, the smallest incorporated village in Wisconsin.

MILTON KNIGHT *(page C-68, F-72)*
Milton Knight claims he started drawing, painting and creating his own attempts at comic books and animation at age two. "I've never formed a barrier between fine art and cartooning," says Milt. "Growing up, I treasured Chinese watercolors, Breughel, Charlie Brown and Terrytoons equally." His work has appeared in magazines including *Heavy Metal, High Times, National Lampoon* and *Nickelodeon Magazine*, and he has illustrated record covers, posters, candy packaging and T-shirts, and occasionally exhibited his paintings. Labor on *Ninja Turtles* comics allowed him to get up a grubstake to move to the West Coast in 1991, where he became an animator and director on *Felix the Cat* cartoons. Milt's comics titles include *Midnite the Rebel Skunk, Hinkley*, and *Slug and Ginger* and *Hugo*. Check the latest news at www.miltonknight.net, and Milt's work in:
Graphic Classics: Edgar Allan Poe
Graphic Classics: Jack London
Graphic Classics: Ambrose Bierce
Graphic Classics: Mark Twain
HorrorClassics: Graphic Classics Volume 10
Christmas Classics: Graphic Classics Volume 19
African-American Classics: Graphic Classics Volume 22
Graphic Classics Catalog of Publications

H.P. LOVECRAFT *(page F-2)*
Howard Phillips Lovecraft was born in Providence, Rhode Island in 1890. His father died in 1898, and his mother suffered from mental instability until her death in 1921. Poor health and his neurotic, overprotective mother combined to make something of a recluse of Lovecraft. Growing up, he had little contact with other children, and as an adult maintained his many long-distance relationships through voluminous correspondence. He was obsessed with dreams, and wrote most of his stories and poems around a central theme of

ancient gods who once ruled the earth and are merely awaiting a return to power. His writings appeared mostly in the "pulp" magazines of his time and received little critical attention outside of the horror genre. Since Lovecraft's death in 1937, his stories have grown in popularity and have spawned a huge cult of both fans and professional writers who continue to expand Lovecraft's themes through stories set in the "Cthulhu Mythos." More stories by Lovecraft appear in:
Graphic Classics: H.P. Lovecraft
Horror Classics: Graphic Classics Volume 10
Fantasy Classics: Graphic Classics Volume 15
Halloween Classics: Graphic Classics Volume 23

ALLEN KOSZOWSKI *(page F-2)*
Allen Koszowski has been published in the SF/horror/fantasy genres since 1973. He has had over four thousand pieces published in such magazines as *Fantasy Tales, Weird Tales, Whispers, Eldritch Tales, Asimov's SF Magazine, F&SF, Weirdbook, Cemetery Dance, The Horror Show* and many others, and has worked for publishers including Subterranean Press, Midnight Marquee Press, Gryphon Press, PS Publishing, and Centipede Press. He has won a World Fantasy Best Artist Award, and has been the artist Guest of Honor at The World Fantasy Convention, The World Horror Convention, The EerieCon, The Albacon and more. He currently edits and publishes his own magazine *Inhuman*.

ALGERNON BLACKWOOD *(page F-4)*
Algernon Henry Blackwood, (1869–1951) was an English short story writer and novelist, and one of the most prolific writers of ghost stories in the history of the genre. His interest in and understanding of "spiritualism" as well as of human psychology is responsible for the impressive power and effectiveness of his ghostly tales. H.P. Lovecraft considered Blackwood's *The Willows* to be "the finest supernatural tale in English literature". Among his thirty-odd books, Blackwood wrote a series of stories and short novels published as *John Silence, Physician Extraordinary* (1908), which featured a "psychic detective" who combined the skills of a Sherlock Holmes and a psychic medium.

ALEX BURROWS *(page F-4)*
Journalist and writer Alex Burrows lives in Oxfordshire and works in London as Managing Editor for *Classic Rock* magazine. His publishing career began with *Arnie*, a comics and punk music zine co-published with artist Simon Gane. He has also written for *Total Guitar, T3* and *Classic Rock* magazines and contributed to the book *Anarchy In The UK – The Stories Behind The Anthems Of Punk*. His previous adaptations appear in:
Graphic Classics: H.P. Lovecraft
Graphic Classics: Oscar Wilde
Graphic Classics: Louisa May Alcott
Graphic Classics: Special Edition
Christmas Classics: Graphic Classics Volume 19

RANDY DUBURKE *(page F-4)*
Randy DuBurke (www.randyduburke.com) was born in Washington, Georgia. "I lived my first few years in rural Georgia with my mother's parents. Then my parents brought me to New York where I immediately decided I wanted to be an artist and spent the subsequent years working for that goal," says Randy. He has now been a professional illustrator for twenty years, having done comics, animation, editorial illustration, book covers and children's books. Clients include Byron Priess, DC Comics, Vertigo Comics, Marvel Comics, *The New York Times Book Review*, MTV Animation, Chronicle Books, Clarion Books, and Lee and Low Books. He was awarded the 2003 Coretta Scott King/John Steptoe award for best new talent/illustration for his first children's book *The MoonRing*. After spending most of his life in New York, Randy now lives with his wife and children in Switzerland.

FRANZ KAFKA *(page F-40)*
Franz Kafka (1883-1924) was born to a middle-class German-speaking Jewish family in Prague, Bohemia (presently the Czech Republic). Kafka trained as a lawyer and, after completing his legal education, obtained employment with an insurance company. He began to write short stories in his spare time. For the rest of his life, he complained about the little time he had to devote to his writing. Only a few of Kafka's works were published during his lifetime. Most were published posthumously by his friend Max Brod, who ignored Kafka's wish to have the manuscripts destroyed. He is now regarded by critics as one of the most influential authors of the 20th century. The term Kafkaesque has entered the English language to describe surreal situations like those in his writing.

VINCENT STALL *(page F-40)*
An experienced screen printer and print designer, Vincent Stall publishes comics and posters as "King Mini" in Minneapolis. His work can be seen in the *Meathaus* anthology, as well as his self-published comics, *5M The Busline Diary* and *Jetsom*, now available at www.kingmini.com. His art can also be found in the pages of *Attitude Lad, Negative Burn, Murder Can be Fun, Rosetta* and *Project Telstar*. Nearing completion, his first fully realized story, *Brass Tack*, is scheduled for publication by Top Shelf. Vincent is also the co-owner of PUNY Entertainment, a digital media group that produces television and interactive pieces with credits that include *Yo Gabba Gabba* and Cartoon Network's *MAD* series.

SAKI *(page F-42)*
Hector Hugh Munro was born in Burma in 1870. He was sent to Scotland to be raised and educated by two aunts he grew to despise. Hector briefly journeyed to Burma in his twenties as a police officer, but returned to England due to health problems. There he began to write for various periodicals and later as a correspondent in Paris, Russia and the Balkans. For his fiction he took the pen name "Saki" from the cupbearer in *The Rubaiyat* of Omar Khayyam. Munro enlisted in World War I, and was killed by a sniper's bullet in France in 1916. Find another story by Saki in *Horror Classics: Graphic Classics Volume 10.*

TRINA ROBBINS *(page F-42)*
Trina has been writing and drawing comics for more than thirty years. She was one of the first female underground comix artists and a co-founder of *It Aint Me, Babe* and *Wimmen's Comix* in the early 1970s. She has drawn for DC's *Wonder Woman*, and scripted *GoGirl!*, a teen superheroine comic illustrated by Anne Timmons. Since 1990 Trina has become a writer and feminist pop culture herstorian. In addition to her award-winning books on comics from a feminist perspective (*The Great Women Cartoonists* was listed among *Time Magazine's* top ten comics of 2001), she has written books about goddesses and murderesses, and her latest is *The Brinkley Girls*, a collection of Nell Brinkley's cartoons from the early 20th century.
You can learn more on Trina's website at www.trinarobbins.com, and find her illustrations and comics adaptations in:
Graphic Classics: Jack London
Graphic Classics: Louisa May Alcott
Gothic Classics: Graphic Classics Volume 14

LISA K. WEBER *(page F-42)*
Lisa K. Weber graduated from Parsons School of Design in 2000 with a BFA in Illustration. Her whimsically twisted characters and illustrations have appeared in various print, animation, and design projects including work for clients *Scholastic, Cricket Magazine*, Children's Television Workshop, and many others. Her work is featured in a series of young reader's books, called *The Sisters Eight*, published by Houghton Mifflin in 2009. She has also participated in exhibitions in New York and Philadelphia. To see more of her art, visit www.creatureco.com. Lisa has provided comics and illustrations for:
Graphic Classics: H.P. Lovecraft
Graphic Classics: Ambrose Bierce
Graphic Classics: Mark Twain
Graphic Classics: O. Henry
Graphic Classics: Oscar Wilde
Graphic Classics: Louisa May Alcott
Gothic Classics: Graphic Classics Volume 14
Poe's Tales of Mystery: Graphic Classics Volume 21

JOHNNY RYAN *(page F-53)*
Johnny Ryan was born in Boston in 1970. As a boy, he says, "First I wanted to be a cartoonist, then I wanted to be a physicist, then I wanted to be gay, and then a cartoonist again." He now lives in Los Angeles and is the creator of the award-winning *Angry Youth Comix*. His work has also been published in *Nickelodeon Magazine, Goody Good Comics, Measles* and *LCD*. "Comics used to be fun and crazy and weird and gross," says Johnny. "Now, they're a serious art form... it's as if everyone was having a big crazy orgy and then your grandparents walked in. They really sucked the life out of the party." Johnny's decidedly unserious work appears in:
Graphic Classics: Ambrose Bierce
Graphic Classics: Robert Louis Stevenson
Graphic Classics: O. Henry
Science Fiction Classics: Graphic Classics Volume 17

EDWARD LEAR *(page F-54)*
Edward Lear (1812-1888) was an English artist, illustrator, author, and poet, renowned today primarily for his literary nonsense in poetry and prose, and especially his limericks, a form that he popularised. Lear was already drawing "for bread and cheese" by the time he was aged 16 and soon developed into a serious "ornithological draughtsman" employed by the Zoological Society. In 1846 Lear published *A Book of Nonsense*, a volume of limericks that went through three editions and helped popularize the form. In 1865 *The History of the Seven Families of the Lake Pipple-Popple* was published, and in 1867 his most famous piece of nonsense, *The Owl and the Pussycat*, which he wrote for the children of his patron, the Earl of Derby.

MARY FLEENER *(page F-54)*
Besides doing comics, like her biweekly strip *Mary-Land*, autobiographical collection *Life of the Party*, and Eros title *Nipplez 'n' Tum*

FELINE CLASSICS
Please flip book over to read

Tum, Los Angeles native Mary has also produced illustrations for magazines and books such as *Guitar Player, Musician, Spin, Hustler, The Book of Changes, Guitar Cookbook, RoadStrips*, and Poppy Z. Brite's *Plastic Jesus.* Her paintings have been shown at The American Visionary Art Museum, La Luz de Jesus Gallery, and the Laguna Beach Art Museum. She is currently painting on black velvet, and makes hand-thrown ceramics. Fleener also plays bass, and sings her own tunes in a band called The Wigbillies with her husband. She loves to surf, and walks a lot.
Mary's website is at www.maryfleener.com. Her art also appears in:
Graphic Classics: Edgar Allan Poe
Graphic Classics: Mark Twain
Graphic Classics: Louisa May Alcott
Adventure Classics: Graphic Classics Volume 12

CARL SANDBURG *(page F-57)*
Carl Sandburg was born the son of Swedish immigrants in Galesburg, Illinois in 1878. He first gained fame for his collection *Chicago Poems*, published in 1916, and is best known today as the author of the poem *Chicago* and his six-volume biography of Abraham Lincoln. A journalist for *The Chicago Daily News* and an active socialist, he was dubbed "the people's poet," twice won the Pulitzer Prize, and was named America's Poet Laureate by President John F. Kennedy. Sandburg died in North Carolina in 1967. *Jack London and O. Henry* was published in 1922, in Sandburg's collection *Smoke and Steel.* Of the subjects of his poem, Jack London died in 1916 of kidney failure, at age forty, and William Sydney Porter in 1910, of cirrhosis of the liver, at age forty-seven.
Another Sandburg poem appears in
Graphic Classics: O. Henry

SKOT OLSEN *(page F-57)*
While growing up in Connecticut, Skot and his parents spent their summers sailing up and down the coast of New England and all over the West Indies. It was on these long trips that he developed his love for the sea which forms the basis for much of his work. A graduate of the Joe Kubert School of Cartoon and Graphic Art, Skot now lives on the edge of the Florida Everglades, where he concentrates on paintings which have been featured in numerous publications and exhibited in galleries in Florida, New York and California. A large collection of his work is online at www.skotolsen.com and in:
Graphic Classics: H.P. Lovecraft
Graphic Classics: Bram Stoker
Adventure Classics: Graphic Classics Volume 12
Fantasy Classics: Graphic Classics Volume 15
Poe's Tales of Mystery: Graphic Classics Volume 21

ROBERT E. HOWARD *(page F-58)*
Texas writer Robert Ervin Howard is best-known as the creator of Conan the Barbarian and the father of the sword and sorcery genre. He also wrote hundreds of poems, three novels, and over three hundred stories in the genres of fantasy, horror, mystery, boxing, historical adventure and westerns. His work was originally published in the pulp magazines, most notably *Weird Tales*, and from the late 1920s to the mid-1930s Howard was the most popular fiction writer in America. In 1930, he began a correspondence with fellow *Weird Tales* author and mentor H.P. Lovecraft, which continued until Howard's death. Howard lived all his life with his mother, who suffered from tuberculosis. When she fell into a coma in 1936, the distraught Howard committed suicide at age 30. The story of his later years is told in the film *The Whole Wide World* (1996). *Knife River Prodigal* was originally published posthumously in *Cowboy Stories* magazine in July 1937. Howard's Knife River Prodigal appears in
WesternClassics: Graphic Classics Volume 20

PETER KUPER *(page F-58)*
Highly regarded by both fans and his peers, Peter Kuper has been active in the comics community since the early 1970s. In 1979 he co-founded the political comics magazine *World War 3 Illustrated* and remains on its editorial board. He has been an instructor at the School of Visual Arts since 1986 and is also an art director for the political illustration group INX (www.inxart.com). Peter's illustrations and comics appear regularly in *Time, The New York Times* and *MAD.* He has written and illustrated many books including *Comics Trips*, a journal of an eight-month trip through Africa and Southeast Asia. Other works include *Mind's Eye, Stripped – An Unauthorized Autobiography, The System*, a wordless graphic novel, and an adaptation of Kafka's *The Metamorphosis.* Peter's recent book, *SPEECHLESS*, collects his career to date. More of his work can be seen at www.peterkuper.com and in
Graphic Classics: Jack London

JOSEPH JACOBS (page F-64)
Joseph Jacobs (1854 – 1916) was a folklorist, literary critic and historian. From 1899-1900 he edited the journal *Folklore*, and from 1890 to 1916 he edited multiple collections of fairy tales. Jacobs was secretary of the Society of Hebrew Literature from 1878 to 1884, and came into prominence as the writer of a series of articles in *The Times* on the persecution of Jews in Russia. In 1900, he accepted an invitation to become editor of the *Jewish Encyclopedia*, which was then being prepared at New York. He wrote many articles for, and was generally responsible for the style of the whole publication, which was completed in 1906.

PAT N. LEWIS *(page F-64)*
Pat N. Lewis is an illustrator/cartoonist from Pittsburgh, Pennsylvania. His work has appeared in anthologies from BOOM! Studios, Top Shelf Comics, McGraw-Hill, and Fulcrum Books. In 2007, Pat's first graphic novel, *The Claws Come Out*, was released by IDW Publishing, and he was a contributing artist to the Eisner Award-nominated *Trickster: Native American Tales.* Currently he is hard at work on a web comic entitled *Muscles Diablo In: Where Terror Lurks*, which you can follow online at patnlewis.tumblr.com.
More of Pat's art appears in
Native American Classics: Graphic Classics Volume 24

JOE R. LANSDALE (page F-67)
Joe R. Lansdale is the author of over thirty novels and numerous short stories. His work has appeared in national anthologies, magazines, and collections, as well as numerous foreign publications. He has written for comics, television, film, and newspapers. His work has been collected in eighteen short-story collections, and he has edited or co-edited over a dozen anthologies. His novella *Bubba Hotep* was adapted to film by director Don Coscarelli, and his story *Incident On and Off a Mountain Road* was adapted to film for Showtime's *Masters of Horror.* He lives in Nacogdoches, Texas with his wife, dog, and two cats.

LANCE TOOKS *(page F-67)*
Lance Tooks (lancetooksjournal.blogspot.com) began his comics career as a Marvel Comics assistant editor. Lance has also worked as an animator on more than a hundred television commercials, films and music videos. He has self-published the comics *Danger Funnies, Divided by Infinity* and *Muthafucka*, and illustrated *The Black Panthers for Beginners*, written by Herb Boyd.
Lance's stories have appeared in
Graphic Classics: Edgar Allan Poe
Graphic Classics: Ambrose Bierce
Graphic Classics: Mark Twain
Graphic Classics: Robert Louis Stevenson
African-American Classics: Graphic Classics Volume 22.
Lance's first graphic novel, *Narcissa*, was named one of the year's best books by *Publisher's Weekly*, and his four-volume *Lucifer's Garden of Verses* series for NBM Comics Lit has won two Glyph Awards. He collaborated with Harvey Pekar on *The Beats: a Graphic History* and *Studs Terkel's Working*, and has recently adapted tales by Mary Shelley and W. Somerset Maugham for *The Graphic Canon*, from Seven Stories Press. Lance moved from his native New York to Madrid, Spain, where he's hard at work on a new and very original graphic novel.

TOM POMPLUN
The designer, editor, and publisher of *Graphic Classics*, Tom also designed *Rosebud*, a journal of fiction, poetry and illustration, from 1993 to 2003, and in 2001 he founded the *Graphic Classics* series. Tom is currently working on *VampireClassics: Graphic Classics Volume 26*, scheduled for May 2015 release, with associate editor Mort Castle.

Please flip book over to read
CANINE CLASSICS